W9-BDX-975

HUNTER'S RUN

By the same author

Fiction

The Five Fingers (with James Hudson)

The Killing House

Nonfiction

The Specialist: Revelations of a Counterterrorist

The War Against the Terrorists: How to Win It

HUNTER'S RUN

Gayle Rivers

G. P. Putnam's Sons/New York

The epigraph and the quotations at the beginning of each chapter have been taken from *The Rubáiyát of Omar Khayyám of Naishapur,* translated by Edward FitzGerald.

G. P. Putnam's Sons
Publishers Since 1838
200 Madison Avenue
New York, NY 10016

Published simultaneously in Canada

Library of Congress Cataloging-in-Publication Data
Rivers, Gayle.
Hunter's run / Gayle Rivers.
p. cm.
ISBN 0-399-13505-7: price.
I. Title.
PR6068.I94H8 1989 89-34771 CIP
823'.914—dc20

Printed in the United States of America
1 2 3 4 5 6 7 8 9 10

Awake! for Morning in the Bowl of Night
Has flung the Stone that puts the Stars to Flight:
And Lo! the Hunter of the East has caught
The Sultan's Turret in a Noose of Light.

HUNTER'S RUN

1

There was a Door to which I found no
Key:
There was a Veil past which I could not
see.

With a crackle of starch, the nurse leaned over him and unclipped the black rubbery bands from his wrists and ankles, then removed the disks from his chest. They made a plopping sound as they came away. She coiled the wires that led to the ECG machine.

"There's some Kleenex in that box on the shelf, Major Yardley, if you'd like to rub the grease off your chest."

"Okay," he said.

"Would you get dressed and then go back to Captain Reynolds's waiting room. Second door on your left down the corridor. When the green light shows over his door, just walk in. No hurry. He'll be about ten minutes."

Yardley said, "Thank you," and with a swish of her white skirt the nurse left, sliding the door of the examination cubicle shut as she went.

The Bethesda naval hospital, he thought, fine for cutting bits out of presidents, but God, how I hate hospitals. That antiseptic smell, the squeaking of rubber-soled shoes on polished floors, the air of defeat and depression. In ten years with the Special Forces, he had been pretty lucky—hospitalized only twice for brief periods, once for a flesh wound and once for a badly sprained neck, the legacy of a parachute drop by night. There couldn't be anything really wrong with him this time. The checkup was just part of the old military routine grinding away.

He tied his tie, slipped on his civilian jacket and gave himself a cursory glance in the cubicle mirror. You're an ugly bugger, Yardley, he thought, but you look fit enough. He walked down the corridor and sat in the waiting room until the green light came on. He knocked on the door and went in. He stood at attention in front of the desk: the heart specialist was a U.S. Navy captain who far outranked him.

"Hey, relax, Major," said Captain Reynolds. "We're not on parade. Sit down."

The specialist had what looked like a graph with a spidery line running across it in his left hand. In front of him on the desk was a bulky file. He was a bit like a spider himself. Yardley was over six feet tall, but when they had met briefly before the ECG test, he had found himself looking up at the doctor, who was skeletally thin—maybe a hundred forty pounds stretched into those lanky arms and legs.

"What do they call you in the mess?" Reynolds asked. "Robert?"

"Lots of things," Yardley said with a smile. "Bob, usually."

"Okay, Bob, let's get down to cases. I've read through your papers but I'd like to hear the facts from your side. Now let me see." He flipped over the top pages. "You're a career soldier, commissioned in 1974, transferred from the infantry to the Special Forces in 1978 as a lieutenant, and have served there ever since, making captain seven years ago and major the year before last. Right so far?"

Yardley nodded.

"I see they awarded you the Medal of Honor—'for services beyond the call of duty.' Want to tell me about it?"

"There's not much to tell. It was a special op in Beirut. I got lucky."

"You damned heroes are all the same! If anyone ever gave me a medal, I'd flash it all over the place." He turned a page of the file. "Before Grenada, your first bit of real action was in the Iranian desert. That abortive attempt to free our hostages?"

"That was a real mess, but it wasn't the Army's fault. Someone in the Pentagon set us up—playing politics."

"Okay, okay, let's keep off politics! There's a cryptic note in your file here that says you were involved just a few weeks back in that World Trade Center mess."

Yardley said slowly, "I think that's still top secret, sir."

"All right, I won't probe. But—it was rough?"

"It was rough."

"These aren't random questions, Bob. I'm trying to establish what we call a profile. I don't want to pry but I have to find out what makes you tick. Or what makes that heart of yours tick—irregularly. Now, on a different tack, you're married?"

Yardley hesitated. "Technically, yes. But my wife—she's British—has gone back to her folks in England. She'll be suing for divorce."

"I'm very sorry. No children?"

Yardley, not trusting himself to speak, shook his head.

Captain Reynolds continued probing. "What about your parents? They in good health? I suppose they'd be in their sixties right now."

"Afraid not," Yardley said. "They would have been—but they died in an accident at sea. My father—he was a career soldier, a colonel in One-oh-one Airborne—retired nearly ten years ago. He was a keen sailor, went to live in Camden, Maine, where *his* father came from, bought a boat and taught my mother to sail. First long cruise they tried was down to the Caribbean. They hit Hurricane Louise on the way. That was what? seven years ago. The yacht was found, drifting, waterlogged—but no trace of my parents. End of story."

"Christ, I'm sorry. Any other family?"

"No, I'm an only child."

There was a pause while Captain Reynolds riffled through several pages in the file. Then he took off his black horn-rimmed spectacles and rubbed the red indentations on either side of his nose. At last, he said, "Right, Bob, tell me in your own words what happened. When you first noticed the symptoms."

Yardley said, "Once a month, everyone in the squad—no exceptions, unless you have a medical certificate—goes through the assault course. I laid it out myself, it's quite tough. Twelve minutes is good going, fifteen is a pass. Seventeen minutes, depending on age and rank, is the absolute outside. One second over seventeen—and you're out."

The specialist interrupted, "It says here you hold the record at nine minutes and some seconds."

"Yeah, well. Like I said, I laid the damn thing out. Well, two weeks ago, on the monthly trial, it took me all of fourteen minutes and fifty-odd seconds. Okay, so I was within the pass limit but I felt drained. My chest felt hollow—like it was empty, no lungs, no heart, no nothing. And I was panting as though I'd just swum fifty yards underwater. I don't usually check my pulse, but this time, when I'd more or less recovered, I did. It was going fast for a bit and then slow and then fast again. My usual rate at rest is forty-eight to fifty to the minute. I know that from annual checkups. Over the last week or two, it's been difficult to check out, what with the sudden surges and then the slowdowns, but it must be up around the hundred mark. Maybe it's something I've been eating. Could that be it, sir?"

Captain Reynolds said, "I doubt it. You've had no stomach upsets, no diarrhea or vomiting?"

"Not a thing, sir."

"Do you drink heavily?"

Yardley gave a dry laugh. "We're talking about the Special Forces, sir. We're trained to the minute—or that's the idea. A drinker wouldn't last a week with our bunch. Okay, I'll have a scotch on the rocks before dinner and maybe a glass of wine with it—but that's my lot."

"Do you smoke?"

"I stopped when I joined the SF. Haven't touched a cigarette or a cigar these past ten years. What do you make of it, Captain? Is this latest ECG all right?"

There was a pause. Yardley felt his heart palpitating, thudding away as though he were a teenager asking a girl for his first dance. Captain Reynolds rubbed his nose again and finally said, "You were examined at Fort Bragg by your resident MO. He gave you an electrocardiogram test—and was not happy with the results. He told you so. Quite properly, you requested a specialist examination, which is why you're here at Bethesda. I've compared your ECG test at Bragg with the one I've just had done—and, Bob, I have to tell you this. There's no improvement. Your heartbeat is still irregular. Now, level with me. You still feel breathless after any real exertion—right? And at night in bed you can feel your heart thumping away like a rock-and-roll tune—right? And I bet that up to a few weeks ago you never realized you had a heart—you just took it for granted. But since then, you're aware of it the whole time. Right?"

Yardley said, "Right. But why? I'm thirty-five, in the prime of life, I train hard all the time, I lead from the front—not the back. What the hell's happening to me, sir?"

"The medical diagnosis is that you're suffering from arrhythmia—irregular heartbeat, in plain English. Why it's come on when it has is beyond me. We know that a severe emotional problem can bring it on. I'm not prying, but perhaps your wife's leaving . . . or the excitement of military action over a prolonged period can have the same effect. Lord Moran, Sir Winston Churchill's physician, wrote a fascinating book, *The Anatomy of Courage.* He reckoned that bravery was like a bank account. You keep on drawing on it—and one day you find you're overdrawn. Simple as that. Maybe the loss of your wife coupled with that World Trade Center business was just too much. I can tell you *what.* I can't tell you *why.*"

"And the solution?"

"There's no simple solution. On the medical side, there are two alternatives. We could put you under for a few minutes and give your heart an electrical jolt. Sometimes that knocks it back into a regular rhythm."

"You say 'sometimes.' What does that mean, sir, percentagewise?"

"I won't kid you, Bob. Fifty-fifty perhaps."

"And the other alternative?"

"The oldest remedy in the world. A foxglove derivative. The ancients knew that the foxglove plant could help to steady and regulate the heartbeat. You take one digoxin pill every morning—let me stress, for the rest of your life—and your pulse will steady down."

Yardley said eagerly, "So I take the pills and report back for duty?"

Captain Reynolds said nothing for a long moment and then looked Yardley straight in the eyes. "Sorry, Bob, that's not the way it goes. Okay, you can go back to duty—but it's behind a desk for the rest of your Army career."

"What the hell—sir!"

"Steady, Bob. Just think about it. You're second in command of one of the toughest outfits in this man's army. Any time a bushfire war breaks out anywhere in the world, you and your men fly out that night. An aircraft hijacking in the Middle East, an insurrection in Central America—you're the boys to mop it up fast. Think of your men. They need a leader who's not just as fit and highly trained as they are, but fitter and better trained. You remember General Montgomery's slogan for the Eighth Army troops—back in World War Two?

'Fighting fit and fit to fight.' Bob, I have to tell you straight. You'd be a liability in your present condition. For your men's sake as well as your own. You just can't cut it."

"But after a break, a bit of relaxing . . . ?"

"Sorry, Bob. I'm going to recommend strongly that you take immediate furlough, thirty days minimum. That and the daily pills should settle you down. You're not going to be a permanent invalid, for God's sake! An occasional round of golf, some gentle swimming, even a spot of running would be fine. But you have to face it—your days as a Special Forces leader are over."

He saw the look of dejection on Yardley's face, the slump of the massive shoulders, and went on more gently, "All you athletes, hairtrigger-trained, are living on borrowed time. Five years from now, ten years at the most, you'd be over the top. You either resign your commission or you become an armchair warrior. That's the strength of it. You follow me?"

"Yeah—but you've just taken ten years away from me."

"I have to, Bob. When you think it over, you'll know I have to. Tell me the truth. However often you go into action, isn't there always a surge of adrenaline beforehand? Don't you feel tense, your heart's pumping away. Right?"

Yardley nodded.

The specialist pressed on. "Well, it's like an engine that's not firing on all cylinders. You hit the gas pedal, rev up the engine and—bang!—it blows. That could happen to you, Bob. Your heart's under pressure. Accelerate it, and vroom"—he made a slashing downward movement with the edge of his right hand—"that could be the end of Major Yardley. I'm not kidding. So right now, it's a rest and a break for you. You'll be reclassified at grade C2, light duties only, when you report back. Six months' time, you can request another thorough checkup, ECG, blood pressure, blood samples, the lot. Maybe they'll upgrade you again—*maybe.* Don't bank on it."

"The old days," Yardley said, "they did it in style. Put you in a room with a revolver on the table and one round in the chamber. Now they get a high-ranking quack in a white coat to blow you away."

"That's enough, Bob. Cut the emotion and face it straight. You've given the Special Forces ten good years. You've passed the course with honors. And you've a lot more to give—as a trainer and teacher in irregular warfare. You can give just as much these next ten years, more maybe. It's up to you, once you stop feeling sorry for yourself."

Yardley stood up. He mustered a grin. "Message received and half understood. Anything else, sir?"

"No. You get on back to Fort Bragg. I'll send a signal through, saying you're to be given immediate leave. I'll also send the prescription details to your detachment MO, so he'll have the tablets ready for your return. My advice is, drop everything at the camp. No one's irreplaceable. Grab a couple bottles of scotch from the PX, jump in your car and hightail it off somewhere. June's nice anywhere in the U.S. of A. You have any place in mind?"

Yardley said, "No. Way I feel right now, sir, any place is as good as any other."

"What about Maine? You said your family came from there. Know it well?"

"I don't know it at all, sir. Never been there, in fact."

"You'd like it. All those forests and lakes. It's kind of peaceful and remote. Interesting seacoast too. You can get a whole fresh lobster, straight out of the sea, for under ten bucks. I'd try Maine."

"That's a thought." Yardley extended his right hand. "I'd like to thank you, sir, and I'm sorry if I sounded like a spoiled brat. It takes some adjusting to."

"Sure, don't I know it. Let me tell you, it's no great game sitting here and playing God to brave young guys like you. You probably hate my guts right now—it's what we call 'shoot the messenger' syndrome—but one day when you look back, you may thank me. At least I'm keeping you alive."

"Half alive, sir." Yardley saluted and walked out of the room.

When the door closed, Captain Reynolds dictated rapidly into a microrecorder, switched it off and pressed the buzzer on his desk. In a few moments, the nurse who'd supervised Yardley's ECG entered.

"Okay, Trisha, you've got the name of that MO at Bragg? And the commanding officer, Special Forces detachment? I've a couple of signals to send," he said, and handed her the tape.

"Is he going to be all right?" she asked. "That Major Yardley, he looked like a real tough guy. Very pleasant, though."

Reynolds answered slowly, as though picking his words with care. "He'll be all right. Maybe in a different job. We'll see."

"Shall I send his file back, Captain, through channels?" She reached out a hand.

"No, that's okay, Trisha. I'll hold it for now. It's signed out to me, yes? That will be all."

The adjutant at Fort Bragg wanted to have a special mess dinner that night, but Bob Yardley was having no celebrations. To be posted on secondment to the SAS in Hereford, England, or with the SEAL teams down the coast would have warranted a party. But without telling his friends, he looked on this as a defeat. He made up some story about having to take compassionate leave to sort out family estate details up in New England. He couldn't just swan around the States and he was privately taken with the idea of visiting Maine to see his father's and grandfather's homes. He had been halfway around the world on military duty—to the Mediterranean, Lebanon, Iran, Britain and West Germany on training detachments, but he'd never been north of Boston. Now was the chance. So after a quiet dinner in the mess that night, he got out a set of maps of the eastern United States and roughly plotted a route. West to hit the Blue Ridge Parkway near Asheville, North Carolina; north to the end of the Skyline Drive at Front Royal; then north again, with a brief detour in Gettysburg, up Route 81 and then Route 87 to the top of New York State, east across Vermont to a little town named Berlin—and then he would be on the edge of Canada and the state of Maine. Twelve hundred miles and more. Four days if he pushed it, five days in a leisurely way. Why push it? he thought with a trace of bitterness. You're just filling in time now, boy. You've no place to go in a hurry, no deadlines ever again.

He poured himself an extra scotch on the rocks and slept better that night.

2

And suddenly, one more impatient
cried—
"Who is the Potter, pray, and who the
Pot?"

After breakfast the next morning, a bright and sunny June day, Bob Yardley locked the front door of his married quarters—that was a laugh, there were too many echoes of Angela in the place, a lingering trace of her scent in the now two-thirds empty bedroom closet—slung a suitcase on the back-seat of his Ford Bronco and drove slowly to the main gate. The sentry raised the pole and threw him a salute. With an acknowledging nod, he swung the car right and accelerated away. No fanfares, no farewells. He knew he'd be back, if only to clear out his things, but he already felt like a stranger. As he picked out the route toward Asheville, he vaguely remembered that the novelist Thomas Wolfe had come from there. Yardley had read one of his sprawling novels in some remote camp when it was the only book available. What was it called now? *You Never Go Home Again*—something like that. Right on, Thomas baby, he thought. You never do.

He sat back and let the car take him. If he saw an inviting side road running roughly westward, he took it and passed through hamlets he would never have seen—Pee Dee and Peachland and New Salem and Fairview—on his way to Charlotte. His thoughts drifted in circles but they always came back to dwell on his break with Angela. That quack was no fool. The breakup had hit him—right in the heart; he could remember how it had seemed to stop dead, then lurch on in a stumbling run when she first admitted to her affair with that psychopath Tim Bell—her lover before she married him. On the rebound, no doubt. He could have killed her right then. Or maybe held her in his arms and hoped it was just a bad dream. Even after he had seen Tim's body cartwheeling to his death in the Hudson River, he had somehow guessed things would never come right again between Angela and himself. In his line of work, when your life might depend on covering fire from a comrade, either you trusted your friends implicitly—or you never trusted them at all. There was no halfway house. And he knew, right down there, that he'd never be able to trust Angela again—in spite of her tears and her vows.

So when living together had become untenable and she had hesitantly suggested a spell apart—there was a reasonable excuse, her mother back in England had been seriously ill—he had sensed it was the end of the marriage. Which had been spelled out in a rambling, almost incoherent airmail letter from Angela several days later. She blamed herself entirely but between the lines he guessed she felt a bit relieved. She would get over it—but would he? He still had the sour taste of failure, almost defeat, in his mouth. Perhaps, if he'd been gentler, more considerate, had encouraged her to share his military life more, he could have kept it going. That last bit was a laugh. How can you share top-secret plans and classified weaponry with a talkative wife? Still, he had to accept the fact that it was basically his fault. He would miss that giggle of hers, the soft breasts and wide mouth, that sort of puppylike affection she exuded. Oh, Christ!

He had stayed the previous night at a motel on Route 40 just outside Marion, North Carolina, twenty miles short of joining the Blue Ridge Parkway. He had not talked to a living soul since leaving Fort Bragg the day before, apart from a brief chat with the waitress at the diner where he had breakfasted that morning and the gas pump attendant when he filled up just before the parkway. Somehow it had been a relief to be alone. Now it seemed to be backfiring on him, his anger was beginning to dominate. It was time to pull over, stretch his legs and get some air—quiet down a little. Yardley steered the Ford Bronco into a scenic turnoff and got out. The road had topped a rise and he enjoyed a view of the wooded slopes and the eerie mist shrouding the Shenandoah Valley. The late-afternoon light played wonders with scattered moist prisms threading through the branches. The tranquillity was broken by a voice behind him. "Excuse me, sir, are you heading north?"

Yardley turned to face a young man in his early twenties. He had long greasy blond hair and acne scars along his jawbone and was dressed in an open-necked shirt and dirty Levi's, with a leather poncho over the shirt. "Sure, I'm heading north. Are you in some kind of trouble?"

"No, sir," he replied. "No trouble, I just got separated from a friend a while back and need a ride to join him, up the road a ways."

"Okay, no problem. Get in and ride with me." Hell, Yardley thought, he'll be a welcome diversion.

As he pulled out onto the parkway, Yardley sniffed a strange smell, part sweat and part something he couldn't define. He hadn't noticed it outside in the open air, only now, in the close confines of the vehicle. The boy had tossed his light backpack into the rear seat and climbed into the front seat. He chatted on about the walk along the Appalachian Trail he and his friend had planned, and about being a student and a lover of nature, and then, looking straight ahead, he lapsed into silence. The smell and the silence irritated Yardley and he began to regret giving the kid a lift.

They had ridden about four miles when the hiker casually said, "You see that overlook ahead? Hundred yards up there on our side. Would you mind pulling in, sir?"

Yardley felt relieved. Maybe the kid had arranged to meet his friend here. He swung the Bronco into the parking area, which was sheltered by some fine oak trees, and came to a stop by a low wall that prevented anyone careless enough from rolling down a steep slope. There were a litter basket and a wooden table and benches alongside. Thirty yards away, in front of a station wagon with a U-Haul trailer attached, an old man wearing a baseball cap and his frumpy wife were gazing eastward, enjoying the view of the wooded plains below.

"You want to get out here?" Yardley asked.

"Yes, thank you, sir," said the young man. "I'm meeting my pal here." He turned in the seat and reached for his backpack. As he lifted it, his grip failed and it toppled into the rear of the wagon. "Oh hell, sir," he said, "would you mind opening the tailgate for me, sir, I don't want to climb all over your upholstery."

"Sure," Yardley said, and got out and walked to the back.

He unlocked the tail door and swung it open. As he reached inside for the backpack, his eyes met the boy's, staring back at him from the front seat. There was an evil smile across his face which widened with excitement. Yardley's brain registered danger, and then the wind was knocked violently out of him and excruciating pain shot the length of his back and changed just as suddenly to a sickening numbness. This traveled down his legs, and as it reached his feet, his legs gave way. With full force, the tail door, its weight doubled by the spare wheel anchored to the outside, had been slammed shut on his outstretched body. Now the unseen hands pulled it open again and Yardley slid to the ground. Gasping for breath and seemingly paralyzed, he was at the mercy of both of them. He looked up into the unshaven face of a man about his own age, with a scar running from the corner of his right eye to the corner of his mouth. There was no smile on this face, only violence. The man was wearing surplus Army fatigues and a camouflage smock. He busied himself searching Yardley's pockets and ordered the young man to go through the Bronco. They worked as a team, with a well-rehearsed routine.

Yardley willed the feeling back into his legs and sucked all the air he could find down into his lungs. He knew he had only seconds. Then the pent-up anger in him exploded. His upper torso came up off the ground and the full energy of his well-aimed head-butt caught the man across the bridge of his nose. As the man instinctively snapped his body back to protect his head and regain balance, he let out a scream. It was cut off by Yardley's left boot, which he buried heel first into the man's groin. The force of the kick sent him flying backward to crash against the wooden table, blood gushing in a fine spray from his smashed nose with every exhaling snort. The younger man's arms locked tight round Yardley's throat. He had seen the action start, and had left the cab and attacked from behind. Yardley lifted both arms and reached behind the kid's neck, gripped hard and pulled him bodily over his head. As the boy came over, Yardley gathered in his legs so that the small of the kid's back made a crunching impact with his raised knees. Releasing his grip, he brought the edge of his stiffened right hand down sharply on the exposed throat. The unconscious body rolled off Yardley's knees like a discarded rag doll. Yardley found his feet and moved in to face the man now raising himself from under the table. In his right hand was a deadly Applegate-Fairbairn fighting knife. It was in the hand of someone who had been trained to use it. Yardley saw all the signs, the stance, the easy grip and the feinting free hand. The one advantage in his own favor was that the man's balls were still up in his stomach.

Sliding inside the man's reach, Yardley clamped his left hand over the thrusting knife wrist, palm outward, and pulled the man into him, simultaneously driving the point of his elbow into his attacker's sternum. Following through, he spun and crouched slightly, put his right shoulder under the man's chin and looped his right arm over, then back under the straightened knife arm, to lock a grip on his own left forearm. Pulling hard and down on the knife arm as he executed a perfectly timed hip-throw, Yardley heard the man's elbow dislocate. The knife dropped from his grasp and he spun off Yardley to land heavily on his back. A scream of pain forced from his lungs came out as a high-pitched whistle as he went down. Dropping to one knee and still gripping the wrist that had held the knife, Yardley delivered one, and then another, pile-driving punch into the man's face. Groaning and the sound of heavy breathing filled Yardley's ears. He realized it was his own. All his wrath had welled to the surface and he fought back the urge to pulp the man's face and kill him.

He left them where they lay. He threw the backpack into the trees and closed the tailgate. Yardley found himself leaning heavily against the Bronco, his heart thumping. He felt drained and thought, What a sick fucking mess, as he moved slowly to the driver's door. The old couple in the overlook were still gazing at the view, oblivious to the drama. He climbed in behind the wheel and drove past their station wagon back onto the parkway going north. After a short while his pulse was beating like a regular drum and he began to feel better—in fact, much better.

On the afternoon of the third day, he left Route 81 at Chambersburg and drove east on 30 to Gettysburg. Fifteen years before, as a student at West Point, he had visited the place when studying the Civil War campaigns but his recollections of the place were hazy. He pulled the Bronco into one of the many parking areas, and ignoring the refreshment rooms and the information center with its videos and illustrated maps of the battle, he walked to the southern point of the cemetery. It was a hot, still afternoon. There were not too many visitors to break his reverie. He stood there among the marble monuments, the snouts of the cannons aiming southward, the uniform heaps of cannonballs, and gazed down the slope. The view couldn't have changed in a century and a quarter.

Half closing his eyes, he could visualize those Confederate troops in their ragged gray uniforms, hungry and desperate, making that charge up the hill against the massed forces of the North, the raking, scything fire of grapeshot that cut them down, the savage hand-to-hand fighting when a handful or more reached the ramparts. They must have fallen back and regrouped behind that green copse of trees down there and come again for yet another doomed charge. Boys who had grown too quickly into men, cousin against cousin—a necessary war perhaps, but a terrible war.

He had fallen into an easy, unthinking regime—a leisurely start in the morning after first working out a route on the map and listing the towns and highways he would pass through. After driving a hundred or more miles, he would break for coffee and a doughnut, then cover more miles in a vaguely northeastern direction. Shortly after six o'clock, he would find a quiet motel, then a shower, two or three large scotches from the almost empty first bottle, a quiet supper and early bed. Sleep came surprisingly easy. He had already begun to accept the fact that when the vacation was over he would be driving a desk for the rest of his Army career. And if he forgot, there was always the little white pill each morning to remind him. The choice was bleak. Somehow at thirty-five, after nearly half his life in the Army, he couldn't see himself entering the civilian rat race. Anyway, who would want him, for Christ's sake? He sketched out a typical job interview in his mind's eye.

"Okay, Mr.—what's your name?—Yardley, just gimme your qualifications." Some fat, balding guy behind a large desk, peering at him through gold-rimmed spectacles.

"Well, sir, I can do delayed parachute drops and kill a man with my bare hands or a knife. I'm a qualified marksman with six different types of small arms. I can swim a mile fully clothed. I can . . ."

"That's enough, Yardley. There's a door behind you. Close it quietly when you go out."

He stopped for lunch on the fifth day at the neat little town of Berlin in northeastern New Hampshire. Porch railings, the small church, many of the houses gleamed white in the strong sun. Ah, he thought, if I owned a paint store in New England, I could start my own private army—the hell with this one. He ate a couple of hot dogs and a slice of blueberry pie and flirted mildly with the middle-aged waitress. Maybe that quack at Bethesda had been right. What he needed was a good break.

After lunch, on an impulse, he headed north, not east toward Camden on the coast. Somehow it seemed too soon to be hunting up the ancestral home. It was early yet to be wallowing in nostalgia, to remember his strong, quiet father with his clipped mustache and slow voice, his mother with her dancing eyes and merry laugh. At least they had been happy when they died—too soon though it was. So he drove on rutted pavements through silent woods and long stretches of brooding water until he came to a signpost marked "Rangeley." It was late afternoon. When he came to the one-street town alongside a big lake, he fell for it at once. He pulled into a motel at the edge of the lake and booked himself a room.

Next morning, after five days of sitting at the wheel of his car, he felt like some real exercise. The sun was sparkling on the peat-brown lake, which was deserted apart from a solitary fisherman in a boat two hundred yards offshore. Yardley had flung a pair of swimming trunks into his bag, and so, without another thought, he changed in his motel room, walked across the mown lawn to a little wooden jetty and slid into the cold silky water. He decided to swim roughly in the direction of the moored boat, just in case his heart played up—although it seemed as good as it ever had been. In a long, steady crawl stroke he cut across the placid lake.

Fifty yards short of the boat, he swung onto his back, shaking the soft water out of his eyes. He glanced at the boat, narrowing his gaze against the bright sun. The lone fisherman appeared to be waving. What the hell, he thought. New Englanders are supposed to be dour folk. It must be the sun in my eyes. He looked again. No, the old boy—he looked old and hunched up in his mackinaw and baseball cap—was definitely waving. With a dozen powerful slow strokes, Yardley cut the distance until he was treading water a few feet from the boat.

From the shadow cast by the baseball cap came the grating sound of a voice he had come to know well. "Major Yardley, I presume."

He spat out a mouthful of lake water. "Christ, General Bradford from the NSC. What the hell you doing here, sir?"

"Waiting for you, Yardley."

"But no one knows where I am. Hell, I didn't know myself until last night."

"There are ways and means, Yardley. Look, you're ruining my fishing. You know the Rangeley Hotel? Big building halfway up the main street on the far side of the road. Dinner there tonight at seven—and don't be late. That's an order."

"Number-one mess dress, *sir*?"

"Don't be insolent, Yardley. You're talking to a general!"

Brimming with suspicions and unvoiced questions, Yardley strode up the main street of Rangeley that evening and entered the old-fashioned hotel with its bamboo chairs and morose-looking stags' heads mounted on the walls. Just to show his independence, he was going to turn up in an open-necked shirt and a sweater, but at the last moment decided to put on a tie and coat. Just as well, because the general was wearing a well-pressed alpaca suit and a familiar-looking tie with dark red and blue stripes. He was sipping sherry in a tulip glass and without asking ordered a scotch on the rocks for his guest.

"Excuse me, sir, but isn't that a British Army tie?"

"Sure is, my boy. The Guards, no less. Never heard about my secondment to the Guards Armored Division? World War Two—under General Horrocks. Looked like a bishop—and acted like one often enough. We might have relieved those poor bastards, the Red Devils, at Arnhem, if he'd shown more drive. I was only a boy—just twenty and first time in action."

He prattled on about his wartime experiences, then ordered fish—"straight from the lake, it says here"—and a bottle of white wine for them both, again without consulting his guest. At last, when he had to pause for breath, Yardley cut in.

"There's something—a lot—I don't understand. First, how did you just happen to be here? It was after lunch yesterday I decided to make for this place. Don't tell me it's one big coincidence."

"Of course not. I had a DF-forty-two transmitter fixed

under the trunk of your car. Ten-mile range. All my boys had to do was travel along a few miles behind."

"You had me followed?"

"Oh, sure. They lost you once. On the Blue Ridge Parkway, when you stopped to sort out that hitchhiker and his mate. Remember that light-aircraft activity later that afternoon around Roanoke, West Virginia? That was them relocating you. Pretty neat, I thought."

"What the hell is all this in aid of? I'm a soldier, not a fugitive on the run!" And then all Yardley's suspicions began to slide into place, like the tumblers of a well-oiled lock. "All those symptoms, the medical tests. Do I really have a serious heart condition?"

"You have a heart like an ox. No, with some help from our medical people at Fort Detrick, Maryland, we had a little something put in your water supply. Sure, you're not much of a water drinker but you like your coffee and your scotch on the rocks. Our funny boys tampered with your icemaker. Don't worry, Yardley, it's just temporary. I'll wager your heart's better already, now you're away from Bragg."

Yardley clenched a big fist. "So you screwed up my Army career. For a joke? I've killed men I didn't even know for less."

"No joke. This is deadly serious. You should know me better by now. I can't afford a sense of humor in my job. Now come on—eat up your fish."

Yardley pushed the plate away. "I've sort of lost my appetite."

"Right, we'll have coffee in my room. I've a bottle of Armagnac there that might interest you. No need to look suspicious, Major. The room's not bugged. This is just between you and me. *Off the record.*"

They went up the wooden stairs to his large, old-fashioned bedroom, which had a small sitting room with a verandah overlooking the lake. It looked brown and sinister, tinged with the red streaks of the setting sun.

Yardley was still on edge, angry and suspicious. "This had better be good, sir," he said.

"Just listen while I tell you. That's all I ask." General Bradford swirled the cognac round his glass, took a long swallow and then continued. "You heard of Chubb's in London? Sure you have. Their safes and security equipment are world-famous. Well, one of their best trained technicians, a man named Peter Shaw—a quiet man who kept himself to himself—resigned a year ago. Nothing strange in that, people come and go in the best jobs, though he looked set for some kind of stardom. It turned out he was a mad gambler and some goons were after him for not paying his debts. They leaned on him—and it's a short step from safe maker to safe breaker. The mob found out where the good stuff was, and in went Mr. Shaw to twiddle the knobs. You with me so far?"

Yardley nodded and sipped his cognac.

"His last job was to do the safe at our ambassador's residence in Regent's Park. You know, the grand big house near the zoo. His Excellency's lady has great taste in diamonds, they tell me. What no one knew—and it's never been announced—was that the secretary of state happened to be staying there that night on his way back to Washington. He placed some very top-secret documents in the private safe overnight. Shaw lifted the lot *including* the secret papers.

"Scotland Yard picked him up soon afterward—*and* the papers still in their sealed wallet. At least so it seemed. We heard through a friend at the Yard that he tried to do a deal. If they didn't square the judge for a lenient sentence, he would pass the contents on to the press. Bluff? Or had he opened the wallet, made notes or even photocopies? The British cops didn't push him—why should they, it was no skin off their nose. So our Mr. Shaw is doing a seven-year stretch at a quaintly named jail, Wormwood Scrubs, in the northwest suburbs of London."

"All very interesting, General. Make a good TV play. But I don't see what it has to do with me."

"You, Major Yardley, are going to spring him."

"I'm—what? And end up in the next cell!"

"Here, not so fast, my boy. Let me replenish that glass of yours. You've only heard the half of it yet."

The general leaned forward in his basketwork chair and went on talking quietly but urgently in that rasping voice of his, like the crackling of dry sticks underfoot. Back in the early seventies, he said, the British had been worried about security in their jails. There had been too many breakouts: Earl Mountbatten had been asked to advise. He arranged for five SAS teams to test the system by seeing if they could break into five of the maximum-security jails and get out again without being detected. They did. Of the men involved, at least two-thirds were out of active service but still around.

Yardley wouldn't have to break into Wormwood Scrubs himself. His job would be to recruit an ex–SAS team to spring Shaw. Once out, the man would be spirited to France, where the local CIA would grill him intensively, find out just what he knew of the documents and whether he'd passed anything on.

"Now I'm going to be indiscreet, Major. This is for your ears only. Some of that stuff is straight out of the Kremlin—so hot it makes hell look cold. An inside assessment of Gorbachev; who's against him in the Politburo; his chance of surviving; what's really happening with the warheads. The circulation of those papers would be restricted to maybe six—the president, secretary of state, the heads of Defense, NSC and CIA. Why do you think the secretary was carrying them personally? They fall into the wrong hands, our contacts inside the Kremlin are blown away. And I tell you, it's taken since Penkovsky's execution—twenty years back—to set 'em up."

Yardley said, "I hear you, sir. But why me? There must be a dozen guys in Langley—professionals—trained for a job like this."

"Correction, Major. There's no one comes near your qualifications. You've proved yourself in action, you're not a talker—and best of all, you have the contacts. We can't have Americans busting into a British jail. It has to be a team from the SAS. Okay, ex-SAS. And you're known and liked at headquarters in Hereford. Don't look surprised—I check things out. No guy's indispensable—we all know that—but you're the next-best thing."

"*If* I accept—I'm not saying I will—and *if* Shaw gets sprung, what happens then?"

"That's about it. Once he's handed over to the Company in France, they'll hoover him inside out. If he's clean, he gets turned loose for Interpol to pick up. If he ain't, then he could be due for an accident. That's not your problem. Your job's done when you hand him over."

"You make it sound easy, sir," Yardley said. "I can't go busting into London and put an ad in the papers: 'Wanted—three strong men to break into a jail. Apply Box so-and-so.' Have a heart."

"I'm ahead of you, Major. You'll be interested to know that through various contacts, I've gotten a New York publisher to put up three-quarters of a million bucks for your inside book on Special Forces involvement in every covert op since the Bay of Pigs."

"My—what?"

"Oh, yes. When they heard a real-live hero on convalescent leave was going to write *the* authentic book on Special Forces action worldwide, not just the Green Berets, Delta Force and Task Force 160, but the British SAS, the French Foreign Legion Second REP, the German GSG 9, and the rest, they were ready to jump without parachutes to get their hands on you. Our contact should have held out for more money."

"You have a nerve, General. How do you know I can do more than write a report to my CO?"

"My boy, you are too modest. Hell, you just start at the beginning and work your butt off till you get to the end. Why, every pinko at the White House and the State Department is into writing books these days. If they can, you can. Besides, I've read your articles released in our services publications and your fine papers on 'surgical operations' and counterterrorism that you presented to SHAPE HQ in Brussels and SOCOM in DC. They made damn good reading. And anyway, publishers have experienced editors to give it a final polish."

"What if—with great respect, sir—I don't play ball and suggest that you shove the whole idea?"

"That's your privilege. After all, we're not in Moscow. But let's not forget the Army *does* own desks in some very remote places." The general paused for effect. "You know how it works, Major. We get very single-minded about these covert jobs, once they get the go-ahead. And we get to feel the same way about the people we recruit to do them—refusal ain't really part of the vocabulary, if you get my drift."

Yardley solemnly nodded and thought, Uh-huh, a permanent medical downgrading and a posting to transport officer, Albuquerque, and oblivion. Those ball-crunchers in DC always did have a sweet way of getting a soldier's acquiescence. Or is this Langley talking? Christ knows what agency our friendly general is fronting for. Sure, I know how it works, and I'm not being asked, I'm being told.

"It all sounds too easy, General," Yardley said. "And as full of holes as auntie's colander. Why don't you get the Brits to grill this man Shaw? Their C Branch people would get him singing in no time—they're no fools when it comes to interrogation. He's *their* man, tucked up in *their* jail."

"Wake up, Major." There was a ring of sarcasm in the

general's voice. "Some things we don't share with the cousins. Have them laughing in their dainty teacups to know such sensitive papers were left in a safe you could bust open with a can opener? Forget it."

"And who carries the can if the op comes unstuck? They do go wrong sometimes, sir, even the best-planned ops. Washington leaks like a sieve—anything can happen."

"That's a naive question, Bob. Why do you think we've gone to all this trouble to get you isolated from Special Forces and on medical furlough? You know the score by now. You will be deniable—the whole operation will be deniable, nothing to do with Uncle Sam."

"Well, there's sure as hell nothing new in that. But what about the SAS guys? The British won't like us using them, and if they get wind of it, they'll apply the usual pressure to make them back out. It could jeopardize everything."

"That's not my problem. You'll have to handle that yourself over there—pick 'em good and set up a smart cut-out plan that disassociates you from the actual jailbreak. Shit! I don't have to tell you."

"Can I think this over, General?"

"Sure, Bob, you sleep on it. And don't be so gloomy, remember, you'll be collecting all those bucks riding on the book. Eleven o'clock tomorrow morning, I'll be out on the lake—same place—tossing a fly over those damned elusive trout. You swim out and give me your answer, right? Oh, and flush the rest of those digoxin pills down the john."

They both got up to leave. Yardley's mind was already sifting through the general's words. Failure or disclosure of the op would be down to him, a major in the U.S. Army—probably ex-major by now. They would have had his medical discharge papers on file and backdated since the day he left the Bethesda hospital. He'd be on his own, the rest of the Yale and brass-hat element would vaporize if the shit hit the fan. Including this General George Patton derivative standing in front of him.

General Bradford stood there and looked him straight in the face, his eyes as hard as flint. As if he had read Yardley's thoughts, he said, "I like your style, Major. That's why I chose you for the assignment. But you cross me up—and I'll make you wish you'd joined the Navy!"

Yardley walked down the quiet main street back to his motel. The little stock theater was closed, dark. He sat in a deck chair on the lawn for an hour, looking out at the silent lake and listening to the slopping of the wavelets against the wooden jetty. Then he shook himself like a dog coming out of the water and went to bed.

Next morning, another sun-blazing day, he saw the solitary boat moored two hundred yards away. He stripped to his swimming trunks, did a racing dive off the jetty and swam out to the boat, his feet throwing up a wake behind him in a steady eight-beat crawl.

"They biting, General?"

"Not now, they ain't. All that splashing."

"Well, here's one sucker who's taken the bait. I'm on."

"Right. Be back at Fort Bragg a week from today. You'll get a call from a guy calling himself a literary agent. Name of Wilkinson. But he's one of mine. He'll have your instructions when you go see him in New York. There's no time to spare, so don't hang around. Oh, and Bob—thanks. I mean it."

3

Come, fill the Cup, and in the Fire of
Spring
The Winter Garment of Repentance fling:
The Bird of Time has but a little way
To fly—and Lo! the Bird is on the Wing.

"Welcome to the Lansdowne Club, Mr. Yardley, sir. If you'd just go up those steps, across the waiting room and book in at reception. I'll have your bags taken up to your room. Nice to have you with us, sir." This from the gray-haired porter behind the desk.

Ah, that old-world British courtesy, Yardley thought as he followed instructions. Even if they carve you up, at least they do it with that well-known *politesse.* He felt crummy and gritty-eyed after the overnight flight, but after a shower and an hour's rest on the bed in the narrow single room, he went downstairs and strolled around what had been an eighteenth-century mansion, the town house of the noble Lansdowne family. He wondered at the grand ballroom with its ornate blue-and-gold ceiling and a minstrel gallery at either end. The house had been designed and built by Robert Adam, the famous architect, whose name was commemorated in the Adam Room, now the bar, with its intricate plaster ceiling. The general, who had put him up for temporary membership, had told him to look out especially for the small anteroom off the bar, a shrine for all patriotic Americans. For it was there, over two hundred years ago, that the then Marquess of Lansdowne, secretary of state for the Colonies, had signed away that obstreperous Yankee one. A small portrait of the marquess hung over the Adam fireplace in the anteroom.

Yardley went into the bar and ordered a prelunch beer. He was privately horrified to learn that the club had only those light, gassy bottled beers and lagers beloved of Americans, not the heavy sour draft English beer he had come to like on his various visits to Hereford. He was not horrified to learn, as he sat quietly at a corner table, that it was a mixed club. From the patio behind the open French windows, he could hear the neighing sound young English girls made when they laughed. Ah, the girls in their summer dresses. For the first time in weeks, he could feel a stirring in the loins, a sense of life and excitement. He was going to get fighting fit again—hence the beer instead of scotch on the rocks. The advantage of the Lansdowne Club, General Bradford had said at their last meeting, was that it had squash courts and a swimming pool in the basement and was only a few hundred yards from both Hyde Park and Green Park. "If some phony modern saint name of Madonna can go running in Green Park, Bob, you sure as hell can. And see you do, what's more."

Sipping his beer, he reflected on all that had happened, so much of it, in the eighteen days since Rangeley Lake. There had been two visits to New York to meet his supposed literary agent, Ken Wilkinson, prematurely white-haired with a soft sarcastic voice. But whether he was a genuine agent or someone from the Company throwing around a lot of big words, he seemed to know his way around contracts—and indeed there was a contract—with all those zeros in clause 5 on page 4. The general had been as good as his word. Maybe the NSC or the Company owned the publishing house. Anything was possible when the cloaks and the daggers came out.

"Are all contracts as tough as this one?" he had asked Wilkinson.

"They fling lumps of lovely dough at you and you call it tough? Let me tell you, Major, sir, I sweated big drops to pull you this deal."

"And I'm grateful. But the way I read it—maybe I'm wrong, being just a clodhopping soldier—one, I cover them against libel, but two, they can settle anytime they like without a how-d'you-do. Three, if they don't like the book, they just say so—I can't argue—and they're liable to get their money back. If I haven't spent it. Four, if they lose or damage the typescript, too bad, no skin off their nose. Five—do you want me to go on?"

"Ever thought of becoming an agent, *Major*?"

"This is a business discussion, isn't it?"

"It is, believe me. I'm on your side, not theirs. But a wise man once said to me, When you go into a negotiation, leave the other side with a slight smile on their faces. Don't just nail 'em to the wall. It makes sense, Major. You may be the best goddamn writer since Saul Bellow. Or maybe you can't write your way out of a wet paper bag. We don't know yet. Either way, we want the publisher at bat on our side, not pitching curveballs at us. You get me?"

Yardley got him, all right. What he didn't get when he came to meet the publishers high up on Madison Avenue was any feeling they knew what the book was about or of what they wanted him to write. The book might be part of a cover plan, but he never did things by halves, and after some thought he had became quite interested in the project. He scribbled out several pages of notes on the Green Berets and their origins, the U.S. Rangers, the SEAL teams, and something of the background, as he had learned it from periods of attachment, of the SAS and its birth in the Western Desert under Colonel Stirling in World War Two. The pale woman editor and the earnest bespectacled young man, her assistant, greeted him with the deference and respect Moses no doubt received when he came down from the mountain with the tablets, but there was no input, no bright ideas for a starting point or chapter headings or suggestions for a main theme to which his many stories should be linked. Well, it was up to them. They were buying.

The first priority was to put together a snatch team for Wormwood Scrubs. At least the publishers had supplied him with an imposing-looking letter announcing "to whom it may concern" that they had commissioned him to write the definitive story of Special Forces worldwide.

He knew from General Bradford's briefing that his first task in London was to emphasize the cover plan. So the first morning after his arrival he strolled from the Lansdowne Club up the west side of Berkeley Square, past the Connaught Hotel into Grosvenor Square, and called at the U.S. Embassy, where he signed the book and chatted briefly with a junior official named Steiner. The same day, he telephoned SAS headquarters at Hereford, a hundred and fifty miles northwest of London on the border of England and Wales. The adjutant knew of him from previous attachments and invited him to have lunch two days later. He had half forgotten the brisk efficiency of the SAS network and how quickly the word got around in that small world. It was something of a surprise, therefore, when the following morning there arrived at the Lansdowne Club an embossed invitation card to dine with other SAS squadron members the next Tuesday evening at their mess at the Duke of York's Barracks in Chelsea, West London. At the bottom of the card were the words "Mess Dress." Luckily, he had brought his number-one dress uniform.

On the way down to Hereford in the train, he thought again of his last meeting with General Bradford at the Waldorf-Astoria on the occasion of his second visit to New York. Over a meal, he gave Yardley his final instructions.

"Just to wrap it up, Bob. You've been fully briefed and now you're on your own. The word's out that you've been given six months' leave to write a book on Special Forces and you're starting your research in England. You take that check from your publisher and open yourself a local account with Barclays Bank, Pall Mall, London. You are to operate all your cash funds out of that account. No checks, no credit cards. The dollars amount to about eighty thousand English pounds, you shouldn't need more. If you do, call Ken Wilkinson. I don't want to hear a word from you. Once you leave this room, we don't know each other. Whatever happens—and I mean *whatever*—don't come crying for the general, he don't live here anymore.

"This op is as deep as they can go. Our ambassador in London, his first secretary and the rest of them, including the company bureau chief, who's billed as the energy attaché, know nothing about this caper. And they mustn't. If you find yourself in the end zone without your pants, don't turn up at Grosvenor Square looking for a new pair. The embassy has got to go on living pure, in London, they must be Caesar's wife. Your only outside contact is Roger Rodel, the agency man at our Paris embassy." He handed Yardley a slip of paper. "That is his current secure number, a direct line. It's manned twenty-four hours a day." He retrieved the paper from Yardley's fingers. "When you call him, use a pay phone—if I know those limeys, they've got most of London bugged."

"When I was last in England, sir, the public telephones never worked. If you could find one without its guts torn out."

"Ah, they've learned the meaning of privatization since then, and phone cards, no more of that crap with those big coins of theirs. You need call Rodel only three times. One, for initial contact and to let him know you've arrived. Two, the day before the snatch and three, as soon as you can when you know Shaw is out of their reach. Maintain your cover story throughout. When you call Rodel the second time, he'll be expecting you to tell him that you'll be finished with your research in England tomorrow—or whenever you've timed the snatch—and you will ask him to arrange an interview for you at the Foreign Legion headquarters at Aubagne. He'll answer, 'It will take a few days to organize.' And the third call from you will be to tell him you're coming to Paris anyway—that day."

"And do I fly to Paris that day?"

"You sure do. With Shaw out and away, there's no need for you to hang around. Don't underestimate the Brits, they'll be onto you by then. Put the English Channel between you and Her Majesty's Government, like you were a one-fifty-five shell out of a howitzer. There's bound to be a few casualties in your smoke. There always are."

The general stuck out his hand. Yardley shook it, stood up and gathered his tunic off the back of his chair. He looked around at the opulence, his eyes fixing on two beautiful bejeweled women. His mind registered that it would all have to wait until he got back. He looked across the table.

"Thanks, General."

"Best of luck, son. Hell—I wish I was coming with you." He blew his nose loudly on a Waldorf table napkin and shuffled awkwardly.

Yardley smiled kindly and walked off. Shit, he thought, that's all I need, a sentimental goddamn general.

Hereford was a pleasant trip down memory lane. It was at least three years since Yardley's last attachment there and he felt a nostalgic pang as he saw again the old familiar places inside the Banbury Lines, the killing houses on the left, where the Pagoda teams trained, the wooden creosoted buildings and, above all, the clock that stood on a wooden plinth in the center. The name of every SAS man killed in battle or covert action was painted in gold on the clock tower. Staying alive in the Regiment was known as "beating the clock." He had learned on previous attachments never to ask after an old comrade unless he was damn sure the man was alive and well. Too often there had been a shrug and a quiet "Oh, he failed to beat the clock." Nothing more.

From his last detailed briefing with the general, Yardley had learned that one of the SAS team who had successfully broken into and out of Wormwood Scrubs on the special op all those years ago was a sergeant named Mike Murphy, an Irishman. Yardley vaguely remembered him from the past. He must be well into his thirties now, pushing forty maybe, and probably on the reserve. So over lunch in the officers' mess, after the usual badinage about pen-pushing and the U.S. Rangers becoming the U.S. Writers, and "Careful, chaps, old Bob's got his recorder switched on," he started asking casually after old friends, including Sergeant Murphy. There was a fractional pause and at the edge of his vision he saw that the adjutant on his left frowned slightly. Then someone answered, almost too heartily, "Oh, Mike's doing all right. He's been out a few years now, must be four or five."

The adjutant cut in, "Yes, Bob, we don't see a lot of Murphy these days. Lives in London, doing some kind of security work, they say."

Yardley could read the signs. He knew they wouldn't be disloyal but something was wrong. Mike Murphy was definitely not the flavor of the month in the Regiment. He changed the subject, saying, "How's Colonel David? Would he give me half an hour, if I asked nicely?" Colonel David Stirling was the legendary founder of the SAS.

"He hasn't been too well—not as young as he was. But I'm sure he'd like to see you. Let's see, you're staying at the Lansdowne Club. He's got a place in South Audley Street, couple of hundred yards from you. Shouldn't be beyond your navigational skills, Bob, to find it. I'll give you the address and phone number before you go."

On his way back in the train to London that afternoon, Yardley assessed the visit. Part of him chafed at the slowly-slowly tactics. Diplomacy was not his strong suit. He would have liked to go straight in to ask direct questions about Murphy and the other guys on the prison break-in. But he knew the SAS had a wide private network. Once their suspicions were aroused, the word would spread secretly—and he would be effectively frozen out. As it was, he reckoned they had bought his cover story. In fact, on bidding him farewell, the adjutant had said he was welcome to return for a longer stay and interview some of the old hands. He could also read some of the closed operational files. Of course, they'd like to see his draft chapters dealing with the SAS before his book went into publication. "No censorship, Bob, you understand. Just to make sure you've got the details right." Like hell, he thought, but he smiled his thanks.

For the next few days, he slipped into an easy routine. After waking up at the club, he would take the elevator down to the basement and swim a dozen lengths of the pool. Then a cold shower and breakfast. Most mornings he would wander around London, getting the geography clear in his mind. Once he took a bus from the Paddington area along Du Cane Road past Wormwood Scrubs Prison. From the upper deck of the bus, he glanced across at the grim building with its turrets and solid gate. It looked forbidding, impregnable. How the hell do you get in and out of that, he thought, without armor-piercing shells and a brigade of infantry supported by tanks? Well, the SAS had done it once; they'd sure as hell have to do it twice. He only hoped the defenses had not been improved too much after that first going-over.

Several afternoons, to confuse possible surveillance, he called in at the Imperial War Museum, south of the river not far from Waterloo Station. It had an excellent reference library, and once he had told the curator of his mission, the library staff was helpful. The book project, which had started as a joke, was beginning to get to him. He had always thought of World War Two as a series of massed actions, twenty or more divisions—maybe a quarter of a million men or more—on one side against similar numbers on the other. "How many divisions has the Pope?" Stalin had asked in his sardonic Georgian way. He had never realized how many small, sometimes irregular, units there had been—the British commandos, the SAS, Popski's Private Army, Force 133 in the Dodecanese islands, Otto Skorzeny's special units on the German side. Once, sitting in the hushed library at the museum, he broke into a loud chuckle and startled the other serious researchers. He had been thinking of the look on General Bradford's face, if he suddenly announced that the real mission was off. He would just keep the money and stay in England to get on with his book.

In the evenings before going to bed, he would put on a track suit and his running shoes and run twice round Green

Park, just a hundred yards south of the club. At the far corner, you could look across at the imposing pile of Buckingham Palace with the sentries in their bearskin hats stamping to and fro across the courtyard. He had a growing fondness for England. Nothing ever changed—at least on the surface. It was like a swan. The feet might be paddling furiously under the water, but everything went gliding along serenely above it.

On the evening of the dinner at the Duke of York's Barracks, he changed into his mess dress, cursing as he fastened the tight collar. Although it was a sultry July night, he put on a light raincoat over his uniform. He didn't want the members at the Lansdowne Club thinking he was going to a fancy-dress ball or parading as an extra in a remake of *The Four Feathers.* The taxi took him down Sloane Avenue and around the square and dropped him outside the barracks guardroom on King's Road, the cradle of the swinging sixties. The man in the window of the guard hut took his name, checked the list and said, "Major Yardley, sir? Yes, they're expecting you. You know your way to the Artists' Rifles mess, sir? It's that building on your left, the first you come to. Up the stairs, second floor."

He smiled to himself. The SAS kept itself so secret that it didn't even admit to having its own headquarters at the barracks but took the name of the resident reserve unit, which had been formed from volunteers in the Great War.

He had deliberately arrived ten minutes early. When he reached what the Brits called the first floor—the second, to logical Yanks—he looked into the mess bar, hoping to spot a friendly face. He was lucky. The bar was quiet, but there were two men chatting in one corner. He recognized one, a sergeant major named Alan Smith with whom he'd trained on his last attachment. Smith knew him at once and offered him a drink. When asked what he was doing in town, Yardley mentioned the book and the names of various squaddies he would like to interview. He slipped Murphy's name halfway into the list. Smith's reply echoed that of the adjutant at Hereford.

"We don't see much of Mike these days. He had that spot of bother."

"Oh?"

"Yeah, well. Don't know too much about it meself. I was abroad at the time. No, we've rather lost touch with old Mike. Pity."

He knew too much to push it. The Regiment had its own brand of loyalty. They didn't split on an old comrade. But something must have gone wrong if Murphy was no longer persona grata at the Duke of York's. Christ, he thought, back to the drawing board. Who the hell do I contact now? He thanked Smith for the drink and went upstairs to the adjutant's office.

Dining in was always an occasion—all those knives and forks and the collection of shining glasses in front of each setting, the silver candelabra and the mess ornaments. He recognized the framed black-and-white photographs of famous men and events: a youthful Colonel Stirling in the Western Desert; Paddy Mayne, who had won three—or was it four?—DSOs in World War Two. He knew that the Distinguished Service Order was Britain's second-highest military decoration. To win one you had to be very good. To win three, you had to be crazy. And there was that picture of the Marbit Fort in Oman, where a handful of SAS men held off hordes of yelling tribesmen. There was a sense of quiet pride about the room.

The colonel was in his blue patrols, as was the adjutant, and even the most junior officers present wore service dress. An ex-commander of the Hereford Squadron, Colonel Alistair McAlister, a Scotsman, wore full Highland dress, the frilly jabot at the neck, silver buttons, a kilt in his clan tartan and even the ornamental knife, the *skean dhu,* in the top of his right stocking above silver-buckled shoes. Yardley noticed that the eyes of several of the more junior officers flicked from time to time to the bright ribbon of the Congressional Medal, which led the top rank of his own medal ribbons—but they were too well bred to ask him about it.

At the end of the dinner, when they had drunk the Loyal Toast to the Queen and another to the Regiment and the port decanter was circulating, Colonel McAlister, drawing on a deadly-looking long black cheroot, asked him where he was staying and how long he'd be in London. "Ever been grouse shooting, Bob?" he asked. "The season starts in a couple of weeks. I'll be having a party up at my place in Scotland. Mainly paying customers—these city slickers'll pay through the nose for the real thing—but you'd be my guest. It's an experience, believe me. We bang away all day and then there's some wholesome traditional fare and good drink in the evening."

He was so insistent that Yardley found himself agreeing to

the visit. It would take him at least another two or three weeks to set up the snatch and a few days in Scotland could help the cover story.

He was nicely muzzy with the good food and the fine wines as he retraced his steps to the guardroom after the dinner in search of a cab on King's Road to take him back to the Lansdowne Club. I enjoyed that, he said to himself, but it was really a wasted evening. Nearly a week in London—and damn near nothing to show for it. But the man on duty, as he was letting him out, said, "Paddy up in the mess says you wanna contact Mike Murphy, sir. Try the Wellington Tavern. It's a pub near Waterloo Station, other side of the railway bridge. He's usually there of a night."

The time dragged by—and there was no sign of Murphy. Knowing he might have to hang around for several hours, Yardley took small sips from his pint of bitter, but even so he could not prolong it beyond half an hour. On the third pint, he fell into conversation with an old man sucking the yellow-stained mouthpiece of a briar pipe, which made disgusting bubbling sounds. The old boy had served in World War Two and went droning on about the Second Front as though he alone had paddled ashore that June morning nearly half a century before. But at least it helped to pass the time.

The only thing to break the monotony happened not long before closing time when Yardley went up to the bar to buy the old man "one for the road." A punk rocker with a studded leather jacket and dyed black hair in spikes was standing at the bar, waving his arms around and shouting raucously to impress the painted-up peroxide blonde in a miniskirt alongside him. As Yardley edged back from the bar with a glass of beer in each hand, the rocker swung his left arm sideways, giving Yardley a glancing blow above his elbow. His arm jerked and a couple of drops from the right-hand glass splashed on the man's tight jeans. "I'm terribly sorry," he said.

"You clumsy cunt!" the punk yelled. "Now look what you've done—ruined me jeans."

"I said I'm sorry. Here, let me buy you a drink to make up for it."

"You sound like a fuckin' Yank. Think you can buy your way out of trouble, just like that. How about we go outside and settle it, man to man?" The punk clenched his fists and squared up to impress his girlfriend.

For a moment, Yardley was tempted to take him up on the offer. Christ, he thought, there must be something about me that gets to these punks, first that hitchhiker on the parkway and now this loudmouthed nothing. Then he realized it would be crazy. Brawling outside a London pub, maybe putting his opponent into the hospital—that would blow the project to hell and gone.

"I have a bad heart," Yardley said. "Any excitement and I might keel over. You don't want a murder charge, do you?" He put the beer down on the counter, pulled three pound coins out of his pocket and said to the barman, "Here, give these good folk what they want." He picked up the beer and went back to the old man in the corner. Behind him, he could hear the punk's jeering comment, "Bad heart, eh? More like no guts!" He sat down at the table and could feel the nails of his left hand digging into the palm. Restraint was part of his conditioning.

The following evening, a Thursday, he struck lucky right off. As he entered the Wellington Tavern, he recognized Mike Murphy at the far end of the bar, deep in conversation with a thin-faced ferrety-looking man. Murphy saw him at once and waved. A few minutes later, the other man went off and Murphy came over.

"Why, it's Major Yardley from Bragg. Welcome to London, Major. Let me buy you a drink."

"A pint of bitter would do fine. And let's cut that rank crap. It's Bob to you, Mike."

He could see Murphy was pleased, more so than he might have expected. Off parade, members of the SAS and its close allies were always on first-name terms, irrespective of rank. He looked at the man casually as he worked his way toward the bar. A short man, maybe five feet, six inches, he had always looked like a naughty choirboy, with flaxen hair that stood up in an untidy clump at the back, innocent-looking blue eyes and round pink cheeks. What was that English saying? "Butter wouldn't melt in his mouth." Yet he knew Murphy's reputation as a hard man among some of the hardest on earth. He had fought with distinction in that savage undercover war in Oman and had been involved in the storming of the Iranian Embassy in London. He was a real gadgets type, always experimenting with new infrared sights or waterproofing weapons or, as an explosives expert, playing around with booby traps. When he came back to their corner table with a pint for his guest and a large scotch for himself, Yardley could see that the first joints of the knuckles on each hand were heavily scarred from bare-knuckle fighting.

For half an hour and more, they talked about old times and old friends. Murphy remembered most of the U.S. Rangers with attachments to Hereford during his time and seemed genuinely shocked when he inquired after an American explosives expert, "Flamer" Brown, only to be told that the Flamer was dead.

"Couple of months ago, Mike. He blew himself up."

"You don't say? Christ, how'd it happen?"

"It was stupid, really. You know those phony light bulbs that are actually grenades—of course you do, you and Flamer probably invented them—well, he had one in the light fixture in his bathroom, must've forgotten, switched on the light and—curtains. Mind you, Flamer'd fallen on tough times. He was living dangerously."

"Why, what happened, Bob?"

"It all started with that accident of his. You know, he was fooling around with an incendiary device, something went wrong—and it burned the side of his face off. The plastic surgery never took properly and he was retired. On a miserable half-pension. I have to say, the Army treated him lousily."

Murphy said bitterly, "Ain't that a fact? Same wherever you go. Wot they used to say—long service in hot stations—and when you've done your time, it's 'Thank you, my man. You get off here. And don't call us—and we sure as hell won't call you.' "

Yardley said, "Here, it's my round." He went up to the bar and ordered another large scotch for Murphy and a half-pint for himself. He wanted to keep his man's vocal cords well oiled. After Yardley bought yet another round, Murphy was in full flow. His "spot of bother," as Sergeant Major Smith had delicately put it, turned out to have been a six-month jail sentence for GBH—grievous bodily harm. There were extenuating circumstances, or else the sentence would have been much longer. He had returned unexpectedly from a spell in Northern Ireland to find his wife in bed—"right on the fucking job," as he put it—with the local handyman.

"I give 'im fucking handyman an' all, Bob. I'm telling you. He wasn't too handy when I'd finished. Knocked his front teeth halfway down his throat an' broke his left arm. The judge said I used 'undue force.' Undue force—I'm asking you. You walk in all nice and friendly, Bob, and find some guy astride your everlovin', giving it to her right up to the hilt, what're you supposed to do? Sit down and suggest a game of three-handed bridge? Course the Regiment stood by. Gave evidence on my behalf. That helped. But when I come out after doing my time, I soon got the hint when I dropped into the Duke of York's. Nobody actually *said* anything, but you could tell from their faces. I felt like a stiff prick in a nunnery!"

From there it was the old inevitable story. In the normal way, he would have been snapped up by KMS or one of the other security outfits that recruited ex-SAS men to act as bodyguards for VIPs. But no one wanted a guy with a criminal record. Nor did employers in Civvy Street, especially a man who was thought to be violent. So he had picked up odd jobs, escort to a dodgy bookmaker, bouncer at a sleazy Soho nightclub. Now he was acting as driver and bodyguard to a man he called the Boss, a major underworld figure. The Boss spent most evenings in a West End gambling club he partly owned. Murphy would pick him up around midnight in the large Mercedes and drive him back to his mansion in Hampstead with the security gate and the video cameras positioned at strategic corners. Although he was a Roman Catholic, Mike had divorced his wife and now divided his time between a furnished room in East Ham, London's tough East End, and his girlfriend's flat in Shepherd Market. Yardley had come to know the Market quite well—it was behind Curzon Street, not fifty yards away from the Lansdowne Club: a strange area of narrow streets and small eighteenth-century terrace houses with several choice shops and restaurants. And yet it was a notorious place for prostitutes who rented rooms for their trade. Over a drink, an old member of the club had told him about the discreet sign on one house: "French lessons given." A respectable middle-class woman with her schoolboy son, who was backward at languages, had once rung the doorbell and demanded some tutorials for her boy from the madam.

Yardley's face must have betrayed his confusion, for Murphy said, "Oh sure, Desirée—that's what she calls herself, real name's Emmie—is a pro. She does it for money—and she gives the punters good value. But ain't that more honest than some conniving bitch who's all lovey-dovey to your face and fucks like a rattlesnake the moment your back's turned? She's a good kid, my Emmie, and no one's goin' to give her aggravation with me around.

"That's enough about me, Bob. What brings you to London? I heard on the old bush telegraph something about a book."

Yardley told him the now well-rehearsed story, then suddenly decided to add a variation. He knew how old SAS hands loved a spot of intrigue.

"Mike, this is for your ears only. I really mean that. No one at Hereford or the Duke of York's knows the real reason. I can trust you?"

Murphy said, "Cross my heart." His eyes were eager.

Yardley looked round the pub, shifted his chair a few inches closer and lowered his voice. Christ, he thought, what a ham actor I'd make. But Murphy looked impressed.

"The book is for real. Okay, it's the cover story but I have to make it stand up. It's about Special Forces, from Colonel David starting the SAS back in the Western Desert to the present day. Worldwide. Not just the Brits, though you've always been out front, but the Yanks, the Krauts, the French Foreign Legion—the lot. One section will be about testing jail security back in the seventies. Don't look innocent, Mike. I know you led the raid on Wormwood Scrubs. I want the real facts on that. What's more—and this is the confidential bit—I want to put you through your paces again.

"Hey, don't interrupt—hear me out. The Company back in Langley, Virginia, is worried stiff about U.S. jail security. Apart from psychopath multikillers, we're holding any number of terrorists around the U.S. If those guys were sprung, there could be a bloody revolution. No kidding. The Company's commissioned me privately to recruit some experienced guys over here to come to the States and repeat what you did in 1974—wasn't it? Big money and all expenses paid. But they won't accept a bunch of old has-beens. They've gotta know you can still cut the corn. You interested in the caper?"

"You mean—go and do the Scrubs all over again? Jesus, Bob, you don't want much!" He paused, then went on with mounting excitement in his voice, "Mind you, with the contacts I've made since I came out of the Regiment—Christ, I was on remand meself at the Scrubs for a week after I done up that sod who was poking my wife—and with all that overcrowding, maybe it could be done again. What a lark! You know last time we left a note on the governor's desk telling him to go and fuck himself. He musta shat his pants when he saw it."

"Yeah, that was great. This time, there's a new twist. You bring a prisoner out as well."

"Pull the other one, Bob."

"I mean it, Mike."

"You know what you're saying? If the fuzz fingers my collar this time, we're talking about five years—minimum. With my record."

"We're also talking about five thousand down—pounds, not dollars—and another five when the job's done. In cash. Twenties or fifties—however you want it. That's the standard rate for each guy in the team. You lead it—you get extra. And if it were to fuck up, which it won't, there's another five grand all round, paid where and how you like, for when you come out. You hear me?"

"Loud and clear, Bob. Boy, it's tempting."

Yardley decided not to push things. "That's enough for one night. Go away and sleep on it. But you promise me you won't say a word to anyone—not even those guys who were on the original raid. Right?"

"My oath, Bob."

"If you decide it's not on, then I have to talk to the rest of them in the squadron. I take it all the original teams are out now? That's fine. But you have first go at it. That's a promise."

"You're staying in London, Bob?"

"Sure."

"You know Shepherd Market? Between Curzon Street and Piccadilly. Like I said, my Emmie's got a flat there. Nice and quiet. I know what you're thinking—but it's okay. She won't be working tomorrow or the weekend. What say we meet there Saturday evening—seven o'clock? I'll give you the address. She's a dab hand with steak and chips. And after supper she can go and see a girlfriend round the corner and leave us to a quiet chat. You on?"

"Like a shot. Sounds great."

That Saturday evening, Yardley strolled the short distance into Shepherd Market through the archway alongside the Steering Wheel Club. He had already bought a bottle of burgundy from the liquor store at the corner of Queen Street, and a bunch of flowers for Murphy's girlfriend. Colonel

McAlister had once said to him, talking of the difference between the Brits and the Yanks, "Always treat a prostitute like a duchess and a duchess like a prostitute. You can't go wrong." He was still to meet a duchess but he hoped the first half of the advice would stand up.

Emmie's flat was a walk-up on the third floor in an alleyway off Shepherd Street. Each of the buttons on the ground floor had an illuminated nameplate—"Lulu," "Monica" and "Desirée." He pressed the right button, the buzzer sounded and the door opened. He had had visions of a French bordello, discreet pink lights, overstuffed cushions and mirrors on every wall, but the sitting room was suburban in its ordinariness. There were two quite shabby armchairs, an oak table with three wooden dining chairs and various knickknacks on a small corner cupboard. There were even three flying china ducks fastened to the wall above the mantelpiece.

The biggest surprise was Emmie herself. He had been expecting an exotic creature in the tightest of leather skirts, tottering on six-inch high heels, her face caked with cosmetics. But he saw a pleasant-looking girl with hardly any makeup, her hair screwed back in a bun, wearing a demure dress that covered her knees. She would have passed muster in any supermarket line. She greeted him shyly and was genuinely pleased with the gift of flowers.

Murphy had not exaggerated. The steaks she produced from the tiny kitchen that separated the bathroom and the bedroom from the sitting room were tender and juicy, the French fries crisply golden. The three of them exchanged platitudes about Wimbledon, which had finished a couple of weeks before, and the way London traffic got worse and worse, and those "bloody wardens" who went around the Market clamping your car if you left it for five minutes, and who was going to win the presidential election in November. Emmie was unassuming and friendly, but Yardley noticed there was always a slight tremor in her left hand; she chainsmoked Silk Cut cigarettes, dragging each lungful of smoke as though it were some lifesaving elixir. Being "on the game" was a great misnomer, he thought. Not much of a game with all those kinky misfits he'd seen wandering around the West End at night.

She served them coffee—real coffee, not granules out of a jar—and then announced she had to go see a friend. "Give me a couple of hours, okay, Mike?" she asked. There was clearly a warm affection between the two of them, maybe love, he thought. Strange world. Here was this whore, a girl from the back streets of Birmingham, and there was his own wife—ex-wife—a clergyman's daughter, who had known only two men, himself and that shit, Tim Bell. And yet he knew for sure which one of them he would trust—and respect.

They heard her clattering down the uncarpeted staircase. Murphy took a bottle of scotch from the cupboard and poured a large slug in each of their glasses. "Cheers," he said, and he took a swallow and leaned forward eagerly.

"I've been thinkin', Bob. I'll do it, you bet. I miss the old mob and the real stuff. Sure, it's a doddle driving that fat slob around the place—but it's not like the old days. I've made a couple inquiries—all very discreet, I promise. There were five of us in the original team. Laidlaw didn't beat the clock, he copped it on a land mine near Crossmaglen. And they say Tiny Smith—remember Tiny, must've been six-feet-six and more?—they say he's got religion. Joined some church when he come out and runs a soup kitchen for down-and-outs in Liverpool. But the other two are around, all right. And there are several other likely lads in the offing. So what's the score? How many do you need, when's it gonna happen, and who do we snatch?"

"Gently, Mike. One thing at a time. First, whatever happens—even if I have to call the whole thing off—you'll get your down payment. I've even brought five hundred for luck." He dug into a side pocket and brought out a thick envelope, which he tossed onto the table. "I'll draw the rest a bit at a time, don't want the bank to start wondering, but you can have the rest of the five grand within the week. Okay?"

Murphy grinned his thanks.

"Now, until I give the word, you don't speak to a soul. It stays with just you and me until we have the op planned right down to the last detail. We don't brief the others until we're good and ready. That's an order. Now, based on last time, you tell me how you see it."

"Right, sir." Murphy was already slipping back into military discipline. "If we're gonna pull a prisoner out, we have to have a bent warder, what you'd call a crooked guard, sir, on the inside. No two ways about it. That ain't a big problem. The Boss has some pals inside—yeah, one or two in the

Scrubs—who he slips extra smokes and things to. He's got a few warders sewn up."

"No way I'm going to have a big crook like him involved!"

"Understood, sir. He don't confide in me and I sure as hell don't confide in him. But don't you see, I can easily find out who the crooked screws are and pick the right one. Fair enough?"

Yardley nodded. Murphy poured some more scotch into their glasses, and for the next hour they argued, cutting across each other's remarks, flinging out ideas, eliminating the crazier ones and gradually hammering the plan into shape. Yardley always had the final word, but he was honest enough to realize that Murphy's inside knowledge was essential. And Murphy, he could see, had an operational cunning, apart from his local knowledge. The combination was a winner.

The whiskey was low in the bottle by the time they had the basic plan ready. The bent warder would secretly feed Peter Shaw, the man who was to be sprung, a measured dose of nicotine concentrate in his late-night drink. He wouldn't like the taste, and the warder would blame it on the bromide, added to lower prisoners' sex drives, and make sure he downed the lot. The effect would be almost instantaneous, causing a constriction of the arteries and inducing all the symptoms of an attack of angina. Shaw would at once be taken to the sick bay in the prison hospital wing for medical tests. He would suffer the effects of the nicotine for at least twenty-four hours, but once it was excreted from the body, he would be as good as new.

Late that same afternoon, a supposed warder and prisoner, both of them in fact part of the SAS team, would arrive at the jail. The cover story would be that the prisoner who was on remand had collapsed in the dock at West London Crown Court and had been sent to the Scrubs, the nearest prison, for medical investigation. The prisoner's belongings, in a large plastic bag, would in fact be another uniform. Once in the sick bay, he could go under escort to the bathroom and there change into the uniform.

Yardley looked incredulous. "For Christ's sake, Mike, that sounds dicey. What about the documentation?"

"You don't know prisons the way I do, from the inside! I tell you, the Scrubs is like a bloody madhouse. There're four prisoners to a cell that is crowded with two; the warders are either bent or ready to go on strike—can't blame 'em; people are coming and going the whole time. And talk about documentation. Why, the other day a guy appeared at the Old Bailey to answer charges as long as your arm. What happens? The judge, spittin' blood, has to find him not guilty. The fucking court officials didn't have the case prepared. All the details had been sent to Leeds Crown Court by mistake! I tell you, Bob, sir, the paperwork's a right fucking mess. All our man with the prisoner has to do is say the paperwork's following. It'll work every time. Hell, the guy on the main gate is there to stop people getting out! He couldn't give a shit for anyone trying to get in."

The rest of the plan was straightforward. The following morning, an ambulance with lights flashing and siren blaring away would come tearing up to the main entrance of Wormwood Scrubs. On board, dressed as London ambulance staff, would be Murphy himself as the driver and one other. They would be there to collect the sick prisoner, Peter Shaw, from the infirmary and take him for investigation to Hammersmith Hospital, next door to the prison. If challenged, Murphy would wave some documents and yell that it was an emergency. Did they want the poor sod to drop dead while they buggered around? Nice court of inquiry that'd make. The ambulance would enter the jail and drive to the hospital wing, where the other two members of the team—the "prisoner" now dressed as an ambulance man—would take Shaw out on a stretcher. The ambulance would drop them off at Casualty and would then head around the hospital to the ambulance park at the back. The other two would push the stretcher along the corridors and out to meet the waiting ambulance, bundle him inside, and then away it would go, siren on and lights flashing, to a suburban street where another car would have been parked since the night before. Shaw would be transferred to the car, which would then drive to a prearranged safe house. His two companions would remain to keep guard over him until phase two of the operation began.

"It sounds good and easy the way you put it, Mike," Yardley said, "but now for the questions. First, where does the ambulance come from? You aiming to steal it?"

"No need. There's a company in West London rents out police cars and ambulances—or look-alikes—to film and TV companies. We rent it for a couple of days, pay cash and give 'em a phony address. Soon as your man is dumped at the safe house, I'll take the ambulance back and pick up the deposit. It'll be back the same day—no problem."

"Okay. Now how about the safe house. Who's going to fix that?"

"Leave it to me, sir." Murphy hesitated for a second or two, then went on. "This is strictly between you and me, Bob, right? At least for now. I know the exact place. You ever meet Nick Baring? No, I thought you wouldn't have. Ex-Rhodesian SAS and Selous Scouts. I met him on an op in Mozambique. Good guy. He owns a houseboat in Little Venice, on the canal. Gave me a key and lets me use it if I'm really stuck. That'd be the place—no suspicious landladies, no porters in the block of flats."

"Little Venice? That's a new one to me."

"You know Marble Arch, sir? Couple miles up the Edgware Road and to your left—that's the Little Venice area. There's a big canal runs across the north of London. Quite a posh place. And it wouldn't be more than three miles, as the crow flies, from the Scrubs. We'd be there in fifteen minutes. An' it's as quiet as the grave. Just the job."

It was getting late and Emmie would be back any moment. Murphy had already mentioned the name of another mate of his, Johnnie McDermid, who had come to the Regiment from the Royal Navy's Special Ops flight and could fly any bloody aircraft. He ran legitimate charters for businessmen in a hurry from East Midlands Airport, but was always open to something "interesting" on the side.

Yardley said, "I'd like to see him early next week—the sooner the better. With you, of course. Can you fix it? I'll pay his expenses to London and back. And a hotel if he has to stay overnight."

"I'll get on to him first thing tomorrow. But how do I contact you, sir?"

Yardley was prepared. He had thought of using a cut-out in young Steiner at the U.S. Embassy but had decided it would be too cumbersome. Besides, General Bradford wanted the diplomatic boys kept right out. So he said, "I'm staying at the Lansdowne Club. Just around the corner from here. The number's 629-7200. But I don't want all the team calling me there. You're the only one to know the number—right? And where's a safe place for us to meet?"

Murphy screwed up his choirboy's face in thought, then

said, "All the lads know the Union Jack Club behind Waterloo Station. You know, sir—dead opposite that pub, the Wellington, where we met last time. The phone number's in the book. You can leave messages for me there."

"I'll probably take a one-room office on a short lease in this area. That'd be easier than having too many calls at the club. But for now use the 629 number. We're moving forward, I guess."

The following Monday, August 1, was a public holiday. The meeting with Johnnie McDermid took place on the Wednesday of that week. Murphy had arranged for them to meet independently at the Terrace Café of the National Theatre on the south bank of the Thames. As Yardley walked across Waterloo Bridge and saw the gray fortresslike bulk of the theater to his right, he mentally gave Mike further marks for his shrewdness. The meeting place was nicely anonymous, the kind of rendezvous that three businessmen from out of town might well choose. He walked down the pedestrian steps to the terrace, where Mike and McDermid were already sitting at a table drinking coffee.

They chatted briefly while he ordered coffee for himself from the smiling waitress, which gave him the surreptitious chance to size up the pilot. He was impressed with what he saw. McDermid exuded a quiet self-confidence. He was slim, clean-shaven, dark-haired, with a pair of bright eyes that seemed to miss very little. And he liked the man's no-nonsense approach.

McDermid said, "Before you tell me anything, one thing I must know. Is the cargo clean?"

Murphy began, "You mean . . ."

"Mike, you know damn well what I mean! In my book, the only use for a needle is to sew a button on. And unless you've got a cold, sniffing is out."

"Can I tell him, boss?" Murphy asked.

Yardley nodded.

Murphy explained the plan as far as it affected the flight. McDermid was to take a genuine passenger on a one-way flight to Marseilles. On the way, the plane would have to touch down briefly somewhere in the south of England and pick up an unofficial passenger, fly the man to the Camargue, a desolate plain northwest of Marseilles, drop the second man off there and then fly on to Marseilles airport, where the genuine passenger would be landed. That was it. McDermid could then fly the aircraft back to the UK on his own. But as far as the air traffic authorities in Britain and France were concerned, it would be a nonstop flight from Johnnie McDermid's base at the East Midlands Airport to Marseilles.

The pilot was silent for a moment. "I need to do some thinking," he said. "Look, you two have another coffee and give me ten minutes. I'm off for a stroll along the South Bank and back. I think better on the move."

On his return, he sat down in the vacant chair, looked Yardley straight in the eyes and said, "Okay, I'm on. But we've got some heavy points to work out. Let's deal with the easy bit first. This genuine passenger—he needs a proper cover story. Special Branch is hot on charter flights these days, especially with only one passenger. Do I know him, by the way?"

Murphy and Yardley looked at each other.

"Oh, come on—don't be coy. I'm going to meet him sooner or later, aren't I?"

Yardley said, "It'll probably be the Honorable Rupert Lycett-Smythe."

"Not old Lysol. For heaven's sake."

"You know him?"

"Oh sure. Well, that's a turn-up. He'll be fine. He looks just the type to charter an aircraft for a swan round France. But he'll need a solid story. Let's see—he's back in the family bank these days, isn't he? Great. He can be looking over some property for sale in or around Marseilles. Leave that to me. I'll get some plans and brochures ready.

"That's the easy bit. The tough side is timing—split-second timing. I'll spell it out. I'll be flying a Cessna 421—the flight time to Marseilles is three hours, twenty minutes. The aircraft will be subject to air-traffic control every inch of the way—first through UK control and then the French. Somehow I have to divert from the flight plan twice without being spotted. Once to pick up the other guy on this side and then to drop him off over there. It can be done—it damn well has been done! But there's no margin for error. There's an airstrip I know in Hampshire—I'll let you have details later—but that guy just has to be there waiting when I put the wheels down. After twenty seconds I'm away again. I'm not hanging around for Prince Charles himself!"

"Prince Charles it ain't," Murphy smiled.

"I don't want to know who it is," McDermid went on. "Long as he doesn't throw up all over my nice clean aeroplane. But the same thing applies to the Camargue landing. We touch down, he goes out like shit off a shovel, and I'm up and away again. So you'd better make pretty bloody sure the reception committee's ready and waiting."

"It will be," Yardley said quietly.

"So that only leaves two things," McDermid said, "the timing and the money. Speak to me."

Yardley and Murphy had already agreed that snatching Peter Shaw should take place in the last week of the month, coming up to the bank holiday on August 29. The Scrubs would be even more in confusion, with many of the regular warders away on their annual vacation and their temporary replacements unsure of local procedures. That suited McDermid as well. The additional package-tour flights in late August would put extra pressure on the air traffic control centers throughout the country.

There was no haggling over money. Payment for the official passenger would have to "go through the books" and his charge for that was 2,000 pounds. His unofficial charge was a further 20,000 pounds, to be paid into his private Swiss account—half right away and the other half on completion. McDermid tore a page out of his Filofax, scribbled the Swiss number on it and passed the slip of paper to Yardley. They also exchanged telephone numbers and shook hands. The endplay looks fine, Yardley thought as he stood up to go. All it is now is a little matter of busting open that jail and extracting our Mr Shaw.

4

The Stars are setting and the Caravan
Starts for the Dawn of Nothing—Oh,
make haste!

For the next eight days, Yardley was busy interviewing likely candidates for the three vacant places on the team. One of them, Peter Parker, an ex-SAS troop leader, was a fitness fanatic, and so the two of them went running twice around the perimeter of Hyde Park early one morning, ending with a plunge in the Serpentine.

Another candidate, the Honorable Rupert Lycett-Smythe, who had held the rank of captain in the Regiment, took Yardley to lunch at the Grill Room at the Savoy. He was clearly a regular; the headwaiter and the sommelier greeted him with familiar deference. When Yardley asked him why he wanted to get involved, he said, "Simple. I miss the excitement." He made a sign to the sommelier, who produced an ice bucket and a bottle of champagne. "Try this, Bob—may I call you Bob?"

Yardley nodded.

"Let me tell you my sad story," Lycett-Smythe went on. "Incidentally, I've always been known as Lysol since Eton days. If you want to call me anything, apart from 'Hey, you,' I'll always answer to 'Lysol.' "

"Okay—Lysol."

"Where was I? Oh yes, the family history. My grandfather had a clothing factory in Bradford, Yorkshire. He was plain Mr. Smith in those days. He made a fortune in the Great War supplying khaki uniforms for the troops and bought himself a peerage. Don't look surprised—Lloyd George, the prime minister, was selling honors to anyone who gave enough to party funds.

"My father was a shrewd young devil. He smelled the Wall Street crash coming, sold off the factories at the height of the boom—and stayed liquid. Come the slump and he bought himself a nice little merchant bank and a large holding in an insurance company. And a nice big estate with a thousand acres in Gloucestershire. He married late, and my elder brother and I came along after the Second War. As the heir, my brother went into the family bank after Oxford. Me, I left Eton, went through Sandhurst, was commissioned into a Guards regiment, found ordinary peacetime soldiering pretty dull, so I volunteered for the SAS. Seven years of that and I went on to the reserve.

"Since when, it's been a doddle—but a boring doddle. I'm just a kind of superior liaison man for the bank. Basically what you Yankees would call a greeter. I chat up rich industrialists from the provinces, buy them lunches here or at Boulestin, listen to their dreary anecdotes, find them tickets for Wimbledon or the Lords' Test Match. It's what in the Guards they used to call poodle-faking. Oh sure, I've a big flat in Knightsbridge and a place in the country and the statutory BMW coupé. But it's dull, dull. I need some action, something to stretch me. Your caper sounds just the thing. Here, how about another bottle of this Krug? Slips down without touching the sides, doesn't it? Tony!" he called the sommelier.

Afterward Yardley wondered about the wisdom of adding Lysol to the team. When putting together an operational unit, he had always asked the men why they had volunteered. Anyone who replied, "I want the chance to prove myself," was automatically out. He needed a team who knew what they were about, not a bunch who were in search of themselves. But he realized that Lysol had proved himself more than once in the tough undercover world of Northern Ireland. So his name went in—as the second man in the ambulance under Murphy's command and doubling as the bodyguard for Shaw on the aircraft's outward flight. After all, he looked like—and was—the kind of upper-class businessman who might well charter a private plane for a quick trip to France.

Parker and the fourth man, a burly ex-sergeant named

Tom Tritt, who had also been on the original Wormwood Scrubs raid and who now did occasional bodyguard duties with one of the top security firms, had remained close friends. They lived near each other in council flats south of the river. They would be the pair to get inside the jail on D-day as the warder and the sick prisoner. Yardley liked the look of them. Parker was slim and quiet whereas Tritt had clearly been the unit joker, always ready with a quip or a dirty story. He would be the warder, who might have to talk their way out of trouble, and Parker would be ideal for the sick prisoner.

The first get-together for the team was set for Tuesday evening, August 9. Yardley decided that he and Murphy should walk the course beforehand. Sunday afternoon, the time-honored day for family strolling in the park, was to be the day. He met Murphy outside the East Acton Underground Station on the Central Line at two-thirty. To add to his cover, Murphy had even acquired a nondescript mongrel dog, which trotted along after him on a lengthy leash.

They walked slowly along Erconwald Street and turned right into Braybrook Street, where they came to the Old Oak Annexe, a low modern structure on the other side of the road that served as a children's playschool. It was on the edge of the Scrubs Park and close to the high rear wall of the jail. Murphy muttered in a low voice that this route kept them outside the range of the cameras high on the west wall of the jail, which covered the lower end of Braybrook Street.

"Don't look up," he said, "but the length of this public path we're walking along is covered by four pole-mounted camera units. The direct-feed video kind. They traverse the whole of the path. There are no obvious blind spots I know of. And the path is fully lit throughout the hours of darkness. This sure isn't the best side to get in—or out of—in a hurry."

It took them six minutes to walk on the path for the full length of the rear wall. Once, as though they were having an argument, they stopped and turned so that Yardley was looking toward the wall of the jail. He could see that across the exercise yard located against the inside of the north wall hung antihelicopter wire stringers with orange balls spaced across them. The inner wall was topped by barbed wire. There was no way a helicopter could set down inside the prison yard. A fully fit prisoner, keen to break out, would have his work cut out to ascend the wall, drop down the other side and avoid capture long enough for a helicopter to swoop down onto the common and pluck him off. The timing would be too tricky. And with a prisoner like Shaw, who was not particularly anxious to break out and who was physically weak, it would be impossible.

They strolled on, leaving the rear wall of the prison behind them as they went eastward on Wormwood Scrubs Common. Their main problem was the dog Murphy had borrowed from one of Emmie's girlfriends. They guessed it must be a bitch in heat, because half the big dogs on the Common tried either to fight or to seduce it. Murphy spent most of his time aiming kicks at Alsatians, retrievers and spaniels. But at any rate, as he argued, it made their cover look more convincing.

They were now behind Hammersmith Hospital, approaching West London Stadium, a sports complex with a running track. There were tennis courts along the rear wall of the hospital and a large car park on the west side of the stadium. Murphy mentioned that there were the usual school gatherings and track meets on Tuesdays and Thursdays at the stadium. It would be easy to park the ambulance overnight without arousing any notice.

They took careful note of the narrow road that ran between the east wall of the prison and Hammersmith Hospital. At each end a red-and-white swing-up pole acted as a barrier, but these were left in the up position during the daytime to allow access to the stadium and for the ambulances leaving the west gate of the hospital. It did not escape their apparently casual gaze that cameras atop the east wall of the prison covered the road. Yardley made a mental note to brief the ambulance team accordingly.

He said, "Now we're here, I wouldn't mind doing a reconnaissance of the inside of the hospital—just the ground floor."

"No problem," Murphy replied. "At least not for you. They'll never let me in, not with this four-legged fucker." He indicated the dog, which had cocked a leg against a convenient lamppost. "But it's visiting hour, Sunday afternoon. Why don't you just mingle with the crowds, boss? I'll go on home. We're meeting the boys day after next, so see you at the Union Jack Club Tuesday."

They walked down the rest of the narrow road together, then departed at the corner of Du Cane Road. Yardley turned eastward and came to the main hospital entrance. He noted the pole barriers stopping unauthorized vehicles entering the hospital grounds and joined the stream of pedestrians who were visiting friends and relatives in the wards. There was a large glowing sign, "Casualty," by the east entrance, with two security men in a cabin inside the entrance. He had a story ready in case one of the staff stopped him—but no one was taking any notice of casual visitors on a Sunday afternoon. He came to reception, a small cramped hatch with two middle-aged women behind the counter. A row of black plastic chairs was lined up against a wall. It was like Piccadilly Circus at rush hour. Nurses in uniform and hospital orderlies were continually passing to and fro; occasionally a harassed doctor with open white coat flapping rushed past and disappeared through one of the numerous corridors.

Looking blank, as though he were lost, Yardley turned right and then left through a pair of double wooden swinging doors and came to the main passage. He saw signs for "Blood Trans" and "Cardiology" and then decided to retrace his steps. No one had stopped him, apparently no one had even noticed his presence. But he had seen enough for his purpose and dared not risk that any hospital official might recall an unauthorized member of the public wandering in that private area—once the snatch had taken place.

At half past six on Tuesday evening, he walked yet again across Waterloo Bridge, going south. He had come to enjoy walking the streets of London, adapting his long stride to the twisting narrow roads and the continual halting at traffic lights or jinking in and out through traffic jams in the wide streets like Piccadilly or the Haymarket. He had quickly discovered that the British are a nation of jaywalkers. A momentary pause, a holdup while a parked truck worked its way back into the traffic flow—and even the sedate matrons were in like Flynn, cutting between rear fenders and front fenders like all-American quarterbacks.

Murphy had told him that the Union Jack Club was opposite the pub where they had first met. It was an allied services club, a place for out-of-town servicemen and -women to use when on leave in the Big Smoke. As part of NATO, U.S. servicemen were also eligible to join the club. In Murphy's words, "The Yanks love it here. It costs thirteen pounds a night for a room without a bath. If you want one, you have to share the bathroom at the end of the hall. A room with a shower costs four pounds extra. The Yanks always take the room with a shower. Hell, they've got the bloody money, right?"

The group had already booked a private room and ordered a case of beer and sandwiches—"for a kind of regimental reunion." Yardley smiled at the Irish doorman and went to reception to check the details of the room. The wall behind reception was covered in regimental shields—he noticed the blue and maroon of Anzuk Force and the shield with crossed daggers of Trucial Oman. Nearby was a vast portrait of Field Marshal His Royal Highness the Duke of Connaught, KG, staring down imperiously at the motley mob beneath him. Those were the days, Yardley thought. Britannia ruled the waves—and most of the land as well. A field marshal gave the order and a hundred thousand officers and men—in India, Australia, New Zealand, South Africa and God knows where else sprang to attention. The ex-squaddie at reception pointed to the green baize notice board on the wall inside the main entrance. Yardley memorized the number of the room they had booked, went down the dimly lit corridor and walked in. Murphy was already there, setting out the chairs around the wooden table and putting out the beer.

One by one, the others arrived, greeted each other casually and slipped into an easy camaraderie over the first pint of beer. Three of the five present—Murphy, Tritt and Parker—had taken part in the previous SAS op in Wormwood Scrubs jail, although with very different roles from those now contemplated. But at least they had "walked the course," as the Army saying went, and would not require much refreshing. Lysol's SAS service had been too recent for him to have firsthand knowledge of that op, but he had been on assignments in Northern Ireland with Murphy and Parker at different times. So it was really a reunion for the Englishmen and at first Yardley felt like the new boy at school. But the others treated him with a kind of guarded respect—they knew he was an old hand, with a "top gong" to prove it—which would ripen into friendship once they came to know him.

After first explaining that he and Murphy had carried out a reconnaissance of the jail and its surroundings, Yardley told them there was no way Shaw could be extracted by force: it would have to be an inside job. Then he went into details of the plan. Everything hung on Mike's ability to get hold of a bent warder who would have Shaw moved into the hospital wing of the jail. Murphy interjected that after making discreet inquiries among his underworld contacts, he had located a likely man and was due to buy him a drink the following evening.

"I remember him from when I did my spell of porridge in the Scrubs," Murphy added. "Nasty bit of work—couldn't lie straight in bed! Bet he'd screw his own grandmother if the price was right. He's our man, I reckon."

After a couple of hours of discussion and debate, they decided to call it a night. Everyone knew his role up to and including removing Shaw by ambulance the morning after, but Yardley decided to leave the details of the safe house and the further shifting him out of the country to another meeting a week later. In any case, the hour was approaching when Murphy would have to go and collect the car and act as chauffeur for his underworld bigshot. Yardley realized that it was an advantage in one way to have a second-in-command with useful criminal contacts, but he wondered what extra pressure might be applied by having the man's head, as it were, permanently in the lion's mouth. One surprised gesture, blurting out the wrong thing—and Murphy might find himself trapped. The guy had his wits about him, right enough, and he'd been tested time and again under fire. He ought to be able to tough it out.

The following week, at their next meeting at the Union Jack Club, with the snatch now a little more than two weeks away, Murphy seemed more and more on edge, restless, jumpy, snapping back at Lysol's weak jokes. Yardley was privately disturbed—but it was too late now to make any changes. From long experience, he knew well that the prospect of action takes men in different ways. They could be tense or relaxed; sometimes those who were the most jumpy beforehand were the coolest when the bullets began to fly. Maybe, once Murphy collected the hired ambulance and set off for the Scrubs, he would become professionally ice-cold. And there would always be the presence of Lysol—once his officer—in the ambulance to calm him down. At least Murphy had fixed his senior warder, a "screw" as British prisoners called them, inside the Scrubs. Everything hung on that man feeding the nicotine to Shaw and having him in the infirmary on time.

A letter with an embossed crest on the flap had already arrived for him at the Lansdowne Club. It was from Colonel

McAlister, confirming the invitation for grouse shooting. The season actually began on Sunday, August 14. The colonel suggested that Yardley turn up on the Saturday to get his bearings and stay over for the shooting on Sunday and Monday. He would be welcome to stay as long as he liked, but perhaps he would have to get back to London fairly soon for his book research. Yardley was beginning to understand the establishment. Reading between the polite lines, he knew the letter was saying, "Up to breakfast on the Tuesday morning, you're my welcome guest. After that, on your way, friend." He scribbled a reply of thanks, warmly accepting the invitation.

Early on Saturday morning, he took the shuttle from Heathrow to Glasgow airport, rented himself a car and drove up past Loch Lomond to the colonel's estate, a long promontory above Argyllshire. It was a wild, romantic and lonely drive. He had read about the Highland Clearances: after the Battle of Culloden, in which the English troops under "Butcher" Cumberland smashed the Jacobite rebellion, the crofters had for many decades been ruthlessly turned off their lands. Scotland, it seemed, was still vastly underpopulated, fertile farms having declined into rough moorland and roofless cottages standing derelict. God knows, he thought, why the Scots always rally round the English when there's fighting to be done. Maybe they just love a fight.

He swung off the road onto a long driveway that led to Castle McAlister, a huge turreted stone mansion forming three sides of a rectangle. He drew up his rented car with a crunch on the gravel drive and a kilted servant came out of the iron-studded oak front door to take his bags. Inside was a vast flagstone hall stretching up to the third story. Before him was a broad wooden staircase that could have taken six men abreast. On all sides hung game trophies, stags' heads with branching antlers, and a tiger or two that some McAlister forebear had shot when the British still ruled India. He blinked and felt that he might have strayed into a time warp. The servant took him up the stairs, down a long corridor and into a cold drafty room with a canopied double bed and gloomy dark wooden closets. The bathroom was farther on down the corridor; the lavatory was like a regal throne encased in shining mahogany, perched on high two steps above the floor level.

When he returned to his room, the servant was already

unpacking his bags. The man said in a lilting voice, "Himself wants you to know the other guests will be dressing for dinner. He suggests mess dress if you've brought it, sir." Yardley was relieved that he had had the foresight to pack his mess kit.

At dinner that night, he felt even more that he had strayed onto some film set, where the host and all the other guests knew their parts and he was the outsider. Colonel Alistair McAlister—"my friends call me Allie"—had greeted his guests in a drawing room with his back to a roaring fire, even though the night was warm. He was dressed in full Highland regalia, as he had been at the dinner in the Duke of York's Barracks a few weeks earlier. Cocktails were out. "This is Scotland, I'll have you know," he had said with a hard edge to one of his paying guests, a fat young City dealer who had brought his "painted lady," an over-made-up simpering blonde with a plunging neckline. "None of your sidecars or Manhattans or Bronxes. Here we drink the straight malt." Yardley was glad enough to sip the peaty-brown malt that slipped down smoothly and then exploded in a riotous glow somewhere amidships. After a couple of large glasses, he felt more in the party.

Ten of them sat down to dinner in the enormous dining room with a log fire blazing at each end. Apart from the colonel and himself, there was a retired major general with his faded lady, the two City couples who were paying for the privilege of dining "with the nobs," and a couple of local Scottish lairds with weather-beaten faces, who poured down the malt whiskey and then the very drinkable claret, glass after glass, with no apparent effect. Yardley found himself between the major general's wife, who spoke so softly he could hardly hear her, and one of the "popsies," who was already halfway drunk. Although the seats were well apart, he soon found her warm thigh pressing urgently against his but managed, when she was being served the fish course, to shift his carved and weighty chair a few inches away. Fortunately, conversation was soon out of the question. With a noise that sounded like a cat being slowly strangled, the McAlister piper, who had marched in in full dress and saluted the host, began to skirl on the pipes. Once the bag was fully inflated, he marched around the room making those caterwauling sounds only the Celts appreciate. The major general's lady picked out the Black Watch regimental march

"The Flowers of the Forest" and even the McAlister Lament, but to Yardley it was like a banshee's wailing. As he sipped his claret and ate the main course of venison, he recalled that the Duke of Wellington had once been asked by some idiot if he thought his troops would strike fear into the French enemy. "I don't know about the French," declared the Iron Duke, "but by God they frighten me!" He must have been reviewing a Highland regiment marching to the sound of the pipes. At least the weird noise saved him from having to keep up an inane conversation with the blonde number on his right. At the end of the performance, the piper marched up to the head of the table and saluted the colonel, who poured him a tumblerful of malt whisky. The piper drained it in one swallow, saluted again and marched out of the room.

The next morning, after a hearty breakfast for those who had the stamina and powers of recovery, the shooting party climbed into Land Rovers and drove on tracks through the heather to the butts. Yardley could see no point in the senseless slaughter of game birds that had done him no harm—and tactfully said as much to his host. He put on his trekking boots and walked cross-country to the butts, arriving as the beaters in the distance drove the grouse out of their coveys to whir like low-flying aircraft toward the shooters. Each of them had a gamekeeper behind him loading a spare shotgun. The idea was to let fly with a couple of barrels at each bird as it rocketed toward the butts, then grab the spare gun from the loader and fire twice more as the grouse swung past—preferably without blowing the head off the loader or one of the nearby guns. Allie McAlister had said to him, "No stomach for the shooting, Bob?"

He had replied, "I'm better at killing a man who's out to kill me." And then he had regretted the retort. But Colonel McAlister had only shrugged and laughed. He was an ice-cold guy, that one. Man, bird or beast, he'd kill anything that came his way and lose not a moment's sleep. And he'd had the *nous* to see through that treacherous shit, Tim Bell. No wonder the SAS were the tops in irregular warfare—with ruthless aristocrats like that to lead them.

On Monday night, after the usual dressed-up dinner where the drinks flowed like Niagara and the paying guests, much the worse for wear, had staggered off to their respective bedrooms, Allie had said to him, "How about a nightcap in the gun room, Bob? Last chance I'll get of a quiet chat, as you'll be off after breakfast."

"Fine with me," he said.

They walked down to the gun room, the colonel's inner sanctum, with its ranks of shining Purdy shotguns, each worth several thousand pounds, standing like guardsmen at attention behind glass doors. There was a billiard table in the center of the room and the brass fireguard had upholstered leather seats where one could sit and warm one's behind against the cold drafts that percolated throughout the stone mansion. McAlister's Irish setter dozed alongside. There were silver-framed regimental photographs on the mantelpiece.

Allie McAlister opened another bottle of malt and topped up his own glass and Yardley's. He had lit one of his black torpedo cheroots and sat for a moment with his back to the dying fire, blowing out fragrant blue smoke and swirling the liquid round and round in his glass. There was a long companionable silence, the end-of-the-world hour.

Then McAlister said quietly, "I don't know what you're up to, Bob—and for God's sake don't tell me. But let me give you some private advice. Drop it."

Yardley was secretly appalled. He reckoned to have covered his tracks pretty well. He managed to blurt out, "With respect, Allie, I don't know what the hell you're talking about."

"Come off it, Bob. I know all about that book. For all I know, you may actually be going to write a book. And I know you may have to interview some of the old muckers. Fair enough. But book writers interview people sitting down at a desk, not boozing with them at service clubs."

"You've got it all wrong," Yardley protested. "Sure, I've had a beer or two with some of the lads. But that's just to gain their confidence. Let's not forget—I'm a Yank, not one of you. Okay, I've done secondments to Hereford and been on maneuvers with SAS teams in the past, but that doesn't make me a blood brother. So I have to chat these guys up, show them I'm serious."

"Have it your way, Bob. I'm not going to argue. All I'm saying is, if there's anything else in the back of your mind, forget it. It won't do you any good—and it sure as hell won't do the Regiment any good. Okay, I like you, but when the chips are down, I don't give a damn about you. You're a big boy, you can look after yourself. It's the Regiment I care about—and I don't want it fucked up. That's it."

It took him a long time to get to sleep that night. He put it down to all the rich food and the whiskey, but he realized inwardly that the colonel's remarks were disturbing him. Had one of his team been gossiping to a mate in the squadron at Hereford? It would be a crazy thing to do, risking the large sums he had promised them. Was there a spy in the camp? It was a nasty thought; in an operation where each man depended absolutely on the others, the prospect of someone deliberately sabotaging it was unthinkable. Maybe McAlister had just been on a fishing trip, expecting him to break down and confess everything. Or it might be that the SAS, with its superb network of contacts, was just that much slicker than even he had reckoned it to be. By the time he had said his adieux next morning and had driven back to Glasgow airport, he had resolved that the plan must go ahead. He would ignore the warning—but he would be doubly cautious to cover his own and the team's traces.

Back in London, he called Rodel in Paris from a public phone and passed on the map reference for the pickup of Peter Shaw in the Camargue. He stressed the split-second timing from the pilot's viewpoint and urged that the reception committee be punctual. He tried to find out who would be responsible at the other end, but Rodel was deliberately evasive.

"Kiddo," he said, "once the freight's airborne, you've done your stuff. Leave the rest to us. But book yourself on an aircraft to Paris that same morning. You read me? One-way flight. Have everything settled up there in London. You won't be back for a while."

"You mean I'll be flying back to the States from Paris? I haven't finished my book research yet."

"What did the poet say? 'Theirs not to reason why.' You'll get your next orders when we meet here."

Yardley retorted, "The poet also said, 'Theirs but to do and die.' "

"Let's not get gloomy, kid. Your death doesn't figure in the Company's plans."

"Delighted to hear it." This Rodel character was beginning to get up his nose. He sounded like a real chairborne warrior, sitting there at a big desk and thinking he was God Almighty calling the shots.

At five forty-five on the afternoon of Wednesday, August 24, a London ambulance, with headlights blazing and blue lamps on the roof flashing, drove fast northward on Old Oak Road, straight across the junction with Western Avenue and onto Oak Common Lane. With a blast on the siren, which sent a couple of pedestrians scuttling for the safety of the sidewalk, it swung right into Du Cane Road and went bullocking eastward until it came to the prison entrance and turned hard left. It stopped with a squeal at the guard hut alongside the red-and-white-striped pole that formed a barrier across the road. Beyond to the left was a shelter where prison visitors waited to be called forward—and beyond that was the main entrance to the jail, a huge iron-studded oak door with turrets on either side.

"What's with you?" asked the man inside the guard hut.

"Prisoner from West London Crown Court. Court appearance prisoner. Giving evidence the poor sod was, when he suddenly keeled over in the witness box. Minor heart attack, the doc reckoned. Or so I was told. They sent for an ambulance to keep 'im 'ere overnight under medical attention." This was from Murphy, the driver, dressed as an ambulanceman.

"Christ," said the man inside the guard hut, "what the hell they think this place is? The Hilton? Where's his documents?"

"Don't fart around," Murphy answered. "I'm off duty at six. I don't fancy 'anging around 'alf the bleeding evening."

"Hang on," the man said. "There's a right way of doin' things and a wrong way. You can't come poncing along and expect me to open up for some sod I've never heard of. You need proper documents to get in and out of here."

"Jesus wept—all you lot think about is documents. This guy could be dying—and you talk of bleeding documents! Me mate in the rear's probably giving 'im the kiss of life right now—straight up. Here—I've got a form signed by the doc. What more do you fuckin' want?" Murphy handed over a form that had been lifted from the Crown Court with a forged signature on it.

The guard put on a pair of wire-rimmed spectacles and started reading it slowly.

Murphy said sharply, "For Chrissake, let's get cracking. Chummie here dies in the back of me ambulance, they'll have your balls for breakfast when I tell 'em you wouldn't let 'im into the hospital wing. I'm trying to get him into prison, not break him out! There's a warder with him in the back of me van. What more do you bloody want?"

"The warder keeps an eye on him the whole time he's in?"

"Natch. Why bring a warder along, otherwise? Chummie don't need a valet. It's only an overnighter. He's due to continue as a witness at the Crown Court tomorrow morning, if he's passed fit."

The guard put down the official form and picked up the telephone. He spoke to the warder on the inside of the main door. After a while he put the phone down and said to Murphy, "You lot think you own the bloody place. Okay, take him through. Turn right inside and you'll see the hospital wing in front. You and your mate can take him up to the emergency ward on the first floor. The ward orderly'll meet you there."

Murphy said, "I'm deeply obliged."

The guard said, "Up yours, too," and went back to studying the racing results in the evening paper.

He must have pressed a button on his desk, for the red-and-white pole swung upward. Murphy nosed the ambulance underneath it and drove slowly toward the main door, which opened at his approach. A warder popped out from a small room, opened up the rear and saw the "prisoner" moving restlessly under his red blanket and the "warder"—Tritt in uniform—watching him closely from the opposite bunk. Lysol, dressed as an ambulanceman, was kneeling close to the prisoner. Satisfied with the tableau, the Scrubs guard waved Murphy through. He drove sedately forward and soon pulled up outside the hospital wing.

He remained inside the ambulance while Lysol and Tritt maneuvered the stretcher bearing Parker out of the back of the ambulance and up to the first floor, where the ward orderly was waiting for them. Lysol said, "We're wanted on another job—swiftish. Can't hang around. He's all yours now."

"Hey, not so fast," the orderly said in a high-pitched voice with a touch of an Irish brogue. He fluttered his hands a lot as he spoke and his lips were never still. "What's the prognosis? And what's this big warder doing here?" he asked, pointing to Tritt.

Lysol said, "Cardiac problem. They say he blacked out in the witness box. 'S' all I know."

Tritt said, "My orders are not to let him out of my sight. I tell you—I'd rather be home with my feet up, watching the box, than sitting up all night keeping an eye on this cunt. Don't worry—I'll keep out of your way."

"Let's get him into bed in your nice ward," Lysol said, "then I can take the stretcher and beat it. Bloody job this is."

Parker was breathing rapidly and shallowly, as he had been taught to do. He had a natural pallor and soon discovered that giving the occasional muted groan would convince the ward orderly, whose name turned out to be Delaney, that he was a genuine heart case. The emergency ward was a long narrow room with eight beds on either side and a passageway in between. Shaw was in the end bed on one side with curtains drawn. Only two of the beds on the other side were occupied. While Delaney was fussing around and making arabesques with his wrists, Lysol and Tritt decanted Parker into an empty bed on the same side of the room as Shaw's, with one empty bed between them. Then Lysol pulled the sides of the collapsible stretcher together, tucked it under his arm and ran down the stairs to rejoin Murphy in the ambulance. He slammed the stretcher into the rear compartment and climbed alongside the driver, who drove slowly out of the jail, gave a two-fingered salute to the man in the guard hut at the outside barrier and then turned left into busy Du Cane Road. The driver went left again up the narrow roadway between the jail and Hammersmith Hospital and drove on, turning first right, then left, until he came to the public car park alongside the West London Stadium. Several coaches were drawn up at right angles to the wall surrounding the car park. Murphy eased the ambulance into an inconspicuous place beside and slightly behind them.

They both already knew that Murphy would have to do his usual stint that night as chauffeur-cum-bodyguard to his underworld boss. The arrangement was that Lysol would remain hidden inside the ambulance all night, making sure that no one tampered with it before the vital next morning.

Yardley had rented a one-room office in a block in Queen Street, just behind the Lansdowne Club, for the duration of the op. So Murphy, on his way to Mayfair, stopped at a public telephone and dialed Yardley's office number. When Yardley answered, Murphy said, "Phase one complete, boss."

"Great. No hangups?"

"No, sir. The consignment is delivered. My friend says that everyone concerned is in position."

"Everyone?"

"So he says. They're all in the same place."

"Good work. You'll let me know when the next move's complete?"

"You bet." Murphy hung up.

Back in the emergency ward at the Scrubs, Tritt knew it was going to be a long twelve hours. A young bearded prison doctor had examined Parker, with Delaney in attendance. The doctor had said sharply, "I can't find much wrong with him. The pulse is regular and strong, breathing a bit shallow—but nothing remarkable. The patient really needs an ECG—but Cardiac's closed for the night. You sure he's not malingering?" This last query was shot at Tritt with a hard glance from under bushy eyebrows.

"Don't think so, sir," Tritt replied doubtfully. "You shoulda seen him keel over in court. In the witness box. One moment he was giving evidence quite normal-like, the next he groaned and swayed—and down he went. Like a ton of bricks. There wasn't a doctor in attendance, but when they called for an ambulance, the guy reckoned he'd had a minor heart attack. Looked the real thing to me, sir."

The doctor said to Delaney, "I'll prescribe a sedative. If he's restless overnight, give the patient a mild sleeping powder. I'll make a note on the file so that when the day staff comes on, he can have a full examination, ECG and all. If his condition deteriorates in the night, you have my number on call?"

"Oh, yessir."

Tritt cut in, "Begging your pardon, sir, but he's due to continue his evidence at ten A.M. tomorrow when the Crown Court reopens."

"If he's fit enough. If he's not, he'll damn well stay here until he's fit to be discharged. My own private feeling is, he's swinging the lead—just wants a good night's sleep in a soft bed. He could probably take part in the London Marathon! I'll take a look at the other prisoner," he went on, turning to the ward orderly, "while I'm here. That man Shaw in the end bed, curtained off, is he?"

He walked to the end of the ward, accompanied by Delaney. Tritt could hear him murmuring from inside the curtains and then he emerged and walked up the ward toward the exit. He said something about taking the man off his IV and keeping him under sedation the rest of the night, then disappeared through the swinging doors.

Parker lay back in the narrow bed, his eyes closed. His belongings were stowed away in the bedside table and he wore a pair of rough serge prison pajamas. A large plastic shopping bag lay half hidden between the side of the bed and the adjacent table. Inside was the jacket uniform of the London ambulance brigade. Tritt sat in a chair alongside the bed, apparently keeping watch on his prisoner. He had refused the offer of a bed in the warders' quarters on the grounds that his orders were not to let the prisoner out of his sight.

They were both experts at waiting—after many a long hour lying motionless under the stars in the Omani desert, where if you watched long enough, a camel-thorn bush in the distance might appear to turn into a turbaned Yemeni scout and move cautiously several feet. Or lying in the wet mud of an observation post in an Ulster field, with the rain soaking through your cover of sticks and leaves and chilling your bones to the marrow. Compared to all that, this was a cinch—but there was an animal alertness beneath their resigned waiting. It was worse for old Parker; he just had to lie there and look ill. Tritt decided the time had come to get alongside the ward orderly. He looked like a real limpwrister, but maybe he went for butch guys in uniform. He'd soon find out.

He wandered along toward the cubbyhole just this side of the swinging doors, where the orderly sat. There were a table, a couple of chairs and a bunch of files sitting in a wire basket. The grimy window looked out onto a blank wall. On the ledge underneath the window were two or three mugs, a jar of instant coffee, some lump sugar, an open box of teabags and an electric kettle.

"Gawd, I could use a hot cup of tea," Tritt said, exhaling loudly. "Court duty's a real bastard—never off your feet. Mind if I sit down?"

"Feel free," the orderly minced. "I could do a nice cuppa myself—the way mother used to make it. Here, I'll plug the kettle in."

He made the tea and took a waxed container of milk out

of a small refrigerator in the corner of the room. Tritt could see it contained a row of medical phials and a dish containing instruments. They sat and chatted, at first in a desultory way, but gradually Tritt thawed the man out. He told him that he had done a long-service stretch in the Army before joining the prison service. One far-fetched anecdote of army life led to another and before long he had Delaney giggling with laughter and saying, "Oh, my!"

"If I'd been in the Army," he said, "I'd have wanted to join the SAS, they're the boys—those dishy balaclavas and leaping through windows."

"Sod that for a lark," Tritt said. "It's too damn tough in the SAS, I reckon. Me for a quiet life."

"But you're a big tough man. You'd have been just right for the SAS."

"Don't you believe it. I met a few of them when I was serving in Belfast. Mostly quite little guys. Wasn't a John Wayne amongst them."

"You don't say. Ooh, I *am* disappointed."

As they chatted about this and that, Delaney confirmed what Tritt already knew from the research. The night staff was on duty till six o'clock the following morning, when the day staff relieved them. Then the patients were woken, washed and given breakfast, and beds were tidied for doctor's rounds, starting at eight o'clock. Supper for the night staff was sent around between seven and eight.

By now they were almost old friends, and Delaney volunteered to keep an eye on his charge while Tritt went for supper at the warders' mess. Tritt refused with many thanks, saying that his orders were to stay with the prisoner at all times. If it meant going without supper, it wouldn't be the first time. At which Delaney, who was clearly a good-hearted soul, said he would telephone the kitchens and arrange for a second plate of supper to be sent to the ward for Tritt, along with his own supper. They had a container of hot soup apiece, fruit, bread and cheese. Tritt pocketed an apple and a banana for Parker, who had refused the tray when an outside orderly brought it around.

Of the two other patients in adjoining beds on the opposite side of the ward from Shaw and Parker, one was a thin-faced morose man who spent his time staring into space. Delaney shrugged and tapped his forehead when he indicated the man to Tritt. The other, beefy and scarlet-faced, snorted and grunted like a pig. Delaney said quietly that his blood pressure had risen off the map and if it didn't improve he'd be shifted to a proper hospital. Both of them were on sleeping pills and so would be unlikely to cause any trouble during the night. Tritt gave a secret smile of relief.

By ten o'clock all was quiet. Shaw in his curtained-off bed had fallen into a troubled sleep, Parker was apparently dozing, and the other two were right out, judging by the stertorous breathing. Tritt and Delaney had had another cup of tea in the cubbyhole and were now the best of friends. Tritt suspected that the orderly was in a confessional mood and would soon start discussing his emotional problems, so he said he would take his boots off and stretch out on the vacant bed next to Parker.

Delaney said, "Here, why don't you get properly undressed and get right into bed? I've got to be awake all night—I'll gladly keep an eye on him for you."

"You're a hero—but no, thanks. If I knew his form, I'd be sorely tempted. But for all I know he could be a slippery cunt. If he *is* faking it, I don't want him causing a ruckus in the night with me snoring my head off! Thanks all the same, but I'll just kick my boots off, get under a spare blanket and doze. If you need any help with my guy—or any of this lot—give me a dig right away. And thanks—you've been a pal.

"By the way," he continued, "if I do doze off, give me a call sharp at five-thirty, would you? I want to be up and about when you go off duty. Maybe we could have another nice hot cuppa before you clock off?"

Delaney gave a smile of genuine pleasure, revealing a gold-edged front tooth. "You bet," he said boyishly. "Be my guest."

At five o'clock the next morning, Thursday, August 25, Murphy paid off the all-night taxicab at Kensal Green Railway Station. He waited out of sight until the driver had made a U turn and driven back down Harrow Road to the center of London. There was a predawn twilight and Harrow Road was deserted. Murphy ran lightly across the road and swarmed over the iron railings into Kensal Green Cemetery, dodging southward between the gravestones and the marble monuments until he came to the wall by the Grand Union Canal. Skirting westward, he passed through the bottom end of St. Mary's Roman Catholic Cemetery, sketching the sign of the cross as he did so. He was still a Catholic, if not a good one. He waited by the Mitre Bridge across the canal until he was sure the coast was clear and then scrambled up onto the embankment alongside Scrubs Lane. Keeping to the east of the main road, he traversed the recreation ground at Little Wormwood Scrubs. At the junction with Delgano Gardens he waited in the shadows until a big truck with blazing headlights ground slowly past, going north. After glancing up and down the road first and reassuring himself it was empty, he ran on his toes across wide Scrubs Lane and up and over the iron railings, and there he was—on the common, a few hundred yards behind West London Stadium with its car park and the concealed ambulance. In the half-light, his watch showed five-fifteen. Perfect timing.

Flitting like a ghost and keeping to the shadows, he traversed the back of the stadium, came to the car park entrance and walked noiselessly past some parked cars and a coach with blank windows until he came to the ambulance behind it. He tapped lightly on the front passenger's window.

Lysol, who had stretched out across the front seat, came alert at once, recognized Murphy and reached over to lift the internal door lock. Murphy gently opened the door, slid inside and sat down. He said in a half-whisper, "Anything happen?"

"Not a peep. Quiet as the grave."

"Don't mention graves. I've just come across two cemeteries. Got my gear there?"

Lysol indicated the ambulanceman's jacket on a peg behind the seats, on top of a white coat. Murphy struggled out of his jacket, put the other one on and transferred the contents of his pockets. His trousers were a gray-blue serge, the London ambulance color.

"Portable phone working?" he asked.

"Sure. I checked it just now by dialing 123 for the time signal."

"Good man. Christ, I could do with a nice cup of tea!"

"Coming right up, Murph. Only thing is, we'll have to share the top of the Thermos flask."

"Suits me—long as you haven't got AIDS."

Lysol rummaged in a medical bag and pulled out the Thermos. They sat in silence, handing the plastic lid to and fro, sipping away and feeling the hot liquid warming their veins. Both men knew that the next hour would be the most crucial of the whole op. It would need precision—both here and more so back at the jail—lots of bullshit and a large slice of luck if they were to pull off the snatch. But there was nothing to be done until the phone call came. Tense, they sat and waited.

Back in the hospital wing at Wormwood Scrubs, the orderly Delaney was as good as his word. Just after five-thirty he tiptoed through the silent ward and gently nudged Tritt's shoulder. Tritt, who was lying on the bed next to Parker, was already wide awake, though with his eyes closed, but he made a good pretense of yawning, sitting up and rubbing his eyes.

"You want that cup of tea?" Delaney asked.

"Boy, could I get round a cup of tea! You're a sportsman. Give me five minutes, will you. I need to take a leak—and better have a shave. Could be on duty again the rest of the day."

"You need a razor?"

"Thanks all the same. I've got a portable electric one for emergencies. See you in ten minutes. I'd better get this sod awake and take him for a pee. After a night's sleep, he could do with some exercise."

"Saves me getting a bedpan," Delaney said. "Fetching and carrying for criminals ain't my idea of the good life. Sure he'll be all right?"

"Yeah. Take a look at him if you like, but I reckon he's been playing up."

Delaney needed no further excuse. He took a cursory look around the ward, then went back to his cubbyhole. Tritt could hear the tinkle of spoons on saucers. As soon as the man's back was turned, he shook Parker vigorously, motioned him to get up and take the concealed plastic bag and started berating him as they passed Delaney's door. In the hospital restroom, Parker quickly pulled off his pajamas and dressed in the ambulanceman's trousers and shirt, which he'd brought in the bag. He slipped on his boots and then the gray-blue official jacket with its lapel badges, while Tritt was operating his electric razor. Delaney still had his back to them as they returned past his glass-fronted door. Fully dressed, Parker got back into bed and pulled the blanket up to his neck. He had taken a slim leather case out of the plastic bag and lay there clutching it in his right hand. Inside the case was a hypodermic needle containing enough morphine to put Shaw out for a further three hours. At ten to six, Tritt walked over to Delaney's little room. The kettle was boiling and three cups were laid out on the wooden table. There was also a plate of digestive biscuits. Christ, he thought, this guy would make someone a good wife.

A few minutes later, the door swung open and the day orderly walked in. He was a fat dark-haired man named Collier. The three of them sat drinking their tea while Delaney, who was obviously an old mate of Collier's to judge by the way they joshed each other, did a cursory handover. "That lazy bugger needs watching," Collier said to Tritt. "Always ducks out at the crucial moment and dumps the problems in my lap."

"Get away," Delaney said. "You try doing nights for a change. Takes years off your life." He held out his hand to Tritt. "Been nice knowing you. Take care."

"You, too. I enjoyed our talks. Maybe you could use a beer when you're off nights?"

"Ooh, I'd *love* that. You can always give me a ring or leave a message here. Bye-bye for now." He blew Collier a mock kiss and swayed out of the room.

Collier said to Tritt, "Most of those so-called gays get up my fuckin' nose. But old Frankie boy's all right. Got a good heart under all that ooh-la-la."

"You bet. He couldn't have been more helpful when I was dumped here last night. Hey, did you hear someone shouting out there in the ward?"

It was Parker, who had taken the opportunity while their backs were turned of getting out of bed, tiptoeing through the curtains of the second bed over and shooting the hypodermic needle into Shaw's thin arm as the man lay dozing. He was now back in bed and covered up.

"Something's wrong," he shouted when they appeared. "I heard terrible moaning and groaning from that bed there—and now he's gone all quiet. You'd better do something—fast!"

Collier rushed down the ward as quickly as his bulk allowed. Shaw was waxy-pale and apparently unconscious. Collier felt his pulse and put his ear to the man's mouth to listen to his breathing. Then he straightened up. Tritt had followed him through the curtains and stood at the foot of the bed.

"Christ!" Collier exclaimed. "It would happen now." He explained swiftly—what Tritt already knew from the research—that the MOs on night duty always left promptly at six A.M. and the daytime doctors usually wandered in anytime between seven and eight, when their rounds were due to begin. The medical side was short-staffed—the job of prison doctor was not a favored one—and they didn't have a full-time heart specialist on duty, anyway.

While he was flapping about, Tritt took control. "Look," he said, "you must have some oxygen on hand. Why not give him a squirt? Can't do any harm—and it might help. Why don't I go and ring for an ambulance from Hammersmith Hospital? It's just next door. They brought my guy in and'll be fetching him a bit later on. They could have an ambulance here within minutes. Let the experts take the responsibility, I say. Jesus, you don't want a bloody corpse on your hands, do you? If he dies, his relatives will sure as hell sue you for negligence. I were you, I'd get shot of the little bastard—fast!"

"But what about the paperwork?"

"Fuck the paperwork! That can always follow on. The trick is to get him off your hands while he's still breathing. Look, while you're fetching the oxygen, why don't I ring for that ambulance? Then I'll call the main gate for you, tell 'em what's happened—and to expect an ambulance from Hammersmith Hospital any minute."

"You reckon they'll wear that?"

"Course they will. There'll be a prison warder sent to the hospital with him. If it helps any, hell, I'll go along as well to keep an eye on things."

"Would you, really?"

"Sure. Anything to help out. Jesus, he doesn't look too good to me. Gone whiter, if anything. Here, you go and grab that oxygen—I'll do the phoning."

Collier clattered off through the swinging doors at the far end of the ward and returned a few minutes later, pushing a cart with the oxygen apparatus on it. Tritt went into the cubbyhole office, dialed for an outside line and then the number of Murphy's portable phone. He answered after the first ring. Tritt said, "Right—come now," and rang off. Then he looked up the extension of the main gate on the prison directory pinned on a notice board. Tersely, he told the warder who answered that he was calling from the hospital wing;

there was a serious heart case who had to be shifted at once to Hammersmith Hospital, which had an ambulance on its way. There was no time to prepare the official discharge documents, but they'd be sent over to the hospital that morning. And there'd better be a warder standing by to accompany the sick prisoner in the ambulance.

The man at the main gate took it all in without comment, then said, "What's your extension number?"

Tritt gave it to him.

"I'll call you back when everything's laid on," he said.

"Okay—but make it snappy. The patient could be dying." He rang off. That main-gate guy was quite smart, he thought. Wasn't going to play ball until he was sure it was a bona fide call from inside the prison.

Murphy drove the ambulance cautiously out of the stadium car park and down the slip road between Hammersmith Hospital and the jail. Only when he turned right into Du Cane Road did he switch on the headlights and the blue flashing lights. He charged in front of an early-morning red bus, drove fifty yards or so and then swung hard right into the entrance road for the jail. He hoped to God the same moron who had held him up yesterday would not still be on duty. He was not. The man in the cabin by the barrier must have been warned in advance. "You come for a heart case?" he asked.

"That's what they told me."

"Okay. Through the main gate, right and then half left. That's the prison wing."

"Thanks."

The striped pole went aloft and, as the ambulance approached, the main door opened in front of it. "Easy as pie," Lysol muttered.

"Wait for it! This next bit's the tricky one."

While the ward orderly was administering oxygen to the prisoner Shaw behind the concealing curtains, and Tritt was busy on the telephone in the cubbyhole, Parker had quietly slipped out of his bed, pulled up the blankets and smoothed the pillow. He folded up the plastic bag and shoved it into a pocket and went out through the swinging doors and ducked into the lavatories. Earlier that morning, while Tritt was shaving, he had located a window that looked out onto the space in front of the hospital wing. He stood there, alert and hardly breathing, holding his white linen ambulance coat in one hand. The wait seemed interminable. At any moment a patient on light duties might enter—and then he'd have to bluff his way out—or worse. But in three or four minutes, he saw with relief the ambulance nosing its way through the main door and approaching the hospital wing entrance. He donned his white coat, ran down the stone stairs and stood just inside the swinging doors. When Murphy and Lysol came through wheeling the stretcher, without a word he tagged on behind them and went back up the single flight of stairs. The ward orderly had hardly taken a look at him since coming on duty, and besides, a man in a white coat always looks different from a patient in bed. The risk was minimal.

Murphy and Lysol pushed the stretcher down the ward, following Collier, who was relieved to see them. He unclipped the oxygen mask from Shaw's face, and they bundled him onto the stretcher and adjusted the oxygen apparatus on the stretcher. With hardly a word, they went back through the ward, with Parker walking alongside the stretcher and making a show of fiddling with the dials for the oxygen. Tritt said to Collier, "Don't worry, mate. I'll keep a watch on things."

"You're a pal," Collier replied, as the whole team, together for the first time since the op began, summoned the elevator. They rode to the ground floor without a word. The stretcher was pushed into place in the rear of the ambulance, and Tritt and Parker went in behind it. Lysol took his place alongside Murphy, who drove. Back at the main door, a grizzled old warder with the Queen's Police Medal above the breast pocket of his uniform awaited them.

"Hey, dad," Lysol called out. "You like to sit in the back—keep an eye on the prisoner. He won't give no trouble."

"Not so much of the dad," the old boy grumbled. "How d'you open these bleedin' doors?"

Out of sight of the prison and close to the main entrance of Hammersmith Hospital, there is a "zebra" courtesy crossing for pedestrians. The ambulance, driving sedately without headlights or flashing lights, pulled up behind a milk truck and a bus, as two or three pedestrians walked across twenty yards ahead. Lysol, who had removed his white coat, slipped out when the ambulance paused briefly, and strolled back nonchalantly past the prison to Fitzneal Street, where he entered the East Acton Underground Station. He traveled eastward on the Central Line as far as Tottenham Court

Road, changed to the Northern Line and got out at Euston. At the main railway station, he walked up to a row of left-luggage lockers, opened one and took out a garment bag, which contained a dark city suit made in Savile Row and a change of casual clothes. He carried the bag into the public lavatory, chose an end cubicle and put on a clean shirt, trousers and sweater. With several hours to kill before he took the train to Derby, he had a shave and a facial massage at the barbershop in the station concourse, then took a leisurely breakfast at the station buffet. He was pleased with life . . . but he hoped to Christ the last vital link in the snatch was going—had by now gone—without a hitch.

The ambulance drove on past the main frontage of Hammersmith Hospital and turned up a narrow road on its east side. Twenty yards along, it pulled up sharply, close to a red neon sign marked "Casualty." Tritt and Parker lifted out Shaw and, with the prison warder trotting along beside them, walked quickly in through the hospital entrance. Once they were clear, Murphy made a U turn with the ambulance, drove back past the main entrance again, turned right up the narrow roadway next to the prison and came out around the back of the hospital near the ambulance park and the London Ambulance Transport dispatching office. He pulled up to the side of the waiting line, got out and lit a cigarette, and then gave a vague wave, as though to a friend somewhere in the back of the line.

The security guards by the Casualty entrance had waved the stretcher through and now it paused a few yards in front of the Casualty office, where a tired-looking gray-haired woman sat, surrounded with rows of buff-colored files on shelves. Parker, as the remaining ambulanceman, took control. "Here," he said, to the prison warder, "you check him in. We've got to get him to Cardiology—fast."

"What's 'is name and number?"

"Name's Shaw, Peter Shaw. God knows what his number is."

"That's no good to me," said the warder. "Gotta have a number. How can they keep proper files without a number?"

"Stuff the number! Look, this guy could be dying. He's hardly bloody breathing. You want me to tell the court of inquiry we coulda saved his life if you hadn't gone farting around about his number?"

Tritt, as an apparent warder himself, chipped in. "He's right, old man. Here, she'll respect someone with your length of service. You register him and I'll help get him into Cardiology. Once the doc's saved his life, we can sort out his number then. One phone call to the prison—that's all it needs. And we'll be just round the corner in Cardiology. See you there in five minutes."

Still shaking his close-cropped white head in doubt, the warder went over to the reception window and started talking to the woman. Parker and Tritt pushed the stretcher down the side corridor right past the "Cardiology" sign and turned left when they reached the main passage. Just as they both felt they were almost home, a hospital orderly who wasn't looking where he was going pushed a cart through a set of swinging doors on the left of the passage. The cart, with various flasks and bottles on it, crashed into the side of the stretcher. Two flasks toppled and crashed on the polished floor. The rank smell suggested they had contained urine samples.

"Christ!" said Parker.

The orderly, a spotty young man, shouted, "You done it now! What you up to?"

"What are *we* up to?" Tritt said with cold menace. "You come bouncing out and smash into us. This is a very sick patient, I'll have you know."

"Where you think you're taking him? The wards are back that way."

Tritt balled his fists and took a step toward the orderly. Parker said softly, "Cool it. You"—to the young man—"if you don't want a bunch of fives in the face, beat it! We're in a hurry."

The orderly hesitated. Something about the set of Parker's face warned him not to go any further. He said, "Why don't you fuck off, then?" and, stooping down, began to pick up the bits of broken glass.

They pushed the stretcher through a passage signposted "To North Side," straight past the new outpatients' reception, and turned left following a sign that read "Transport." On they went through a pair of light gray swinging doors to the transport waiting room. They ignored the waiting London Ambulance Transport dispatching staff room and pushed the stretcher out through the external swinging doors.

They were now in the parking area, and there was Murphy, waiting beside his ambulance. Without a pause they steered the stretcher toward him, stopped to lift it into the rear and then climbed inside themselves. Murphy drove calmly past the Abbot Security guards at the west gate. They took no notice. The whole operation, including the unexpected holdup from the accident in the passageway, had taken less than three and a half minutes. They could not be sure but they guessed that the grizzled old warder would still be dealing with the registration forms back at Casualty reception.

Murphy drove down the narrow pathway next to the prison wall and turned sharply left into Du Cane Road. Then he switched on the headlights and the flashing blue lights and drove fast in an easterly direction. They were still not home and dry. As the ambulance rushed toward the traffic lights to make a left turn on Wood Lane, there was a green baker's van illegally parked close to the light. A double-decker red bus, halted at the bus stop twenty yards back, pulled out in a leisurely manner from behind the van and stopped at the traffic lights, blocking the eastbound roadway. Murphy, with sirens blaring, pulled out onto the wrong side of the road, intending to turn left to cut across the front of the impeding bus. And just then from the side road, with the traffic lights in his favor, a young man in dark glasses driving a red BMW came out, swerving left and aiming straight at the ambulance's front fenders. Murphy pulled the ambulance hard in a controlled skid as the young man braked. He slid across the front of the bus, missing it by an inch. "You cunt!" he yelled at the yuppie BMW driver, who had done nothing wrong. The ambulance powered north on Wood Lane, the bus driver gasping when the dark bulk zipped across his vision. Murphy, alone in the front compartment, muttered a prayer of relief under his breath. Half a second—two inches' difference—and the ambulance would have been wedged between the bus and the front of the BMW in a tangle of screeching metal and breaking glass. And then the police would have turned up, statements would have been taken, the sick passenger in the rear investigated. And that would be the whole op written off and the three members of the team arrested.

Switching off the headlights and the blue lights, Murphy drove more soberly, right into North Pole Gardens and on into Barlby Road until they reached the junction with the broad Ladbroke Road. Already the traffic was thickening up, and at the traffic lights he exchanged pleasantries with the driver of a milk truck on his early-morning deliveries. He turned north again when the lights went green, then east into Harrow Road, one of the main arteries to the center of London. Close under the Westway, high on its vast concrete-and-steel stilts, he went left into Westbourne Terrace and, after a couple of hundred yards, pulled up under a plane tree in Blomfield Road. The arc of branches with their broad maple-shaped leaves would act as a shield against prying eyes in the upper windows of the houses. He tapped the bulkhead dividing the driver's compartment from the rear.

Tritt, having jettisoned his London ambulance jacket, got out from behind and strolled over to the Warwick Estate, where they had left an inconspicuous gray Ford estate car parked among those belonging to the council tenants. He drove it across the road and pulled up alongside the ambulance. Murphy and Parker lifted the half-conscious Shaw out of the ambulance and into the back of the car. Parker got in the front and Tritt pulled away. It had taken ninety seconds from the moment the ambulance first pulled up.

He drove the short distance into Warwick Place and stopped at the white gate leading to the canal at Little Venice. He stepped out, unlocked the gate and, with Parker supporting Shaw on the other side as though he were a drunken reveler returning from an all-night party, they maneuvered the man down the path and up the steps to the hideout barge. Tritt went back to the car and drove it a few yards to a lock-up garage at the rear of the Warwick Castle pub. He then went on foot to rejoin Parker aboard the barge.

Murphy meanwhile drove the ambulance quietly back to Harrow Road and, reversing the route he had just taken, back to the West London rental company. It was still early, and he had to wait out in the road until eight o'clock, when the gates opened for business. The rental company clerk inspected the vehicle, took the mileage, then conducted Murphy into the untidy office with half-empty coffee mugs on the wooden table and ashtrays overflowing with cigarette butts.

Murphy had paid cash in advance. He signed the release form in the same false name he had used when booking the ambulance, cracked a joke or two about taking expectant mothers shopping, shook hands and walked away.

Up to now, he had deliberately kept his mind cold and

unemotional. Even in the near collision with the bus and the BMW, his reflexes had been honed, just as in the good old days in the Regiment. But as the enormity of what had been done began to sink in—four men had beaten both the prison and the hospital system in the space of twelve hours—his natural exuberance began to bubble over. It was all he could do to stop himself dancing a little jig as he walked along Fulham Road. He came to an unoccupied telephone booth and dialed Yardley's Queen Street number. When Yardley replied on the third ring, he said, "Major, we did it. We fucking did it!"

Jack had been sitting in the dark and deserted car park for about ten minutes. They were late and even the plush leather interior of his Jaguar XJ6 was beginning to feel cold and a little uncomfortable. Shit! They were only two minutes late, relax. At one-thirty in the morning, being alone in a vacant car lot nestled beside the A3I6 Twickenham Road had him feeling like a naked doll on top of a Christmas tree.

This was a heavy job, real heavy. It had come to him in the usual way. Two nights earlier he had downed his regular pint of IPA beer at the Golden Lion Pub in Fulham High Street, then crossed the road to the Fulham Snooker Club. He had a high-stakes game on with two of the regulars from the Halfway House Pub at Fulham Cross. He had taken their money on the tables many times and they were always relaxed about losing it. Hard bastards, all of them. Their solution was to go straight out and steal some more. The antiquated club rooms squatting at the eastern end of Putney Bridge were second home to many like him. A contact point for a wide range of under-the-table expertise. His far-reaching reputation heralded two activities: playing pool and driving highly tuned cars for illicit purposes. The external appearance of the place made him feel safe: the front wall covered in posters and the windows down the Church Gardens side protected by wire mesh, the thick brown wooden double doors at the entrance with the oversized cast-iron padlock hanging limply in its bracket. It was all sufficiently unwelcome to keep the bullshit out. That was on the other side of the tracks, at that fucking flash drum next door. Fulham Palace, the only bleedin' balls they played with in there were their own.

He had entered the club and strolled the length of the pool

hall, passed the sixteen immaculate tables, each highlighted by an overhead lamp. The usual greetings sang out from shadowed faces. His two challengers were already at the table chalking the end of their cues. As he lifted his prized customized cue from its usual container, chained in a rack of similar cylindrical containers, he had seen the note taped inside. A telephone number and two words. "A Grand."

The snooker game had been easy. His secret fix of adrenaline, injected by the note, and their drinking had made him dominant. A bloody pushover, they were. Afterward he had made the call from a public phone in the Kings Arms, opposite in Kings Road. On the way he had collected a copy of the London A-Z street directory from his car.

"It's about that game of pool, you're on."

A brief silence, then a clipped, hard cockney accent. "Page eighty-eight, four D, car park behind the church. Monday morning, one-thirty, three bags. Fucking be there!" The phone went dead. The menace in the voice did not. It still vibrated in his head.

For his twenty-five years, he had been around. Hardened, street-wise, confident, and he knew the rules. You didn't fuck with these boys.

He had positioned the car close to the footbridge that led across the wide dual roadway of Twickenham Road to the Old Deer Park recreation ground. If the police or any other trouble came into the parking lot from the single narrow entrance down the side of the church, he was off. Forget the car, and over that bridge like a scalded cat.

The crunch of tires on the gravel surface alerted him to the small van rolling furtively through the Park Lane entrance. As it passed under the one and only streetlamp at the end of the lane, he noted the cleaning company advertising splashed along its side. He slipped his driver's door open an inch and started the Jaguar's engine to a quiet idle. The van, with lights extinguished, moved to a parked position in the far corner. The driver first got out and satisfied himself that it was a Jaguar he was looking at and then gave the nod to two others seated in the back. The rear doors opened and closed smartly, and three men walked briskly toward him. As they drew near, the front man signaled with his palm facing down that he should close his door and stay in the car. Without a break in stride the rear door of the Jaguar was opened and two men slid into the backseat. The third man, obviously the leader, was suddenly in the front beside him.

Without introduction he slapped a brown envelope across the steering wheel. "This is for you." The low, no-nonsense voice was full of authority. "What do they call you?"

"Jack." He ran his thumb across the notes. Used fifties sleeved neatly in two bundles. The full one thousand pounds up front.

"Let's go, Jack." The speaker was looking straight ahead and wasn't expecting a reply.

Jack had the car sliding out to Twickenham Road and away from Richmond before the money had settled inside his leather jacket.

"Take the M3 all the way to the Winchester bypass. I'll direct you from there." The voice remained level and detached.

By the time they hit the M3 at Sunbury it was clear to the three passengers that this was no run-of-the-mill Jaguar XJ6. The acceleration and the distinctive whine of a turbocharger being emitted from under the hood confirmed otherwise. The young driver in the leather driving gloves knew his stuff. No drama, very fast and in total control.

Jack had been around hardened underworld types all his life. They looked tough, acted tough and in most cases were tough. These three geezers didn't look tough, but he knew, or more, sensed, that they were as hard as nails. He had observed the escort sitting in the back keeping the thin man between them upright and awake. He was obviously on something. The leader up front next to him constantly studied the road map on his knees and checked his watch. None of them had spoken a word since they left the parking lot in West London an hour earlier. He had kept their speed over the 100 mph mark all the way down the motorway. Approaching Winchester he had eased up a bit.

"I'll tell you when to slow down," came the voice next to him.

This lot is military, thought Jack. I'm carrying one of the funny mobs. They were all wearing industrial overalls, but he had seen his passengers' footwear. Bloody commando boots. Except the sleepy one in the back, he had on those rubber boots that the toffs prance around their yachts in.

"Take the Romsey Road." The clipped order gave him little time to digest the array of road signs.

The Jaguar smoothly changed lanes and slipped off the main A3 road.

A short time later: "Two miles to a hard right-hander.

There will be a farmhouse on your right. There should be a country road sign saying 'Farley Mount.' " The map reader turned to the rear passengers. "If Fangio here can keep the pace up we have eight minutes to run. Make sure he's awake and ready to move."

"He's awake, boss," came the first words from the back-seat.

They raced past a sign saying "Hursley." The winding road sliced through a valley with farmland rising gradually on both sides. The road was fast but patches of fog appeared, making Jack nervous. As the car emerged from one such patch, an order snapped from his left.

"Hard right here, now!"

By reflex the car was sideways, down two gears and gunning into the country lane. The dancing Jaguar accelerated into a straight arrow between parallel hedgerows. The twisting road began to climb, the gradient increasing sharply. Then they were in it. Thick fog.

"Okay, slow it down, we're in good time. Continue up here for three miles." His head dropped back to the map. "There's a crop of trees on your side at the top of this rise. Pull over when you see it. It's a tourist lookout spot, so there should be some kind of overlook."

The car continued on through the eerie fog. The foliage seem to be closing in on them from both sides. The road widened and Jack felt without seeing that it dropped away on his side. The crop of trees, only their trunks visible, suddenly was there. He pulled over beneath the hanging branches.

Jack turned to his passenger for confirmation, maybe a little congratulation. Shit, he had gotten them there from London in just over an hour and a half. And in fucking fog.

Expressionless eyes stared back at him from two holes in a black balaclava. Jack turned and saw another head in the same gear and another with a woolen fisherman's hat pushed down almost covering his eyes.

"Right, Jack, get this clear. We'll be gone for four hours. With him along it's slow in and fast out for us. You be here! If you have to move, don't go off this road; you'll get lost in this damn fog. Zero your mileage meter before you move. Just make sure you are on this spot at oh-seven-hundred hours. Got it?"

"Yeah, I've got it."

The group in the back were getting out of the car. One of

them took three camouflage jackets out of a carryall. He tossed it back onto the seat, catching Jack's eyes with his.

"Be here!" The muffled firmness in the voice left nothing in doubt. The rear door closed.

His front passenger was now out of the car and leaning back in. A Silver compass hung from his neck on a red string. Two cold eyes zeroed into Jack.

"I'll be here! I'll fuckin' be here for fuck's sake!" His voice seemed to have risen in the delivery.

The left eye under the balaclava winked. The head withdrew and the door closed firmly.

Parker led his men across the road and up the embankment into the tangled undergrowth. He was smiling to himself. Pausing briefly, he found his compass bearing, stuffed the map and compass inside his jacket and struck out toward the farm airstrip. Out there in the fog somewhere.

In the small hours of that same morning, Murphy had driven the Boss back to his home in Admiral's Walk, Hampstead. The man stayed in the car until his resident "gorilla" opened the front gate by remote control and switched on the floodlights between the flagstone path and the front door.

Grunting as he levered his bulk out of the rear seat, he had said, "Mike, I'll need you later this morning. We're going for a little drive. You be here sharp on eleven."

"Sure, Boss," Murphy had said.

So here he was, waiting outside at five to eleven. The bright sun hurt his eyeballs. Emmie had been working late—he had had to celebrate on his own, but he'd sunk at least half a bottle of scotch. He'd been tempted to call up Major Yardley to share the celebration but the caution born of many operations had prevailed. It was finished, you kept well apart. Still, with all that dough in the bank, now was the time for a fresh start. No more bleeding driving for a fat, ugly pig. And no more of "the game" for Emmie. They could cut loose, go abroad, start all over, live in comfort for a long time.

He wondered vaguely what all this was about. The Boss usually slept late, never rising much before noon, putting in an appearance at one of his West End clubs for champagne and a snack. Murphy hoped to God that there was no rough stuff in view, where he might have to go and in the Boss's presence beat up some poor sod who was behind on his payments. His master was a proper sadist, just loving to hear the victim yell and weep before the hitting began. Now maybe he and Emmie could make a clean start. But inside he knew it was only a dream. With his record, he'd never get a visa for the States or Australia—and there were too many pals of the Boss's lolling on the Costa del Sol. Why the hell didn't someone start a nice little private war where there was room for an ex–SAS man?

Mr. Big was ready at last. "Where to, Boss?" Murphy asked.

"Down to Arkwright Road and then into Finchley Road. On down past Swiss Cottage, and I'll direct you again when we get there."

As the car was approaching St. John's Wood tube station, Murphy was instructed to turn right at the lights. At the next junction, it was right again. Just short of the crossing at Hamilton Terrace, the Boss said, "You see that guy there near the corner? Pull up, we're giving him a lift."

Thank Christ for that, Murphy thought. Now there's someone to do the dirty work. He stopped the car and the man got into the front passenger seat. He looked a nasty bit of work, with a shiv mark, a long scar made by a knife or a cutthroat razor, down the length of his left cheek.

The Boss said, "Right, Mike, just drive on and pull up in that gap over there, by the big tree."

Murphy wondered what the hell was going on. The Boss wasn't one to hang around once he was in the car. But he did as he was told and drew the big car to a halt in the space under the tree.

"Now we're just one happy family. That right, Mike? No secrets, no funny business?"

"No secrets, Boss."

"You're a fuckin' liar! What d'you think, Tony?"

The man with the scar, who was chewing gum, said, "You're right, Boss. In my book, he's a fuckin' liar."

The Boss said, "You're not only a liar, Mike, you're fuckin' stupid with it. That warder, Barlow—he's *my* guy. You think you can pull your little stunts on my patch? He got the word to me yesterday you'd sprung Shaw. You and your bleedin' fancy-Dan ex-soldiers. I didn't *want* Shaw outside. He knows too much. All the safes got cracked in the last two years, what was in 'em—the lot. Now you just keep both hands on that steering wheel—if he don't, cut 'im, Tony."

"Right, Boss," said the man in the passenger seat alongside Murphy.

"So let's have a quiet little talk, Mike. Like, you do the talking, I'll just listen. First, where you got him?"

Murphy's pulse had been thudding like a voodoo drum but he was rapidly getting control of himself. The operational side of his brain told him the Boss's tactics had been too slow. As soon as the evil-looking Tony had gotten into the car, he should have slid a knife against Murphy's neck and shocked him into blurting out the facts. Now he'd had the vital few moments to think. He had to get the car rolling again—it was his only hope. And he knew that Shaw would have left the houseboat five hours back. He'd be airborne by now.

"Christ, I'm sorry, Boss," he said. "I had no idea that Shaw meant anything to you. It was just a job. Some geezer from up north—Scottish, he sounded—gave me five grand in cash to spring him. I wouldn't have touched it—honest!—if I'd known Shaw was one of yours. You gotta believe me."

"I don't 'ave to believe anything. Not from a lying hound like you. But I'm still asking—where is he?"

"Not far from here, Boss. Other side of Maida Vale."

"Okay, let's go. But listen good. No one screws me twice. Got it? Tony here is rodded up—that right, Tony?"

"That's right, Boss," said the gum chewer.

"And it's got a silencer. So you drive nice and careful, Mike. You just take us to where you've stashed Shaw—and he'd better be there. You read me?"

Murphy said, "You bet, Boss. Jeez, I'm sorry about all this."

There was no point in arguing. He had to let them think he was broken, submissive. But he knew he was doomed if he didn't do something fast. The Boss would snuff him just as soon as light a new cigar—and with as much enjoyment. As he drew away from the crossroads, he wondered if it would be worth crashing into the back of another car and trying to make a break in all the confusion, but the Mercedes was built like a tank and might suffer little damage. If they reached Little Venice, he knew he would have had it. Once out of the car, he could easily handle the Boss but not this villain with a silenced pistol at the same time. God curse that bugger Barlow, who must have blown the whistle as soon as the break was complete.

As they swung hard left into the Edgware Road, he allowed himself to swing with the car. His left elbow nudged his passenger's right side. He could feel the bulge of the pistol in its armpit holster. So this Tony was a southpaw. His first lucky break.

Just short of the Maida Vale tube station, he saw a milk truck pulled over at the side of the road. He swerved in front of a bus, slammed the car toward the curb and stamped on the brakes. As Tony was flung forward, he hit him once—hard—on the side of the neck beneath his right ear with the edge of his hand. Tony slumped with a groan. Murphy snatched back his coat, yanked the pistol out and in one quick move ejected the magazine. Then he ripped out the wires of the car phone, switched off the engine and pulled out the ignition key. He opened the back door and tossed the empty pistol into the Boss's lap. He looked quite green under his swarthy beard growth.

"I ought to bend that gun over your head," Murphy said. "But I'm in a hurry. You don't look well. Why not buy a pint of nourishing milk from the milkman here?" He dropped the bunch of ignition keys and the loaded magazine down a drain just in front of the car and ran lightly toward the underground station. He ducked into the entrance, but as soon as he was out of the Boss's sight, he emerged and flagged down a cruising cab, telling the man to drive to the Dorchester Hotel in Park Lane. He gave the impression of entering the hotel, but when the driver had picked up another fare and had driven on toward Hyde Park Corner, Murphy walked rapidly the few hundred yards to Emmie's flat.

It was not yet twelve-thirty and, luckily, she had no customer but was puttering about in her dressing gown. He had walked past the lower end of Queen Street on his way and had been tempted to call on Major Yardley and explain the catastrophe. But pride and the feeling that he could still somehow sort things out unaided had stopped him. After all, it was he who had introduced Barlow. Bob Yardley was a hell of a guy who would never bawl him out, but he could just imagine that half-concealed look of contempt that would silently be saying, "Right cunt you turned out to be." And anyway, Shaw would be airborne by now. The operation had worked, hadn't it?

"What's the matter, Mike?" Emmie asked anxiously. "You look terrible—all white."

"It's nothing," he said airily.

"Oh yes, it is. You don't fool me. Something bad's happened. I can tell."

"All right," he said. "It is bad." Quickly, he told her what had happened with the Boss, leaving out the snatch from Wormwood Scrubs. If that blew up in his face—and he wouldn't put it past the Boss to blow the whistle on him—the less she knew, the better.

She was twisting the cord of her dressing gown round and round in her fingers. Like a bleeding Arab with the prayer beads, he thought. Christ, I could use a rosary right now. She said, "What you going to do?"

"First, I've gotta call my friend in Marseilles. He owns the bloody houseboat. He'll give me a right bollocking but I must tell him it's blown. Then I'm going to skedaddle—fast. I'll grab the money I've got stashed and go to ground, God knows where. The Boss knows all my haunts. You start packing, love. Tomorrow we could maybe take a plane to Dublin—and think again. The Boss don't give up easy."

He went to the telephone and dialed the Marseilles number, spoke briefly and then obeyed an instruction to hang up. He paced up and down the small sitting room, chewing the flesh around his left thumbnail.

After an age, the telephone rang. He snatched it up and said, "Nick? Thank Christ I got you." The words came tumbling out as he explained his predicament. There was a long silence at the other end. Then the cool, almost faintly amused, voice in his ear said, "Relax, Mike. Take it easy, boy. You know Tooley Street, south side of the river, just off Tower Bridge? There's a block of council flats, Clement Attlee House, just along from the police station. They'll give you protection! You go see the caretaker on the ground floor, slip him a fiver and say you're booking eight C. Got it? If he asks any questions, tell him the man from Salisbury sent you. He'll give you the keys—but it's only for forty-eight hours. After that, you're on your own."

"God, you're a friend, Nick. That's all I need. A day to sort it out and then I'm away. You're a mate!"

"Anything for an old friend, Mike. You know that."

5

'Tis all a Chequer-board of Nights and
Days
Where Destiny with Men for Pieces plays:
Hither and thither moves, and mates,
and slays,
And one by one back in the Closet lays.

After the heart-churning moments of getting that ambulance into and out of the Scrubs, and then that neat dodge of driving around the hospital mulberry bush and away again, the Honorable Rupert Lycett-Smythe had welcomed a return to almost normal living. A first-class reserved seat on the 12:05 train from St. Pancras to Derby, a seven-mile taxi drive to the Donington Thistle Hotel, a room with a view of the East Midlands Airport Terminal—and a large gin and tonic from the refrigerator alongside the television set in the hotel bedroom. This was more like the life.

The receptionist had handed him a sealed parcel when he checked in. He tore off the wrapping as he sipped his gin, and found several brochures and the plans of a large industrial land-purchase project on the northern outskirts of Marseilles. There was an unsigned note attached: "Expect a call at eighteen hundred hours."

The call came right on time. A girl with a bright voice welcomed him to East Midlands on behalf of Macair Charters. A taxi would collect him from the hotel at 0530 hours the next day and drive him to the airport terminal. His pilot, Captain McDermid, would be waiting at the general handling desk, on the left as he entered. "Have a nice evening, sir," she said as she hung up.

Fat hope of that, he thought. Up with the birds, instructions not to leave the hotel, not knowing a soul north of Watford except for a few hunting friends in the Shires—it sure cramped a man's social life. So he ordered a meal to be sent up and watched an old movie on television. It would be *Birdman of Alcatraz.*

He had brought a city suit with him on the train, and after his early-morning call and a cold shower, he put it on. His role was now the keen young entrepreneur, off to make a killing in property while the opposition slept. He spotted McDermid at once in the terminal and went over to shake hands. McDermid wore the uniform of a charter pilot with four gold stripes on each sleeve. He was friendly and polite but formal and briskly efficient. On the table in front of him were various documents—the company flight log, the flight plan, weather briefs and customs papers.

Matter-of-factly he said, "Please fill in this general declaration with your personal details. Make sure they correspond with your passport details."

Lysol made a face as he reached for his pen. "Bloody forms—are they really necessary?"

"Absolutely. This is a legitimate charter. The C-284 is for Special Branch, antiterrorism and all that. This other declaration is for customs."

McDermid attached the papers to his clipboard. "I will explain the flight operation to you out at the aircraft. First, let's get the formalities over with. We clear customs and immigration in the normal way. Jack Rogers has Special Branch duty this morning, he will probably give us the once-over. Just relax, there's nothing to it."

He led Lysol across the deserted terminal and into a narrow corridor. They made their way into a glass-paneled room. Behind the panel were three customs officers, one of whom slid open a window and accepted the declaration forms from McDermid. The window closed equally abruptly and the officer conferred with a tall man, the type that looks like a policeman at any distance. The usual flamboyant thumping of rubber stamps took place and the tall, plainly dressed man returned to the window with the pilot's copies.

"Morning, Johnnie, off with the birds again, I see." He turned to Lysol, looked and missed nothing. "Business in the sunny south of France, is it, sir?"

"Yes, that's right. I don't envy you chaps being up this early every day in a place like this. It's hardly Heathrow."

McDermid saw the danger and stepped in.

"Morning, Jack. My passenger has early appointments outside Marseilles this morning and I'm getting concerned about this fog making a mess of the usual heavy morning arrival traffic. If that paperwork's in order, I'd like to get moving."

He handed both passports to the Special Branch officer, who inspected and returned them.

"Have a good flight, Mr. Lycett-Smythe." The glass window closed firmly.

McDermid led Lysol through a door out into the dark morning chill. The noise and bustle of turbine engines, ramp vehicles and human activity swam around them. East Midlands is a hub airport for the large volume of mail, newspapers and night-freight flights going on yearlong and it comes alive between midnight and seven in the morning.

Lysol and McDermid walked out across the light-aircraft parking area, past various executive aircraft, toward their plane. The Cessna 421 sat low on its wide undercarriage, sandwiched between a bright red helicopter and a Peregrine Airways Gulfstream 1. The tarmac was bathed in light from high lamps spaced along its edge.

McDermid shouted above the scream of a taxiing Vanguard Freighter of Airbridge Carriers, which was being maneuvered into a loading bay by its four powerful turboprop engines. "We'll talk in the plane."

They approached the port side of the plane. McDermid pulled a lever out of its recess in the fuselage and the top half of the split door opened upward. In familiar fashion he lowered the bottom half, exposing steps into the main cabin. He gestured Lysol into the plane.

"I've already preflighted her; I'm just going to do a quick walk around."

Lysol observed that McDermid seemed to be almost caressing the plane with a light touch as he inspected this place and that surface. These bloody pilots are a funny lot. McDermid disappeared around the nose of the aircraft and Lysol sat and took in the lush interior.

Hmm, this is not a bad way to go to war, Major Yardley. The thought amused him.

McDermid joined him in the cabin and drew up the steps behind him, leaving the top half of the door open. He sat in one of the passenger seats, reached across to a locker cupboard under a small utility unit and extracted a flight bag and a mail sack. From the sack he took a steel U lock, the type used by motorcyclists to secure their machines against theft. With efficient movements he attached it to the frame of the middle seat and demonstrated how it was free to swivel up to be level with the sitting position. He also took out a pair of plastic gloves, a pair of medical overboots and a pair of overalls adorned with the logo "Volvo Marine Engines."

"Our flight-plan departure is for six, that's in twelve minutes' time. I'll be briefing you as we go along. Our flight time to our first target, position Pickup, is thirty-two point five minutes from takeoff."

"I'm very impressed with the point five of a minute, the Army . . ."

"Shut up and listen, Lysol! This is the part of this operation I am paid for. I don't give a fuck how you screw it up on the ground, but the air op will be precision down to the last turn of those propellers. You will act on my orders and question nothing. If I demand, you respond. Is that clear? With a bit of luck on our side we'll slip in and out of the system like a fart in the House of Commons. The luck we get is the luck I make."

Lysol did not miss or underestimate the firmness in McDermid's quiet voice.

"Message received very loud and very clear. Consider my sense of humor shelved for the duration."

"We are on the ground and I have repositioned for takeoff. Parker knows the routine. He will have our passenger at the door when you open it. They have been in the dirt most of the night. I don't want a trace of that Hampshire cowshit in my aeroplane, and that is not because I'm house-proud. They'll have him held clear of the ground. Pass out the overalls. As his feet appear, you put the overboots on them. When he slides in, they'll offer up his hands. You put the plastic gloves on him and be sure to pull the wrist strings tight. Throw him in this seat and handcuff him to this U lock. On my instrument panel is a light indicator telling me the door is open. When I see that light out, I'm up to takeoff power and we go. You get yourself strapped in the best you can. The boys on the ground will have thrown themselves flat before then. You have two point five minutes to get it done. If you hear the engines go to power before then, don't worry. If you hear me shout "Time," close the fucking door regardless, because we will be moving. Got it?"

"Got it."

"Let's get airborne."

They moved toward the cockpit. McDermid slid both cockpit seats fully back on their rails for easier entry and swung himself easily into the left-side pilot's seat. He was strapped in and flicking switches before Lysol had found a home for his legs. To Lysol the cockpit looked like that of a Boeing 747 crossed with a TV ad for British Gas. To McDermid it was home.

From the moment he flicked on the master switch, the instrument panel had become an array of dancing needles, indicator lights and whirring gyros. This soon settled down into some sort of order. McDermid completed his cockpit checklist in a brisk, precise manner and appeared to be asking somebody for permission to start engines.

McDermid signaled to Lysol to put on the headphones hanging behind his head. He heard:

"Golf Echo, X-ray Echo Charlie cleared start. Cleared taxi holding point runway 09 wind 085 degrees 05 knots QNH 1019 confirm Alpha."

"Golf Echo, X-ray Echo Charlie cleared taxi 09 QNH 1019 affirmative information Alpha."

McDermid's left hand immediately dropped to the waist-high sidewall panel at his left. He moved the left-right electric primer switch between the two starter buttons to the right. His right hand simultaneously moved the red-topped mixture lever for the right engine to the full-forward rich position on the center pedestal between the seats. Having noted a positive fuel-flow reading on the instrument panel, he moved the mixture lever back to idle, cutoff position. He glanced outside toward the starboard prop and saw that it was clear, and then switched the ignition on and pressed the starboard starter button. As the starboard engine fired, he moved the mixture lever again fully forward to the rich position, bringing it to full life. His right hand gently adjusted the throttle setting for the starboard engine, his experience allowing time for the turbocharger to spin up to its much higher revolutions beyond that of the engine and thus to create a lag in response to throttle movements. A glance at the manifold pressure gauge confirmed all in order, and oil pressure and temperature gauges were instinctively noted. Already the procedure was being repeated for the port engine and they were soon rolling toward the holding point.

Lysol recognized he was in the hands of an expert. The whole process had taken seconds.

They fell in behind another taxiing aircraft, becoming framed in the red arc of its rotating beacons, and turned left along the taxiway. Lysol was surprised at the volume of traffic at this airport. He looked across at the dark red silhouette of McDermid, aware of his voice in his headphones.

He seemed to be making sense out of the crisp and clipped exchanges coming out of the cacophony of radio traffic. Following McDermid's gaze outside he could see the landing lights of an approaching aircraft cutting a swath through the drifting fog toward the runway.

It crossed his mind: How the fuck do we land at some remote farmer's field in this damned soup?

As if reading his mind, McDermid's voice came through the intercom. "Don't worry your head about the fog. This is perfect for us. When I checked the weather earlier and saw that the temperature and dewpoint spread was within five degrees I fully expected this. I checked out our weather down route and London Gatwick's TAF—that's a trend forecast—was full of good news." He leaned over and pointed out with his pen a row of numbers and letters on his clipboard. "This row of zeros after the letters EGKK, the indicator for Gatwick, tells us that the surface wind is calm. Now '0200' tells us their visibility is two hundred meters and 'R0400' that their RVR, runway visual range, is four hundred meters. '43FG' says they have fog with the sky obscured and this '4CU020' that there are four oktas of cumulus cloud at two thousand feet. There is a layer of stratocumulus up higher at eight thousand feet helping to keep the ground temperature warm. The letters GRADU indicate that this will all improve into the morning. What interests me is the depth of this fog. Outside temperature is just above freezing, so it will begin to lift and drift as the sun rises and wind increases. While it sits there it will delay daylight to our advantage. This soup covers the south of England. Gatwick reports a vertical visibility in the fog of about a hundred feet. I reckon it's about four to five hundred feet deep. Our target is on the rising ground close to Farley Mount, the highest spot in the county of Hampshire, at five hundred eighty-four feet above sea level.

With a bit of that luck I was talking about, we'll be landing with only our wheels in it."

They moved to halt by a low sign—"E Hold Cat 11." The aircraft in front was moving onto the runway. McDermid concentrated on his power checks, moving his propellers to 2,000 rpm to circulate and warm the pitch-operating oil trapped in the airscrew hub. Setting prop rpm to 1,500 rpm, he moved the propeller levers to the top of the feather arc, checking that there was no change in rpm. Had there been, it would have indicated a faulty constant speed unit and the engine would have to be shut down. He then moved each prop into the feather position, checked that the corresponding engine was slowing and confirmed to himself that the blades were moving past the coarse position into feather. This was vital, should they suffer an engine shutdown in flight. An unfeathered prop indicates that the blade is flat onto the airflow and is producing a dramatic increase in drag. The aircraft would probably not maintain level flight at their AUW—all-up weight—in that configuration. He completed his vital action pretakeoff checks and noted the time at 06.00.

"Golf Echo, X-ray Echo Charlie, are you ready to copy clearance?"

"X-ray Echo Charlie is ready to copy."

"Golf Echo, X-ray Echo Charlie is cleared to leave the zone to the south Special VFR not above two thousand feet initially, direct Delta Tango Yankee. Onward clearance with London on frequency 127.7 prior to joining Red 25."

McDermid read back the clearance accurately.

"Golf Echo, X-ray Echo Charlie that is correct, you are cleared to contact Castledon Tower on 124.0."

"Roger, ground 124.0." McDermid pushed a button on the radio cluster in the instrument panel beneath the row of engine dials. The stored frequency for the tower popped up in the LED readout.

"Castledon Tower, X-ray Echo Charlie with you."

"Roger, X-ray Echo Charlie, you are cleared to line up and hold runway 09. Wind is 085 degrees, speed 05 knots."

The brakes were released and the aircraft wheeled right, onto the active runway. McDermid moved the control wheel through all planes of movement as a final freedom-of-movement check and brought power up to takeoff on the brakes, and Lysol heard in his headphones:

"X-ray Echo Charlie cleared takeoff wind 085, 05 knots call approach on 119.65."

"X-ray Echo Charlie rolling."

The surge forward as McDermid released his brakes took Lysol by surprise. The engines snarled, passing the blue-line speed of 80 knots in seconds. At 95 knots McDermid smoothly rotated the nose skyward, and with 100 knots indicated, they lifted clear of the runway. In one flowing movement of his right hand he activated the undercarriage lever, adjusted throttle and propeller levers, touch-checked that the flaps were in the full up position even though they had not been used for takeoff, and pushed the button to dial up the required approach frequency. His eyes checked temperature and pressure gauges, scanned across the instrument panel, checked that the three undercarriage lights had changed from green to red and noted the stopwatch in the wheel center was running. His left hand lightly gripped the wheel, thumb nudging forward the electric trim control on top of the left handgrip, trimming out the control forces as speed increased, rolling the aircraft into a climbing right turn onto 175 degrees and nailing the cruise climb speed at 120 knots. They were climbing at fourteen hundred feet per minute and passing one thousand feet of altitude. McDermid flicked off the electric fuel pumps and called approach. It was 06.04.

"Approach, X-ray Echo Charlie, with you passing one thousand feet on heading 175 degrees."

"Roger, Echo Charlie, you are cleared to climb on course, flight level 055 direct Daventry call passing flight level 030, squawk standby."

As he acknowledged, McDermid reached forward and confirmed that his transponder was set to the four-figure code of 4321 and the single control knob on its face was in the standby position. He felt happy with this, knowing that in the standby position the transponder, with its 4,096 individual codes and mode C capability, would not be undergoing continuous interrogation by the ground radar operator along their route. Later, when they entered controlled airspace and activated the Instrument Flight Rules segment of the filed flight plan, G-EXEC would be issued an identity code from one of the 4,096 available. This, together with the mode C altitude readout facility, would have their position and height clearly defined on radar screens all the way to Marseilles.

"X-ray Echo Charlie passing 3,000 for flight level 55 on 1013 Victor Mike Charlie."

"Roger, X-ray Echo Charlie, you are cleared to your en-route frequency London Information available on 124.75. Good-day, sir."

Lysol, sitting observing the smooth professionalism of his pilot, sensed the last exchange sent them on their way. McDermid was obviously well ahead of this machine and the system. He made it look easy. Lysol nurtured no fear of air-craft, but quite frankly preferred to jump out of them. The SAS had given him the taste for that. Right now he was feeling like a spare prick at a wedding. Those first 500 feet were completely blind, with fog and darkness beyond the cockpit glass. McDermid's eyes had been firmly glued to his instruments. Suddenly, pop! They burst out into a wide tran-quil world of gray tinged with the pink of a distant sunrise. They were sandwiched between the fog layer and scattered cumulus cloud several thousand feet above them. Looking down at the fog layer gave the only indication of their speed across the ground below it. The two 375-horsepower Conti-nental engines protruding from the smooth bonded wings had been accurately adjusted to their climb power and syn-chronized. As they leveled off at flight level 055 McDermid's right hand, already resting on the control levers, retarded his two throttles to give him 32.5 inches manifold pressure, and the two propeller levers to a rev counter reading of 1,900 rpm. An even hum replaced the harsher noise the engines had given, pulling for altitude. The twin three-bladed McCauley metal propellers rotated to the course position and bit into the air. As the airspeed indicator needle climbed toward 200 knots he reached forward and pointed to the instrument. Lysol followed his finger. The face of the airspeed indicator was turning, changing the reading under the needle. "This beauty self-corrects itself for temperature and pressure. I'm looking for a TAS, true airspeed, of 210 knots."

It meant little to Lysol, he looked out and down. "Christ, this thing performs!"

Level in the cruise and heading south, it had taken three minutes and six miles across the Leicestershire countryside.

"London Information Golf Echo X-ray Echo Charlie, good morning, over."

"Golf Echo X-ray Echo Charlie good morning, go."

"Golf Echo Charlie is a Cessna 421 out of East Midlands at

06.04 Zulu, west abeam Loughborough, 175 degrees, flight level 55, VFR, estimating Daventry VOR at 15 over."

"Thank you, Echo Charlie. There is no LARS [low altitude radar service] available from Brize Norton at this time, you are a little early for them. I suggest you give Upper Heyford a call on 128.55 before entering their MATZ [military air traffic zone]. No known conflicting traffic."

"Will do. Golf Echo Charlie out."

Lysol heard the high-pitched tones of a Morse signal in his headset. —·· — —·—— DTY. McDermid had tuned in and confirmed his healthy navigation signal from the Daventry VOR beacon. They tracked toward it, above the white blanket that seemed to cover England. McDermid was happy with their progress. They had crossed the Daventry beacon at 0.13. A good ground speed aided by a little increase in the tailwind component was working in their favor. He reported to London that their time at Daventry was 0.16 and had updated his flight plan estimate for the Goodwood VOR on the south coast, accordingly. They would be joining the airway Red 25 there and entering controlled airspace. He knew that from the moment he accepted London's airway clearance, there would be no room for ambiguous altitude and position reporting.

He had made it a habit over past weeks to depart East Midlands on a Special VFR clearance and join airways at a convenient point en route and away from the congested terminal areas. Air traffic control had appreciated this as it avoided suffering the delay in departure, sitting on the ground waiting for a slot in the airway system. He had also been calculating his flight log entries to hide the actual amounts of fuel uplifted. Spread over a lengthy period an inflated fuel burnoff would not be detected by some clever inspector from the CAA [Civil Aviation Authority] if this little caper should go wrong. On inspection of fuel records and the receipts he would produce from Marseilles, it would be found that the aircraft would have been too heavy to have flown into the confined strips they were heading for. He had in actual fact taken on minimal fuel for the flight and removed the underseat toilet system and one or two other luxury items to make the plane as light as possible.

Although this model was fitted for using one of the baggage compartments in the engine nacelles as an extra fuel tank, McDermid had only used the main tanks. Allowing for taxiing on the ground, climbing to cruise altitude and descending, he had uplifted 156 Imperial gallons. This was less than the 172 gallons the mains could hold, but even including some reserve fuel for the unexpected he knew the short field performance would be tight.

He had calculated that of the 1,407 pounds of fuel onboard, 177 pounds would have been burnt off by the time they reached the Hampshire airstrip. This meant that taking the extra man on board, at an estimated 165 pounds was not increasing their all-up weight. He had filed his flight plan based on speeds and arrival estimates using a 65 percent power setting. The slower en route speed of 190 knots notified to air traffic control would give a narrow margin, measured only in minutes, to make the off-route diversions and still meet his legal route arrival times. As he explained this to Lysol it became very clear why the two and one half minutes on the ground were critical. There was only eight stray minutes to play with over the whole three hours twenty-nine minutes of the flight.

As they covered the eleven and one half miles to fly over the grass aerodrome of Finmere, McDermid had chattered briefly with a cheerful and very professional lady manning Upper Heyford radar control. Lysol was aware that somewhere in the banter McDermid's charm recognized that the 20th Tactical Fighter Wing of the United States Air Force was in excellent and lovely hands. She liked that. He had also asked her for the Cotswold regional QNH, without it sounding too important. At their cruise level they were flying on an altimeter pressure setting of 1013.2 millibars, the international standard atmospheric pressure being used by all aircraft flying above the transition level of three thousand feet in Europe. The regional setting was needed to give McDermid safer altimeter indications relative to his tricky approach to the airstrip. The height above sea level minus the airstrip's elevation is what mattered now.

Returning to the London frequency, but saying nothing, McDermid rolled the aircraft into a right turn onto 196 degrees and smoothly intercepted the inbound radial to Compton VOR. They had eight and one half minutes before they began their descent. The visibility within their suspended sandwich of white and pink moisture had improved as they flew south. The upper cloud had become more scattered and daylight, at their level, was upon them. It made Lysol feel a little exposed.

"Don't worry, sunrise on the ground here in the south is officially posted for 06.02 hours. In reality, with this fog it's still dark down there. The farmer will be up but with luck he won't hear us above the noise of his machines, or the BBC. No one will see us above the fog." McDermid spoke in a totally relaxed manner. His eyes were constantly scanning the instruments, looking outside the plane and then passing over the scribblings on his kneepad.

Lysol had heard stories about him and his exploits during the war in Rhodesia. Citations read out at medal-pinning ceremonies had not told half of it. It was obvious to Lysol that the flying member of the team had done a lot of this. The cool bastard probably thinks it's too bloody quiet. There's nobody taking potshots at him.

His thoughts were interrupted.

"Do you see those columns of steam rising up about ten miles ahead in your one o'clock position?"

Lysol could see them. They rose in twin pillars from the fog and then lazily drifted southwesterly away from their flight path. McDermid continued.

"That's steam from the cooling towers at Didcot. If, when we get closer, we can see the rims of the towers it will be a good indication that we'll be just clear at the strip. If we can't, we are probably fucked." His last sentence seemed to drift off into concentration. He passed the topographical chart to Lysol. "Just below my finger, and off to your right, is a red circle indicating the Beckley antennae north of Oxford. Can you see them down your side?"

Lysol, not really knowing what he was looking for, replied that all he could see was a lot of cotton wool.

"Those antennae are five hundred forty-two feet above ground level, and we can't see them. The Didcot power station cooling towers are six hundred fifty-four feet above ground level. See what I'm getting at?"

Lysol ran his finger down the line on the map indicating their track across the ground. His finger stopped at the spot height circled in blue ink. The number declared a height above ground level of five hundred eighty-four feet. About a mile to the northwest, a cross was inked in. "Bloody hell if that's our target, it's in the damned fog." McDermid gave a suppressed chuckle.

"That, laddy, is what this game's all about." He retrieved the map from Lysol.

"I will begin our descent just south of Newbury. We will

have fifteen miles to run and it will take us four and one half minutes. I'll be keeping the speed up in the descent and maintaining a reduced but constant power setting, all the way to the target. The locals are used to hearing transiting air traffic in the area and we don't want them recalling an erratic engine noise at an exact time. Also, these engines do not like to suffer shock cooling, but that needn't concern you. This baby has two things going for us. The gear-limiting speed is high, at 175 knots, and the flap-limiting speed is 146 knots. That means I can go in fast, dump the wheels and, soon after, most of the flap. That slows us up nice and quick. I'll be doing that as we overfly the field in a westerly direction. I will be pulling military-type turns, so expect it. It's then a turn back toward the field. Once I have stabilized the approach I'll lower full flap and go to full fine pitch with the props. That's when anyone down there will know it's a landing. Unless they are close to the field boundary they shouldn't see much. Our approach speed will be a little high and I'll be on the brakes as soon as the wheels hit grass. The brakes are bloody effective on this thing so be ready for that, too. When I tell you, go and buckle yourself into the cabin seat by the door. Do you remember the technique for opening the door from inside?"

"Captain Johnnie? You have here one of the best kickers in the business. You get this racer on the ground and leave the rest to me."

Both faces cracked open in broad smiles. "As the old Indian trader used to say, before they scalped him, 'Why, by golly . . . every time is just like old times.' " McDermid's voice was a good impersonation of the old trapper.

McDermid banked the Cessna and they both looked along the starboard wing into the gaping chimney stacks. Vertical visibility was good enough to see the rims. Wings again level, they sped across the Thames Valley. High ground of the Chiltern hills rose out of the fog to meet them. The white flag in the face of the VOR dial tumbled from a TO indication to FROM as they passed overhead the Compton beacon. The aircraft banked right again. This time to track outbound on the 205 degree radial, direct to the target. Time checked at 06.23.

Using the area navigation equipment on board, McDermid had tuned his second VOR set to the beacon located at Southampton Airport. By dialing in the 331 degree radial and moving the beacon signal from its source to a position 12.5 miles along the radial he had placed the ghost beacon on the target field. As both VOR needles centered they confirmed the field was on the nose. The DME confirmed fifteen miles to run. McDermid came back on the power and nudged his thumb forward on the electric trim. They were in the descent. In his visual scan outside the cockpit he mentally noted the high mast off to the port side on the hills above the town of Kinsclere, its point reaching one thousand two hundred twenty-six feet above sea level. The high ground slipping behind under the port wing meant they were now south of the Newbury gap. The fog was becoming more patchy in its density. He heard Lysol claim sighting of a railway line through the mist. Instinctively his forefinger moved down the map and covered the main Andover to Basingstoke railway line. Time to talk to the master.

"London Control, Golf Echo, X-Ray Echo Charlie on 127.7."

"Golf Echo, X-Ray Echo Charlie, London strength 5 go ahead."

"Golf Echo, X-ray Echo Charlie, Compton at 27, flight level 55, VFR, Goodwood at 41, request onward clearance, over."

"Roger, Golf Echo, X-Ray Echo Charlie, I have your flight plan, you are cleared to join Red 25 at Goodwood at flight level 110. Call level on reaching before entering controlled airspace and advise any change of ETA."

By now it was clear to Lysol what game this chatter related to. McDermid had cleverly advanced beyond the flight plan positions he was reporting to air traffic control and was buying them the time for the diversion and pickup.

They were now at fifteen hundred feet, and descending. The distance readout showed five miles to run, just over two and one half minutes. A large white satellite-type dish suddenly loomed out of the fog on Lysol's side.

"That's the Chilbolton Radio Telescope." McDermid was leveling off at one thousand feet on the altimeter. "Go and get strapped in back there. Make it quick." The flags in the VOR dial were dancing as if drunk. They were there.

Farley Mount was a faded green wart on a white blanket. The fog was still thick in the valleys but thinning on the high ground. Lysol, looking out of the cabin window, had now lost the visual perspective. He had sensed the almost indistinguishable reductions in power as the plane leveled out. Suddenly it was on its wing tip. He felt the downward G-force as they pulled through a hard right turn. He heard the electric whine and thump as the wheels swung down and locked. The flaps were now running out from the wings' trailing edge in jerky stages. To him they were still flying at a hell of a pace. Over they went. A hard left turn that seemed never to end. "Holly shit! I hope our Johnnie gets this right." Lysol began to make crumping sounds to himself, imitating antiaircraft fire. This was living.

McDermid saw he was right of the center line for the field. He used his left rudder to skid the aircraft into line. All the engine controls were now full forward and the flaps were at their full forty-five degrees. Airspeed was nailed to 95 knots. He had washed off the last of the unwanted speed in the final turn and they were now rushing in over damp crops leading to the landing strip threshold. No movement was detectable on the ground from above. That was good. Parker would have them half buried in the dirt.

Round-out, back on the wheel, back on the throttles, thump, they were on. Progressive braking, flaps retracting fully up, now braking hard. Slow enough, full left rudder, power up on the starboard engine to help it around. They backtracked down the strip, nobody in sight. Here on the ground they were in poor visibility. The crops they had just approached over were now only partly in view, the fog swallowing the surrounding fields.

McDermid felt the cold rush of air around his neck as Lysol opened the top half of the door. The door warning light glowed on the annunciator panel in front of him. The stopwatch ticked away. Reaching the end of the grass strip he wheeled the aircraft around to face the direction for takeoff. Engines were brought up to half power against the brakes. The far end of the strip was out of sight in the fog. It was now 06.31.

Lysol lowered the airsteps, raised his head and looked into three pairs of eyes staring back at him from black balaclavas. Parker didn't mess with words.

"You're a minute early, that's how I like it. Overalls!" he demanded. Lysol threw him the Volvo overalls as other hands lifted Shaw bodily off the ground and offered him up feet first. Shaw's feet appeared. Parker tied off one of the overboots, Lysol got the other one. The gloves were rammed onto his hands and his arse hit the cabin floor. By the second bounce his left wrist was held fast in the handcuffs attached to the U bolt. The bottom half of the door slammed shut. Lysol spun around to secure the top section and to yell his goodbyes. They were already gone.

The door latched shut and simultaneously the engines were up to takeoff power. Lysol was thrown to the floor. Shaw had worked out what seat was his. He was attached to it. They were off the ground before Lysol fell into his.

McDermid was aware of the three men running at a crouch into the crops, in his peripheral vision. The door light flicked out. His right hand advanced to full power, the left stopped the clock. Holding it against the brakes, he checked his instrument readouts, eyeballed the compass heading and let her roll.

He knew that the high ground fell away beyond the boundary. There were two fences and a hedge to think about in the takeoff path. He eased the nose wheel off the grass as soon as he felt the rudder responding to the airflow and raced along on the mains. Speed was building nicely. He held it on the ground a little beyond the moment the plane told him it wanted to fly. The far fence came into view. Time to rotate. The main wheels broke from the surface. He had them retracting as they did so. McDermid kept the nose down looking for speed. The wheel retraction time was counted off in his mind. Five seconds from liftoff they were tucked away and the Cessna cleared the fence by inches. They had used all the seventeen hundred feet the airstrip had to offer and now they needed just a little more. He converted speed to height with firm back pressure on the wheel and climbed. Sticking the airspeed needle on 110 knots for best rate of climb, he shook off the fog. It was 06.33.

Lysol stuck his head into the cockpit, a little flushed. "Jesus Christ, old boy, I believe you had no illusions as to the disposition of the natives."

"How's our passenger?" McDermid was busy with the airplane.

"Well . . . he appears somewhat confused by it all. I will sit with him for ten minutes and we can exchange travel horror stories. That last airport leaves a lot to be desired." He retreated with a nod from the pilot.

He was climbing due east, passing the northern edge of the city of Winchester. Back at fifty-five hundred feet with twelve miles to run for the interception of their original track south, over the town of Liss. From there it was a right turn onto a southerly heading of 161 degrees and direct to Goodwood.

Aware that he was encroaching on the base level of the east-west airway Red 8, McDermid decided to give London a premature call, revising his ETA at Goodwood by three minutes to 06.44 was appreciated and clearance to climb to the cruising flight level of eleven thousand feet was approved. He was asked to squawk a four-number transponder code and mode C, on reaching cruising level. It was just what the doctor ordered. Reporting passing Goodwood corresponded with the green light on the Cessna's transponder beginning to blink. London Radar were interrogating them. They were now a block of numbers on a radar screen. Back in the system.

"Lysol, how about some cabin service on this airline?"

The flight had been unproblematic all the way down through France and the French controllers had left them well alone. A bit of chat as they flew the airways to the west of Paris and that was about it. Their filed flight plan had remained unaffected. Airway R25 had become A34 to the Chartres beacon and then it was a rejoin to R25 and on to Nevers. They could not see it, but the Loire Valley had run beneath their flight path since passing the Châteaudun beacon northwest of Orléans. The beauty of the region, now blanketed by low cloud, was now the running subject of conversation.

Lysol waxed lyrical about his dirty weekends at various châteaux and in one careless moment admitted to having fallen in love. The change of mood, not without some design, had served to relax Shaw and bring him out of himself. The drugs, having left his system, were without aftereffects and he was now well aware of what was happening to him. He had vaguely recalled a nightmarish drive in the fog followed by a forced march through thick clinging undergrowth. He knew he would not have survived it without the powerful pairs of hands that never let him go. The hour he had spent lying half buried in the muddy crop field had been a welcome relief. His escort, either side of him, let him drift in and out of sleep. He had felt too numb from the last twenty-four hours to really feel the cold.

The luxury of this executive airplane was much more to

his liking. It was the sort of luxury he had originally dreamed of when he entered the world of crime. It had seemed the perfect answer. For a while he had enjoyed feelings of revenge over past corporate executives who seemed always to win the prizes from his expertise. The feelings were short-lived. Naiveté had got him caught. He had lost everything.

Lysol detected a mood of self-pity coming over Shaw. He moved forward to the cockpit.

"I say, Mac, old chap, I think our Mr. Shaw can up anchor from the shackles and join the land of the free. What do you say?"

"Yes, why not. He's been in that seat for an hour and twenty minutes now. Keep an eye on him. Any sign of trouble he goes back in the handcuffs." McDermid lowered his voice, bringing Lysol's head farther forward.

"We have ten miles to run to Nevers. Then fifty minutes' flying time to our top of descent point abeam Montélimar. I'll soon have to talk to Paris for a handoff to Marseilles Control. It will be better for all of us if he is a willing and relaxed participant."

"Don't worry, old boy." Lysol spoke from the side of his mouth in a low and mischievous tone. "Getting on like a house on fire. We support the same rugger team, you know." His smiling face withdrew.

McDermid downed the last of his coffee, reached back and dropped the plastic cup into the waste bag hanging on the partition. He glimpsed the rapport exchanged between Lysol and Shaw and felt reassured that the fighting aristocrat was the right man for the job.

He felt comfortable with the way things had run so far. The aircraft had performed as expected. Fuel burnoff and speed equations were conforming to his preflight calculations and the winds aloft, although swinging around to a southwesterly direction had not punished his ground speed too badly. They were traversing a weak cold front and at flight level 150 had been flying in and out of cumulus cloud. Icing had not been a problem and what was there was easily managed by the heated props and windshield. The automatic pilot and integrated flight control system made the single-pilot operation of this machine a joy.

The upper airway traffic was becoming busy with the dawn arrival of long-haul jumbos and heavy domestic schedules into the Paris airports. It made them conveniently insignificant at their middle flight level. McDermid was relying on the Marseilles controllers being similarly preoccupied with overflights across the southern region and weekenders scurrying to leave the relative tranquillity of Lyons, Nice and the Riviera, and more important, Marseilles. A more ambitious hope was that the French air force, based at the large military airfield of Istres-Le-Tubé fourteen miles to the northwest of Marseilles would be slow in wakening on this damp and drizzly morning.

"Lysol, can I have a word?"

Leaving the comfort of his reclined sherry velour seat, Lysol checked the dozing Shaw, switched off the reading lamp at his table and went forward to the cockpit. Settling in beside McDermid he remarked, "May I suggest that you are going to tell me that it is time for our second little jolly."

"You're absolutely right, my blue-blooded friend. How is our passenger?"

Lysol, with some reflection replied, "I have the distinct impression that our man Shaw is overcoming his fears of the unknown and is beginning to consider us the bearers of his salvation." He paused. "I somehow fear his perception will dissolve when his feet are back on mother earth."

McDermid detected in the dry statement laced with wit the hallmarks of this type of soldier mentally preparing for action. It occurred to him that the Lysols in this game always managed to articulate or dig up a bloody quotation just before joining battle. Some Freudian link there for sure. Probably something to do with generations of short arms having to draw long swords, while the cannon fodder looked on. He chuckled to himself as his mind imagined bets being wagered among the ranks that the dashing young officer would cut his balls off in the process and then they could all go home.

"Do you see that high ground in the mist over to starboard? That belongs to the 'Massif Central.' We passed the Thiers beacon on schedule at 08.27. That puts us midway between Clermont Ferrand and Le Puy-Lourdes."

Lysol interrupted. "Well then, let's all drop into Lourdes for a spot of faith healing." His words fell like a damp squib, and he wished he hadn't.

McDermid continued. "We have thirty-four miles to run to checkpoint 'Agrev.' We're flying down airway Red 31. The checkpoint is not a compulsory call to Marseilles Control, but I'm going to call them anyway. Passing 'Agrev' takes us clear of the highest ground around here, particularly Mount Mezenc. That beauty climbs to a height of five thousand seven hundred and fifty feet. It's the source of the Loire River, which may interest Mr. Shaw. What interests me is that it signals the safe beginning of our letdown into the Ardèche towards Montélimar. At that point I will start my little charade with Marseilles. We are on an instrument flight plan. That means in controlled airspace in this region this aircraft has to operate a mode C transponder."

"This does not mean a lot to me, Johnnie. But carry on, I'm all ears."

"It's important, Lysol, and you have to have a sense of timing. I won't be able to explain this once it begins." As he talked, McDermid was busy with tuning in the Montélimar VOR beacon and responding to a French voice in the headsets giving permission to change frequency to 123.9. From this terminal controller there would be one more en route handover to Marignane approach radar at Marseilles Airport.

"Mode C is the facility that gives our altitude readout to the ground radar controller. I am going to simulate losing mode C by switching to our number-two transponder, which only has mode A. I will then lose that and register a general electrical problem with the controller. He will grant me clearance to leave controlled airspace and I will request cancellation of our instrument flight plan. The weather information for Marseilles broadcast a short time ago indicates recent rain showers clearing from the south and generally clear conditions. The front is well behind us now. My request to continue to Marseilles VFR, in visual conditions, will be accepted. I'll take it down low and advise them that I will route due south to this checkpoint named RHONE. It's an entry point suspended in the air just off the coast and is used for controlling aircraft approaching Marseilles from the west."

Lysol looked across at the Jeppeson airways chart under McDermid's finger. It looked like an aerial photo of a plate of spaghetti, but he got the idea.

"Once we are outbound from Montélimar beacon, I'll descend in the cruise to flight level 090, that's nine thousand feet. It is then a stepped descent down the Rhône River to the city of Arles. We cross the junction of autoroute 113 and route 570 on the western outskirts. We hit that junction at one thousand feet and a speed of 110 knots. From there it's two minutes to touchdown. Got it?"

"Got it!"

The VOR needle on one set had swept across the dial, indicating "Agrev" had passed underneath. The flags on the other VOR box were beginning to jerk in their windows. Montélimar was closing on the nose.

"Time for me to chat with our French friends. Go back and prepare Mr. Shaw. I will call you forward when I need you."

As Lysol climbed out of his seat, McDermid was already talking to the invisible Frenchman below.

One of the joys of flying in France is that they do not overcontrol, as the British tend to. If they sense that a pilot is ahead of the business and not likely to become a problem to them, the controllers leave him to get on with it. McDermid's experience of this showed in his selection of route, flight levels and what he said to whom along the way.

With an instruction to stay clear of controlled airspace and to observe restricted areas, an unworried French voice had cleared him to RHONE. The same controller had confirmed no conflicting traffic operating out of Istres and having talked to them by land line, had got him clearance through Istres zone. This was with a proviso that he keep to the western zone boundary and above thirty-five hundred feet. All very accommodating, thought McDermid, and he was only too happy to oblige. Yes, he would report when reaching RHONE.

They were now heading 190 degrees outbound from Montélimar. The southerly course took them eleven miles west of the city of Avignon and put Arles on the nose. Six and one half minutes after the beacon they had covered the twenty-four miles to his first landmark. This was a high chimney standing five hundred thirty-five feet high on the west bank of the Rhône. He did not see it. They were scud running. He quietly cursed the puffy gray clouds suspended two thousand feet aboveground. Their precipitation, being dumped in scattered showers over a wide area, was limiting his visibility. Quickly cross-checking his position with an NDB low-frequency beacon at Orange, he felt happier seeing the ADF arrow fall from an easterly indication to stern.

Trimming a touch nose down, he increased the rate of

descent from nine hundred feet per minute to one thousand eighty-six. Having descended through nine thousand feet he advised the controller that he was now passing through flight level 075. The controller appreciated this and as this now put them below controlled airspace he was cleared to change frequency to Marignane Approach on 120.2.

"Marignane Approach, Golf Echo, X-ray Echo Charlie, with you on 120.2, leaving flight level 75, Victor Mike Charlie, estimating RHONE at 20."

"Roger, Golf Echo, X-ray Echo Charlie, maintain Victor Mike Charlie and report RHONE."

The relaxed accented English confirmed to McDermid that a little luck was riding with them. They were moving fast, and McDermid felt a tightness in his guts. He must see the next high chimney on the northern bank of the Rhône, just beyond Avignon, or they were in deep trouble.

"Lysol! Get up here." It was an order.

As he seated himself, Lysol felt an urgency in the cockpit. This seemed to be emphasized by the low cloud layer rushing up to meet them. He observed McDermid working and concentrating with crisp efficient purpose. He showed some frustration with one of the navigation instruments.

"I want your eyes outside the cockpit, Lysol. We just passed abeam the Avignon VOR beacon, it's northwest of the city. I have tried to move the beacon down its two-hundred-degree radial to put it on our target, but I'm not getting a reliable indication. That could be for a number of reasons, but I don't have the time to fuck around with it." McDermid's words were clipped and precise.

"Where has the blessed river got to? I see only tree cover below the cloud." Lysol felt that his words had not exactly helped.

"Forget the bloody river. We have two minutes to run to a chimney stack. It's eight hundred sixty feet high and we must see it, for course correction. The river is off to our left in that rain shower. It winds its way around through the city and meets our track again to the south, immediately beyond the chimney. The river is wide at that point so don't be distracted by it. Find the chimney!"

McDermid's right hand disengaged the autopilot. He was now hand-flying the Cessna and arresting their rapid descent at four thousand feet.

"I just saw a railway line. Double tracks." Lysol shouted it out.

"We are almost on top of it. I have to . . ."

Lysol's raised voice cut across McDermid's. "There it is. Over to the right, almost on the riverbank, to the right of that small town." His finger jabbed at the cockpit glass.

"You little beauty. Got the bastard. Well done the Duke." McDermid rolled the plane toward the chimney, checking that his altitude was nailed at four thousand feet. The relief in the cockpit was almost physical.

The chimney, then the river swept beneath them. McDermid stabbed the stopwatch into action and adjusted the rate of descent to seven hundred fifty feet per minute. The terrain below had now flattened out as the vast Rhône Valley leveled to meet the Golfe du Lion and the Mediterranean Sea. He kept the speed up; the sleek machine responding to every twitch of his wrist. This was the part he lived on.

"The river should be running with us down your side, Lysol. That's Tarascon and Beaucaire towns on the nose. The river splits them. From there it's five and one half minutes to touchdown. Tell Mr. Shaw to buckle up."

As Lysol instructed Shaw, McDermid began to reduce speed. They were now at one thousand feet and running beneath the scattered puffs of cloud. The rain showers were behind them and visibility in the thin lingering mist had improved. The twin towns slipped under the port wing and McDermid took the plane down to almost river level. Arles was ahead, but not yet seen. The land all around them now unobstructed and practically at sea level. They had been illegal for some time now.

McDermid dropped the Marseilles Carte Aeronautique Number 6 into a side pocket. The area chart had served its purpose. He now focused on a faxed copy of the local survey map. The target road they were heading for highlighted in fluorescent yellow. He clipped the map to a chrome holder on the control wheel in front of him, bringing it within his instrument scan.

"Arles left of the nose. River splitting, Petit Rhône going right. Railway line coming up running east to west." McDermid was talking softly to himself.

Simultaneously his eyes and right hand were scanning and touching their way through vital prelanding checks. Speed was reducing to peg on 175 knots. He mentally noted the roads below, dampened by the earlier rain showers. Would they affect braking action at the target?

Lysol knew the routine expected of him and had moved back to strap himself in next to the cabin door. Shaw seemed strangely calm. Perhaps he was even enjoying the whole thing.

McDermid's voice shouted from the cockpit. "Two minutes!"

The familiar whine and thump of the wheels pushing into the airflow and locking down in chorus with propellers going to fine pitch signaled to Lysol that McDermid was into his lever-pulling routine and they were on stage.

The road junction of the 572 and 113 appeared where it should. The expanse of the Camargue stretched out in front, to the sea eleven miles away. A vacant land of waterways, boggy ground and tall flaxlike swamp grass. The region's beauty lay in its vacuity and mystery, perpetuated by Romany myth and wild horses. A perfect safe haven for the large colonies of rare and protected bird life. McDermid hoped they would be the only species disturbed by their arrival on this bleak morning.

"One hundred and ten knots, three greens, temperatures and pressures, leaving river to left, with small road running parallel, the D36." McDermid's utterances were born of deep concentration. Anticipation rising by the second.

"Small cluster of houses, cross road, second cluster avoided to the right. That's Saint Cecile. A red barn, a red barn. Where is the bastard?" He knew they were on top of it.

"There's my red barn!" His voice now audible in the rear cabin. "We're on, Lysol, I have the road!"

McDermid dumped the last of the flap, yawed the aircraft to line up with the narrow road. It was going to be bloody tight. The flax seemed to want to snare the wing tips. The Cessna's forty-one feet of wingspan left no room for error. He held it off until he saw the blue car, reversed into a side track flash past his left shoulder. Levers back, they were on.

Lysol was up and opening the door. He could feel McDermid working the rudder pedals hard to keep the plane in the center of the road. As they slowed he was suddenly aware of the blue BMW hugging their slipstream. The lights flashed off and on. He pulled his head back in and shuffled Shaw to the door. No one was standing on ceremony.

Over the blare of increasing engine noise he shouted into

Shaw's ear, "When you hit the road, get well clear or you will lose your head on the elevators. Now go!" The last command was supported by a firm push.

Shaw disappeared with a dumbfounded expression across his face and the door was closed. Lysol knew the damn wheels were probably already in bed.

The departing white bird stayed low and banked sharply into a left turn. The wing tip appeared to cut through the reeds. The double chocolate-colored cheat lines running the length of its fuselage seemed to give it speed.

Behind, on the deserted road, Nick Baring got out of the BMW and walked toward the pathetic figure standing in the roadside mud. Shaw's head was turning backward and forward, alternating between the disappearing plane and the approaching stranger. Clothed in blue overalls and plastic extras, he looked like someone out of a Woody Allen movie.

"Don't hang about, get in the car. Snap out of it. Move!"

The Rhodesian accent conveyed authority, but no threat. A relieved Shaw scurried toward the BMW. He was now used to these SAS types. They didn't say a lot, but they did not expect to repeat what they did say.

Earlier that same morning, Nicholas Baring had strolled casually along the stone and concrete jetty of the Vieux Port. He had parked his small white Renault 5 at the end of the seawall the previous evening, after bringing on board several boxes of supplies. It was still dark, but at six o'clock in the morning the marina was alive and the Marseilles fishermen had already done a day's work. The south coast and most of the Provence region had been rained on heavily for the past month, and suffered for it. Sea conditions had only improved in the last few days and the fish and the fishermen were both rising to the occasion.

He returned, in perfect French, the jocular greetings coming from down in the colorful boats. He held the seafarers' respect as a man who understood the sea and the life they all lived at its mercy. As part of the local port community, it was readily accepted that Baring had a past. Not unlike many of the ex-Legionnaires who considered the port area their haven. No questions were ever asked. That was not the way here. But there was talk and reputations gained by association.

The old men sitting in the array of dockside cafes always

got excited when he set sail and disappeared past the ancient Fort St. Jean at the harbor entrance. They did not care if their beloved steaming dishes of bouillabaisse were cooling from neglect, the spectacle warmed their hearts, and was a good enough event for a wager. Baring was a traditionalist. He always maneuvered the immaculate fifty-foot ketch with a deft skill through the crammed anchorage under sail—he was not known to succumb, and use the on board engine. The old boys never told him of the money riding on his skills. The winners who had kept their faith in him quietly found a reason to buy him a drink on his return. He enjoyed belonging and they coveted their secret sport.

Baring steered the Renault slowly out of the port and threaded his way into the African quarter of the city. He knew the busy narrow streets well and would be able to shake any close surveillance. The chaotic mélange of shops piled high with garments, carpets and exotic Arab candy and the teahouses crowded with men dressed in every kind of regional costume, from Algiers to Ivory Coast, eliminated any feeling that this was France. The unique contrast the quarter offered was what made Marseilles a unique city. Turning into the Cours Belsunce, the scenery became France again. Blending with the flow of traffic, he rode with it around the square toward the domineering structure of the Gare St. Charles. Driving faster now, he slipped down a small street behind the railway station and turned into an underground car park. The black face in the ticket office cast a disinterested look across at him as he halted the car next to a blue BMW 323i. Locking the Renault, he knelt down out of sight between the two cars and ran his hand up under the BMW's wheel arch. Feeling the small obstruction, he ripped back the Velcro strip and two keys fell to the ground. The BMW started easily. Leaving it to idle, Baring approached the ticket office and paid the outstanding amount as well as a generous tip. He knew it did not buy any loyalty, but at least it secured a continuing disinterest.

The city streets opened out onto the wide A7, and he was soon speeding through the outer suburbs. Crossing to the A55, he left the city behind as it took him around the south of the inner waters of Étang de Berre in the direction of Martigues. The Camargue rendezvous was 93 kilometers to the west and he was in plenty of time to make the aircraft's ETA of 09.15.

To the onlooker, the Rhodesian's casual behavior did not reflect his hectic activity of the last twenty-four hours. The surprise telephone call to his boat had set off an unwanted chain of events. Murphy was a London contact, whom he had met during the usual camaraderie exchanged in the mess bar at the Duke of York's Barracks. He had passed his telephone number to Murphy with an invitation to come aboard the ketch anytime. The floating possibility of some mercenary work had been the real reason behind the mutual contact. Murphy was not his type, and their last meeting had been over two years ago. Now this unwelcome phone call. Coming straight to the point, Murphy had declared himself in trouble, and sounded panicky. Baring took his number with a promise to call him back in ten minutes. The ship-to-shore line to the boat had big ears hanging on it, like pegged-out laundry. His return call from the pay phone in the marina terminal to Murphy's London number had been answered first by a female voice. Then Murphy had snatched the hand receiver from her and spilled his problem down the line. The names he dropped and his cryptic explanation made it clear to Baring that the Londoner needed a place to hide and fast. The underworld name was familiar to him. Murphy had upset some bad people. They would have his balls.

Thinking on his feet, he gave Murphy a south London address. Told him to go there and wait for him to telephone. Contact nobody, and say nothing to the hooker. As he stepped out into the cool sea air, Baring had already guessed that he had a big problem to deal with. Buried in Murphy's frantic words had been an alarming reference to "some fucking geezer named Shaw."

Baring's fingers tightened around the steering wheel as he recalled the events. He spoke aloud in the empty car. "That bloody idiot was out of his depth. He should have stayed on in the Muscat of Oman. That was more like Murphy's type of war."

Murphy was probably dead by now. It had been immediately obvious to Baring that the operation he was now involved with had been compromised in London. Murphy, recruited on "a need to know" basis, would have been ignorant of Baring's link with Shaw, and now he had become a threat.

Flood's coded orders, received three weeks earlier, had

been very specific. They included irreversible advice that the London end was to be a total closure. That meant no overlap with the England operation, a total cut-out. This tactic ensured that any investigation by the British authorities would meet a dead end. Baring had made a snap decision. Returning to the pay phone, he had called another London number. The cheap little hustler who took the call was not surprised when his small talk was interrupted.

"Shut up and listen, you little weasel. You don't need to know who this is, so thank Santa Claus. I hear a certain Murphy is sweating south of the Thames."

He had hung up the phone before the excited voice had finished reading back the address, the one he had given to Murphy. Walking quickly back to the mooring, he had already begun focusing on the wider implications. The underworld connection between London and Marseilles was a potent force. The Corsican soldiers were probably already on the streets.

He swung the BMW off the N568 onto the N268 Port-St.-Louis road. The morning traffic had been easy. The route had been chosen for good reason. It wound its way through an industrial zone and across the Canal d'Arles. A short distance later the road met the west bank of the Grande Rhône River and paralleled it northward for six kilometers and intercepted the D35. Here, Baring followed the D35 across the bridge at the riverside town of Solvay and into the empty Camargue. This was the most southern crossing of the Rhône and he was confident that no city boys were on his tail.

Now the D36, the secondary road had narrowed and ran north through the swamplands and crossed numerous canals. The occasional small villages along its route seemed completely deserted, as did the road. The whole area had an aura of resignation—that it should capitulate and let the vast patchwork of ponds wash over everything. The people who lived here harvested a culture and wealth all their own. Strangers were ignored, as long as they were passing through. Inquiry always met with taciturnity. Baring had gambled that their activity, although bound to be seen, would be deemed harmless to the community, and favored by its customary blindness.

He knew the road, having driven it a fortnight before. His duty then had been to find a suitable landing strip for the incoming aircraft. The type and dimensions of the plane had been relayed to him in the form of a sales brochure depicting the Cessna range of executive aircraft with a circle scribed around the caption for the Cessna 421 Golden Eagle. It was the cautious way Flood did things. In subsequent communications confirming the location secured and establishing times, the word "brochure" meant aircraft. Baring had not asked, but he had a fair idea who would be flying it. If it was McDermid, he was sure it would arrive regardless of weather or risk. Once located, the ideal stretch of road had been paced out and a thorough reconnaissance made of the approach path and departure route. He then worked out a return route to Marseilles, north via Arles and away from the Camargue. Information for the pilot was then faxed to a fax bureau in Soho, London. It was disguised as one of three pages of real estate particulars. Each page had been topped and tailed with the letterhead of a local Arles property agent and addressed to a bogus client, for collection. The same day the fax was received in London, one of the many motorcycle courier firms received a call to activate a prepaid instruction. To send a rider to the bureau and have the fax retransmitted to a hotel in the city of Derby, marked for collection.

Approaching the tiny village of Mas du Cabassolle, on the northern edge of the Étang de Vaccarès, more than twelve kilometers across and the largest pond and nature reserve in the region, Baring reminded himself that just beyond lay the turnoff. It was then a short three kilometers to the straight stretch of tarmac selected for the landing. He mentally agreed with himself that all was in place. He smiled. His air hostess girlfriend argued openly with him in the port customs office, the day before, against flying alone to Majorca, Spain. In a raised voice she had protested for all to hear that it was a stupid idea. That she should sail down with him on board the ketch. If there was some little bitch going near him or his boat, she would kill him. He thought she had responded, predictably, in the best French tradition. A good public display of old-fashioned jealousy. Snatching the air ticket from his hands, she had turned on her heels and stormed out. Her parting shot was a cocky shout.

"I take a taxi. I don't need you. *Cochon!*"

It amused all present, but he thought pig a bit strong. Still the kiss and makeup should be dynamite. The customs officer had made fun of him as he ordered some duty-free whiskey and cigarettes to be held in the bonded store.

His thirty-two years did not show. Bronzed good looks topped with thick sun-bleached blond hair made him younger. That was until a closer look into the pale eyes. They held a hint of tragedy. Life on the coast kept him fit. His killing instinct was kept sharpened by three sessions a week with a martial arts master. A crazy exile from Cambodia. The Oriental's hatred of Pol Pot gave amazing speed and force to every punch and kick that penetrated Baring's defense. The tranquil tea drinking after each session, with the bustle of the African quarter in the street below, had forged between them a mutual understanding of their past. Many times they sat in silence throughout, the sipping of tea the only sound. Talking out the memories of violence, loss, atrocity, did not always need words.

Born and raised in British colonial Rhodesia, he had spent his youth on the family farm in the Cashel Valley, a rich land south of Umtali, close to the border with Mozambique. The location had made their property vulnerable early in the troubles. His father wouldn't leave the land or desert his black workers, which meant his mother took an equally stubborn stance. A younger sister was well out of it, in a school in England. His entrance to university had been indefinitely delayed by the draft. His knowledge of the area that became known as operational area THRASHER, and fluency in the Shona and Ndebele dialects made him a natural choice for the Special Forces. Nineteen seventy-six saw him deep in the Chimanimani Mountains inside neighboring Mozambique on reconnaissance missions against Nkomo's ZANLA terrorists. By now a very experienced member of the elite Selous Scouts. August of that year they had carried out a highly successful raid on the ZANU Chimoio headquarters at Nyadzony on the Pungwe River. Of the five thousand terrorists training there, operation ELAND killed one thousand of them and wounded many more. He and a partner had been accidentally left behind after the raid, as had one or two others. They had to walk a two-day hike back to the border. Avoiding parties of heavily armed marauding guerrillas, all the way. There had been many bold raids through the years of bloody fighting. Remembered by their exotic names, Long John, Aztec, Ignition, Vodka and others.

Flood had entered his life during these times. He had heard of the man, and rubbed shoulders with him from time to time and heard talk of his operational involvement since the troubles started. Flood had served Rhodesia both within and outside its borders. It was openly known within Special Forces that he had been instrumental in setting up the intelligence for the raid on Nkomo's house in Zambia in April 1979, a failed attempt to assassinate the terrorist leader. The resupply of badly needed helicopters, despite crippling sanctions, also had his mark on it. Late in 1978, Baring and two other scouts were hiding in the scrub alongside the Malvernia/Maputo railway line. A deep reconnaissance mission had gone wrong because the Rhodesian air force had refused their commander the use of aircraft to extract them. Their radio requests for exfiltration assist from their side, just north of Jorge Do Limpopo, fell on deaf ears. Groups of FRELIMO and ZANLA fighters were closing a net around them. Flood, at that time supervising business interests across the border in South Africa's Kruger National Park, took it on himself to come and get them. He flew a small two-seat Piper P18 SuperCub aircraft covertly into Mozambique. Landing the plane some five kilometers from the Scouts' position and hiding it under slashed branches, he walked through enemy positions to link up with them. By now it was night. Baring recalled vividly the moment Flood's calm voice whispered out of the darkness, "Well lads, your boss was right. You have screwed up, haven't you?"

He had led them through the enemy, crawling, killing and finally walking their way to his hidden airplane. With the sound of Nkomo's pack crashing toward them in the surrounding bush, they clambered on board the little high-winged monoplane. Flood had removed one of the two seats. It still meant two of them sitting out either side of the cockpit sides. The flight to the South African border had been a thrill a minute. Overloaded and underpowered, they had collected scrub all the way to Kruger Park. Flood's only comment had been that they were lucky there were no giraffes about.

Before returning to Salisbury by road, the three Rhodesians had enjoyed a good breakfast with Flood. The food was a luxury. The recon group had existed on *sadza,* the terrorists' staple, and very basic diet, for the past several weeks. When they went in among them, it was live as they live.

Taking Baring aside, Flood had quietly mentioned how things were going to change dramatically in the coming year. He had asked him to pass on to his unit commander, Lieutenant Colonel Reid Daly, that Com-Ops was infiltrated.

Alarmed at hearing this, Baring questioned the improbability of any ZANLA or ZIPRA people getting in that close. Flood ended the conversation with a sigh of resignation.

"No, Nick, not Nkomo's or Mugabe's lot. The bloody Brits. MI6, on behalf of the British realm, are going to send you down the proverbial Zambezi."

A few months later, in March 1979, the terrorists put to maximum use the Sam 7 missiles they had acquired with Soviet help. Orders were given to commit an atrocity. To shoot down a civilian Viscount airliner as it departed the town of Kariba. The terrorist leaders publicly rejoiced. They had finally killed their archenemy, General Walls, The Commander in Chief of Rhodesian Forces. As it happened, Walls had changed planes. On board were defenseless black and white Rhodesians, American, French and British tourists. Eighteen of them had survived the captain's brave attempt to crash-land the stricken plane. Eight walked for help. Ten, including the injured and children, had remained by the wreckage. They were butchered by the terrorists who came out of the bush to finish the kill. Baring's mother and sister, on vacation from her English school, had died in the crash.

The Lancaster House Agreement signed in London later the same year, by Nkomo and Lord Carrington, representing the British government, had been the final betrayal to Baring and many like him. The British had embraced the obese Joshua Nkomo, terrorist leader. The man had lived up to the tribal name given to him by his elders in 1962. *Chibwechitedza,* "the slippery rock." Baring had left the country, his father stayed on. Working for Flood had been the natural progression.

The turnoff took him through the village of Mas d'Agon. The only movement was two peasant women standing outside the small pâtisserie, their long and fresh baguettes of bread tucked underarm. A low mist hugged the watery waste either side of the road. Finding the side track at the upwind end of the landing run, he reversed the BMW into it and switched off the engine. There would be a twenty-minute wait.

6

For in and out, above, about, below,
'Tis nothing but a Magic Shadow-show,
Play'd in a Box whose Candle is the Sun,
Round which we Phantom Figures come and go.

At the entrance to customs and immigration at Marseilles Airport, Lysol and McDermid shook hands formally, Lysol thanked him in a loud voice for an uneventful flight and then they went their separate ways, McDermid through the air-crew channel and Lysol through the passenger channel. There were no problems. The official glanced at Lysol's passport, quickly checked his face against the photograph and handed the passport back without a word.

He was going to order himself a *pastis* at a bar in the main hall and then thought, Duty first. He changed some French notes into coins, lined up at the rank of telephones and dialed Yardley's number in London. It only rang twice, and Yardley was on the line. He said, "The parcel's delivered."

"Everything okay?"

"Smooth as a baby's bottom." He hung up.

Yardley cradled the phone in his rented room in Queen Street and in spite of himself his features creased into a big grin. He smacked his right fist into the open palm of the other hand. They'd done it—they'd bloody well done it! He got up, went over to the cupboard and took out a bottle of scotch, poured a large dollop into the mug he had been using for coffee and took a long swallow. That Mike was okay—they were all okay. It's not every day you beat the system and walk away. Right, walk away—that was the next move.

He put down the mug and picked up the phone again, dialing Rodel's private number in Paris. "Is that the Commercial Secretary?"

A woman's voice answered. "Liz Hall here. I'm Mr. Rodel's personal assistant. Who is speaking?"

"Robert Yardley from London, England. I'm an American citizen, working on a book here." He thought, Christ, where's that damned Rodel when I want him?

She picked up the cue at once. "Of course, Mr. Yardley, sir, Roger said you might be calling. He asks me to apologize—he's been called to an urgent conference with His Excellency."

Yeah, more like he's still at lunch. And on first names, are we? I must have hit the Fawn and Ollie network. He squeezed the handset in irritation.

She said, "Roger mentioned you might have a message. It's all right, Mr. Yardley—I *am* his personal assistant."

"Sure. Would you tell him, please, I've completed my research on this side. I was thinking of coming to Paris to tackle the French side."

"That *is* good news. He *will* be pleased." Does she have to emphasize one word every sentence? he thought. How does dear Roger stand it? She went on, "He thought that might be the message. He has one for you. He'd like to see you as soon as possible. Could you take an early flight out of London tomorrow morning, please? And he would like you to pack up the London end altogether, if possible. You may need to stay here quite a few days. We've fixed some accommodation, so all you need do is call here at the embassy on arrival."

"I've already booked myself onto the nine-thirty Air France flight out of Heathrow tomorrow morning. Let's see, you're one hour ahead of London time. I should be with you around noon tomorrow."

"That's fine, Mr. Yardley, just fine, that will be flight AF809 into Charles de Gaulle."

Yardley looked round the small rented room. He had taken it for six months—the minimum time the landlord would accept—so that smooth-looking, dark-jowled type would be a few hundred quid, as the Brits called it, to the good. But so what? It had paid off fine. He took a duffel bag out of the bottom drawer of the metal filing cabinet and started packing his few belongings, the bottle of scotch, the mug, a jar of instant coffee, his notepad and pencil. He had already warned the Lansdowne Club reception that he would be leaving tomorrow, anyway. If the op had come unstuck, he wouldn't have wanted that fine old club to get bad publicity through the arrest of a temporary member on the premises.

He zipped up the bag, locked the door and handed the keys to the super on the ground floor. As he walked to the bottom of Queen Street and turned left for the fifty-yard stroll to the Lansdowne, past the gray MI6 building that adjoined it, he was thinking that tonight he would dine at the Special Forces Club in Hans Crescent and tie a small one on. Pity he couldn't celebrate with Mike and the lads—but they all knew the drill. Once the op was over, you all split and went back to ordinary life. Sometime, somewhere, there might be a kind of reunion, a chance meeting in a bar or at the Duke of York's and you would buy one of the lads a drink and he might say, "Cheers, Bob, remember the old Scrubs?" And that would be that. Keep it low-key and casual. That was the SAS way.

Lost in such thoughts, he didn't register the big black Mercedes parked on a double yellow line just near the Curzon Cinema.

Tony with the scar on his cheek kicked in the door of Emmie's flat. Reg, another heavy, crashed in behind him. She was in bed with a john, a weedy little man with a Hitler mustache. Tony grunted, "Out!" The little man leapt out of bed, snatched up his trousers from the bedside chair, and held them like a shield in front of his private parts. Tony's long knife slid into his hand. He waved the knife at the man.

"You," he said, "get your clothes on and beat it. Hang around—and I'll slice your balls off and stuff 'em up your ass!"

The man hopped around on one foot as he struggled to get his trousers on. He snatched up his coat, shirt and tie and scuttled out into the sitting room. It was an experience he'd never forget, all the more because there'd be no one to share it with. Forgetting his socks, he thrust his bare feet into his shoes and ran down the stairs, almost banging into the Boss, who was ponderously mounting the narrow staircase. The Boss gave him a contemptuous backhander that sent him stumbling to the foot of the stairs.

Emmie sat up in bed, clutching the bedclothes to her chin. "What the hell," she started to say.

The Boss came into the bedroom. His bulk loomed in the doorway. "Where's Mike?" he said.

"Who's Mike?" She was defiant, but there was a quaver in her voice.

"Cut the crap, you slag, I want the facts—and I want them fast. I'll start again. Where's Mike?"

"Honest to Gawd, I dunno anyone named Mike."

The Boss said, "Cut her, Tony. Not too much—on the cheek. Refresh her memory."

Tony leaned forward almost casually and flicked the point of his knife against her left cheek. There was first a thin red line and then the blood oozed out. A trickle ran down toward her chin. She screamed.

The Boss said, "You don't play games with me, sister. That's just for starters. Next time Tony'll slice off your left nipple. That really hurts. Right, Tony?"

"Right, Boss."

"Oh, Christ," she sobbed. "Don't hurt me anymore. I'll talk."

"That's better. I like people with sense. Now where the fuck is Mike?"

She started to gabble in a high-pitched voice. He'd come in that very morning, something had gone wrong, he was very pale and nervous. He'd made a phone call and then left. He wouldn't tell her where he was going. His friend on the phone had suggested a hideout. She'd heard part of the phone conversation and thought it was near Tower Bridge, but Mike wouldn't say where. What she didn't know wouldn't hurt her, he'd said.

"Christ, how wrong can you be?" the Boss said. "You'll get plenty hurt if you don't keep talking. Where was that phone call to?"

"Marseilles." She pronounced it "Marsales." "I 'eard him ask the operator for the area code for Marseilles."

"So that's where they're taking that fuckin' Shaw. Anything else?"

"I 'eard him call the other man Nick."

"We know any Nicks in Marseilles, Tony? You, Reg?"

The two heavies shrugged. Tony said, "Don't mean a thing to me, Boss."

The Boss said, almost in an aside to himself, "I got some

good friends in Marseilles. They move the stuff around as slick as spitting. They'll know any Nicks on their patch. Let's get back to the car. I've got a call or two to make."

"You want me to sort this one out, Boss?" Tony asked.

"Not this time, Tone." He turned to Emmie, who was holding her left hand against her wounded cheek. The blood was welling through her fingers. It was crimson in the afternoon sunlight. "You got lucky, sister. Tony here has a score to settle with your Mike. And you'd do just as well. You keep buttoned up, you may live a bit longer. Here," he took a crocodile wallet out of an inner pocket and slid out some notes. "Here's a couple of big ones. You find a bent quack and get that cheek fixed. But one cheep out of you—and Tony'll be back to do a real job on you. His big trick is cutting girls' titties right off. Ain't that so, Tone?"

At 12:20 P.M. next day, Yardley checked in at the U.S. Embassy on Avenue Gabriel, in Paris, and asked for the Commercial Secretary. There had been one minor crisis when he had arrived at Terminal 2, Heathrow, to find that the Air France flight had been overbooked. A special smile to the pretty girl at the desk and a quickly invented story about his sick mother in Paris had ensured him the last seat in front of a pompous English businessman, whose bullying tactics had got him nowhere.

One of the guardians at the front desk in the embassy had carefully looked over his credentials, had called through to the commercial secretary's office and had then conducted him through the security checks to the room on the third floor. And now he had his first sight of Roger Rodel. He saw a large man, plump rather than fat, bald with a wisp of light brown hair dragged across his scalp in a vain attempt to hide the shining dome, horn-rimmed spectacles and a chubby, well-fed-looking face. I'd like to have you on an assault course for a couple of weeks, Yardley thought. That'd tighten up that ample waistline.

"Major Yardley, sir. Good to meet you at last." The soft hand that Yardley grasped had a heavy signet ring on the little finger. "I take it things went well?"

Yardley looked questioningly around the room.

"Good thinking, Major, but we're okay. This room is swept for bugs every day. You can talk freely."

"It worked fine," Yardley said. "The team went into the

jail, lifted your man out, the aircraft picked him up on schedule yesterday morning and he was collected from the Camargue a few hours later."

"No alarms or excursions? No police cars with sirens going and lights flashing?"

Yardley said, "Not from where I was sitting. Mind you, Her Majesty's Government must know by now they've lost a valuable prisoner. But nobody's felt my collar." He saw the questioning look on Rodel's face and added, "That's what the Brits call it. Feeling your collar means a police arrest."

"Quaint turn of phrase those cousins have. I must remember that one."

Yardley went on, "So that should see me out. I've discharged General Bradford's orders. While I'm here I might as well contact the French Foreign Legion and do some interviewing for my book. You have any useful numbers I could call, Mr. Rodel?"

"Hey, not so fast. And do call me Roger. They tell me you prefer Bob. That was just phase one, Bob. You did well—we are pleased. But there's more to come."

"There's—what?"

"Oh yes, lots more. Here—let's get Liz in. I'd be lost without that lady." He pressed a buzzer on the underside of his desk. A few moments later, a brisk, middle-aged brunette in a severely tailored costume walked in. "Liz, meet Major Yardley. Bob, this is my PA, Liz Hall. You spoke to her yesterday." They shook hands. "You got the tickets, Liz?"

"Right here, Roger." She had a wallet in her left hand and extracted two flight tickets, one of which she handed to Yardley. He flicked over the page and saw it was a single ticket to Geneva that same afternoon. He could feel a slow anger welling up from inside. These damned government officials—they think they bloody own you.

Liz Hall was still talking. "Oh, Roger, that nice Mr. Flood called. He says there'll be a helicopter to collect you both from the Trans-Air terminal, Geneva Airport, when you arrive."

"What the hell's going on?" Yardley demanded. "And who's nice Mr. Flood? I signed on for one op—to spring that prisoner—and I did it. That's my lot." He stood up and made to leave the room.

"Sorry, Bob," said Rodel. "We couldn't tell you before.

Need-to-know and all that. You're still on the team. In fact, you're still *leader* of the team."

Yardley said through a tight mouth, "Don't give me that horseshit! Who's Flood and what the hell's going on?"

Rodel said, "You've met Flood—at least once, maybe more."

"A quiet guy. Fairish-haired, medium height—you could lose him in a crowd. Ex–New Zealand SAS in Vietnam. That Flood?"

"That's the very one."

Yardley began to feel a little better. He still didn't like being pushed around, like a pawn on the chessboard, but at least if the Flood he remembered was somehow involved, it couldn't be all bad. Flood was something of a mystery man—now you saw him, now he disappeared for months on end, but it was a name that cropped up in the higher circles of the Special Forces. When he, Yardley, had done that snatch in Beirut, the one that gave him the Medal of Honor, word was that Flood had been there before—undercover—setting up the op. And he had wiped out one of those Basque ETA terrorist teams around Biarritz. He was beginning to feel quite interested.

"So what's it all about?" he asked.

Rodel grinned. "No point in telling it all twice. Look, Bob, you deserve a vacation. I'm coming with you. We're off to Geneva this very afternoon—and tonight you'll be meeting Flood and maybe a few of the guys. We'll be up in the mountains at a place called Château d'Oex. That actor guy, David Niven, used to live there. He was a friend of Flood's in the few years before he died. You can clear your lungs in the mountain air and take a short break. You've earned it."

"Hell," said Yardley, "what do I do about General Bradford? He was running me on the prison break."

"Don't worry about the general. This is a Company do—and was from the start. We wanted you, and the general was useful in getting to you. That's for the history books now. Langley'll keep General Bradford posted."

"Or tell him some fancy story."

"Or tell him some fancy story," Rodel repeated with a grin. "You know our methods, Watson—or you soon will. Let's go have a quick lunch. You got the car standing by for de Gaulle, Liz?"

She nodded. "You both have firm bookings on Air France

966 in separate rows. Just in case. That's a 16.15 departure, gentlemen."

"That's my girl. Well, as the guy said in *The Wild Bunch,* let's go!"

"Monsieur Baring, *s'il vous plaît?*" The thin wiry little Frenchman stuck his weather-beaten face into the Renault's window. Baring felt the impact of the strong garlic traveling on the old fisherman's breath.

"*Bonjour,* Monsieur Petan. How are you this fine morning? Are your sea bones telling us anything about the mistral today?"

"Ah, monsieur! It is not the wind and the weather I have to speak with you about." He looked across at the diminutive Shaw and wondered if he should continue in front of this stranger.

Baring got out of the car, closing the door behind him. "You have a problem, Monsieur Petan?"

"Not me, Monsieur Nick. I think you have a problem." His callused forefinger tapped the side of his nose. "When you approach the jetty you will see a man standing against the rack of fire buckets. He is making a *theater* of reading the *Provençal.* He watches your boat—and he did not take breakfast today."

Baring took the warning. "How can you be sure he is not waiting for an incoming vessel?"

"Monsieur Nick." The old boy leaned forward with arms spread wide, an expression of being pleased with himself crossing his face. "A man like this does not read such a newspaper, he never risks his cheap shoes at sea, and he never misses his *petit déjeuner.*"

His last reference to breakfast was emphasized by a stabbing of his gathered fingers toward an open mouth.

"*Merci,* Monsieur Petan. *Merci beaucoup.* I hear your warning." They shook hands.

As Petan turned away he left some advice.

"Be careful with this one, Monsieur Nick. He is out of a rat hole."

Baring recognized the French phrase *un trou au rats* for what it meant. The Corsican underworld were on the hunt.

Shaw had hardly spoken during their return trip from the Camargue. The different route, although a similar distance, had been motorway practically the whole way back to Marseilles. It had meant the BMW was not seen on the road or in a village by the locals at the same time the aircraft was overhead. It also placed them on the safe side of the river Rhône before police roadblocks could be set up.

Baring noticed the gray hallowed look that Shaw carried. This was the mark of prison life. Men in prison never quite stayed clean. The tension never really left them. A red cold sore to the side of his nose that prison life gave no chance of healing. Eyes that had receded, starved of real daylight. He detected that the man was going along with events, reacting to discipline, orders, from an ever present guard. It suited Baring. Less trouble that way.

As they had approached the underground garage behind the station, Shaw had protested.

"Do I get to be relieved of my ball and chain now?" He raised the weighty mechanic's toolbox off his knees.

"You carry that until I decide that you don't. Until then, shut up."

From the moment Shaw had seated himself in the BMW, Baring had reminded him that this was no game of comfort. The metal box, with tools inside, had been placed on his lap. His left wrist snapped into a set of handcuffs attached to the handle. Shaw was not going anywhere with that. Any thought of running off evaporated. After a few kilometers he had read all the funny stickers stuck all over the box and decided to accept his lot. A central sticker on the box lid was a facsimile of the Volvo Marine badge on the pocket of his blue overalls. Transferring to the Renault had increased the discomfort.

Approaching the boat, the watcher was not in sight. Baring guessed that he had seen them coming and gone to the phone. The pair of them looked the part. A boat owner escorting a marine engine service mechanic to his mooring. Once on board the toolbox was set aside. The handcuffs stayed on. Shaw was now attached to a forward bunk bed complete with blanket and pillow.

"Here, take this glass of whiskey and relax. I have some formalities to attend to in the terminal. The door will be locked. If anybody comes along, make no sound and stay away from the porthole."

It was two hours before Baring returned. He found Shaw fast asleep. Without waking him, he prepared his captive some lunch in the small galley in the stern. During his absence the Rhodesian had walked the marina, outwardly appearing to shop and attend to the bureaucracy for leaving the harbor. He had also been assessing whom and how many he was up against. They were under surveillance all right. It had been easy to spot the three watchers positioned where they could cover the boat, his Renault and the terminal. But he was not being followed. This told him that the Corsicans had orders to watch and not touch. It meant someone had not yet arrived to positively identify Shaw if he did show up. Baring guessed a heavy would be on the way from London. It gave them some time.

He himself was expecting someone to arrive within the next hour. Flood had instructed that he would have help with the escort of Shaw to Switzerland. The signal had simply read that a "previous buyer" had agreed to a viewing appointment.

Shaw welcomed the food. He chose to ignore the danger he was in. As he had said to Baring in the car. "The safest place for me was Wormwood Scrubs. Whatever this is all about, outside those prison walls I have no chance. I'm scared, Mr. Rhodesian, but I'm not stupid. Types like you kill easy and quick. Room service isn't included in the price. You're being paid to keep me alive, for the time being anyway. That makes you my best protection from those cut-throats out there, doesn't it?" Shaw's voice was an attempt to sound strong. Somehow it did not sound so convincing as it was intended.

"Mr. Shaw, you seem to understand the situation. I personally don't give a damn who you are or where you have been. I only care about where you are going. If I get you there, you'll be alive. If I don't get there, you will be dead." With that, Baring moved farther astern and opened one of a row of leather-lined cupboards set at head height into the expensive mahogany fascia.

Sliding out a custom-fitted box, and setting it down on the captain's table, he released the combination lock and lifted the lid. Looking up from his plate Shaw saw him extract a handgun and a submachine gun and several magazines of ammunition. His appetite suddenly gone, the locksmith swung his legs up onto the bunk, the food discarded. He felt a wave of depression sweeping over him. Life was coming to an end.

"Ahoy on board the *Udaka!* Can one come aboard?" The

very English voice jerked Baring's eyes away from the firing mechanism of the MP5 submachine gun, the cleaning cloth dropped to the table.

With the 9mm Browning automatic at the ready in his right hand, he signaled Shaw, with a finger against his lips, to be quiet. A look through the spy hole in the cabin door showed a pin-striped suit and a briefcase.

"Lysol, what the hell are you doing here?" Baring emerged and closed the door behind him. The Browning was now in his jacket pocket. His finger remained on the trigger.

"Well, old boy, is that the usual welcome you give to all your previous buyers?"

Seated at the captain's table, a bottle of whiskey placed between them, the two Special Forces veterans got down to business. Lysol had explained the successful arrival at Marseilles airport and the smooth way McDermid had led him through customs and immigration. The property brochures had saved a lot of chat and his visit had not been challenged. McDermid had gone off to the Bureau de Piste to have a little talk with "Monsieur le Chef de District" about his electrical problem, and that was that. Lysol had arrived at the marina more than an hour ago, but had not approached the boat. He had seen the watchers.

Lysol knew that the Mediterranean sun falling away pulled most Frenchmen into the bar for a quick drink of *pastis.* He chose this moment to come aboard. Acknowledging Shaw, whose eyes lit up in recognition, he said nothing to him. There was no continuation of the airborne bonhomie. This was Baring's part of the operation, it would be played his way.

"This is how we are going to do it." Baring spread a map of the region across the table. "We are up against the Guerini crowd. They are a legacy left by the Guerini brothers, the underworld bosses who used to run this city during the 1950s. The hard core that will be on our backs are professionals and organized. They control the narcotics traffic, which means they have the weapons, the soldiers and the corruption on the streets. There will be no soft options, these scum will be doing a favor for the London end. If they hit us, we take them out."

He handed Lysol a Browning automatic from the box and two thirteen-round magazines.

"The ammunition load in these is soft nose and Geco mix.

I've measured the grain fill myself. I don't have to tell you the damage the soft will do to the body. It will go in and stay in. The Geco has a titanium-coated round. It will rip through any engine block or car body they throw at us."

Lysol extracted two rounds and inspected them. A smile crossed his lips as he reloaded and rammed one of the clips into the butt of the handgun. "And the MP5?"

The sinister submachine gun so favored by the SAS lay on the table. Its curved thirty-round magazine, designed to prevent the weapon jamming, was beside it.

"In mine, a one-in-four mix." Baring reached inside the box. "This one is for you."

He held a briefcase identical to the one Lysol had arrived with. As he stepped back from the table, his right hand gripping the case's handle in the conventional way, his right arm suddenly jerked up and straightened sharply downward. The briefcase fell away and exposed the snub-nosed MP5 machine pistol concealed inside. The continued sweep of Baring's arm movement brought the weapon up into the firing position, cocked and ready to shoot.

"I believe you are familiar with this lovely little toy, Lysol."

For the next forty-five minutes they briefed down to the last detail. Lysol would take a taxi to the Gare St. Charles. He would agitate with the driver to hurry so that he did not miss the train to Avignon. At the station he would make a show of concern about missing his connection there, the Geneva to Barcelona express at 15.46. The Marseillais are proud of their railway service, particularly the TGV that would run to Avignon on its way to Paris. A few raised voices for the ears of the watchers should not be hard to encourage. He was then to shake them off and collect, unseen, the BMW from the car park and proceed to a rendezvous with Baring at the "Calanque de Morgiou" along the coast to the east.

Baring would set sail on a heading for the Spanish Balearic Islands. The customs would record his destination as Majorca. Out of sight of land he would alter course back to the coast. If they got underway within twenty minutes, he estimated arrival at the R/V at 17.30 hours.

The wooden ketch *Udaka,* named after the Matabele word for the Rhodesian clay used by the people to build houses in their tribal villages, was prepared for sea. Baring had scrubbed the varnished deck and laid out the immaculate white ropes vital for his single-handed operation. The Mistral wind was expected, confirmed as the prevailing wind had gradually backed around to the northwest, forecast to eventually be gusting force six or seven. He had learned from the old sea dogs to check the boat's deck early in the morning for moisture. Its presence together with limited visibility inland indicated a high pressure system and not good sailing to the south. But as they told him. A dry deck in the morning, sailor take warning. Earlier that morning he could see well inland to the clear outline of the Alps-de-Haute-Provence. As he had walked the jetty, the rigging of the boats nestled in the shelter of the harbor was clanking as if under a conductor's baton. Checking the *mauvais temps,* he knew the cooled air descending the mighty Rhône Valley to collide with the warm air of the Midi would bring the Mistral.

He had accepted an invitation to join a table of fishermen taking their daily routine bottle of Calvados and canapés of raw fish. Staying long enough to agree that the Mistral was a fair wind for the Balearics and on a broad reach with a double-reefed main and a storm jib he was in for a good sail. Collecting his duty-free supplies from the customs bonded store helped spread the deception. Any observer would be convinced that Baring was catching the Mistral to the Balearics.

With the sun hanging low in the sky, now cleared of the wet shroud of recent weeks, Baring hauled up the mainsail and jib. The old sea salts, wrapped in scarves and hats to catch the last heat of the day at the cafe tables, placed their bets. With the sails luffing in the wind he slipped the mooring, allowing the wind to push the yacht to port. Catching the drift, he quickly pulled in his main boom and then urgently winched in his jib. *Udaka* played out on a port tack and serenely glided out of the harbor entrance. Behind, at the tables, glasses of Calvados clinked together and money changed hands. The scene belied the violent reality beneath the tranquillity.

Beyond the harbor mouth experienced hands loosened the jib and mainsails, letting the yacht run free until the compass settled on 225 degrees magnetic. Now on a comfortable broad reach with the wind abaft, gusting force six, the boat quickly built to a hull speed of 9 knots. The yacht's motion was rough, but exhilarating. From experience Baring knew to leave his mizzensail lashed to its stern boom. This was the most comfortable for this sea state.

The sound of Shaw throwing up belowdecks jolted him out of his indulgence. Lashing the wheel to maintain the compass heading, he made his way below. The pale man was more pale than ever. He lay facedown on the bunk filling his pillow with lunch.

"I see that I have a real sailor here." The handcuffs were released. "You had better come up on deck and find your sea legs. If you go overboard, you can stay overboard."

The fresh air changed Shaw's complexion to a healthier green. Seated in the stern the spray and wind hit his face and soon took his mind away from the trouble he was in. Baring observed the sea applying its therapy on the drained features and dismissed any threat. His attention returned to navigation. On this heading they were on course for the Île de Planier, thirteen miles off the coast. Off to starboard lay the double islands of Îe Ratonneau and Îe Pomègues. Running before the wind like this would keep him at the wheel until past Planier. A journey time of one and one half hours. Then, well out of sight and beyond the wind effects of Cap Croisette, he would make the course change to Les Calanques.

Lysol boarded the orange-and-gray TGV express. The surveillance had closed in. He wondered if Nick had left harbor safely. Seeing one of the two watchers climb aboard, he opened the door on the blind side and dropped down onto the track. Slipping through the traces of a freight train alongside put him on the adjacent platform. Out of view of both followers. With unobtrusive speed he descended the grand stone staircase leading from the station to the Boulevard d'Athens and the thoroughfare of the Canebiere beyond. Doubling back down the side of the building had him at the BMW inside four minutes. The keys were where Baring had left them. In his haste he left skin from his hand inside the wheel arch. The traffic in the Canebiere was heavy and there seemed an abundance of traffic police on points duty, all of whom seem to be looking hard at him. He recognized a touch of paranoia. The wide road was not unlike Fifth Avenue in Manhattan, without the pedestrians.

Leaving it behind, he headed east toward the Parc Chanot, Baring's road map and directions on the seat beside him. A glance in the rearview mirror satisfied him that the Corsican heathens had lost his tail. He thought of the conditions that existed in Marseilles Baumettes jail, home most of the time for these underworld lackeys. He had experienced it first-hand for a short time. Arrested while acting as bodyguard for a Greek businessman, who unbeknown to the London security firm that had hired him was involved in narcotics trafficking. It had not been the happiest of interludes. The ex–SAS officer who ran the London company had felt his wrath on being released. Breaking his nose and putting him in a neck brace for a month had given Lysol some small degree of satisfaction. It had not been sufficient recompense for what he had suffered while incarcerated. The Marseilles criminal element was vicious.

It had taken Baring two and a half hours to sail from the island of Planier to his present position at the mouth of the Calanque de Morgiou. He had jibed from a port to a starboard tack and winched the sails in to pinch as closely to the wind as possible. Maintaining a steady crawl windward on a compass heading of 095 degrees eastward to make his landfall some way around the coast from Marseilles. The ten nautical miles of this second leg had been very slow, but had achieved the deception. He had explained the plan to Shaw, who had failed to find any comfort at sea. At one point he had suggested to Baring that he should end his misery and simply hand him to the Corsicans. He had not been joking, and was now lying on a bunk below, making a low groaning sound. An aroma of vomit floated on deck. Baring felt nothing but disgust for this useless individual. Light was failing now as he approached the sheltered anchorage. The Calanques were a series of inlets along the coast between Marseilles and the town of Cassis. Beginning at Cap Croisette, the fiordlike cuts into the deserted stretch of coast varied in length, some quite shallow, while others created coastal peninsulas. Baring had selected one of three that cut into the tree-lined rocks and did not offer easy access from the land side. A single road ran from the outskirts of Marseilles to a small village at the top of the inlet. This was Morgiou, a lonely cluster of whitewashed peasant housing. A forestry dirt track left this road before it reached the village and ran along the top of the ridge that formed one side of the Calanque. At the tip of the peninsula the track dropped down some two hundred and twenty meters to the sea. Four kilometers, and out of sight of the village. Completely sheltered from the northerly wind, the yacht lay bobbing up and down with the slight swell, as Baring made several attempts to throw his bow rope around a pine tree jutting out at an angle from the rocky shore.

It had not escaped his mind that Lysol might have trouble finding this place. Daylight was in its last fling as the boat, now secured at the stern as well, was eased closer under the rocky outcrop. He did this with Shaw's help, shortening each rope in turn. If their business there had not been of such a serious intent, it could almost have been enjoyed. Going below, Baring gathered up the prepared weapons. The Browning went into a customized belt holster, concealed under his leather jacket. The MP5 into a small underwater-diver's bag. After collecting some personal effects and taking a last glance around his pride and joy, he left the cabin. As he locked the door, Shaw was commenting on the beautiful evening song of the birds filling the trees above. Baring mentally agreed with him.

"Get yourself back to the stern, we're going ashore." It was an order.

They clambered up the rocks toward the track. Looking back down, Baring thought *Udaka* would now make a perfect advertisement for those Bacardi people. Reaching the dusty track they found no sign of Lysol. The yacht was going to stay in its secluded berth for some time so Baring decided to leave the location so as not to draw attention to its presence. They began to walk inland. A dust cloud warned them of the approaching car. Baring pushed Shaw into the trees and worked the action of the Browning. The blue BMW crawled slowly toward them.

With Shaw seated in the back and Baring now driving, the BMW negotiated the twisting dirt track at speed. Shortly after, the tires gripped tarmac again as they descended down from Mount de Luminy and met the beginning of the urban road. Lysol glanced to his right. They were passing the monastic buildings of Les Baumettes.

"You should have mentioned that luxurious landmark. It's not unfamiliar to me." The ugly gates of the prison slipped by.

"Any trouble along the way? None of our friends seems to be with you." Baring's eyes were seeing everything, every face, every vehicle.

"No trouble, I left it all at the station." Lysol's eyes were also alive. The briefcase stood upright between his feet and the Browning lay under his hand on his lap. Baring swung the car out onto the main D559 highway and accelerated toward Cassis.

Pushing the BMW hard Baring raced through the climbing turns of the Col de La Gineste. The elevated road paralleling the coast but separated from it by the Massif du Puget, offering a challenge to any driver attempting to cover it at speed. They had to gain time. The surveillance teams would remain fooled for some time, but not forever. As soon as the TGV reached Avignon, the man tasked with sticking with Lysol would be on the phone to his Marseilles bosses, reporting that the tall Englishman was not on the train. A single sighting of him slipping out of the city, by any of the thousands of pairs of eyes paid to watch for such events, would blow their game. Secrets were not secrets for long in the melting pot of Marseilles.

"We might not have the time you think we have, Nick." Lysol spoke in knowing tones. "Those TGVs are equipped with national telephones these days. If he walked the train, he's made the call already."

"Shit! You're probably right. There were a few curious eyes outside those prison gates as well." Baring paused and glanced across. "Be ready for them."

Lysol, by way of professional habit, ejected the loaded magazine from his Browning. A cursory inspection and it was rammed back into its place in the handgrip.

"Oh, don't worry. I'm ready for the little garlic suckers." There was no trace of his usual flippancy now.

Behind them, Shaw said nothing. He sat braced against the car's motion and looked on. The night they were driving into was filled with threat. He was not overconfident that he would see morning.

"Are you all right back there, Mr. Shaw?" Baring was eyeing the nervous man in the rearview mirror. "If we run into trouble, you stay down and don't move unless you are ordered to. If you have to move, at any time, you stay on the heels of Lysol here. You don't follow me because I will be drawing fire. Do you understand?"

"Yes, I understand." Shaw's reply drifted away in his fear.

The tussock-covered rocky terrain spread inland, becoming the Camp de Carpiagne. Here and there the road ran through patches of dry pine forest and then swung north behind Cassis. They had covered the twenty-five kilometers easily. To avoid the town Baring took the D41 past the large military camp and joined the main autoroute fourteen kilometers farther north. It was now motorway all the way to Aix-en-Provence fifty kilometers away. The A50 soon became the A52 at Aubagne and ran on to the A8 a few kilometers east of Aix. They were making good time. The smoother ride had sent Shaw to sleep.

The lights of Aix-en-Provence sparkled in the dusk light as they followed the motorway around its southern suburbs. Slipping through the junction with the A51, Baring joined the dual carriageway of the N296 and again headed north. It became the N7 and they had to make a turning to Manosque in three kilometers. Beside him Lysol was confirming their progress on a road map. Only Baring had taken a mental note of the two cars parked illegally on the overpass of the last motorway junction.

The alpine route they were taking to Geneva offered a good single carriageway and light traffic. It followed the Durance River through Château-Arnoux as far as Sisteron where it changed to follow the river Buech and the railway line to the city of Grenoble. To most travelers it was the scenic route.

"Our total distance to Grenoble is four hundred and eighty-one kilometers. Then it's a one-hundred-and-sixty-kilometer run to Geneva. That last stretch is motorway and takes us past the lake at Annecy, and across the Swiss border just past Annemasse. If they are going to hit us, I reckon it will be before Grenoble, at the latest, Chambery sixty kilometers beyond."

"What's your reasoning behind that, Nick?" Lysol's attention stayed with the map.

"These bastards, if they have figured out our route, will set up an intercept. They will bring in people from Lyons to cut us off. There's a fast motorway linking the three cities. Get my drift?"

"Yes, it makes sense. We should be all right until then." Lysol looked out at the passing main street. "This is Sisteron, the road turns off to Gap a short distance from here."

"We will stay on this road. There is a series of tunnels up ahead, if I remember rightly and I suggest we use one of them to have a chat with our newfound friends." Baring's thumb was indicating behind his shoulder.

Lysol lowered the sunshade on his side and used the vanity mirror to check the road behind. A pair of headlights was leaving the town a short way behind and appeared to be moving briskly through the few local vehicles. He said nothing.

The river and the railway line separated and soon after they entered a tunnel that was the first of several that threaded the railway backward and forward over the road. Baring took a right turn along a parallel road signposted to Veynes. One of the cars in the line behind them also left the main road. This secondary road continued in a circular direction back toward Gap. The car following could only be going to Veynes. Before the town Baring turned off left, back across the railway and rejoined the Grenoble road. The car followed. "It's them," he said. "I feel it tickling my scrotum." His hand changed to a lower gear and he smoothly increased speed. So did the other car.

They were approaching the highest section of the route, the pass at La Croix-Haute. Entering the town of St.-Julien-en-Beauchene, Baring allowed the car to gain on them. Under the streetlights he could define it as a brown Citroën with Marseilles registration; three men, two in the front seat, one in the rear. Lysol resisted turning around. By doing so he would signal to the men behind that they had been noticed.

"I saw that car way back above the motorway at Aix. They've kept their distance and I lost sight of them. Now they're moving in, which means they made contact with Marseilles." Baring was stating facts, not making conversation.

"Do I wake Sleeping Beauty in the backseat?" Lysol's tone was agreeing with Baring's thoughts. Let him sleep. It will be over in seconds anyway.

"Next tunnel." Baring had placed his Browning on his lap. "I'll put our nose on them, then reverse. You know the routine."

"Gotcha, old boy." Lysol set his briefcase aside and reached behind Baring's seat, taking the MP5 from the diving bag. He would need the advantage of the Geco armor-piercing rounds and the longer weapon length. The tunnel entrance appeared ahead. The BMW had powered up the last rise to its mouth more easily than the Citroën. They had drawn ahead by half a kilometer. It was all they needed. The well-lighted tunnel curved slightly midway.

"I'll put us just in the dark at the other end." The car was traveling ninety miles per hour and the front windows were on the way down. As they took the curve Baring saw the Citroën's lights enter the tunnel.

The cold mountain air now rushing into the car snapped Shaw awake. He felt the speed, and the tension.

"What the hell is going on?" His voice was excited. He began to sit up.

Lysol barked out without turning, "Stay down, you bloody idiot, and shut up!"

The wheels suddenly locked. The sound of tires screaming under the torture of Baring's braking action seemed to fill the tunnel's cavity. The car was sideways across the road. Then it flicked around and they faced back into the tunnel. Baring's left hand yanked the hand brake on, locking the wheels solid, and then in an eye-beating wrist movement, the gearshift found first gear. The BMW was still sliding backward in a controlled skid. The Citroën appeared, moving very fast, headlights on full beam. Lysol's passenger door was now open as the BMW slid almost to a halt. He hit the road and rolled once. Finding his feet, he went into a crouch on one knee and fired. As he did so, the Citroën driver jumped on his brakes. They were all dead before the tires lost their grip. The MP5 spat two precise three-second bursts, then a slightly longer burst raked down the length of the Citroën, now rushing side on toward them. The third burst had ripped open the head of the man emerging from a rear door. He joined the other dead, bucking in death's spasm in the front. Baring had executed a skillful hand brake turn and had the BMW faced out into the darkness. Lysol threw himself over the hood and scrambled into the car. His door crashed shut with the momentum of violent acceleration. Lysol changed magazines. The action was over but his juices were pumping. As Baring had said, it had only taken seconds.

"You're mad, you're crazy, mad, killers, killers! We're going to die!"

Lysol turned to the hysterical Shaw and hit him hard across the face. The barrel of the MP5 rammed into his throat.

"Shut your fucking mouth, now! One more outburst like that and I'll put your blood on the road with theirs!" His voice was loud and deadly. He meant it.

Behind them the Citroën had finished its metal-wrenching ride between the tunnel walls. Now helpless, on its roof like an upturned insect, it careered into the darkness in a shower of sparks. A trail of debris followed the car off the road and down the plunge to the river.

The speeding BMW was already out of sight, climbing toward the high pass. Baring did not lift his foot until they were across the mountain bridge spanning the Col de La Croix and descending the other side.

They drove on toward Grenoble in silence. Shaw nursed his bewilderment and fear without utterance. These two men had not said one word about what happened back there. As if it happened every day. A trip to the supermarket. He didn't know whom to be more frightened of, the killer nursemaids in the front seat or the unknown predators from Marseilles.

The night sky was clear and the mountain air crisp and dry. A good moon silhouetted the high Alps of the Dauphiné surrounding them. They seemed to have the road to themselves and were again making good time.

Baring broke the thoughtful quietness.

"I want to get clear of Grenoble as soon as possible. The local police are probably at the tunnel by now. Their confusion will buy us some time before the roadblocks go up. We're vulnerable until Grenoble."

Lysol agreed and checked his watch. "I have 21.30 hours. Do you intend to push right through to Geneva?"

"No. I want to cross the border with the morning rush hour commuters traveling into Geneva. We'll take a rest at a service area at Le Touvet, well north of the city. Then push on with the sunrise."

"The gendarmerie won't get our description from the losers in the Citroën, Nick."

"You're right about that. Even if one of the bastards was found breathing, he wouldn't say a word. They follow the Mafia code of silence all the way."

"That leaves the boys from Lyons. Is that what you're saying?"

"That's exactly what I'm saying, Lysol. After that shit back there, they will come at us like a torpedo. No messing." Baring glanced at Shaw in the mirror. "Do you hear me, Mr. Shaw? That includes you. No messing."

"I hear you, and I understand you. Just tell me what to do and I'll do it." Shaw's voice had a fresh tone of realization about it.

While Lysol had fetched hot coffee and pastries from the service area restaurant, Baring felt it safe to exercise Shaw's legs in the car park. Walking in close radius to the car, their breath floating in the cold air, Shaw nervously sought reassurance from the silent mercenary.

"Nick, look . . . Nick, I can call you Nick, can't I? Yes, I'm sure I can, after all if we . . ."

"Get to the point, Mr. Shaw. Say what you have to say." Baring's full attention was elsewhere. His eyes searching for threat in all quarters of the parking lot. The Browning hung loosely in his right hand.

"Nick, I just want to say categorically that I will not be any trouble to you. I accept the picture now for whatever it all means and I accept that my life is in your hands. I'm out of my depth with all this and I confess to being frightened, but . . ."

Baring cut the awkward little speech short. "I get your drift, Mr. Shaw. Maintain that attitude and you increase your chances. Ours too for that matter. Now let's get back to the car."

The BMW was repositioned at the far corner of the parking lot. The coffee and food had brought welcome comfort. Lysol came to from a shallow sleep. He surveyed the car's interior and then ran a cautious eye around outside. Shaw slept like a baby. He had obviously come to terms with himself. Baring, slumped low in the driver's seat, scanned the area constantly. Watching the night traffic of heavy trucks come and go and other car park dwellers like them, attempting to grab sleep on the move.

Lysol spoke quietly. "I guess this is going to screw up Marseilles for you, Nick? Lose that damned fine ship of yours too; I expect."

Baring thought on it before answering. "There's bound to be some hassle from this. It's down to the bosses. If they say let it go there won't be any vendetta." His tone was unworried and affection crept into his words for *Udaka.* "She's my home and I really don't want to live any other way. The Calanque mooring is safe enough, they won't touch her there. The bastards will be right in thinking I'll be going back to get her." He turned to face Lysol, his expression showing his resigned acceptance of all the odds. "Flood will help to sort it out, he has a long past in that city."

They both sat silently and dwelled on events for a while. Then it was time to move.

"I'm going to the gents. I'll bring back some coffee and we'll hit the road. If he wants to piss, it will have to be by the car." Baring climbed out.

"I say, what about me, old boy? Are you suggesting I submit *my* family sword to the same indignity and rigors as a French peasant?"

"That's the straw you draw, Lysol." Baring chuckled and strode away.

As Lysol made to get out of the car he turned to the wakening Shaw. "Did you hear that, Shaw old lad? That wild bloody colonial called my dick a straw."

The humor was lost on Shaw as he obeyed Lysol's gestures to get out and stretch his limbs. How could they joke around at a time like this?

They drank the coffee on the road. Lysol took the wheel and headed the car north to the ancient spa town of Chambery. The forty kilometers to its outskirts were busy with trucks grabbing a headstart on the pedestrian townsfolk still in their beds.

The night had not been so cold as expected. Even in the mountains the late autumn temperatures remained unusually mild. But with the strong northerly wind it had been cold enough. The convoys of trucks prevented any fast driving and they agreed to just go with the flow. To do otherwise would have attracted unwanted attention. As the road began to descend toward Chambery almost an hour later the three of them were only beginning to feel the long night's fuzz and chill leaving their bodies.

"We'll take the new ring road around the town, Lysol. It joins a motorway spur that links up with the A43 Lyons to Annecy motorway. Then it's motorway all the way to Geneva."

"Okay, Nick. I suggest you take the wheel the other side of the town. That trouble you're expecting may show and your hands are better at this grand prix game than mine." Baring nodded in agreement.

Clear of Chambery, Lysol pulled over to the hard shoulder of the spur road and exchanged places with Baring. Shaw took the opportunity to relieve himself beside the car. The rush and roar of the heavy traffic beating a frantic path to the motorway washed around them. With Baring now behind the wheel, Lysol waited by the open rear door for Shaw to finish his ablutions.

Baring had seen the car approaching on the opposite side of the road. The sleek black Renault 25 had run onto the motorway from an overhead bridge about two kilometers farther on. It caught his attention because from a distance he thought it was the police, and they were illegally parked. As it got closer it appeared to be traveling unnecessarily fast. Not the way of the French gendarmerie coming to help motorists in distress.

"Lysol, get in the car." He said it quietly, still uncertain that any threat existed.

The black sedan drew nearer. Baring could now see it was not the police. He recognized the car's model and the traffic cops were not provided with such luxury. He began to relax, executives heading for the office probably. Lysol closed the door behind Shaw and dropped into his seat beside Baring. He had heard the disguised alertness in the driver's voice. Momentarily their view across the road was blocked by passing trucks. A sound of screeching tires reached their ears. Baring started the engine and engaged gears. The BMW began to roll forward as Baring searched his mirror for a gap in the traffic. The gap appeared, and so did the two armed men running toward the median from the other side of the road. The black Renault had skidded to a halt on the far shoulder.

"Go! Go! Go!" Lysol's voice boomed in Baring's ear.

He did not need telling. The BMW fishtailed its way down the shoulder, leaving strips of rubber in its wake. He hugged the inside protection of the three huge trucks running in convoy until he was certain they had distance. The lead trucker blasted his double Klaxon horn as the blue car swept across under his nose and accelerated out into the fast lane. Lysol looked back. The two crazy bastards were now running and dodging their way back to the Renault, waking a lot of the early-morning drivers from their habitual sleep at the wheel, as they went. Chaos reigned among the traffic flowing toward Chambery, as the Renault accelerated through the panicking cars.

"They're pissing off in the other direction, Nick. What the hell was that all about?"

"The Lyons crowd." Baring's voice was strained in concentration as he guided the speeding car in and out of the busy lanes. The speedometer was climbing past 190 kpm. "They must have been sitting on that bridge all night, and given up.

Our bad luck, but I think they saw us by accident. Otherwise they only had to wait until we passed under them and slip down behind us. They were going for breakfast, I expect. Their mistake, our luck."

"They won't be gone for long." Lysol was checking his weapons. Closing the briefcase, he replaced it between his legs. The Browning got the same treatment.

"If they were alone, we've bought some time. They will have to go some way before they can turn around. He'll probably throw it into a U-turn at those road works about five kilometers back." Baring's voice was raised above the noise of the racing engine. "That Renault 25 is a mover. Faster than us at the top end, so they'll catch us on this open road." He was flashing the headlights and riding all over the rear bumpers of the other cars. "We're also going to attract the law driving like this."

"What are our options, old fruit?" Again the pampered dialogue of the upper-crust Englishman appeared, wrapped as before in a deadly tone.

"We have to get off this motorway. Draw them in. We can't risk a situation close to the border." He beckoned to Lysol for the map. His finger stabbed at it. "Annecy is our option. The turnoff is about fifteen kilometers from here. I reckon we will be seeing them before then."

Lysol left him alone to think, and turned to Shaw. The little man looked prepared. He gave a silent nod to Lysol as if to say so.

"Lysol, this is the plan." Baring knew Annecy well and outlined their only option.

"But it's a single road down there, and what if they overshoot us and head straight for the lake?"

"If they do they'll turn back and look for us. These guys are smart and they know this place as well."

The traffic had spaced out more now. They were breaking loose from the commuter clutter. The clear bright morning was in their favor.

"Here they come." Baring spoke in a calm expectant voice.

Looking behind, Lysol saw the Renault some kilometers back down the motorway. It was in the fast lane with its headlights glaring bright on full beam.

"These fuckers don't give a shit about anything, do they?" He was almost chuckling as he spoke.

"That thing is faster than any police car around here,

Lysol. The mob have the best mechanics in France." Baring paused and assessed the approaching road signs. He slowed the car in the fast lane and then pulled it violently across to the exit road. "I hope they saw that."

He swung off down a steep hill past the signpost showing Talloires to the right. There were high walls on either side, a corkscrew twist in the narrow road and then a tiny village square. Baring drove on down and indicated to Lysol a large house on the left. The early sun now reflected on the lake and the surrounding copse of trees. He suddenly turned through a gateway at the rear of the house and parked abruptly between an immaculate Rolls-Royce and a gleaming Mercedes. "Right, let's get on with it. Shaw, you're with Lysol. Get moving." The combatant's order had its usual galvanizing effect.

Lysol got out. Shaw followed. Taking him by the arm, he led the scared locksmith in a stumbling walk along the road some thirty or forty yards until they reached a low-walled garden. They entered and made their way through the wooden chairs and white tablecloths. A scene of civilized tranquillity nestled under the shading trees. Behind the garden was an old gray abbey—the famous Hotel L'Abbaye.

"Listen hard, Shaw." Lysol spoke firmly through his clenched teeth. "There's no time to repeat it all. You know these people chasing us are killers. There is no guarantee they still want you alive. I strongly doubt that they do. Even if they do, you wouldn't be for long. A rusty knife behind your balls is about all you can look forward to. So do your stuff. Sit here and drink your coffee, and keep your head. There's three of them, but one will stay in the car. When you see them walk into the garden, attract their attention like we told you. Ask the waiter for the toilet. *La toilette, s'il vous plaît.* Get it?"

Lysol guided him to a table convenient to the plan. "This will do, sit here."

"I'm frightened, Lysol. We are in a trap here." Shaw's voice was almost inaudible, quavering like a child's.

"Don't be damned stupid. We are the trap. Pull yourself together and do it!" Lysol's mouth was against his ear. The tightened grip of his hand hurt Shaw's arm. "You will be in my sight all the way to the toilet. For Christ's sake, don't look around for me."

Lysol pushed a couple of ten-franc coins into Shaw's shaking hand. "Relax, you'll do all right. Order the coffee, they'll be here any minute."

With that he walked away toward a drinks table across the garden. He hoped Baring was in position, as he casually approached the drinks waiter. He set down the briefcase and in faultless French ordered himself a Chambery with ice. He ignored the waiter's joke about taking a liquid breakfast. He glanced around, mentally clearing his field of fire of innocent and unsuspecting civilians; the scene struck him as if it were an Impressionist painting. A fat well-kept man sat drinking champagne with a beautiful blonde girl young enough to be his daughter, but damned well wasn't. A couple of children with a nanny were making play of their fizzy drinks and at a nearby table an elderly couple, impeccably dressed, were chatting courteously. It was an idyllic scene.

The two heavies arrived. They didn't fit at all. Menace transmitted from them like loud music. With dark swarthy faces and thin groomed mustaches, they looked like twins walking on the set of an old movie. Well dressed, one in a three-piece blue suit without a tie and flash shoes. The other more casual in a silk polo neck pullover and light worsted trousers, his shoes less ambitious. Lysol summed up their mentality by the gold extras flashing on necks and wrists. Stopping by the entrance, they took in the surroundings. Shaw was being served his coffee. For Christ's sake wait, Shaw. Wait for the waiter to leave so you have to call him back.

After a pause that seemed too long, Shaw did so. His impossible French rang out across the tables. He then got up and followed the waiter's pointing finger. The waiter was now approaching to welcome the two arriving customers. He was unceremoniously shoved aside by the one in the suit. *"Merde!"* The word escaped his mouth as his tray and its contents clattered to the ground.

The two men fell in behind Shaw as he entered the men's toilet. Counting off the seconds, Lysol followed them in. Fuck, I hope Nick's got this right. His words were to himself.

Rounding the door of the toilet, Lysol met the backs of the two men. One held high his hand in a strike position. A long stiletto knife left no doubt about his intent. They were crowding Shaw against the far wall. His mouth was wide open, trying to cry out. Turning to the sound of his entry, they got in each other's way. The rapid action of Lysol's right arm surprised them. The snub-nosed MP5 appearing out of the briefcase, now sliding along the wet-smelling floor, froze them completely. The only sound for a split second was the cocking action of the weapon, completed automatically by the lever release attached to the case. Death was milliseconds away. Lysol's eyes were fixed on them, his trigger finger already had the order to fire.

Baring crashed out of the last cubicle and drove the double-edged blade into the throat of the suited gangster. The man's hand that had been closing around the gun under his arm stiffened. His other hand went up to try and stem the wild fountain of blood gushing out from his neck. His terrified expression reflected in the old mirror had suddenly disappeared behind an artistic splash of crimson. His scream arrived as a ghastly gurgling sound. Baring didn't break his momentum. In one stride he was past the falling man and dragging the head in the polo neck backward in a viselike grip. This time his knife hand swung around the target and plunged deep and upward into the rib cage. The reverse stabbing movement was practiced and efficiently done. Death was instantaneous.

"Get him out of here now!" His muffled shout to Lysol wasn't needed. The MP5 was back in the case and Lysol had moved by him to gather up Shaw. The eyes of the locksmith were screwed up tight. He couldn't take all this. Baring was wrenching the dead man's stiletto from his hand. He pushed it firmly into the small entry wound his own knife had just left. Turning his attention to the kicking body in the suit, now jammed between two urinals, he took the cheese wire garotte from his pocket and looped it over the man's head. He pulled it tight, the wire slicing into the gaping cut opened by his blade seconds before. The job was done. Quickly and coolly, he washed his hands and knife under the tap and stepped past the bodies to the door. The toilet looked like an abattoir.

Exiting into the garden he tried to move as normally as possible. He could see Lysol passing Shaw off as unwell in sign language to the waiter. He didn't care, still sulking from the rude treatment suffered at the hands of those two pigs taking a piss in the gents. They wouldn't get any service from him when they showed.

Catching up, Baring indicated the black Renault parked along the road. It was between them and the BMW. The driver sat at the wheel, conspicuous in dark sunglasses.

"You go ahead with Shaw. Walk on past the driver." Baring was talking in clipped urgent sentences. Lysol did not hesitate or question.

As they passed the Renault, the driver sat up with recognition and reached into his jacket. Baring from a crouched stride wrenched open the passenger door behind him. Both arms traveled in a sweeping arc over the driver's head. The garotte, identical to the one wrapped in the blood of his friend, gathered his neck like a paper doll's. Baring gripped the small wooden toggles at each end of the cheese wire firmly between his fingers, anchoring his forearms against the rear of the driver's seat. The man's shoes were now climbing the inside of the windshield, kicking in the instrument panel and breaking the steering wheel—the last massive strength found to fight death. It wasn't enough. The hands now tearing out the roof lining fell away. Baring tied off the garotte around the headrest and got out. Closing the door he walked away at a normal pace. To an onlooker, the driver could have been sleeping off the night before. He was, in a sense.

Baring peeled off his light gloves as he reached the BMW and dropped them into the diving bag behind the driver's seat. He reversed the car out of the driveway and drove slowly back along the way they had come. A few yards away some boys and girls were fooling in fun on a narrow stone jetty, much to the annoyance of an old fisherman fixing his hooks. All were oblivious to the carnage close by.

"I can't say I'll cherish fond memories of the Hotel L'Abbaye." Lysol spoke as Baring took them toward the main Geneva road. A feeling of tiredness was hanging between the two men. They both recognized it and resisted its temptations. Succumbing to post-combat fatigue, as the adrenaline drained away, got you killed.

"Well, that would be unfair on yourself, Lysol. The owner of that little urinal and the establishment it is attached to has made L'Abbaye one of the finest hotels and restaurants in France. The plush house next door? That's another one. The Au Père Bise has a reputation for being one of the greatest restaurants and hotels in the country. The French do things in style. Two great restaurants within a hundred yards of each other. Perhaps we'll taste them both when this caper is over."

Shaw in the backseat was shaking with suppressed hysteria. "You're a terrible man," he said, "terrible, frightful.

You kill two men in cold blood—and those back in the tunnel—and here you are, talking calmly about restaurants. Human life just means nothing to you. To either of you."

Lysol started to answer the allegation. Baring stopped him with a hard look and turned to Shaw. It was pointless explaining the method in his violence and why the killings had been dressed to simulate a fatal gang argument. "They knew the rules. We played them better and they lost. You had better hope that continues, Mr. Shaw." The look on Baring's face signaled the subject firmly closed.

They drove quietly back to the town of Annecy and onto the autoroute leading to Geneva, sixty kilometers away. Baring drove, preoccupied with himself. Shaw sat huddled alone in the back, chewing at his knuckles like a small child. The scene they had left would not leave him. Lysol sat back and enjoyed the view as the car swept down the long curving road. He felt good, relaxed and yet superbly taut. The wave of tiredness had gone and now he was like a sprinter back on the starting blocks. He was a million miles away from London and the city where egos needed constant stroking and greed reigned supreme. This was real adventure, on-the-line living—like the old SAS days.

Baring drew up at the border post. The French gendarmerie had waved them on through a few yards back, but the Swiss official had other ideas. The stomach in the gray uniform filled the driver's window. The outstretched hand had come down from the salute and waited for their passports. A head appeared and threw a keen if cursory look at the other two occupants.

"Monsieur, *s'il vous plaît.* Would you step out of the car, please." The border guard stepped back, opening the door for Baring as he did so. Lysol watched tensely as he led Baring to the cubicle in the middle of the road. Shit! They're onto us. Shaw gave a muffled whimper in the back. "Stay calm, Shaw, stay calm." Lysol wondered if it wasn't himself that his voice meant to calm.

Baring was strolling back to the car. He got in and dropped the passports onto Lysol's lap. Bending forward he stuck a white label with a green cross on it to the inside windscreen.

"That little beauty cost thirty Swiss francs and we are on our way."

"You bribed the Swiss with thirty francs? Impossible." Lysol spoke with disbelief.

"Motorway tax, Lysol, motorway tax. The man wanted paying for the privilege of putting our rubber on his tarmac."

The laughter in the car as they drove into Switzerland was filled with relief. Following the signs for Lausanne, Baring guided them out of Geneva and onto the autoroute running along the northern edge of the lake. The lakeside city looked serene under the clear blue sky. The towering water spout easily visible as they left the city. Fifteen kilometers beyond Geneva, Baring pulled off the busy autoroute to the town of Nyon.

"We're in good time now," he said. "Let's stop for an early lunch at the Hotel du Lac. It's a nice old hotel alongside the lake with excellent *pêche du lac*."

It was an ancient town with narrow streets and a grim castle on a height above the town. They parked opposite the hotel with its glass-fronted dining room overlooking the sparkling lake.

Baring said, "Hey, you take our friend inside and settle him down, get us a table by the lakeside window. The view and food will do him good. I've got a phone call to make." He answered the questioning look on Lysol's face by adding, "Just to let Flood know we're on our way."

He dialed a number in Canton Fribourg. When it answered, he said quietly, "It's Nick. Just stopping for lunch the other side of the lake."

He heard the even voice say calmly, "All okay?"

"Sure. Couple of local difficulties—but no major problems. Tell you all when we meet. Give us two hours from now."

"Nice timing," said the voice. "I can hear the chopper outside. That'll be our other friends. Have a good lunch—this one's on me."

7

And, as the Cock crew, those who stood before
The Tavern shouted—"Open then the Door!
You know how little while we have to stay,
And, once departed, may return no more."

Bob Yardley tried to look patient and even feel patient, but inside a mounting irritation was turning into suppressed anger. He and Rodel had sat well apart on the flight to Geneva and the clatter of the helicopter that had whisked them from Geneva airport to a landing pad up in the mountains was not conducive to a conversation. Now here they were, walking into a large wooden chalet with a steep-sloping roof—and he hadn't an idea what the hell it was all about and what the hell was going on. An experienced leader himself, he hated the thought of being a puppet on someone else's string, dancing to an unheard tune. He was about to make a sharp comment to Rodel when the front door swung open—and there stood Flood.

He saw a man of medium height, fair-haired and with the most penetrating blue eyes. He wore a short-sleeved open-neck shirt and a pair of Levi's. His forearms were broad with a glint of blond hairs and the legs were solid muscle and bone. Yardley knew the physical type well—the compact fighter who could kill a bigger man in two blows.

Flood said, "Hi, Roger," and held out his hand. He turned

and said, "You must be Bob Yardley. Welcome, Bob. I've heard a bit about you. Come on in."

He led the way through the hall into a long room with rugs on the polished wood floors and half a dozen easy chairs scattered around with low tables alongside. "I rustled up some beer and sandwiches when I heard the chopper circling. We'll dine early tonight. Nick and Lysol and their babe in arms will be here in an hour or so. Miller and Morton should turn up tomorrow and the twins in a day or two."

Yardley said, "With respect, I feel like a novice in a brothel. What the hell's going on?"

"So you haven't briefed him yet, Roger?"

"Not yet," Rodel said. "It seemed best to wait till we made it here."

"Okay, let's eat and have a beer or two. Then we get the well-known Rodel lecture. If it's any consolation, Bob, no one else on the team, even including Nick, knows the project yet. So you're literally the first to hear."

They drank the light Swiss Cardinale beer in earthenware steins and ate some BLT sandwiches. The conversation would have seemed desultory to an outsider but Yardley sensed Flood's cleverness in casually raising Special Forces topics, making him feel at home and drawing a bond between them that excluded the desk man, Rodel. At last, Flood said, "Okay, Roger, the floor's yours. But keep it tight—Nick and Co.'ll be arriving in under an hour."

Rodel lit a long Havana cigar, drew deeply and expelled a plume of blue aromatic smoke. You could tell he liked to be center stage with the audience looking to him.

He said, "Bob, you did a hell of a job back there in London. Springing Shaw was classy—and no one got hurt. It was an ace operation."

"You can thank Mike Murphy for that," Yardley said. "He put the team together and worked out most of the plan."

"Sure—and good of you to give him the credit. By the way, my London contacts have lost touch with Murphy. Seems to have gone to ground in a big way. But that was that—really just phase one of the big plan. Before we get on to that, I have to give you a history lecture. So sit tight.

"We have to go back to before World War Two," he began, drawing on his cigar until it glowed. "Reza Shah had been an officer in the Turkish cavalry when he set up a coup, took over the throne of Persia and declared himself to be the

Shah-in-Shah, the true heir to the two-thousand-five-hundred-year-old Peacock Throne, which was a load of bull, as indeed was the Throne itself. At first, the Brits, who had a major interest in Persia because of the Anglo-Iranian Oil Company, backed Reza Shah because he had brought a stable if despotic rule to the turbulent country and had savagely put down the warring nomadic tribes, the Qashgai and the Bakhtiari, whose travels took them too close to the oil wells in southern Persia.

"But after Britain declared war on Hitler in 1939, the Shah had become very pro-German. If the Wehrmacht were to invade neutral Turkey, seize the oil fields at Mosul and Kirkuk in northern Iraq and then strike into Persia, backed up by a ruler friendly to them, they could take the Persian Gulf and the oil fields in the south, depriving Britain of a lifeline and cutting the essential sea routes to India and the Far East. So in 1941 British troops entered Persia, deposed Reza Shah, who was sent into exile in Madagascar, where he later died, and put his young son on the throne as a puppet ruler under close military and political supervision.

"The young Shah never forgave the Brits for what he held to be their insulting behavior. So, a few years after the war, the Shah encouraged his prime minister, Mossadeq, to nationalize the oil industry and push the Britons out, except for a few advisers. With all that revenue pouring in, he turned to the Americans for support—and to provide tanks, guns and aircraft to modernize his forces. If the silly bugger had spent half the dough on helping his poor bloody civilians, he'd probably be there still—but he had to put on a show.

"He didn't have a drop of royal blood in his veins," Rodel went on, "but he made great play with the Pahlavi dynasty. He even divorced his first wife and later his real love, Soraya, the daughter of a Bakhtiari chieftain, because neither bore him a son. His third wife, Farah, did. The centerpiece, the symbol, of the dynasty was the Peacock Throne.

"That was also a fake, like the rest of the dynastic setup. The real Peacock Throne had been seized by Nadir Shah from the Red Fort in Delhi in 1739, but had been captured later by the Kurds. The present throne had been constructed from ancient bits and pieces in the nineteenth century. But it was truly priceless, encrusted with over twenty-six thousand precious stones and pearls. It had six cabriole legs and two bejeweled steps to mount it by, and the back had a statue of the dove of peace set at each corner. And everyone in Iran believed it was the real thing.

"The Shah," Rodel continued, "abdicated in January 1979, but in the year before he got out, realizing opinion was turning against him, he did a secret deal with Chubb's of London for a ten-million-dollar contract. It was to build a special safe around the Peacock Throne, down in the basement of the Ghulistan Palace in Tehran, and then construct a fortified vault around the safe. The Shah's brief to Chubb's was that nothing short of a direct hit with an intermediate ballistic missile should be able to penetrate the basement fortress. What he said in effect was 'If I can't sit on the throne much longer, then positively no one else is going to polish his ass on it.' He took the combination codes into exile with him when he abdicated and of course died of cancer not long afterward."

Rodel concluded, "It'll soon be ten years since the Ayatollah and his crowd took over. Have you heard a damn thing about the throne? Or seen any recent pictures? Of course you haven't. Don't you reckon the fundamentalists—if they could have put their cotton-picking hands on it—would have had it on display? As a sign of the old decadent times? Or as a symbol of the shining new regime? Take your pick. Seems the Shah had the last laugh on them. They must be mad as hell."

Yardley said, "It's a great story. *The Washington Post* would pay good money for it. But, as my English friends would say—so bloody what?"

"So this, Bob. You're going to lead a team that steals the Throne for us."

"Christ! So that's why Peter Shaw was snatched from jail."

"Right first time. He was one of Chubb's guys who built the safe in Tehran."

Yardley sat back in his easy chair, took in a deep breath and exhaled it slowly. For a moment he was at a loss for words, his mind reeling and racing to grasp the whole crazy idea. At last he asked lamely, "Why?"

"I'd better answer that one," Rodel said. "There are several possible answers. Some you can guess, some even I don't know. Why don't we just say that, back in the White House, there's an old man who won't be there much longer. An actor needs a good last act. You know, the big gesture, the exit line. Now that the guy in the Kremlin's beginning to play ball, the only evil empire left is Ayatollah-land. Teach them a thing or two, wouldn't it, to steal their damn throne from under their eyes? You with me?"

"You're saying we risk the lives of some good men—mine too, come to think of it—for a caper? That's shit, Rodel."

Flood said quietly, "Let's not push it, Bob. There are other scenarios. I'll give you one. There are three American hostages in Beirut. The French bought their man back and so did the West Germans. Two months' time, there's a presidential election, right? Carter could have won eight years ago if he'd managed to end the U.S. Embassy siege in time. You lift that throne, the U.S. government has one big bargaining chip. Rafsanjani's a guy who knows the power game. Word of our little 'caper' gets out and he'll be drummed out of power so fast his head will spin. But, if he puts pressure on the Hizbollah to release the Beirut hostages, he gets the throne back, no questions asked or answered. And George Bush walks into the White House come November. Whatever the motive, your government wants that throne."

"You must both be out of your minds," Yardley said. "Take a team into Tehran of all places and steal this priceless throne? It's sheer madness. What's the plan—parachute down onto the palace and ask a few thousand howling revolutionary guards to back off while we're fiddling with a vault and a safe you say are unbustable? Ah, come on."

Flood said quietly, "Wait on a moment. You haven't heard it all. Of course, it can't be done from outside—but we've got inside help. There's this young woman named Sharqi Zachin . . ."

"God, there's a woman involved now," Yardley began.

Rodel cut in, "Bob, give Flood a chance. Let him tell it all—okay?"

Yardley nodded. He was angry with himself for acting like a schoolboy.

Flood said, "She's no ordinary woman. In her early thirties, a widow, the daughter of a wealthy Iranian Jew, married to another young Jew. In the purges after the Ayatollah took over, the revolutionary guards chopped the two men. She was in disgrace for a while but she pretended to be in sympathy with the regime—and they found they needed her."

He saw Yardley's questioning look and went on, "Yeah, she's a trained art expert. She was educated at a Swiss boarding school—that was in the Shah's day—and then worked at Christie's in Geneva and did a spell at their Bond Street office before she went back to Tehran to get married. She speaks English, French and German fluently, as well of course as Farsi. She hates everything about the Khomeini regime—naturally—but she knew she had to act a role if she wasn't to be stuck in Tehran the rest of her life. So a year or two back she pretended to convert to Islam. Recently, the mullahs have made her curator of the art collection at—wait for it—the Ghulistan Palace."

"You see," Rodel chipped in, "we're not just a pair of pretty faces."

Flood continued, "Seems she sold them the idea that it was their divine duty to restore Persia's great heritage. So they turned the palace into a people's museum. It's full of priceless tapestries, Bokhara and Isfahan rugs, those wonderful delicate paintings on ivory and bone. There are so many rugs, they overlap on the floors like tiles. And of course Sharqi has to make trips abroad periodically, whenever Persian *objets d'art* come up for sale at the auction rooms.

"Now this is the juicy bit. Tehran's over six thousand feet above sea level. So you get stiflingly hot summers and very cold winters. The air conditioning system at the palace was installed forty years back and it hasn't been working properly for quite a while. There's a big risk the valuables will be ruined if nothing's done. Already, some of the ancient parchment books have started cracking and flaking. So Sharqi's been given permission to order a new system from Switzerland—and have it installed in the basement of the palace."

"Is the penny beginning to drop?" asked Rodel.

"Oh, sure," Yardley said. "Our team goes in, pretending to be Swiss engineers. While we're installing the new system, Shaw opens up the safe and, when no one's looking, we take out the throne and beat it. Sounds simple if you say it quickly. To me, it's as full of holes as a Swiss cheese. One—all I know about air conditioning is you turn on a knob and either cold air or hot air comes out. I couldn't fool an expert for five seconds. Two—how do we know this young Persian woman isn't a double agent? If she could turn from a Jew to a Moslem—just like that—why wouldn't she turn another way if it suited her? Three—will Shaw remember enough about the safe after ten years? Four—shall I go on?"

"You've made some good points there, Bob," Flood said. "I reckon we have the answers. Two of the team who will be joining—subject to your approval—are engineers and they've just had a special course on installing air conditioning. As for Sharqi, you can decide for yourself. She'll be arriving here tomorrow. There'll be time to thrash the whole thing out, believe me. The point is—are you willing to take the operation on?"

"Sure, I'm willing. It's a hell of an idea. Tell me some more about this team of yours."

"They're handpicked," Flood said. "I picked 'em. First, there's Nick Baring. Ex-Rhodesian SAS and Selous Scouts. He's tops—you'll meet him any minute now. Then there's your friend Lysol coming with him and Shaw. Next, Jacques and Claude Moulins, two Belgian twins, ex-Foreign Legion. A couple of hard nuts. They're the trained engineers I just mentioned. They'll be here tomorrow. There's an ex-Marine named Miller—he served with the Special Boat Squadron in the Falklands. A good guy who speaks Farsi. He was seconded to help train the Iranian Marines in the last days of the Shah—knows Tehran and most of the country intimately. And to make up the team, we've borrowed a sergeant major from the SAS. Name of Morton."

"Big fellow? With wonderful tattoos on his upper arms?" Yardley asked.

"That's Archie Morton, right enough. You know him?"

"Sure. He was on attachment at Bragg two, three years back. A real nice guy—and handled himself well."

"Well, the others are on a par with Archie. But don't take my word for it. We have a week in hand for some training in the mountains. Anyone you reckon's not up to it, physically or mentally, you give the nod—and he's out. Like that. As of now, you're the leader. Hey, there's a car outside. Sounds like one of those hot rods Nick's always renting."

This guy's got ears like a bat's, Yardley thought. At first he could hear nothing and then he just caught the sound of the engine and a faint laugh that sounded like Lysol's high-pitched cackle.

"Okay," said Rodel, stubbing out the remains of his cigar, "let's break it up, shall we? Bob has enough to think about, and Flood, my boy, if this dump of yours has a bathroom, I could do with a shower before we dine."

"How do you like your shower? We've two varieties for hard men like you, Roger. Cold—or icy."

The chalet was on a steep green slope half a mile above the village of Château d'Oex. There was another smaller wooden chalet at right angles alongside and a driveway that led through a gate to the rough lane that jinked down to the village. After a brief meeting with Baring, who impressed him at first sight, and a joke with Lysol, Yardley excused himself, saying he needed to stretch his legs and clear his head. He decided to walk down the hill, take a look at the main street and generally get his bearings before returning up the green slopes to his temporary home.

And he did need the rhythmical exercise and a chance to think on his own. The last few days had been spent sitting at the telephone in the small rented office in Mayfair or sitting in aircraft or just sitting. London seemed like a generation ago and a distant country. And yet it was not twelve hours since he had checked out of the Lansdowne Club. General Bradford's briefing back in Maine had been crazy enough—but this new development was right off the wall. So there were signs in the breeze that the Iraq/Iran war was edging toward an uneasy peace and maybe the climate in Tehran would become less hostile to the "foreign devils." But what would happen back in peaceful England if a bunch of outsiders went to the Tower of London and tried to walk away with the Crown Jewels? It would be ten years' jail at the least. Try the equivalent in Tehran and you could easily end up with your body in one place and your head on a spike somewhere quite else.

And it all rested on two people. One a young unknown woman and the other Peter Shaw. Judging from the glimpse he had just had of the "hostage," Shaw was on the brink of a nervous breakdown. Great asset he'd be if his fingers shook too much to tackle those intricate lock mechanisms. Maybe some rest and recreation would steady Shaw up, but he'd need to have several long quiet sessions with the man to see what made him tick. When he turned crook, he'd carried out several daring burglaries by all accounts—but you didn't aim to go tiger-hunting with a man unless you knew he wouldn't curl up when the first low growl was heard.

And the same went for this Sharqi girl—in spades. Flood was an expert—Yardley knew that from the man's reputation and the impression he'd already made. You didn't survive in that shadowy world of intelligence and special missions without being extra tough and cool. Flood reckoned she was okay—and that was a good start. But it wouldn't be Flood's head adorning that spike on a wall in Tehran if the mission went terribly wrong. So when Ms. Sharqi turned up, by God, she'd go under the microscope.

His long loping stride had brought him down to the main street of Château d'Oex and he walked the length of it, past the railway bridge and up the shopping area to where the street petered out in a huddle of private houses and chalets for visitors. It was early September in that lull between the summer vacation season and the winter sports that would not begin for another three months, but already the more optimistic shops had installed après-ski clothes in their windows. The coffee shops were nearly empty but there were half-hearted posters up for *Glühwein* and fondues.

He circled round and started back up the long slope toward the chalet in the upland fields. He was feeling strangely irresolute. Part of him yearned to be back at Fort Bragg, set in a nice tidy schedule he knew and understood. That was one thing about the Army; it ran on well-oiled grooves. You followed orders and passed on the orders and everyone saluted someone who was senior and stood to attention at the right moment—and it worked. And here he was—in a strange country, about to go to an even stranger one, and there was no set drill and the operation was a mad one . . . and, he had to admit to himself, he was quite excited at the prospect.

That night, they had a relaxed dinner. Nick Baring sat back like a lazy jungle cat, saying little but sipping a glass of malt scotch with a stein of beer as a chaser. Lysol was in his element, holding the floor as he repeated to anyone who would listen a highly colored version of their journey from Marseilles. It began to sound as if the two of them had seen off a panzer division back in the tunnel—and, as for Annecy, it had been "a one-man wave of destruction." Even Shaw, morose and silent, gave a wan smile as the Honorable Rupert warmed up to his saga. Rodel was clearly enjoying himself. For a desk man, the ultimate pleasure was to rub shoulders with genuine hard men. Rodel was due off early next morning, back to Paris and a further stint of driving his desk, but he would long remember the camaraderie of this night.

Without appearing to, Bob Yardley was all the time trying to assess Flood, discover what made him tick under the cool exterior. When the conversation paused, he said, "One point interests me. Why this place?"

Flood replied, "I could give you one answer—why not? It's reasonably central and quiet. Visitors come and go, they rent chalets for a week, two weeks, and then they disappear. Let's say it's nicely anonymous."

"Is that the only reason?"

"Frankly, no. There are half a dozen or more places like this in Switzerland that'd do equally well. No, for me there's a sentimental attachment. David Niven used to live here in the winter months—he had a chalet a couple of hundred yards away across the fields. He needed some advice on a book he was going to write and a friend introduced me. And then he fell ill. Motoneuron disease—a bit like Parkinson's but more deadly. David knew he had a year or two at the most. He was bloody brave. He could have sat out the war in Hollywood making a fortune but he gave it all up, came back to England and joined Number 4 Commando under Lovat, and ended up with GHQ Phantom. He had a damn good war. We used to sit and talk—toward the end his vocal cords had gone, so I did most of the talking—about his war and my wars and men in action. He liked that. He was a friend—I miss him."

There was a silence. A burnt-out log crashed into the grate around the open fire and the blaze lit up the faces of the half-circle of men. Yardley realized in his heart that Flood's short speech had stilled any qualms he might yet have. He was confident now. He'd lead that team into Tehran and, by Christ, they'd come out with the Peacock Throne.

The Home Secretary sat at the head of the table in his Whitehall office. He was in an icy mood. On his right was the Commissioner of the Metropolitan Police, splendid in his dark blue uniform and silver badges. On his left the head of MI5, gray-haired, gray-suited, wearing an Old Etonian tie. A couple of senior civil servants sat farther down the table and in front of a small desk in one corner sat the Home Secretary's PPS, taking notes.

"Gentlemen," the Home Secretary began—he made the word sound like an insult—"let us start from what we know. A long-term prisoner named Shaw, a safe breaker, you say, decides he wants a change of air from Wormwood Scrubs and coolly walks out of that impregnable prison. No one tries to stop him—indeed, the gate guards help him on his way. And now he's disappeared into thin air. That was three days ago and there's not a trace of him. The Press and TV have made a meal of it and the government is made a laughing-stock—yet again. You can thank God, each one of you, that Parliament is still on vacation. If I'd had to answer Opposition questions in the House, your heads would have rolled by now—and mine, too. This is a damnable business. Now what do you have to say?"

One of the senior civil servants raised a hand. "Yes, Cruttenden?" the Home Secretary said.

"Home Secretary, I have a report from the prison governor. It arrived just before you called this meeting. He says that four nights ago Shaw was suddenly taken ill in his cell. It seemed genuine—like a heart attack or the onset of a stroke. Apparently the prisoner was—is—a very nervous type, intense, didn't fit in well with prison routine."

"I want the facts, not his medical history."

"My apologies, Home Secretary. He was transferred that night to the hospital wing of the Scrubs. Next morning his condition had worsened and the ward medical orderly had to fetch some oxygen. A warder who happened to be there looking after another sick prisoner on remand volunteered to call an ambulance from Hammersmith Hospital, a few hundred yards away. The ambulance arrived and Shaw was taken under guard to the hospital. While the Wormwood Scrubs warder was reporting in at reception, the ambulance staff wheeled the prisoner off to Casualty. None of the three ever arrived there."

"And the warder who made the phone call and *his* prisoner. Have they been questioned?"

"They disappeared."

The Home Secretary grimaced and turned his hands palms upward. "That ambulance—was it kosher? From the hospital allotment?"

"'Fraid not, sir. The Commissioner here had them checked out. All accounted for."

The man from MI5 raised a finger. "May I say a word, Home Secretary? Over a dozen years ago, there was a special inquiry into the security of Her Majesty's maximum-security prisons. Lord Mountbatten ran it. The SAS was brought in to test the defenses, to see whether they could get in and out again without being detected. I'm afraid to say they did—with ease. As a result, prison security was greatly improved—or so we thought."

"History, Kershaw, history. What has that to do with our problem?"

"This, Home Secretary. Wormwood Scrubs was one of five prisons infiltrated by the SAS using a not dissimilar strategy."

"You're not trying to tell me that Hereford is still at it?"

"Not Hereford, Home Secretary. But it could have been organized by *ex*-troopers from Hereford. The Commissioner of Police and I have been following this line of inquiry. He can tell you more."

"What have you got, Commissioner?" demanded the man at the head of the table.

"So far only pointers, sir, more than hard facts. But there's a shape to them—I feel it. There were twenty SAS men originally involved—five teams each of four men. We've checked them out with Hereford and London Group HQ—and further, rather fruitless inquiries were made at the Duke of York's Barracks. Two died subsequently on active service, three emigrated to Australia or Canada, one got religion and four are gainfully employed as VIP bodyguards abroad. Each of those four can be discounted. One of the others is a permanent invalid—emphysema—and another farms a croft in the north of Scotland. He was there three days ago. So that's eight—more than enough to pull this caper."

"It's a bit vague," the Home Secretary commented.

"There's more to come, sir. One of the eight, Sergeant Michael Murphy, has form. He was sent down for grievous bodily harm—*in Wormwood Scrubs,* if you please. He's been doing odd jobs since he came out, as a nightclub bouncer or driving for a known underworld figure. The Regiment don't want to know these men who go off the rails. Yesterday, his body and that of a known prostitute were found in a council flat near Tower Bridge—in suspicious circumstances, presumed murder. He'd put up a hell of a fight. There was blood all over the place including the ceiling."

"Spare me such detail. So you think the springing of Shaw was a gangland business?"

"It could be, Home Secretary, and, again, it might not. You see, in conjunction with our friend here from MI5, the Special Branch has been keeping tabs on Murphy since he came out. In the last few weeks he was seen a few times with an American Special Forces major named Yardley."

"Oh God, don't tell me the Yanks are involved! That means we'll have to call in the Foreign Office—and you know how the FO can talk. Who is this Yardley?"

"He appears to be an upright, all-American boy, sir. Mr. Kershaw checked him out with his Pentagon friends—they're rather proud of him. We have not alerted our CIA friends in Grosvenor Square to the problem as yet. He has a fine record in the U.S. Special Forces, won the Congressional Medal for exceptional bravery, had a spot of bother recently with his heart and is on six months' sick leave. We hear he's writing a book about irregular warfare and has a good contract with a well-known New York publisher. He sounds the right thing."

"Well?"

"He's been staying at the Lansdowne Club. Off Berkeley Square. He checked out yesterday. Left no forwarding address."

The Home Secretary said, "He could have flown straight back to the States. And interviewing this Murphy could have been part of his research."

"We've checked all the passenger lists of flights out of Heathrow and Gatwick bound for the USA. He wasn't booked on any one of them. And the porter from the Lansdowne Club who helped him out with his bags heard him tell the cab-driver to go to Terminal 2 at Heathrow. Continental flights, sir."

"Could have flown to Frankfurt. Lots of U.S. troops there to interview. Or to connect with a U.S. Air Force Military Air Transport flight home."

"He could have, sir. But there's another point. Naturally, once we knew Shaw had skipped, we alerted all the ports and the airports to keep a close watch, and got the Airports Authority to give us a printout of all charter and private flights out of Britain. I have a whole team out—with the help of local police forces—questioning every single general aviation pilot who filed a foreign-going flight plan in the seventy-two hours since Shaw broke jail. I have the list here, sir"—he held up a sheet of paper from his open file—"and there's one very interesting name on it. John McDermid—an ex–Royal Navy Special Forces pilot. He flies charters mainly from East Midlands Airport. He took a passenger—the Honorable Rupert Lycett-Smythe—to Marseilles the day after the break. He left him there and flew back same day to East Midlands."

"And what's so special about that?"

"Lycett-Smythe has been an officer in the SAS. He served with Murphy."

"You don't say? Could be very interesting. On the other hand, it could all be a coincidence. I hear it's a tight little world, that Special Forces crowd. After all, if you're going to hire a private plane, you might as well keep it in the family. And, as for this Lycett-Smythe knowing Murphy in the SAS, that doesn't make him suspect. God, I was at Eton with some of the biggest thugs in Christendom—including our secret friend here"—he jerked a thumb across the table—"but that, I hope, doesn't make me one! Have your boys given this McDermid the heavy pressure?"

"Oh yes, sir. The works. But he's a cool one, they tell me. His flight plan is all in order, he flew straight to Marseilles and back, he was in touch with air traffic control at all the right times. He's been very civil and helpful, they say, but he's no virgin who's going to burst into tears because some copper asks him questions."

"You sure it really was Lycett-what's-his-name who was his passenger?"

"Afraid so, sir. Our Special Branch man at East Midlands remembers him and the Marseilles police and Interpol have been most helpful. He disembarked at Marseilles Airport and showed his passport at immigration. It was him all right."

"Where is he now?"

"We've lost touch, Home Secretary. He told the pilot he had a day's business in Marseilles and was then going to take a break with some friends along the Riviera. In Cannes, the pilot thought."

"And what's his business?"

"He works for the family merchant bank, sir. He has a lot of contacts. His grandfather was a rich financier—made a fortune in property and banking. Bought himself a peerage."

"Oh, one of those." All of them sitting around the table knew that the Home Secretary's family had lived in the same crumbling Palladian mansion for over two hundred years. "No doubt Lycett-Smythe *père* was plain Smith before he made his packet. So where does all that leave us? Sum up for me, Kershaw."

"We think it could be one of two quite separate capers, Home Secretary. Either way, there has to be a crooked warder inside Wormwood Scrubs and the governor is concentrating on that. But, as you know, sir, there's been a lot of trouble just lately with HM Prison Service, union grievances, rumors of strikes. The governor can't ride roughshod over his men—but he is having a detailed investigation."

"Someone must have alerted that warder to get Shaw out of his cell and into the hospital wing. Is he working on that?"

"Oh yes, sir. But first he's got to identify the warder."

"They can't all be crooks guarding the other crooks! So what are your two alternatives?"

"The simple one is this, sir. Before he took to crime, Shaw was one of the most highly trained safe men at Chubb's. He probably knows more about safes than any other three men put together. One of the underworld leaders could be planning a really big heist somewhere and has need of Shaw. So he arranged to spring him."

"Any thoughts on that, Commissioner?" the Home Secretary asked.

"It's feasible, sir. My Serious Crimes Squad has been down on the streets shaking all its contacts around London and the Midlands but there's been nothing on the grapevine so far. It's early days, of course."

"It's never early days, Commissioner. It's too damned late already! Three days've gone by—and here we are, sitting in a row guessing. It's just not good enough."

There was a threatening silence. None of the men sitting down the table from the Home Secretary glanced in his direction. They sat looking down at the papers in front of them.

At last, the Home Secretary said, "And what's the alternative plan?"

The man from MI5 said, "It's a long shot, sir, but we do just wonder whether our friends in the CIA aren't playing games."

The Home Secretary groaned and cast his eyes to the ceiling. "Oh no, not that!"

"Well, it could help to explain Major Yardley, sir. According to the SAS, twice—at Hereford and the Duke of York's—he asked after Murphy. And now Murphy's dead."

"You're not trying to hint that was an SAS job, are you?"

"Good heavens, no, sir! But we know Yardley's worked closely with the National Security Council in Washington. And he disappeared neatly the day after the springing. SAS circles had some vague suspicion—apparently, Colonel McAlister, who used to command the squadron at Hereford, gave him a gentle warning a few weeks back. And the Americans have been very active in London recently, trying to set up an embassy defection with our people."

"We won't go into that here, Kershaw." It was a rebuke, all the more because it was delivered in a soft voice.

"Of course, sir, I apologize. The other interesting fact—or coincidence—is that the last job Shaw pulled before his arrest was at the U.S. Ambassador's private residence in Regent's Park."

"Was it now? The plot is beginning to thicken. So you think—*maybe*—this Major Yardley could have been freelancing for the CIA, comes to the UK, already has a lot of contacts with the SAS, puts together a team from ex-members, including our friend Murphy, springs Shaw and then disappears. Something on those lines, eh?"

"Something like that, sir."

"So why does Murphy get bumped off—along with some prostitute? Sounds a bit messy. Not the sort of thing you'd expect—even from a Yank officer."

"We've discovered, Home Secretary, Murphy was engaged as driver and bodyguard to a gang leader, Ronnie Hawkins. It could be some internal quarrel. Perhaps Hawkins ran the prostitute and Murphy was trying to muscle in on the racket."

"Or we're back where we started, and the springing of Shaw was a gang enterprise. At least, we don't have to reckon with the KGB, as when George Blake got sprung by that mad Irishman, Sean Bourke—also from the Scrubs, I'd remind you. Commissioner, when will your men have finished questioning those eight ex-SAS types?"

"We'll need another few days, Home Secretary." He saw the frown and quickly added, "Some of them genuinely are on holiday. It is late August, after all. So far, we've checked out five of them."

"Anything interesting emerged?"

"Two of them, named Tritt and Parker, are still very close friends. They often go racing together. They were at Goodwood the day of the escape and at Sandown Park the following day."

"Any proof of that?"

"One of them—Tritt—had kept some of his Tote tickets. The other had a badge into the Silver Ring at Sandown, sir."

"That sounds suspicious in itself! Do any of you ever keep losing tickets on the Tote? Of course, you don't—you throw them away in disgust. And any fool could get hold of a badge for the Silver Ring without ever turning up at the races. I suggest, Commissioner, you put these two men in the frame and keep watching them. See if they start flashing wads of money around, change their lifestyle—heavens, I shouldn't have to tell the experts how to run their show.

"So that's it, gentlemen. I have to say I'm not impressed. Not one bit. We'll meet again within the week—fix the details, will you, Cruttenden? And then I'll want some answers, not sheer conjecture. Luckily, the Press is starting to concentrate on the Gibraltar inquest next month, but you'd better pull the stops out on this one. The SAS has enough problems on its hands. If the Shaw case has anything to do with the SAS—even long retired members—and the Press makes the connection, there'll be hell to pay. For each one of us. Remember that."

The Home Secretary stood up, gave every man in turn a cold stare and then strode out of the room.

By midafternoon next day, the rest of the team had turned up. First to arrive, half an hour after Rodel had driven off to Geneva in a rented car, were the Belgian twins, Jacques and Claude. As soon as he had shaken hands, Yardley knew the type: low-browed, broad-shouldered and squat—the peasant stock that would always endure. Their hands were hard, callused by physical work. The only way he could tell them apart easily was because Jacques smoked Disque Bleu, always with a saliva-stained stub in the corner of his mouth, while Claude was a nonsmoker. Both of them spoke passable English with a heavy accent—and both looked highly competent. If Flood said they had had a crash course in installing air-conditioning equipment, he was prepared to believe it. They looked as if they could take a Crusader tank apart and reassemble it without a shrug. They would be okay.

And he had no qualms either about Archie Morton, who had recognized him at once and given him a bear-hug in greeting. He knew from attachments to the SAS that virtually the hardest rank to attain was that of sergeant major. If you had been at Eton and served with the Guards, like dear old Lysol, you still had to pass the most stringent tests but there was that invisible thing the Brits called "the old boy net" to help you on your way. But to enter as a squaddie and make it to the top noncommissioned rank, as Archie Morton had done, meant you were something special indeed. That put a firm tick against his name.

Miller was new to him, although Flood had given him a rundown on Miller over breakfast that morning. He had done well in the Falklands campaign, winning a Military Medal for a special operations on the Argentinian mainland. He had also done an attachment with the U.S. SEAL teams in training in the Gulf of Mexico. Miller, it seemed, spoke Farsi fluently but with an accent that showed he was not a native of Tehran. But, as Flood had said, he might well pass as a southerner from Bandar Abbas. Since the Ayatollah had taken over, Iranians did not travel far from their hometowns and so were more likely to accept a strange accent as coming from a distant part of the country. On first sight, Miller seemed to be the right kind of guy for the job—quiet, composed, no bullshit or loud attempts to impress. All the same, Yardley decided to watch him closely over the next few days. For his own sake and that of the others, he had to make absolutely sure that each and every one would stand up when the pressure came on.

Late that afternoon, Flood took him to one side and said, "Bob, we've got a dinner date tonight."

"Yeah?"

"Yes. In Évian-les-Bains. With young Sharqi."

"I thought you said she was coming here?"

"Well, here or hereabouts. It could be awkward if she's spotted in a small place like this. She's staying in Geneva tonight, and has business in Lausanne today—and Évian's only a short hop away, on the French side of the lake."

Yardley said, "I take it we're not dressing up?"

"God, no. A tie and a jacket is all you need. The season's almost over and we're meeting at a quiet little restaurant I know alongside the lake. Half past six do you?"

"Fine. What about the others?"

"I've got some extra beer and hamburgers in for them. They can have a quiet booze-up while we're working."

Yardley showered and changed and was waiting down in the long living room when he heard the throaty rumble of a high-powered car on the driveway outside. It was a silver-gray Porsche Carrera with Flood at the wheel. He went out and slipped into the passenger seat alongside. Flood nosed the car into the laneway and ambled down to the main street, easing in and out of the traffic at no more than walking speed. But once clear of the village they surged ahead, speeding down the metaled valley road. The Porsche was still in third gear and passing 130 kph when the power came off, a racing change down into second gear and a flick of the wheel had it through a sharp left turn. They were now accelerating hard up the side of the valley toward the Col des Mosses. Yardley realized that he was being driven by a master; it was high precision at high speed.

"The valley road runs on down to Gruyère and Bulle. Our business isn't cheese so we'll take the faster, more interesting route." Flood was smiling. "Interesting" meant from the driver's point of view.

Yardley relaxed and watched the shadows lengthen on this side of the mountains and the tops of the peaks reflect a beautiful shade of orange from the setting sun on the western side. Flood was taking quiet delight from the twisting, climbing road up to the pass. He was completely at home speeding between a rock face towering above his left shoulder and the sheer drop on Yardley's side. They were soon through the Col and descending the tortuous route down to the town of Aigle, out of sight on a valley floor far below. The bottomless gorge was now on Flood's side and the road hugged its edge faithfully. It was a companionable silence. Yardley knew that if Flood had something to say, he would say it, and he for his part needed to gather up his thoughts at the prospect of the meeting ahead. What would she be like? he wondered; and what if, after all, he felt she was untrustworthy?

They had descended and crossed the wide valley floor at the entrance to Canton Valais and followed the road under the brow of the Dents du Midi to the southern shoreline of Lac Leman. Flood had helped Yardley with the geography along the way and they had both marveled at the sight of the sun's fireball sinking below the Jura Mountains way to the northwest; the vast expanse of the lake appearing as a sea coated in clear varnish. The pristine white paddle steamer, its large Swiss flag fluttering at the stern, plowing toward Évian added the final romantic touch.

Évian-les-Bains was shining white in the evening glow when they arrived. The border formalities at the previous village of St.-Gingolph had been nonexistent. Évian provided a popular escape for Swiss wanting a flutter at the Casino tables. France's more liberal gambling laws ensured a regular flow of punters. The grand casino and hotel were white and so were the buildings alongside. The long flight of steps that led up to the great building were also ostentatiously white. It was an artificial town, with flowerbeds neatly arranged and a clean and tidy little park between the main road and the lake. The brushed and scrubbed look to every bush and stone seemed an attempt to mirror the immaculate Swiss on the other side; and yet it felt like a ghost town. The high windows in the spa were blank; only a few cars scuttled furtively along the straight roads. Yardley felt he was watching the opening shots of one of those futuristic French movies—*Last Year at Marienbad,* perhaps.

Flood pulled off up a side street and parked near a small restaurant with red check curtains and, when they entered, red check tablecloths. There were perhaps a dozen tables, and more than half of them were occupied. The waiter greeted Flood with a smile of recognition—he was clearly a welcome, perhaps regular, visitor. They were shown to a quiet corner table, already laid up, Yardley noticed, for three.

"We're quarter of an hour early," Flood said. "I told Sharqi eight o'clock. That's one of my failings. Put me in a fast car and I tend to drive quickly. Let's have a drink while we're waiting. She shouldn't be long."

Yardley ordered a scotch and Flood a *kir royale.* They started to chat about the upcoming inquest in Gibraltar into the shooting by the SAS of three IRA terrorists. Yardley was fascinated to hear something of the inside story and, in particular, how lousy coordination within the Gibraltar police had blown what should have been a neat operation. Still, it had put the small Mediterranean community on the world stage momentarily. The armchair warriors of the British Press had had a field day.

Flood broke off his story, looked up and said, "Ah, here she is. Punctual as ever. Sharqi keeps Swiss time." He rose to greet her. Yardley got to his feet and glanced toward the entrance. He saw a woman with long dark hair standing there. A waiter was relieving her of two large carrier bags with the name "Bon Genie" boldly printed across them, and he was hesitating to take her coat. It was a full-length cloak-type affair with friar's sleeves, made of some expensive-looking red fabric. She was dressed in a fitted plain black dress that hugged her slim curves to just below her knees. The only adornment was a jeweled clasp high above the left breast;

this rode easily with the matching earrings framing her bright face. Even he in his ignorance realized the lady was hung in haute couture. She was looking round the small restaurant and then saw Flood. She smiled and walked over to them. The mixed gaze of diners followed her as she came.

"Don't tell me I'm late," she said, as she leaned across and kissed Flood first on one cheek and then the other. Her smile was infectious and made the introductions easy.

"Of course, you're not. We were early. Sharqi, my love, I would like you to meet Bob Yardley. Bob, this is Sharqi Zachin."

They shook hands. For a moment, he could feel the small palm with the long manicured fingers in his big paw. "It's a pleasure to meet you, Mr. Yardley. Or is it Captain Yardley?"

He was struck by her elegance and charm and it made him feel awkward in forming a reply. Flood cut in, "Major, actually, but just call him Bob, it's easier."

They sat down and she ordered a glass of white wine from the patient waiter. As she enthused to Flood about the shopping she had done in her favorite boutiques in Lausanne and then ridden the small metro down the hill to Port d'Ouchy to catch the steamer across the lake—"Look Flood, look what I have brought you"—Yardley looked at her. Her hair was soft and moved gracefully around her thin neck and shoulders. Hazel-colored eyes under thick dark eyebrows. Her nose was long and straight but fitted with proud cheeks and lips that seemed to form a natural bow. She was slightly sallow but there were becoming touches of pink on her cheeks. He knew little enough about women's makeup, but if the coloring was not natural, it must have been expertly applied. He would not have called her beautiful but she was certainly a striking young woman. She wore a simple gold ring on the third finger of her right hand.

"Bob, please forgive me." Her hand touched his arm. "It is just so long since I have seen Flood." Her happiness was obvious to him.

They ordered their meal—Flood insisting on sharing a bottle of champagne—and fell easily into casual chat. On the drive down, Flood had suggested that the point of the dinner was to break the ice. Yardley needed to get to know Sharqi and, in effect, she needed to get to know him. There was no point in discussing the operation if there was a clash of personalities. Indeed, it would be dangerous to do so. "Let's not forget, Bob," he had said as he negotiated the road above Château d'Oex, "you're putting your neck at risk—but our planning will give you a fighting chance to get out if things go wrong. Not so Sharqi. If the operation screws up, her neck will end up in a mullah's noose. Literally. She has to trust you and you need to trust her."

Sharqi spoke English as if it were her native tongue, even though the slight charming accent would have placed her as neither American nor English. Her family came originally from Poland. When Hitler invaded Poland in 1939, the Russian forces had moved in on the eastern front and had overrun her hometown of Lvov. They had rounded up the defeated Polish troops and had effectively demobilized them by herding the officers and the senior noncoms into the Katyn Forest, shooting them all and burying the bodies in mass graves. For years, the atrocity had been blamed on the Nazis until the truth emerged a long time after the war.

Then the Russians took the old men and women and the young boys and girls from the Poles they had captured and had sent them on "the long march"—many hundreds of miles south alongside the Caspian Sea and through Iran into North Iraq, ending up around the town of Kirkuk. Thousands had died from disease and privation but enough had survived to be trained as fighters for the British forces. The survivors became the Polish Corps that fought with great distinction in the Italian campaigns from 1943 onward. Sharqi's mother, then an orphan in her early teens, had come through the march but had fallen ill with typhus when the column had reached Tehran. She had been taken in by a Jewish family of leatherworkers, nursed back to health after nearly dying and grew up to marry the son of the family. They had flourished during the Shah's reign and had grown rich. Although not wholly accepted by "the hundred families," the socialites around the throne, because of their beliefs, they were allowed to practice their religion without persecution. Sharqi's father made frequent trips to Paris and London to market his goods and order imports from Rue Vendôme and Bond Street. She was his only child—after giving birth to a stillborn son, her mother was told she must never become pregnant again—and he lavished all his love and care on her. Sharqi had been sent away to school in England in her early teens, enjoying a gay life at Cheltenham Ladies College in the heart of the

Cotswolds and then going on to a finishing school in Glyon, high above the Swiss city of Montreux. There she had studied languages and art.

Her mother was, by this time, a permanent invalid. Her father's best friend, another Jew named Izak Zachin, was one of the richest silversmiths in Tehran. He died while she was away in Europe at school. On her return she found Zachin's business now being run by his son, Zacky, who had been one of her childhood companions. It was her father's dearest wish that the two families should be united and, although she felt more like a sister than a potential bride to the young man, there seemed no other option. The hundred families might accept Jews and several of the young blades would have grabbed her as a mistress—but "marrying out" would have been immediate ostracism. So she obeyed her father's wishes. And then the Shah departed and the bearded Ayatollah arrived, bringing decrees of vengeance and promoting his fundamentalist mullahs and revolutionary courts.

"If you were rich or foreign or both—exotic in any way—you stood out," Sharqi said. "The underdog felt it was his turn to growl and bite. The guards broke our door down one night and took Zacky. He was pleading and crying for mercy, but these times are without mercy. I never saw him again, he was shot after a mock trial at the people's court, along with hundreds of others. The night they came, some of them wanted to take me but, for whatever reason, the leader ordered me left alone. He had screamed my father's name at me and taken his fanatics to Father's house. After taking him they daubed his house with filth. We heard nothing of him for days and then they forced me to see him hanging from the public gallows. That finished my mother. They did not hurt her—but the life just oozed out of her and she died inside the year."

She told the story in a calm matter-of-fact manner, but Yardley had caught the hidden catches in her tone and could see that her knuckles were white on the stem of the glass. She turned and looked him full in the eyes. "Do you see now," she asked, "why I have my reasons for being here?"

Impulsively, he leaned across the table, conscious of her perfume and everything about her. He squeezed her hand gently between his. "I see," he said.

She smiled gently as he pulled his hand back. "There's not

much more to say," she went on. "That first year was hard. The mullahs confiscated our silverware business and I sat at home nursing my mother, though I could see from day to day she had lost the will to live. We had friends—but they could only help us a little—and secretly. You've no idea of the crazy suspicions and the spies and the false accusations when the regime was new. To be seen helping an accused family was to be part of the imaginary plot. You were lucky to get away just with financial ruin. It was a dark terrible time. It still is—living in Tehran is like holding a time bomb ticking away in your hand. But as Ayatollah Rafsanjani became more influential, things did ease up. He realized the West would not go away just because the crowds burned the American and British flags and shouted 'Death to the foreigner.'

"Four years ago, they even set up a Cultural Department. It was part of the drive to get back to the ancient honor and glory of Persia, wiping out the whole Pahlavi dynasty. Some months later, the mullah in charge sent an emissary to offer me a junior post in a small museum. I accepted—it would not have been very clever to refuse. The man running it was an ignorant idiot, which they quickly realized. So I was soon given his job. Of course I worked hard and got terribly interested. Don't forget I'd spent five years virtually under house arrest. This was like a breath of fresh air. After six months I was promoted again—to a post in the Ministry of Culture.

"One night, my boss, a man named Sohrabi, asked me out to dinner. He put a proposition to me. They needed someone who spoke English and French fluently to travel abroad on their behalf, to visit the auction houses and the dealers in Zurich, Geneva, Paris, London, and buy back the Persian heirlooms that had been taken from our country by friends of the Shah. I had all the credentials but there was no way the mullahs would trust such a confidential task to a non-Muslim. The job was mine—if I would only convert.

"Jehovah, forgive me—but I'd made up my mind before we drank our coffee. I was never orthodox, nor were my family. Even if I'd wanted to practice my faith, the synagogues in Tehran had all been closed down and the rabbis murdered or deported. The thought of getting out of that repressive atmosphere and going back to sanity and fun! But I pretended to wrestle with my conscience for some days—and then accepted. A week after I'd formally converted, they sent me to Monaco. Oh, the bliss of it! For the first two or three trips, they sent a bodyguard with me, a young man who spent half his time spying through the keyhole and the other half trying to get into my bed. But I managed to keep him friendly and for the last few trips they've trusted me to travel alone."

Flood cut in, "And on one trip she found herself bidding for some special Persian silver filigree work against one of those plunderous foreigners who got chatting with her, asked her out for a drink—and here we are. When this op came up, she went straight into the frame."

"One thing I don't quite understand," Yardley said. "Why didn't you cut and run the first time you were abroad on your own? It's a hateful regime, you've no family left there. Why go back?"

"Two reasons," she answered. "I do in fact have some uncles and cousins on my father's side, and several friends in the Jewish community. How long do you think they'd last if I defected? The mullahs would reckon they'd abetted my escape. Prison and torture to wring confessions out of them is the least they'd suffer. The other reason's equally simple. Revenge. You've never had that boot against the door after midnight or watched your wife snatched out of your arms, taken away and shot. Or had your father first tortured and then executed. Both of them eliminated—just like that"—she snapped her fingers—"because they were Episcopalian or Methodist or whatever. The Jews are supposed to get used to it, are they? Because they've had centuries of practice at being victims. Is that it?"

Her eyes were bright as she looked at him, but whether with anger or unshed tears he could not tell. "I'm sorry," he said. "I really am sorry."

Flood waved to the waiter for the bill and then said, "Perhaps we should leave it at that for tonight. Tell you what. If Sharqi's free tomorrow evening, Bob, why don't you invite her out for dinner? Just the two of you. That'll be the chance to get to know each other better."

"I'd love that," Yardley said. "If Sharqi will forgive my stupidity just now."

"Nothing to forgive." She smiled.

"Right," said Flood. "I'm the local expert. Why don't you two dine at the Beau Rivage in Ouchy, across the water. Sharqi can take one of her favorite steamers and, Bob, I'll lend you the Porsche. But please don't bend it. I'll book—they know me at the Beau Rivage. Quarter of eight. It's a huge hotel, so you'd better meet in the lobby."

The following morning after breakfast at the chalet, Yardley called Flood aside for a private talk. On the drive back from Évian, they had discussed the meeting with Sharqi Zachin and Yardley had said that, although she had impressed him greatly at first sight and was clearly a bright and intelligent girl, he welcomed the chance to get to know her better—to try to discover what really lay beneath that sophisticated surface.

"I think you'll find she's a great kid," Flood had said. "But you're the one who's got to make up his mind, not me."

Yardley had gone on, "Stop me if I'm talking out of turn, but there's nothing special between you, is there?"

Flood had chuckled. "I'd like to say yes—but the answer is no."

"I just wanted to make sure."

"Don't tell me you're getting interested. Love and war don't mix."

"Interested? After one dinner party? Ah, come on." But Yardley knew inside that he was not uninterested. His wife's unfaithfulness and the subsequent divorce had left a raw wound and for several months now he had steered clear of desirable women. But there was something about Sharqi Zachin. He found himself looking forward to the dinner the following night with more than professional interest, dammit.

Now there was another urgent matter he had to talk through. When the living room was empty—Shaw was reading a book in his room and the others were "on the hill" toning up their fitness—he said, "You've put together a damn fine team, Flood. My congratulations. They'll do the fetching and carrying—and the fighting, too, if there's any to be done, which I hope not, for all our sakes. But the rest of us are really the electric charge. The two contact points to blow it properly are Sharqi and Peter Shaw. Sharqi to get us into the palace and look after us there—and Shaw to do the vault *and* the safe. They're the vital links—agreed? I have to make up my mind about her—tonight will help—but Shaw we're stuck with. If he flops, we all flop."

"What are you saying?" Flood asked.

"This. Up to now, Shaw's been treated like shit. Or like a

parcel in a sorting office. He gets grabbed out of jail, held against his will, dumped on an aircraft, taken for a wild drive when Nick knocks off two lots of French thugs in front of his eyes—Christ, it's enough to give a tough guy a nervous breakdown! And Shaw's no toughie. If you agree, I aim to be very nice to Master Shaw. Treat him with some kindness for a change. Make him feel part of the team."

"That's good," Flood said. "That's very good."

"And I aim to start right now. We'll take a gentle stroll down to the village and have a quiet lunch at one of those cafe places. He says he doesn't drink but I'll try a few glasses of *Glühwein* on him—tell him it's nonalcoholic, like warmed-up Pepsi-Cola. We must know what makes him tick, if anything does."

Yardley went upstairs and knocked gently on the door of Shaw's room. He went in and found him reading a thick paperback book, *Noble House,* by James Clavell. Shaw was hunched in the big armchair, with his knees tucked up. He looked like a small boy, sheltering against life's hard knocks.

"Peter," Yardley said, "it's time we got to know each other a bit better. How about a stroll down to the village—and I'll buy you a cup of coffee? What do you say?"

"I'm quite happy here, thank you all the same, Mr. Yardley," Shaw replied primly.

"Oh, come on. It's a great day outside—the walk'll do you good." He could see Shaw hesitate and pressed on, "The others have all gone off. They won't get in our way. Just you and me—how about it?"

"Well, if you say so, Mr. Yardley."

Shaw put a marker in his book and then fussed around, looking for a topcoat and a scarf, although outside it was a balmy autumn day. At last, he was ready and they left the chalet and walked slowly down the lane to the main street. Yardley started telling anecdotes about his life in the Special Forces—nothing grim, just the more light-hearted episodes. He even made his audience grin once or twice.

Down in the village, he walked into a half-empty coffee shop and ordered coffee for two, a plate of cakes and two glasses of *Glühwein.* Shaw said, "I hope that's not an alcoholic beverage, Mr. Yardley. You see, I don't touch alcohol."

"Oh, it's some kind of Swiss concoction—you know, spices and things. Go on, it'll warm you up."

They chatted away. Yardley ordered two more cups of coffee and two more glasses of the hot, spicy wine. This time there were no queries or complaints from Shaw. His cheeks were flushed and he began to open up to the first sympathetic listener he had met for many months. Soon the whole pathetic story came tumbling out.

Peter Shaw had been an only son, who lived with his widowed mother. She had been forty when she gave birth to him. His father had died when he was in his early twenties and for the next ten years, he had been a middle-aged "mother's boy." She had done his cooking and had washed and ironed his shirts and underwear. She had bought his clothes for him, arranged the holidays that the two of them took together and had bound him with an iron hoop of maternal love. Once or twice early on, he had stopped off for a drink after work with some of his mates and when he arrived home in Perivale an hour later than usual, it had been like a grand inquisition. After a long harangue, she had burst into tears, saying that he was taking after his poor dead father whose life had been shortened through drink. Shaw himself could never remember seeing his father the worse for a drink or two but he felt guilty all the same and, to please her, took a pledge against strong liquor.

Throughout this time, his work at Chubb's had prospered. He had a flair for mechanics and the logical mind that enjoyed the cause and effect of high precision machinery. In his teens, he had been an accomplished amateur pianist and possessed the delicate fingers that could easily put together or dismantle the most complicated locks. Gradually, he had been promoted to deal with the top-level range of safes and locks—assignments for very important clients including various government departments. "They don't just want good locksmiths, Mr. Yardley. Firms like Chubb's and Banham and Yale keep a close eye on you as well. Out of office hours, I mean. Even though they split the work up, so that one man builds the lock and someone else he's supposed not to know makes the keys, they still need to be sure you're sober and honest, walking the straight and narrow. Who can blame them? I was a real Boy Scout—a nondrinker who went home to mother every night when the office closed.

"At times it was really strange. Oh, I could tell you some yarns, Mr. Yardley—going to some of these great mansions in the country like Castle Howard and Chatsworth to sort out their safes. Once I had to be flown by helicopter to a castle in Northumberland to open a safe in a hurry. Some old dowager had been tippling and she'd forgotten the combination for her private safe. Royalty was due to arrive shortly and she had to have her diamond tiara to greet them. And there it was, tucked away in the safe, and she couldn't for the life of her remember the combination. And then there was that Tehran job. Oh, I could tell you some stories."

"And how did it all go wrong?" Yardley asked gently.

By now there was no stopping Shaw. In 1984 his mother started complaining of pains in her stomach. She had always been a great complainer, but this time it was different. He finally managed to get her to see her doctor, she went into hospital for tests and never came out again alive. She was diagnosed as having inoperable cancer of the bowel. Every day he went to see her in hospital, she was shriveling up before his eyes. She was dead in a little over a month.

He had often dreamed guiltily of the wonderful freedom when she was dead and gone. But there he was, close on forty, alone and miserable. His mother had never encouraged him to bring a friend home and prevented him from having a social life away from her. So for a month or two he moped around, watched television, ate warmed-up meals covered in tinfoil, went round to the laundromat each week with his washing and was beginning to wish that his mother had never died.

Then one day he was told to go to a large block of flats off Curzon Street, where a young actress, a Miss Julia Lindsay, needed a safe installed for her jewelry. He went round to examine the place and met the occupant, a tall blonde with large breasts and voluptuous hips. She was very friendly and offered him coffee after he had made his inspection and taken notes. He had to return on several other occasions—and each time she became friendlier. She asked him about his career, said how exciting it was and oohed and ahed at the right places in his narrative. She seemed genuinely interested in him as a man. He never paused to wonder why if she was the successful actress she claimed to be she was always lolling around her flat in a negligee. When he had finally installed the safe, she invited him to have dinner with her at a Mayfair casino. He accepted eagerly.

It was a strange new world, the men in dinner jackets, the impassive Arabs in their robes, the cigar smoke swirling under the lights, baccarat tables, banana-shaped blackjack dealing tables, roulette, the girl croupiers in their low-cut dresses—and the sumptuous restaurant where his hostess persuaded him to have a glass of champagne, and yet another. "It's all just bubbles, hardly alcoholic at all." He was not supposed to gamble—you had to register as a member forty-eight hours before you could buy chips—but Julia had a word with the friendly house manager, who shrugged and smiled. She suggested he try the blackjack table and told him it was a simple game—what they used to call as kids pontoon or *vingt-et-un.* As he only had a couple of five-pound notes on him, she even bought him fifty pounds' worth of chips and said he could pay her back out of his winnings.

And he won—and won again. Even after repaying the loan, when they left he had won nearly three hundred pounds. She squeezed his hand and said he had a real flair, a gambler born. He joined the club there and then and invited her as his guest two nights later.

Looking back now, he could see that she had played him like a fish, directed by the men behind her. She would press up against him in the taxi, let her hand rest high on his thigh, kiss him with open mouth when they parted, once letting him put his trembling hand down the front of her dress and encounter a heavily armored breast but the ultimate was always tantalizingly near and yet so far away. One night, she told him in a warm whisper that she wanted his arms round her in bed but she was desperate for sleep. Another time, they had arranged to spend the night together but at the last moment she had a dreadful "tummy upset."

By now he was losing heavily on the tables. He had lost the small legacy from his mother and had eaten into his own savings. There was still a mortgage on the house in Perivale but he was able through his friendly bank manager to take out a second mortgage. He had switched to playing roulette; blackjack was a slightly more scientific game, but there were few chances of winning the kind of big pot that would put him straight again. In roulette the risks were greater but so were the rewards.

In four months he was wiped out. He did not dare borrow money from his employers or ask for an advance on his comfortable salary. If they started asking awkward questions and the truth came out, he could be fired—and that would be total ruin. But now he owed the casino ten thousand pounds. Julia was most sympathetic but there was no way she could help.

And then one night he was scared out of his wits. Late in the evening, there was a heavy knock on the door of the Perivale semidetached house. When he opened it, two bulky men pushed past him. One, named Tony, was fingering a knife with a long shining blade. They told him the Boss was very upset. He didn't like pikers, guys who welshed on bets. If he didn't pay up the ten grand within one week, they would call again. "But next time naughty boys get punished . . . know what I mean, Peter?"

He sat up trembling the rest of the night, wondering what on earth he could do. There was no way he could raise the money—in one week or fifty weeks. He was tempted to go to the police but they would start inquiries, the word would get back to his firm and he would be fired with loss of pension rights. And for the same reason, he couldn't go to his directors and ask for help. There was only one answer. He would have to throw himself on the mercy of the so-called Boss and plead for time to pay, even with interest.

Which, he now realized, had been the ploy all along. The fish had been hooked, gaffed and was now thrashing about in the net. He called at the casino next evening and asked to see the Boss. He was shown into a paneled room; it had been the graceful eighteenth-century home of a famous admiral. Shaw saw a big, fat, dark-haired man sitting behind a large desk, smoking a torpedolike cigar. He was given two brutally simple alternatives. He could either have an arm or a leg broken and his face carved up for starters, or he could open a safe or two after hours, as it were. For each job he did, two thousand five hundred pounds would be knocked off his gambling debt. Once he'd done four safes, the slate would be clean and his credit at the casino would be renewed. The Boss took out a large gold watch and placed it on the mahogany table. "You have two minutes," he said, "Make your choice." It took him ten seconds to decide.

Over the next few months, he did half a dozen jobs for the Boss, a couple in Bishop's Avenue, North London, known as "Millionaires' Row," three in Home Counties mansions and one or two in luxury apartments in Mayfair itself. At first, he was scared out of his wits, his hands trembling so much that he had to take beta-blockers to steady them. But gradually he became used to the excitement, the thrill of danger.

"You see, Mr. Yardley," he said earnestly, "they really were professional. The men helping me out, I mean. And the nerve. D'you know, once in Bishop's Avenue, we turned up in a moving van in broad daylight. One of the servants had tipped them off. The family had arranged to have some furniture moved to their place in the country while they were abroad. So we turned up in our white coats as bold as brass and, while I was doing the safe, the others walked out with a set of Hepplewhite chairs, some Chinese vases and a couple of Old Masters off the walls!

"And some of those safes were a breeze. The family would have the latest burglar alarms installed on the outside and forget they'd had the same safe for maybe fifty years. It didn't need someone of my experience to open them. Mind you, I never let on. But it was weird. Once, I'd done a job the night before and was in the office the next day when the phone rang. It was the secretary of the rich man who'd been robbed. He wanted someone to come round at once and change the combination. I couldn't face it, so I sent my assistant. I'd have had hysterics if I'd gone!

"It was all too easy but I should have realized the luck would run out. That was the night I did the American Ambassador's place in Regent's Park. We'd had the tip-off that he and his missus would be away. What we didn't know was some government high-up had arrived suddenly and was going to stay with the ambassador. They'd doubled the security. I always had a strong-arm guy with me in case the servants or the family got rough. I cleared the safe all right and handed him the emerald necklace we were after, and some rather nice diamonds, and stowed the rest of the stuff in my grip. It was mostly a lot of old papers. We managed to get away out of the back and across the tennis courts into the park itself. Then we split up. I walked across the park to the Marylebone Road and caught the Tube back to Perivale. But two days later, the police arrested me at the office. I'd lost a glove in the rush and they'd found several of my fingerprints at the scene. You see, Mr. Yardley, all top safe men have their fingerprints registered with the police, so that if one of the safes they service is burgled, their prints can be eliminated at once. But this time that's how they got on to me so quickly. And then the whole story came out."

"You never read the papers you'd stolen?"

"I glanced at 'em but they seemed a load of old rubbish. All about Gorbachev and Moscow."

Yardley glanced at his wristwatch. "We'd better be getting back." He waved at the waitress for his bill. "There's a briefing on for later this afternoon."

Shaw clutched at Yardley's sleeve. "What's going to happen to me, Mr. Yardley? Oh, I know there's some job they need me for. They'll all be as nice as pie while I'm wanted. But what happens after that?"

Yardley put an arm round the other man's thin shoulders. "Don't worry," he said. "I'm going to be in charge. I'll look after you."

"But afterward? What happens afterward?"

"You'll be okay. That's a promise."

The meeting that afternoon lasted less than half an hour. It was more like the board meeting of a medium-sized manufacturing company than a gathering of tough professional soldiers. Shaw was not invited, but Yardley and the others saw a stranger sitting in the shadows in one corner behind Flood, who briefly introduced him as "Mr. Rainer, my *fiduciaire.*" The man was thin-faced, with fairish hair going gray and dark horn-rimmed spectacles. He wore a gray suit and clutched a large gray folder. He did not speak throughout the meeting.

Flood stood up. "Gentlemen, this need not take us long. I am going to hand out individual folders to each one of you. Inside you will find a copy of the operation order with the estimated duration. There is also a copy of the financial terms and the insurance arrangements—through Zurich Assurance, as usual. Finally, there is a blank sheet in case any of you want to alter your list of relatives and beneficiaries. Take the documents back to your rooms and, please, go through them carefully. Tomorrow morning, breakfast is seven o'clock sharp. At eight, we'll go through the whole briefing step by step. Major Yardley here, Bob, is team leader, as you all know. He'll take over the briefing tomorrow, but I'll be on hand to cover the admin details. Any questions?"

No one spoke. Each knew he was getting that much closer to the action.

"Okay then, we'll break it at that. Bob and I'd prefer it if you don't start discussions among yourselves when you've read the op order. If you've got questions, jot 'em down for the briefing after breakfast tomorrow; and I don't really have to remind you, but those papers don't go out of the chalet. Strict security from this minute on. Right, chaps, that's all."

Flood nodded to Yardley, who followed him into his study. He read through the dossier, admired the professionalism of the clean-typed orders and wondered at the blank sheet.

With his divorce, no children and his parents dead, he had no one to leave the cash to. One hundred thousand pounds sterling, live or die, and the same amount in insurance if he copped it, with fifty thousand pounds for the loss of an arm, a leg or an eye. There must be some Special Forces charity back at Bragg that could use the dough if he didn't come back from Tehran.

"Is it the same for all of them?" he asked Flood.

"No. You're the boss, you get extra. The others get forty thousand pounds apiece, apart from the twins who get fifty. They've got extra responsibilities, like driving the trucks and organizing the air-conditioning equipment."

"It doesn't seem a fortune. Not to risk your life."

"These boys are free-lancers but some are still serving. You've got to remember forty grand is about three years' Army pay for the likes of Miller and Morton. That's a real nest egg for when they retire. Tax free, sitting safely in a numbered Swiss bank account, drawing interest. Archie Morton'll be out of the Regiment in five years. That'll be worth sixty, maybe seventy thousand, when he comes to draw it; and he could have pulled four or five other jobs in that time. You just concentrate on getting them out of Iran in one piece!"

That evening Yardley enjoyed the drive through the mountains to the beautiful historic city of Lausanne. Once he had mastered the Porsche's tendency to oversteer and the threat of the heavy tail end to swing past him on the more acute bends, he delighted in its performance. It was a balmy September night and as the lights came up on the far side and a breeze ruffled the skin of Lac Leman, it felt like magic. He wanted to get down among it and pulled off the autoroute at Villeneuve to follow the lakeside road round the northern shore. As he approached Montreux the somber castle of Chillon loomed ahead. His military mind agreed with the strategic choice of the château's defensive position, which looked impregnable on its rocky perch alongside the lake's edge. There'd been a famous prisoner kept there for years. He couldn't remember who it had been, but he did vaguely recall some lines from Byron's poems, something about "My limbs are bowed, though not with toil / But rusted with a vile repose." They didn't write them like that anymore. Humming to himself, he squeezed the car through the main street of Montreux and on past Vevey to the outskirts of Lausanne. The city, built on three tiers, spread over the low hills to his right, its skyline dominated by a magnificent seven-hundred-year-old cathedral. The signs for Ouchy led him along a tree-lined street past couples and children strolling at the water's edge to the suburbs center. The yellow canvas awnings of the Hotel Beau Rivage Palace appeared, and following Flood's directions he turned right up the hill and found the main entrance at the rear.

It was like a vast Edwardian palace with great marble columns, staircases sweeping down from lofty corridors and parklike ornamental gardens beyond the giant French windows at the far end of the lobby. He went to the desk and discovered there were several restaurants, but Flood had reserved a table for two in the main one overlooking the gardens. A voice behind him said, "Bob, perfect timing." He swung round—and there was Sharqi. She wore a fashionably short olive green dress. He had never seen more exciting ankles.

They drank champagne and lingered over dinner. Normally a trained observer, he could not have said afterward whether the restaurant had been full or empty. There was something about her that drew a man in, shut out the surroundings. She told him more about life in Tehran, the strain of feeling under constant surveillance, of Sohrabi, her boss at the Ministry of Culture, who clearly wanted to start an affair with her but was hesitant, partly out of risking a blow to his male pride if she were to refuse him and partly because he too was being watched by one of the mullahs. "Spying is a way of life there, Bob," she said. A slight shiver seemed to go through her. "No one is really safe—except perhaps the Ayatollah Khomeini. And you can be sure all his lieutenants are watching him, waiting for him to die, jockeying for position around him. Oh, it's hateful!"

And when she began asking him about his life in the United States, he found himself talking freely for the first time in many months. He skirted around the operations he had undertaken, many of them still top secret, but he did tell her about his life as a boy, of his mother and father who had died at sea, of how on an attachment to the Special Forces in England, he had met and married a local girl, who had later betrayed him with her previous lover, of his mixed feelings—love and anger and pity and something of guilt—

when the divorce finally went through. Even as he was telling the pathetic story, he was wondering inside how he could tell all this to a stranger, things that he would not easily tell his trusted friends in the Green Berets.

She put her slender fingers gently across the back of his hand. "It has to get better, Bob. The hurt becomes an ache and then finally the ache goes. I know. I've been there."

"I hope you're right."

"I know I'm right." There was a brief silence, then in a lighter tone she said, "You know the story of the man who fell out of the window on the eighty-fourth floor of the Empire State Building? As he was dropping past the fortieth floor, he saw someone looking out of the window and he shouted, 'So far so good!' Tell me, Major Yardley, do you dance?"

"Like a man with his legs tied together. Why?"

"I saw a notice in the lobby when I came in. There's a special bar on the lower ground floor with a three-piece—what do you call it in America? a combo? I haven't danced for years!"

"Me neither. As you'll soon find out. Great, I'll just settle the bill here and we can have a brandy downstairs."

It was dark and warm in the bar with its soft armchairs and squelchy banquettes. In one corner there was a polished postage-stamp-sized dance floor and above it on a slightly raised platform a pianist, a drummer and a clarinettist playing smoochy old standards. Yardley took a sip from his goblet of brandy and then stood up, wordlessly holding out his arm to Sharqi. The combo, if that was the right word, was playing "Smoke Gets in Your Eyes." There was only one other couple on the tiny floor, a thin elderly man with rivulets of wavy white hair and a Roman profile dancing sedately at arms' length with a plump woman of about the same age. She was wearing a diamond bracelet and a diamond choker around her wattled throat. Shaw should have been here, he thought.

And then for nearly half an hour, he stopped thinking. To be holding a woman again after all those months, to breathe in that subtle woman-smell, part scent and part the woman herself, to share if only in a stylized way those rhythms that were as old and basic as breathing—he found himself swept away on a strange tide. He could feel a lock of her hair against his cheek and her warm breath, when she spoke softly, against the side of his neck. He moved as if in a dream, the old steps somehow came back and she moved with him, lightly and easily. There was a roll on the drums to signify a break. They stopped, stood at arms' length and looked at each other strangely.

Yardley felt his mouth was dry. He cleared his throat and said haltingly, "Shall we sit this one out?"

She nodded. They walked back to their table and he waved to the waiter, indicating a refill of their glasses. She stopped him.

"Let's take a walk by the lake, it's beautiful out there." Her words were a thinly veiled plea to be alone with him.

She knew the way and led him through the hotel and out past the boutiques on the lower level into the night air. Looping her arm through his, they walked across the road toward the hotel Château d'Ouchy and followed the path next to the water. Their closeness was obvious to both of them, but neither wanted to speak of it and risk scaring it away. Yardley had to suppress the urge to come forward and proposition her, the way he was used to doing. Damn it, he wanted her, he could feel it in his groin and time was running out, he felt panic, was he missing the signals, there was only tonight. Words that were all wrong stopped in his throat, he felt angry at himself for feeling like a kid on a first date. She affectionately tightened her grip on his arm.

"Just look at the beautiful moon, Bob. The way it reflects across the lake, it is like a bridge, I feel I want to walk on it." Her voice was almost a whisper and yet he was jolted out of himself.

He stepped back from her, he had to or the enormous desire to wrap his arms around her, to protect her, would have taken him over. Goddamm it, he thought, what the hell's going on with you, Yardley. The last thing you need is this kind of complication. He unknowingly shook his head as if to clear it.

"Oh Bob, you're laughing at me, you think I'm talking like a romantic schoolgirl." She was facing him and bending forward, her hands clasped in front of her face in girlish embarrassment.

"No, no, I'm not laughing at you." He recognized a happiness welling up inside, in his guts somewhere. "I'm enjoying you."

She gathered into him and they laughed together. His body was warm inside his coat and she didn't want to let go. The shiver that ran through her this time was of a different kind.

"Let's walk down past the lake steamers." As they moved

away she rested her head against his shoulder. "You know, Bob, I feel safe, here and now with you I feel safe," she paused, "and sure."

A reply wasn't necessary, and his arm gently pulled her to him and they strolled on in silence. Small talk had been replaced by something deeper.

Stopping to watch a group of teenagers playing under the streetlights that illuminated the gardens and hedgerows and danced on the water, Sharqi said, "It frightens me, Bob—these children play naturally here, they're happy, and look at that." One of the boys came sweeping toward them, zigzagging through a row of Coca-Cola cans on his roller skates. "Having fun and being creative." She was thrilled at the boy's skill. "In Iran this no longer happens, happiness has become a sin." Her voice had become serious again.

Yardley didn't want her to slip away, of that *he* was sure.

"Look Sharqi, and stop me if I'm out of order, I'll understand." He didn't care how clumsy this was going to sound, "Tonight was very special for me, I haven't felt so light in a long time. I've loved being with you and I want more of it, I don't know how and I don't know when, but that's how I feel." He stopped her from interrupting. "We are all going into something heavy with this operation, but it will come and go like they all have." He paused to construct his words.

"Bob, you're a lovely man." Her fingers touched him lightly on his cheek and then her forefinger gently rested on his lips. "Whatever happens I will not forget tonight or my feelings, but tomorrow I must fly back to Tehran and the next time I see you any such feelings between us will kill us both. I . . ."

"Sharqi, you don't have to say it, that's why I'm speaking out now, I want you to know my feelings before this thing begins." His own voice surprised him, the words calm and firm.

"When it's over," she spoke looking directly into his eyes, "and you are sure you still want to, I will meet you. Please understand that I have no room left for false hopes or too many dreams. Living in Tehran does that to people, but I wish it to be."

Yardley wanted to let out a yell but swallowed it instead.

"No Ayatollah is gonna stand in the way of us meeting up again, I don't care where your Mr. Sohrabi sends you." He held her at arms' length and smiled. "You are looking at one hell of a determined hombre." They hugged each other for what seemed minutes.

"Promise?" she asked.

"Promise. Cross my heart. And now I'm going to drive you back to Geneva."

They drove west alongside the lake in a comfortable silence. He did not hurry, delaying the separation. Rolle and Nyon slipped by and then they were in the rich suburbs of Geneva. The grand houses, discreetly tucked away behind thick hedges and high iron gates, insulated by large manicured gardens, gave way to important-looking buildings and fashionable hotels strung along the Rue du Lac. She motioned him to pull up. "That's far enough, Bob," she said. "The Ambassador Hotel is only a few minutes' walk from here and we cannot risk being seen together. I am afraid even as a trusted member of the Revolution I am not immune to surveillance."

"I'll wait and watch you to your door."

"You're sweet. But no, I'll approach the hotel from the other side so it appears that I have walked down from Cointrin railway station."

She leaned across, took his face in both hands and kissed him on each cheek. Still holding him she said in what could have been a throaty chuckle or a half-sob, "Till Tehran."

"Till Tehran," he said.

He sat for a while after she had disappeared into the shadows feeling robbed, as if something valuable had trickled through his fingers. Shaking it off, he headed the Porsche back along the lake. The distinctive fragrance of Sharqi's perfume filled the car, her presence was right there. A tune began nagging at his brain until it finally became a humming "We'll meet again, don't know where, don't know . . ." He thought, Jesus, Yardley, you damn stupid romantic.

8

The Worldly Hope men set their Hearts upon
Turns Ashes—or it prospers; and anon,
Like Snow upon the Desert's dusty Face,
Lighting a little Hour or two—is gone.

Next morning after breakfast, at eight o'clock sharp, the team reassembled around the big table. Yardley noticed how in just two or three days they had slipped into easy partnerships. The Belgian twins sat together at the foot of the table, Nick Baring and Lysol were along one side and Miller and Morton along the other. But there was none of the usual joshing, the leg-pulling when the aristocratic Honorable Rupert was the usual victim. This was serious business. He and Flood sat at the head of the table and the gray Mr. Rainer was almost invisible in a corner behind them.

Flood tapped the table. "Right. If you're ready, Bob, shall we start? Let's clear the admin first. You've all read the op order and the terms of service. You know the score. If anyone wants out—for whatever reason—now's his chance. No excuses, no arguments. All he has to do is stand up and leave. Mr. Rainer here will pay him off to date and give him a return ticket. No hard feelings. Anyone?" He gazed slowly down one side of the table and up the other. "Great, everyone's in.

"Now, you've all received a pay sheet with your individual bank account numbers on it. And the address of the bank—Crédit Suisse, Geneva. Here's a letter"—he held up a sheet of paper—"with your test code numbers on it." He turned to the administrator and said, "Here, do it right away, will you? Hand each man a copy." The gray man took the sheet of paper without a word.

Flood went on, "Inside fifteen minutes, those accounts will be in operation. And for Christ's sake, don't lose your test code numbers. That's the only identification the bank'll accept. Now, after the meeting's over, if you've got any changes to make—next of kin and so forth—if the married ones, come to that the single ones as well, have any extra kids to support since we were last together, for God's sake tell Mr. Rainer and he'll make the necessary adjustments."

Lysol said, "Nick, what about that hooker in Marseilles you were telling me about? The one who does it swinging off the chandelier? You won't forget her, surely?"

"Cut it, Lysol," Flood said. "Another time, if you don't mind."

It was all new to Yardley, who had never been on a mercenary operation before. Glancing around the table, he felt, as he had done the previous afternoon, that they might as well be the board of directors of a manufacturing company discussing the annual dividend for the shareholders. And yet he could sense the tension in the air, Lysol's enforced gaiety. Making your will was an everyday occurrence, but people usually did it when the possibility of death was remote.

"Any questions so far?" Flood asked. The twins shook their heads in unison, the others were silent. "Okay, I'll ask Bob to run through the operational side, and then we can deal with any further admin. It's all yours, Bob."

Yardley said the plan was to infiltrate the Ghulistan Palace in Tehran, remove the Peacock Throne and transport it to Turkey, where it would be handed over to the U.S. military base. He sketched the history of the throne and how the Shah had arranged with Chubb's of London to build a special safe around it—and then a reinforced vault around the safe. "Which meant, to get it out, we needed one of the guys who had built the hardware round it. The one we found was doing a stretch in Wormwood Scrubs jail." He went on to say that the first phase of the plan had been to snatch Peter Shaw from the Scrubs, and Mike Murphy—"most of you'll know old Mike"—had put an ex-SAS team together, "including young Lysol here," to work the snatch. And it had worked.

Miller cut in with his soft Hampshire burr, "Why isn't Shaw sitting in? He's the key figure."

Flood said, "He comes in later. After we've talked it through. He's a passenger until he's let loose on that safe. Okay?"

Yardley continued, "We drive there in two DAF trucks, I think you call these juggernauts over here. Jacques drives one and Claude the other. It's a four-, maybe five-, day run, depending on the delays we suffer at customs and border queues. The Turks could be a problem at the Iranian frontier. Now, gentlemen, if you would refer to the route maps in your briefing folders. You will join the trucks at St. Galen; from there it's only a short run to the Swiss/Austrian border post at Feldkirch, east through Bludenz, the new St. Christoph tunnel, Innsbruck, then the northern autobahn loop via Salzburg to swing south again to Spittal. I want to push to there as hard as we can, having said that, it's up to you twins to indicate your fatigue factor. We lose autobahn at Spittal and pick it up again at Villach for the short run to Klagenfurt. We cross the Yugoslavian border south of there at the Loibl tunnel."

He briefed the route in detail and the question-and-answer routine covered all the possible risks and logistics they would face. Zagreb, Istambul, east through Turkey and over the tense border with Iran. Then skirting south of Kurdistan and, with luck buried in a convoy of other trucks, they would follow the truck route through the religious capital of Qazvin and on to Tehran.

"Okay, you've all got that clear, it'll be a long grind." The door opened and Yardley paused. Flood had quietly rung for coffee, they had been at it for over two hours. As the white gloved hand of the servant began to pour from the silver pot, Flood dismissed him.

"That's all right, we'll help ourselves." The old Swiss nodded respectfully and closed the door carefully behind him. Flood played mum, the coffee aroma helped to relax their mood.

"The backup truck has all the air-conditioning plant on board. Claude's the driver, as I say, and Miller, Lysol and Morton will be his crew. Jacques drives the lead truck and Nick, Shaw and myself will ride with him." Yardley's crisp delivery showed his experience and the men in the room were feeling comfortable with him. "We must try to keep in close formation; if the trucks do get separated, the rendezvous will always be the stopover designated for that night. The first truck in waits. Clear?" Heads nodded and Lysol raised his hand. "Hold the question for a moment, Lysol, I want to move on a bit. Once we hit Tehran, we make for the bonded truck park close by the railway station." He pointed to one of the three enlarged maps wall-mounted behind him. The street map of Tehran had their entry and exit routes for the city overlaid on clear plastic. They discussed it thoroughly.

"To finish up, the hotel we're all booked in is close to the truck park. The palace is less than a mile from there." Yardley placed his folder down on the table.

Lysol said, "Can I raise one concern? Seems to me we'll need some inside help. If we're all tied up pulling out and replacing the air conditioning, Christ knows how, I wouldn't know an air-conditioning pipe from a hole in the wall, while Shaw tinkers away at the safe, who watches our backs? To me we look damned exposed in there."

"I'll deal with it, Bob," Flood said. "They're good points, but we're ahead of you, Rupert. As usual." He grinned. "First, as I've said, the twins have done a proper course on the air-conditioning equipment and how to install it. Before you set off from St. Galen, the twins will put you through your paces—show you what has to be done. Most of you will just be fetching and carrying but you've got to look like genuine workmen. So get some calluses on those lily white hands of yours, Lysol!

"*And* we have someone inside. A very capable lady named Sharqi Zachin." He gave a brief resume of her career, the execution of her father and husband and her present job as curator of the Ghulistan Palace museum. "She's the one who's insisted on having new equipment installed as some of the exhibits are falling to pieces with the erratic system they have right now. So, naturally, she'll have to keep inspecting progress once the work starts. That satisfy you?"

Lysol nodded.

Then Baring asked, "Can you elaborate on the passports, please?"

"Yes, Mr. Rainer has a Swiss passport for each of you. They've been used, immigration control stamps all over the place. You're Swiss workmen who've done this job all over Europe and you've got the passports to prove it."

Baring smiled his approval, then asked, "Is there a backstop if the museum authorities got suspicious? Can the documents be verified?"

"Yes. Some friends bought a controlling interest in an air-conditioning firm in Berne several months back. The names on those Swiss passports are all accredited employees, some of them for years past. There are worksheets, pay slips, expense accounts, to prove it. Iran security can check all it likes, the cover's solid. Berne even submitted an estimate that the Ministry of Culture in Tehran accepted in writing."

"Nice work," Baring said.

"Now for the weapons," Yardley said. "Let's hope we don't have to use them. Jacques has brought an assortment in from Belgium, in a special compartment in one of the trucks. There are four Heckler and Koch MP5s, two of them with silencers. Then six Browning 9mm Hi-Powers and two .22 Berettas with silencers. And Nick's special Italian job—a shortened Franchi Spas 12 pump-action shotgun."

"You've got no soul, Nick," said the Honorable Rupert Lycett-Smythe. "Sawing up a good shotgun, for God's sake."

"This is not for pheasants," Baring replied, "when the bloody birds can't shoot back. If the shit starts flying in close, give me the pump any day."

"Peasant," said Lysol.

"Okay, okay," Flood interrupted. "Let's keep the song and dance act till afterward. Bob, would you like to hear from the twins?"

Yardley dipped his head and Jacques began to describe the giant DAF trucks. There were hinged bunks for three inside, right behind the driver's compartment. The driver himself could sleep, lying across the three seats in the front of the cab. He explained where the gun compartments, padded to avoid any rattles, were situated and how even a close search would hardly reveal them. Each trunk had had extended tanks welded on, which would allow them almost 50 percent extra mileage between refills.

His twin, Claude, cut in, "Oh yes, Monsieur Flood, we 'ave that spare set of German number plates for the return journey."

Archie Morton said, "German? I thought you said we finished in Turkey."

"So you do. But the trucks will eventually have to return to Germany."

Flood had rolled smoothly with the punch, Yardley felt, but he also sensed, though not from the man's impassive face, that Flood was annoyed with Claude for talking out of turn. There was no need to have mentioned the number plates.

"If there are no other questions," he said, "it's about time we brought Peter Shaw in. Would you like to go and collect him, Lysol?"

"That little prick," Lysol said, but he stood up all the same.

"Hark at who's calling someone else a little prick," Morton remarked. "Be nice to him, Lysol. We need the little blighter."

Lysol came back after a few minutes, shepherding the safe expert into the room. Shaw looked puzzled and even apprehensive when he saw them all sitting around the long table and staring at him. Yardley pulled up a spare chair and said, "Here, Peter, you come and sit down with me. We need some advice from you." Shaw gratefully took the chair.

Flood said to him, "Tell me something. When you've set up a safe—a real big one, I mean, not one of your wall jobs—do you remember the mechanism a long time afterward?"

Shaw replied with dignity. "That's like asking a great pianist whether he remembers a Beethoven sonata. You ask Alfred Brendel if he remembers the *Hammerklavier!* Once you've done it, Mr. Flood, it's always here, and here." He tapped the fingers of one hand against the other, then tapped his forehead.

"That's all I wanted to know. You see, we're going to take you back to Tehran to open up that safe and the vault you installed for the Shah."

"Oh, God," said Shaw. He went pale and his lower lip quivered. "What about the Ayatollah? And those revolutionary guards? They're animals."

"Forget them. It's all worked out and you've got this bunch here to look after you."

Shaw gave Yardley an appealing glance. "Is that right, Mr. Yardley?"

"You bet it's right. I'll be there all the time with you."

As Shaw still looked undecided, Flood pulled his master stroke. From under the table, he produced an aluminum case with a handle and locks. He placed it on the table, snapped back the locks and opened back the outer case to reveal a set of tools framed in foam rubber slots on both sides of the case. "Here, take a look. Remind you of anything?"

"Why, that's my set of tools. Where'd you get it from?"

"It's not the original, but I think you'll find everything there."

Wondering, Shaw took out from their slots a tuning fork and a doctor's ivory-headed hammer for testing reflexes.

Miller asked, "Is this a music lesson?"

Shaw seemed to grow in importance. He said, "I wrote the music for that safe. This is what I tuned it with. And I've got a stethoscope, see? With the hammer and the tuning fork and the stethoscope you can tell minute differences in the resonance of metal. And that always tells the expert something."

He could feel the growing respect of the hard men around the table. Experts in their own field of weapons and covert warfare, they recognized and admired expertise in someone else, especially the man on whom the whole venture hung.

Flood said formally, "Welcome to the team, Mr. Shaw." He shook hands gravely. Each of the others in turn got up, came close and shook Shaw's hand. He squared his shoulders and looked as if he had just had a medal pinned on his scrawny chest.

Yardley gave him a quick resume of the traveling plans and Shaw's eyes lit up when he heard that he would be accompanying the leader in the first truck. Then his face drooped again and he asked in a plaintive voice, "That's fine, as far as it goes. But what happens afterward? After I've helped you get the throne out of the vault and the safe? After that, I'm no more use to you. Do you just hand me back to Scotland Yard or Interpol?"

"Not likely," said Lysol. "They'd arrest us too as accessories. Grow up." Privately, he knew that to be nonsense.

Flood cut in. "You're a man of intelligence, Mr. Shaw. Those are good questions. And here are the answers."

He picked up a thin file with pink covers from the heap on the table in front of him. He took out a Swiss passport and flicked it open so that Shaw could see his own photograph on the inside page. Then he produced an official buff form, in Afrikaans as well as English, which was a residence permit for South Africa. And then he held out another official-looking document in both languages, a South African work permit. Shaw put out a hand to take them, but Flood gently removed them from his reach.

"When the job's done, Mr. Shaw," he said. "That's when you get them. But I can tell you, you're a new man with a new life ahead of you. As of yesterday, you took up an important job as special security adviser to a government department in Pretoria. You're on a month's leave right now, so that you can sell your apartment here in Switzerland and take a break before starting the new job. It's in the file—the bill of sale for the apartment, transferring your Swiss bank balance to a bank in Pretoria—the lot. Once that safe comes out of the palace basement, Peter Shaw disappears forever. There's no way Scotland Yard could connect up Timothy Holt in Pretoria with that fugitive Peter Shaw."

"But, just supposing they did, Mr. Flood? What if one of my associates in London happened to be in Pretoria and bumped into me in the street. What then?"

"Nothing," Flood replied. "So he flies back to the UK and reports you to the police. There's no extradition from South Africa on political grounds. Our South African friends would consider any case against you as political."

Shaw looked blank. Then he grinned slyly when the point struck him; and Yardley, the onlooker, felt increased admiration for Flood's thoroughness. Hell, he thought, I wouldn't fancy my chances at chess with this guy. He covers all the angles, and the straight lines as well.

The meeting broke up after another hour. Every member of the team had closely studied the Tehran street map and another 1:500,000 scale map of the Iran, Iraq, Syria, Turkey, USSR terrain map that hung alongside it. Tomorrow, they would leave Château d'Oex in ones and twos to rendezvous in Basel for a solid twelve-hour nonstop course on the air-conditioning equipment. And, the day after, the long drive would begin. Meanwhile, Yardley, having first consulted Flood, said that a couple at a time could stroll down to the village and have a drink and a look around before the real work began. He knew there was no need to tell them to keep out of trouble and not drink too much. They were hardened professionals, they would look after themselves and each other.

At ten past six that evening, Yardley, Flood and Baring were sitting in a half-circle around the fire, having a presupper drink. Miller and Archie Morton were still down in the village and Lysol was sitting at a card table with Shaw, trying to teach him to play two-handed brag and cheating monstrously as he did so. Flood and Baring were chatting in a desultory way. Now and then Bob Yardley joined in, but most of the time he was watching the flames curling and leaping around the logs in the open fireplace. His mind was back in time to yesterday and in distance to the Hotel Beau Rivage, to the tiny dance floor, the feeling of Sharqi in his arms and their strange conversation afterward. He knew he had to toughen up his mind-set, close out the emotions and concentrate on the journey ahead and then the fraught job in the heart of Tehran. It was all this hanging around, he told himself, this waiting, that broke the concentration. Maybe he should have taken a chance and come on stronger with her, made it just another fling. But he knew in his heart that there was no easy out with Sharqi. What was one of those old numbers the trio had played? "I've Got You Under My Skin," wasn't that the one? Too bloody true, he thought.

Just then Mr. Rainer came noiselessly into the room and over toward the fireplace. "There's an urgent phone call for you, Mr. Flood. I think you'll want to take it in the study."

Flood stood up and waved a hand to the others, as much as to say, Never a dull moment. He followed Rainer out of the room and was gone for at least five minutes. Baring grinned across at Yardley and shrugged his shoulders. Neither of them felt the urge to talk, but Yardley did wonder what it could be at this late hour. Hell, what if the operation were to be postponed—or abandoned altogether?

Flood put his head in the door and said, "Bob, Nick, would you mind coming to the study? There's something we've got to discuss. Hey, Lysol, don't keep looking at his hand! Hold your cards up, Peter. Those old Etonians'd steal the pennies off a dead man's eyes."

The study was Flood's private sanctum and Yardley had not penetrated it before. In spite of the easy chairs and the low tables, it looked more like the bridge of a new naval frigate than a gentleman's reading room. There was a steel table with telephones on it, two computers and a word processor, a fax machine and a photocopier. The filing cabinets had an intricate locking device. Everything was modern, purposeful. The one homely touch was a small cluster of framed black-and-white photographs. Among them, a picture of two men in camouflage gear against a jungly background. Peering closer, he could just see that one was Flood and the other Baring.

"Grab a chair," Flood said. "We have a problem. Nothing

too serious. But it does mean I'll have to borrow Nick here for a day, maybe two at the outside. So he'll have to link up with you on the road. Let's see now, today's the fifth of October. You leave on the seventh, you'll be in Istambul by the tenth. That's easy. Nick can easily fly in and meet you there. No problem."

"I don't like it," Yardley said. "We're a team now. We should travel as a team."

"Sorry, Bob. I wouldn't do this to you if I didn't have to. Something really special has cropped up. I need Nick. It's only for a day or two."

"But what'll the others think? What do I tell them?"

"Just tell 'em Nick's had to stay back but he'll catch up. They know the score. They'll understand."

"Do I get to know what all the fuss is about?"

"Sure. That's why I asked you in here. That was your friend Rodel on the phone."

"God, I might have known it. His clammy hand's all over this op."

"Take it easy. Let me fill you in—and Nick as well."

Flood gave a quick and concise rundown of the telephone call. An hour earlier, Rodel had had his opposite number from the British Embassy in Paris "on the horn." MI6 had discovered that two Hizbollah hit men from Lebanon were due to arrive in Geneva this very night. They were to check in at the Hotel Ambassador by the lake—"the one where young Sharqi's been staying. Pure coincidence, of course." They were being run by a contact in Amsterdam—"the flowerman"—an Iranian who was into drugs and supplying arms to terrorist groups like the IRA, and was related to one of the influential ayatollahs back home in Tehran. The British plan was to wait until the three men came together in Geneva, then grab them without notifying Swiss authorities and slip them the few miles over the border into France. From there they could be extradited into the UK and used as a bargaining lever to help get British hostages in Beirut released. They had tipped off Rodel in the hope he could help put some pressure on the French government if things got difficult.

"It's a bloody stupid plan," Flood continued. "And they've hired some real clowns to pull it off. Someone tried to get me interested through a contact a couple of weeks ago and I told them politely to get lost. Playing cowboys and Indians on my home patch isn't my idea of good business. Even if it worked—which it won't—it would screw up relations with the Swiss. And probably the French as well."

"So if it's that stupid, why are you getting involved now?" Yardley asked.

"I'm not. Rodel has a very different plan for Nick and me."

The Yanks, he said, wanted the two Lebanese hit men eliminated. They needed to keep the flowerman at large—but running scared. The CIA had a ploy of its own, which would involve him when the time came. The flowerman was booked on the last flight out of Amsterdam's Schiphol Airport that night, bound for Geneva. But Rodel had pulled a quick one. He had called a contact in the Dutch antiterrorist outfit and had reported a bomb scare. Word had reached him, he claimed, that a delayed-action device had been planted on the Geneva-bound aircraft, probably in the luggage. That would mean an automatic twelve-hour delay for all the passengers who had checked in for the flight, including the flowerman. They would have to be cordoned off in a secure building, their luggage offloaded, and every trunk, suitcase and bag that had been put on board would have to be taken off and matched with the luggage tags attached to its owner's ticket. Then, even if there were no discrepancies, every item would have to searched thoroughly, as would the aircraft itself.

"It's an old security trick, Bob," Flood explained. "Rodel's bought himself—which means Nick and me—fourteen, fifteen hours. That aircraft won't take off before nine tomorrow morning and the delay shouldn't alert the flowerman. He's a pro, he'll know these bomb alerts can happen from time to time. He'll just take it in his stride. But he won't get to the Ambassador before eleven-thirty tomorrow morning at the earliest. The beauty is, he won't risk asking to make a phone call to tell his friends he'll be late. By the time he does get there, Nick and I will be long gone."

"But why do you need Nick here? Couldn't you do it on your own?"

"I probably could. Though don't underestimate these Lebanese guys. They can be good. Hell, Bob, you should know. You had a taste during your Beirut exploit. No, I have a plan building up. I need an Arabic-speaker. Like Nick."

Yardley thought for a moment, then said, "Okay, Flood. But Nick, when we check in at the Istambul Hilton, I want you there to greet us. And all in one piece. You hear me?"

"Loud and clear, skipper." Baring gave a wolfish grin. "All in one piece—my sentiments exactly."

As soon as Yardley had left the study to rejoin the others, Flood picked up a telephone and tapped out Rainer's extension. When the man answered he said, "Come to the study at once, please." A few moments later, Rainer tapped on the door and walked in. He was carrying a notepad and pen.

"This is urgent," Flood said. "First, get on to the Hotel London in Geneva and book two rooms *together.* Doesn't matter which floor, though the higher up the better. But they must be side by side. Book them in the name of Rothschild. If the desk clerk thinks it's *the* Mr. Rothschild, that's okay. But book them, even if you have to bribe the desk clerk. That's top priority.

"When you've done that, call up Geneva airport and book two separate one-way tickets for tomorrow afternoon. Use one of our offshore company's American Express card numbers, not one in my name. The first is a single for Mr. Baring here to Vienna and the other's for me—to Paris via Zurich. I must see Sharqi tomorrow morning before she boards the Tehran flight out of Zurich. Tickets to be collected an hour before boarding. Nick, do you have any money with you?"

Baring said, "I've a bit under a thousand francs, French money."

"You'll need more. Rainer, get some Amex traveler's checks out of the safe. What've we got, fifties and hundreds, aren't they? In dollars. Prepare fifteen hundred dollars' worth for Mr. Baring and the same for me. That should see you through the next few days, Nick." He turned to the gray administrator. "Would you get on with that immediately—we're leaving within the hour."

When Rainer had left, Baring said, "After Vienna?"

"Hang around for a day and a night. *The Marriage of Figaro*'s on there. Go and enjoy it. Then next day, fly to Frankfurt and stick around there for a day. The book fair'll be on. Get some culture, boy, it's not too late."

"And up yours, too. After Frankfurt?"

"Take a direct flight to Istambul. I reckon you'll be there a day ahead of the team. Do some sightseeing, take in a few mosques."

"You trying to make a gentleman out of me?"

"God forbid, you Rhodesian heathen. Let's go and get

ready. Pack a small bag, enough for one night. You can buy anything else you think you'll need when you get to Vienna."

"What about weapons?"

"We'll take a silenced Beretta each, with low-velocity ammo. This one's got to be quick and quiet."

A light flickered on the central telephone board. Flood picked up the handset, listened for a moment, then said, "Fine, and also prepare an itinerary of Mr. Baring's flights for him, thank you." He replaced the receiver. "Rainer's booked the rooms, so let's get going. See you downstairs in twenty minutes. I'll talk over the plan once we're in the car, we've got a couple of hours' driving ahead of us."

Darkness had fallen when they drove west out of Château d'Oex. They went down the valley, through Gruyères and onto the Bern-to-Lausanne highway at Bulle. The road ran south to the lake and linked up with the other autoroute near Vevey. This fast road continued west behind the lakeside towns to Geneva. There was little traffic and the headlights flung long arrows of light up the two-lane highway as Flood cruised the Porsche at ninety miles an hour. Like a big cat, Baring relaxed in the passenger seat. Flood knew the signs, he had been in action often enough before with Baring. The man was most dangerous when he appeared to be almost falling asleep with boredom. They were flashing through one of several tunnels when Baring asked casually whether the Porsche wasn't a bit conspicuous to leave parked near the hotel. Flood said that he permanently rented a locked garage near the main railway station. The car would stay there under cover until he returned from Paris to collect it. Baring nodded, as if to say, Fair enough, and then half closed his eyes again.

They left the autoroute as it merged with the city and were soon mingling with the evening traffic in the suburbs of Geneva. Flood wheeled left two streets before Cointrin railway station and pulled up in a narrow service road behind some shops. A quick turn of the key, a heave on the overhead door and the Porsche slid into the garage. The Hotel London was only a couple of hundred yards away and they strolled down the hill toward it, inconspicuous among the throng of commuters.

"We going to have much trouble locating the two boys?" Baring asked.

"No problem. God knows what came over British Intelligence. They're overexcited about this one. To get Rodel's help, they even told him the boys' room number in the Ambassador."

"They're not pulling a fast one—like giving him a phony number? Diverting his attention."

"They wouldn't dare. They're smart enough to realize he could pull the plug on the whole Beirut deal if they screwed him up."

"But he's going to pull the plug on these two anyway, and the Brits aren't that stupid not to know he had a hand in it."

"It's imperative the flowerman stays in Amsterdam. The MI6 operation is crossing Rodel's. He's just keeping everything tidy. We're not attributable. He will confuse them, say it must have been a pair of free-lancers, or maybe Mossad who made the hit."

"Will they be fool enough to believe that?"

"Probably not, but they'll have a result, two dead terrorists, and they need Rodel and the Agency too much to make a great hue and cry about it."

"What's the connection with these two?" Baring asked. "I don't mind killing a couple of unknowns—but I like to know how they fit."

"They're a couple of pawns in the big game. The usual volunteers for the chessmasters in Tehran. The flowerman, as far as I can tell, is playing broker for this killer team. He floats here in Europe for the Ayatollah as paymaster and controller for cells carrying out selective assassinations. He's a nephew of a rather nasty mullah in Tehran and is into political advantage in a big way. We know he's not averse to a little private enterprise."

"Why here?"

"There are a number of wealthy Iranian exiles around here and in France that are waiting for the patriotic call now that the war between Iraq and Iran has subsided and Khomeini's all but dead. They're a threat to the mullahs jostling for power in Tehran. Bani Sadr, the ex–prime minister living in Paris, has a following, and he and many others like him are seen as traitors and targets."

"So these Hizbollah boys are the hired guns."

"You could say they have a few Beirut favors to repay."

They walked into the Hotel London, as any two well-dressed businessmen, and checked in at reception. They took their separate keys and courteously declined the services of the hall porter, as they only had a small bag apiece. The time was eight-ten. Baring chose room 410 and Flood room 412 next door. Riding the elevator silently to the fourth floor, both men donned thin leather gloves and gathered their concentration. The doors opened onto a carpeted corridor, empty except for a chambermaid at the far end, who was collecting trays from outside various rooms. Flood said in an undertone, "Give me five minutes and I'll come to your room. Leave the door unlocked."

Five minutes later he slipped into Baring's room. He said, "Set up a few bottles of drink from the minibar on that table, soft drinks and beer." As Baring rose from the chair by the window, Flood made a quick inspection of the room and bathroom. Nothing had been disturbed. "Bring your bag and leave it in my room," he said.

Baring hung a "Do Not Disturb" sign on his door and closed it behind him, and they slipped into Flood's room unseen. He tossed his room key across to Flood's outstretched hand and dropped his bag on the bed. Flood checked his watch and they made their way silently down the fire stairs to the lobby, avoiding contact with the porter. The pair stepped out to the busy road that ran alongside the lake, and a few minutes' walk brought them to the Hotel Ambassador. They made no attempt to talk above the noise of the traffic and the rushing icy water egressing the lake to become the Rhône. Flood skirted round the entrance of the hotel and ducked down a side ramp that led to the underground garage. Baring waited by the ramp while Flood scrutinized the parked cars carefully and finally chose one which had a film of dust on the windshield, a silver-gray Mercedes 190 with a Swiss license plate—VA-199-0043. There was no one in the garage; he worked quickly and placed Baring's room key behind the hinged rear plate. Anyone approaching the Mercedes would not see it. Flood gave a nod and they moved noiselessly out of the garage to the street above.

Back in Flood's room at the Hotel London they prepared themselves. Flood unzipped his bag and withdrew one of the sinister black Berettas, its familiar shape distorted by the six-inch cylinder screwed into the barrel, and handed it to Baring. He removed an identical weapon for himself. Instinctively both men checked the handguns—eject and check magazine loaded, tighten silencer down, work the action, check empty chamber and barrel, ram home magazine, safety on, then off. Completing the routine simultaneously, they played a metallic duet as each of them jacked a round into the chamber.

"Nick, I spotted a linen closet at the end of the corridor, three rooms away. I'm going to cover your back from there. I'll have the whole corridor covered. I hope they'll both come in here together, I want to take them out in here if we can." His voice was quiet, methodical. "You know the drill. They'll go to the Mercedes and find the key, walk here and let themselves into your room. You give them a couple of minutes to feel safe, then call them through to this room, that puts them here approximately twelve minutes after your initial call. They'll do the walk in a greater hurry than we did. All set?"

"Yeah." Baring squeezed his fingers into his gloves and flexed his hands, like a surgeon. He sat down beside the phone and lifted the handset—and waited. He thought briefly about how many times in the past he had set up such an ambush, then sat and waited for the unsuspecting prey. His finger tapped out the number of the Ambassador. The efficient receptionist connected his call to the boys' room and the phone purred loudly in his ear, perhaps for twenty seconds. Baring glanced at Flood and shrugged. Then a raucous voice, which even Flood, standing a few feet away, could hear, answered in a staccato rush. Saying nothing, Baring replaced the handset.

"Okay," Flood said. "They're there. It's on. Now let's try your Arabic on them. This time, when he answers, just say the Arabic for 'garage,' then the plate number of that Mercedes. Got it? 'VA-199-0043.' "

Baring nodded. He dialed again. This time the voice answered on the second ring. Baring overrode the voice with a domineering mutter in a guttural language and then abruptly hung up. "Right! The clock's running."

Flood placed the two bags on the table, away from the door but clearly visible to anyone entering. He then moved to the bathroom entrance and sighted the field of fire, satisfying himself that it covered the main door. He touched Baring's shoulder as he walked across the room. Once in the corridor he turned left, away from the elevator, and concealed himself in the linen closet.

Baring checked his watch. Ten minutes had passed and he had not heard the elevator stop at the fourth floor. Maybe they hadn't taken the bait? He moved to stand against the bedroom door and put his eye to the spy hole. Nothing. Flood saw them first. Crouched low among baskets of linen with the door slightly ajar, he saw one, then another, head of black hair appear level with the top of the stairs beside the elevator. They weren't amateurs after all. The two men, dressed in new-looking suits and shiny shoes, edged their way into the corridor. The leading Arab was tall, with a thick groomed beard; the other was shorter, with the contemporary designer stubble common to pop videos. The tall one seemed satisfied with the empty corridor and signaled his partner forward. They both stood toe to toe and inspected the room key, then looked directly at the door shielding Flood and strode toward it. Flood's pulse rose. Had they seen him? Four doors away the short Arab took the other's arm and steered him to the door of room 410. The tall one knocked lightly, careful to stand to one side. He inserted the key and they furtively entered the room. Flood willed Baring to hear them.

Baring heard the door of the room slam hard. He was startled—Jesus, the bastards are in there. He had moved away from his door for a few seconds. With the waiting, his thoughts again drifted to reflection. Waiting for the prey, what a life, he thought. Orders come, you go and kill people, convinced they're the enemy—but always strangers. They could be young, old, married, single, happy or sad. Who knows? Who even cares? You did the job, quickly and neatly, the way you had been trained. And so you went on. One day maybe the game will be reversed on you, Nick; you'll be the bloody prey in the trap. The noise next door had snapped him out of it. Christ, he thought, forget this morbid bullshit. He was already reaching for the phone, and dialing room 410. It rang once, twice—he could hear it faintly on the other side of the wall. When the call was answered, he said sharply in Arabic, "Come quietly to room four twelve," and hung up.

Baring picked up the Beretta, clicked the safety off and walked silently into the bathroom. He left the door ajar and turned on the cold tap in the shower. The main door leading to the corridor opened to the right. The bathroom was situated in the corner on the opposite side of the room. He had placed a coin in the pile of the carpet to stop the main door from closing under its own weight, and now he concentrated on it, across his field of fire, watching for the slightest movement. The door was suddenly pushed half open and the short Arab knocked feebly as he appeared nervously from behind it. Baring had to draw them both in, and in muffled Arabic he shouted a welcome just loud enough to be heard above the noise of the shower. The Lebanese smiled broadly and stepped into the room, letting the door slam shut behind him. He turned to catch it and was startled by the coin spinning up from the floor and ricocheting off the wall. *Phut, phut*—the first two bullets entered the left side of his chest and he turned to face back into the room; *phut*—the third hit him below the left eye. Baring remained rigid, one pace from the bathroom door with arms outstretched ready to fire again. He watched the man's shocked expression distort as his head swelled like an inflating balloon. His top row of teeth seemed to eject onto his chest; blood gushed from his mouth. From eight feet away, Baring's frozen eyes saw danger in the Arab's jerking arm; he shot twice more, breaking each of his elbows in turn. It was a trained reflex: a brain-dead victim can still pull the pin from a grenade; he had seen it happen. Baring now stepped forward past the dead body and reached for the door.

Flood had watched the short man enter the room from his concealed position twelve yards away in the linen closet. Then the door had slammed, surprising the tall one, who stepped back and reached into his jacket. He had turned to face the stairs and elevator, the route to safety, and for a second had his back to Flood. It was all the advantage Flood needed. As the Arab turned back to face the noise, Flood was coming to a halt ten feet away, Beretta raised and aimed—*phut.*

Baring appeared from the room to see the tall Arab crumple to a heap against the wall. He quickly stepped to the body and confirmed him dead, looked along to Flood and drew his forefinger across his throat. Flood remained in the firing stance, ready to shoot again. He said urgently, "Check inside the jacket. Careful!" Baring lifted the man's lapel with his silencer; a long stiletto, half out of its armpit sheath, gleamed dully in the subdued corridor lighting.

"Okay," Flood said, "let's get him into the room. Take his legs would you, Nick?" As he spoke, Flood took the Arab's silk handkerchief from his suit jacket's top pocket and quickly wiped away the thin smear of blood at the base of the wall. It was the only evidence of the man's death slide. A single bullet through the bridge of his nose had killed him instantly.

Baring propped the door back with one foot as he stooped

to grasp the corpse around the ankles. At that moment the door of room 411 opposite opened and an elderly woman with spectacles, wearing a fur coat, emerged. She gave a look of horror and her mouth opened to scream. Flood moved like lightning. In one stride he had her held in a viselike grip, one hand across her eyes, the other clamped to her mouth. Equally fast, Baring had dropped the corpse's ankles and aimed his Beretta at her heart. Flood froze Baring's action with a deliberate shake of his head, as he spun the panicking woman to face the wall and dropped the hand covering her eyes to grip her behind the neck. Two efficient fingers found the arterial pressure point close to her ear and pressed. She went limp in his grasp. He heaved her over his shoulder and rushed her across into 412, dumping her unceremoniously on the bed. The dead Arab quickly followed and was dropped next to his partner in the middle of the floor.

"Whip the sheets off the bed, Nick. Tie her up where she is."

As he did so, Baring asked, "You going soft? The dead don't identify people."

"Leave it, Nick, we've done what we have to do. The poor old bitch just walked right into it. Not her fault, she was too mortified to remember faces." Flood's tone signaled that the subject was closed. Swiftly they checked the room over and retrieved the bags. Flood took Baring's room key from the body and wiped it clean. "I'll check next door, meet me at the stairs," he said.

They took the stairs to the sixth floor and called the elevator. When it arrived, two hotel guests stepped out, ignoring them completely. Flood and Baring rode to the first floor, peeling off their gloves and depositing them with the weapons into Flood's bag. They took advantage of the bustle of arriving guests to leave the hotel unnoticed—the hotel they had checked into only an hour and twenty minutes earlier.

As they unhurriedly walked up the hill toward the station, Flood dropped the hotel keys in a trashcan. "You go directly to the Penta Hotel at the airport," he said. "Rainer has listed your reservation details. Your Vienna flight departs tomorrow morning. Keep your head down, and no women."

"What about you?"

"I'm organized here in town. If you see me at the airport tomorrow morning, you don't know me and I don't know you, okay? Oh, and good luck in Tehran." Flood walked away across the road.

Two days later, Sir Denis Stiffkey (pronounced "Stew-key"), the permanent undersecretary of state and head of the cabinet secretariat, was lunching at the Athenaeum with his old friend Arthur Best, formerly Brigadier Best of the Ministry of Defense and now seconded to a department that no one mentioned on an open telephone line.

"We're lucky to get a window table," Sir Denis said. "Especially this one. Jim Callaghan always bags it when he lunches here. What are you going to have? Tomato-and-thyme soup and the lamb cutlets? Very nice too—I'll join you. And a selection of vegetables? Excellent. I think a bottle of the club claret would go down well with that lot. All right with you?" He wrote out the order in a neat, small hand.

"We might have some of that Stilton afterward, though, mind you, the sweets trolley is worth a second look. I really must say the food's improved enormously since I first joined. It used to remind me of prep school—you know, spotted dick and jam roly-poly for puddings. But now the cooking's quite something."

"Stiffy, you're burbling," said Best.

"Pure self-defense, I assure you. We haven't spoken for weeks, and then you suddenly call me up, must see me pronto, matter of vital importance, can't wait. Arthur, they say I have a good nose for claret. Let me tell you something. I have a better nose for trouble. And you spell trouble to me—with a very large *T.* A bull's-eye, would you say—or at least an inner?"

"Slap in the middle of the bull."

"It can wait half an hour. Trouble is best confronted on a full stomach. Let us eat and drink while you wonder whether I will grant you that favor you—should I say 'desperately'?—need. What do you make of the presidential election? First it was all Dukakis and now Bush is running ahead. What do your friends at Langley say? Our man in Washington is being very poker-faced. He keeps sending dispatches saying, 'On the one hand the Democrats are doing well in the Northeast and on the other hand the Republicans should sweep the Midwest.' I like a man who comes out and backs his fancy, don't you?"

Teasing his guest like a picador with a surly bull, he spent the next half-hour, as he had threatened, in gossip and anecdote. At last, when they had been served their Stilton and biscuits and a small glass of club port apiece, Sir Denis said, "I have been all tongue. Now I am all ears. Tell me the worst, Arthur."

The brigadier told him of how they had set up a clandestine operation in Geneva, where two Lebanese would-be assassins were due to meet the flowerman, the Iranian from Amsterdam who ran them. Of how two British field agents, who had been shadowing the Lebanese, had been tipped off through an anonymous telephone call, to break into a room on the fourth floor of the Hotel London. The plan was to spirit the Lebanese and the Iranian a few miles over the border into France, and then into the UK. If there were to be any problems in France, the French authorities had agreed unofficially to expedite their extradition.

" 'And I, Teresias, have seen it all.' Arthur, I'm all agog. This is going to be a horror story that makes Boris Karloff look like a Boy Scout. I can't wait to hear the worst."

Looking even more sullen, the brigadier stubbornly plowed on. He described how his team in the field had turned up at the Hotel London at five in the morning—an hour when the opposition might still be in bed—to find all hell broken loose on the fourth floor. The room in question contained two extremely dead Lebanese and no sign of the flowerman, and an elderly Swiss woman having hysterics in the loudest possible way. And all over the place, squads of the extremely efficient Swiss police and the Sureté counterintelligence. It turned out that the woman's husband, a *very* influential Zurich banker, had been waiting for her down in the bar the previous evening for a predinner drink. When she failed to arrive after nearly an hour, he had gone up to her room but got no reply. The hotel had supplied a pass key but the room was empty, though it was clear she had been occupying it. Her clothes were hung neatly in the closet, her toilet things in the bathroom and her modest, high-necked nightgown on the bed. So the husband had insisted on calling the Geneva police. By the early hours of the morning, a room-by-room search had begun. The woman had been discovered in the room across the hall, gagged and tied by bedsheets. And on the floor beside her those two dead Arabs, presumed Lebanese, although they had no identification on them. The woman had been rushed to the hospital in a state of shock but she managed to say something about two men shooting the Arabs—and then nothing.

"Just a story of everyday Swiss folks," Sir Denis murmured. "Your boys wanted to extradite them, someone else comes along and kills them. All terribly neat, what? Why are we supposed to grieve, Arthur, wipe away the furtive tear?"

"Once we got them and the flowerman back on British soil we'd have had a wonderful lever for releasing our own hostages in Beirut. And first we'd have grilled them to a turn, found out their contacts, who was on their hit list, the lot. The worst is, our field men blundered right into it. I'm not excusing them, they'll get a right bollocking, but they got up the nose of Swiss counterintelligence, who soon discovered we were running a clandestine operation on their patch. If the Swiss government takes it up officially, there'll be hell to pay. What do you think Herself will do if it comes to her notice?"

"That is too awful to contemplate. The least she'll want is your head on a noncorrosive platter."

"Exactly. Now do you see why I'm metaphorically on my knees to you, Stiffy?"

"Let's have another glass of port while we finish this excellent Stilton. Which gives me time to think." He waved to the wine waiter, then picked another biscuit off the tray.

He wiped the crumbs off his mouth with the damask napkin a few minutes later and asked, "Do you have any idea who killed the two Arabs and tied up the old woman?"

"Nothing firm. But a free-lance operator, a New Zealander named Flood, was seen at Geneva airport quite early the following morning. It was the kind of shut-out job he's good at."

Sir Denis gave a pseudo-groan. "Oh no, not him again."

"Why, do you know Flood?"

"Not personally—thank God. But, as you know, a prisoner named Short—or something like that—was spirited out of Wormwood Scrubs a few weeks back. Since then, he's totally disappeared. The Home Office and your opposite numbers at MI5 reckon that Flood was somehow involved. And every now and then his name crops up at secretary-of-state level. Anything else that might tie this operation to Flood?"

"Only that he sometimes undertakes 'assignments' for a CIA executive, Roger Rodel, at the U.S. Embassy in Paris."

"Rodel? Fat man with horn-rimmed glasses and a wet handshake—that the one?"

"That's him," said the brigadier.

"But what ties him in with Geneva?"

"This: Unknown to me—which won't happen again!—the man I put in charge of the French end wanted to be on the safe side. So he goes and tells this Rodel about the op and asks for his help in case the going gets rough. We know the Frogs will always listen more to the Yanks than to us—but that was nonsense. Rodel's a crafty bugger and he probably had plans of his own. So what easier than to call up his chum Flood and put a marker on the Beirut boys?"

Sir Denis said, "You haven't explained what happened to the—what did you call him—flowerpot man?"

"The flowerman. I wish he was on our side. He's smarter than our boys. He must have spotted the kerfuffle at the Hotel London and gone back quietly to Amsterdam. Not a whisper of him in Geneva."

The cabinet secretary glanced at his wristwatch. "We may have to skip coffee. I have to be back at two-thirty sharp—for an audience with Her Highness. Let me sum up quickly. Your department has been caught in a public place with its trousers down. The Swiss may or may not lodge a formal complaint. In case they do, you've got to act first—and fast. If you haven't done so already, you must disband that team. Send them on leave, drop them down a salt mine for all I care, but get 'em out of circulation. And this very afternoon, you write a special report. You had a team on surveillance pursuing those two Lebanese—you'll get full marks for being ahead of the game. They tracked them down to Geneva and discovered that a rival gang—probably Amal—had knocked 'em off first. End of story. No mention of bloody Rodel and even bloodier Flood. It was purely surveillance, no funny stuff. Mark the report top-secret and personal to me, copies to the heads of MI6 and MI5. I want the top copy on my desk first thing tomorrow morning. Leave it to me. There are two long reports from Education and Manpower due in—and two formal dinners in the next week at Number Ten. I'll slip your report near the bottom of the pile for Herself. With luck, she'll skim it. If she wants to know more, I duck out. You make your own excuses! *Capito?*"

"Stiffy, when you were head prefect at Winchester, I thought you were an awful shit. You've improved over the years. Seriously, I'm enormously grateful. You may have saved my neck."

"Don't think it won't cost you. If you're still holding down the job in a month, you buy me dinner at Le Gavroche with a bottle of Dom Perignon to start with, a nice Lafite for the main course and at least one large Delamain to round off. A deal?"

"It's a deal."

Two days later, Nick Baring was sitting in the ground-floor bar of the Hilton Hotel, Istambul. It was early evening and the place was as yet only half full. The occupants were mainly European businessmen, a bunch of raucous Germans at a table to his right and two Swedes sitting thoughtfully over their schnapps in a corner at his other side. He had by instinct selected a table at an angle to the room, with his back against the angle and the widest possible range of vision in front of him. He was sipping a scotch on the rocks, waiting.

Twenty minutes later, he spotted the Honorable Rupert Lycett-Smythe standing in the archway, looking around. He waved and Lysol came over. He had an open-necked lumberjack's thick shirt and jeans.

"Christ," he said, "the idle rich. I might have known."

"Surprised they let you in, Lysol. Boy, do you pong! Stand well upwind, if you please."

"The others went up to their rooms to have a shower. All right, I need one too, don't tell me. That Yardley's a great guy, but why didn't someone tell me the Yanks run a dry ship when they're in the field? For pity's sake, order me a large scotch, Nick. I'm busting for a drink."

Baring summoned the waiter, who was wearing a red fez and a red cummerbund across his long tuniclike uniform. When the order had been given, Lysol said, "Do you know the story about the Cairo bus conductor who went up and down saying, 'Fez, please'? Okay, forget it. Where the hell you been, Nick? Bob got all mysterious when you never turned up in Basel. He kept saying you'd been called away—or some shit like that. What goes on?"

"Something you wouldn't know about. Culture. I've been to the opera, looked at dozens of books, even spoke to a publisher or two—and here I am."

"Bullshit. You wouldn't recognize a book except at the races. Come on, cut the crap. Tell your old Uncle Rupe all about it."

"I *am* telling you. I flew to Vienna and saw *The Marriage of Figaro*—do you remember Mozart?—and then went on to Frankfurt for the book fair."

Lysol said, "You mean you're not going to tell me."

"There's nothing else to tell. Look, I'd flown out of Geneva while you and the rest were still up at the chalet. You saw me late-ish the previous evening—when you were cheating that poor innocent at cards. What the hell could I have done in that short time?"

"Well, maybe enjoyed the juices of some gorgeous girl for a start."

"Okay, Lysol, if it helps your dirty imagination, let's say I've been spending my time gyrating with a bunch of women."

"You brought any of 'em with you?"

"No way. This is serious business from now on."

"To hell with serious business. Let's have another scotch before I go off and shower."

9

—Of my Base Metal may be filed a Key,
That shall unlock the Door he howls
without.

As he relaxed under a warm shower in his bedroom in the Istambul Hilton, washing away the sweat and grime of three days on the road, Yardley felt that this was the last frontier. The two giant trucks had driven slowly into the city and had been parked in a vast truck compound near the outskirts. He and the others had taken their overnight grips and driven in a couple of taxis to the Hilton. He had a superficial impression of an age-old town that straddled East and West. The taxis were American Chevrolets, the driver had a portable recorder alongside him, blaring out Michael Jackson and Madonna hits. And yet there was the smell and the pace of the East as they drove along. Once, in a narrow street, the leading taxi was held up while two donkeys yoked tail to head were urged across the street by a man with a *keffiyeh* wound round his head. At the end of a wide avenue with glittering modern shops, you could see a bulbous mosque with its finger of a minaret pointing vertically to the sky. It was, he felt, an interim world, neither one thing nor the other.

He was keen to press on, to get into Tehran, get on with the job, finish it and get out. Part of the urgency, he admitted to himself, was to see Sharqi again, to find out whether the image he had been building up in his mind and memory as the miles rolled by under the wheels of the leading truck was matched by reality when he met her again.

He looked around the hotel bar as they were having after-dinner drinks. The Belgian twins were at one small table, finishing a bottle of wine between them. They were silent but they seemed quite happy. Yardley guessed that somehow they communicated on a deeper level than mere speech. Nick was at the bar ordering a round and Lysol was with him, to help carry the drinks back. Yardley sensed some emulation there. Lysol would have liked to be a free-lance operator, no commitments, moving from one job to the next. One day if his elder brother died without having a family, he would inherit the title and the vast estates and the obligation of finding a wife who would bear him a son to carry on the line. His was the obviously enviable position, but he was still free to envy someone else at the opposite extreme, someone with no lands and no big house and no wife and family, just quick reflexes and a cold nerve.

Miller and Archie Morton were sitting with Yardley, each drinking a pint of lager, "weasel water," as Miller, the ex-Marine, called it with contempt. Peter Shaw, who on each day of the journey so far had become embedded more and more in the team, had excused himself five minutes before to go "and have a leak," as he put it.

Yardley suddenly thought, Five minutes for a piss, it's too long. The men's room was only down a short flight of stairs. The hairs on the back of his neck stiffened.

He said to Morton, "No panic, but Peter's been gone quite a while. He can't have passed out, can he?"

"No way, skipper. He had a glass of wine and some mineral water at supper. I was sitting next to him."

"Let's go have a look. Will you come along? Won't be a moment," he said to Miller.

They went down the flight of steps through the swinging door to the men's room. Shaw crouched with his back against a wall between the two banks of urinals. There was a look on his face like that of a rabbit just before the stoat plunges its sharp front teeth into its victim's throat. Three large Germans were surrounding him. The largest held Shaw against the wall with his left hand. His right had unzipped the small man's fly and the big paw was feeling inside his open trousers.

Yardley said, "What the hell? . . ."

The leader said, "No problem, friend. This man *mein Gott* he make improper suggestion. We teach *sehr gute* lesson. You make scarce, *ja*?"

"Ja," Yardley said aloud. In a conversational mutter, he added for Morton, "You left, me right, then both for the big one. Don't kill 'em."

He turned on his heel, as did Morton. Shaw shrieked, "Don't leave me, Bob!"

Yardley swung back and swerved into action. Using the edge of his right hand like an axe, he hit the first man on the right a chopping blow on the side of the neck. As he jack-knifed, Yardley swung his left foot across, kicking him flush in the groin. The man collapsed with a half-groan. At the left edge of his vision he saw Morton give his target a deadly backhander at the base of his nose and then a stiff two-fingered prod in the diaphragm. The German went down with a crash.

"And then there was one," he said softly. "Let's cope with this big shit, Archie."

They closed in on the remaining German. He held up his hands and tried to contort his face into a smile. "It was a joke," he said. He pronounced it "yoke." "A joke, no?"

"No," replied Yardley. He feinted with his left hand and then kicked the man in the crotch. As he lurched convulsively forward, Yardley hit him almost nonchalantly across the bridge of his nose. There was a crunching noise, the nostrils spouted blood. The man groaned and rolled to the marble floor, hunching himself into a fetal position, his hands between his legs.

Yardley stepped over him and put an arm around Shaw's quivering shoulders. "Christ, I'm sorry, Peter. Those bastards! Still, the U.S. Cavalry arrived on time."

Shaw looked up at him with naked admiration. "I can't thank you, Bob, and you, Archie. I swear I didn't lead 'em on. I just came down for a pee, that's all. They followed me in and crowded round me, honest."

"Sure," said Yardley. "We know you're not gay. They thought they'd have a yoke. Well, the yoke's on them." He stirred one of the groaning bodies with his toecap. "Here, better zip yourself up, and let's get the hell out of here. The ice is melting in my scotch upstairs."

Yardley ordered an early start next morning. He was confident that the three Germans would not risk a formal complaint and any member of the hotel staff who came across them in the men's room might well conclude that it had been a private fight. But he wanted to take no risks; the Turkish police were held to be a suspicious crowd and official statements, with the need of an interpreter, would at the least consume precious time. So, soon after dawn on Tuesday, October 11, the two big trucks nosed out of the park and drove slowly eastward across the Bosporus.

Jacques, the driver of the lead vehicle, humming tunelessly, was hunched over the steering wheel, a Gauloise clamped to the corner of his mouth. He had the gift of companionable silence. There was never any need to scratch one's head and think of a topic to discuss with him. If he had something to say, he would say it, briefly. If not, he kept silent. An ideal traveling companion, Yardley felt.

Nick Baring had taken the bunk in the gap between the seats and the hood of the truck's cab. His eyes were closed, his breathing even and his limbs relaxed. As a very raw member of the Green Berets, Yardley had been sent on a winter mountain course at Leysin in Switzerland, where Dougal Haston ran the climbing school. Haston was one of the greats; he had climbed the North Face of the Eiger in winter and Mount Everest by the hitherto unclimbed Southwest Face. He had taught Clint Eastwood mountaineering and had doubled for him on the more hazardous climbs in the film *The Eiger Sanction.* Tragically, he was killed soon afterward in a sudden avalanche; but thinking of him reminded Yardley of Nick Baring. Each was like a wild puma. In action, sinuous flowing motion; out of action, totally relaxed, apparently dozing. He had seen Haston front-pointing on his crampons with an ice-axe in each hand up an almost vertical glassy ice-wall. It was the outer edge between success and disaster. He guessed that Baring would come through equally well if they ran into a dicey situation in the next week or two. That Flood was some picker.

His mind came back to Shaw, who was sitting alongside, keeping up a running monologue on the sights and scenery they were passing. Poor little Peter! He was going through a bad attack of hero worship right now. Yardley was not heeding his flow but now and then threw in a noncommittal "Uh-huh" as he tried to weigh up the prospects. Would Shaw stand up to the pressure? Once they were in the hostile city, potential spies and enemies on all sides, spending hours every day in a claustrophobic basement, would the safe man crack up? If it was certain he would, the two trucks might just as well pull off the highway right now, turn around and drive back to St. Galen. Shaw was the one trump card in the whole pack. He had around him a fighting force that could not be bettered. But only he had the expertise to crack that vault and open the safe inside. If he fell apart, the op was doomed. Yardley decided there and then to take advantage of the hero worship and make Peter Shaw his close ally. "Hey, Peter," he said, "that sounded interesting. Say it again."

The trucks kept to the old military routine, driving on for an hour and fifty minutes, then taking a ten-minute break and then on for another hour and fifty minutes, and so on until they halted for half an hour in the middle of the day. A ten-minute break was enough for everyone on board to get out, stretch his legs and change drivers, where required. They drove ever eastward, through the winding passes to Erzincan, with the eleven-thousand-foot-high jagged peaks of the Munzur Daglari range to their right, and then to Kandilli and Erzerum, threading past further sawtooth ranges until they came to the plateau. The air was thin, crisp; it hardly filled the lungs. Outside the warmth and coziness of the driving cab, Yardley noticed that Shaw was panting a little, like a small dog after unaccustomed exercise. He would have to get used to being at altitude. Tehran itself was 3,850 feet above sea level.

They camped the first night at Dogubayazit, fifteen miles from the Iranian border and only thirty miles from the USSR to the north. Ten miles away from the truck park, to the northeast a conical peak rose to a height of almost seventeen thousand feet. The setting sun stained its western profile blood-red. As they began to cook up their evening meal, even the talkative Lysol fell silent as he contemplated the sight. "I'd love to climb up there," he said. "What a fantastic view there must be."

"Hark at him," Miller jeered. "A guy who can hardly climb upstairs. You know what you see from the top? I've been up those mountains farther east, I know. Miles and miles of fuck-all, that's what."

Lysol said to Yardley, "Skipper, you didn't pick this mob carefully enough. That man's got no soul."

"Soul, soul? Arsehole to you, Lysol," Miller said.

"What do you expect from a pig but a grunt," Lysol replied, and that clinched the conversation.

Yardley called them all together after supper and ran through the drill for the following day. They would be crossing the frontier into Iran within half an hour of starting off. There should be no problems with the Turkish customs, as all the new air-conditioning equipment was sealed in bond. Nor should the Iranian customs be suspicious. They were bringing goods into the country and had a whole raft of impressive documents, signed and sealed by the Tehran authorities to prove it. The only problem was the weaponry secreted in the second truck with the other equipment. Metal detectors would not be able to distinguish one load of goods from the other at least, he reckoned not.

All the same, he cautioned the team to be patient and keep quiet while passing through both sets of customs posts. "For God's sake, no English," he said. "Don't forget, we're all honest Swiss workers. Those of you who don't know any German or any *Schweizer Deutsch,* just keep your mouths shut. Nick will do all the talking that's required at the Turkish end and Miller can parley Farsi to the Iranians. If anyone addresses you directly, act dumb, avoid conversation, and show him your Suiza passport. Okay? There are lots of foreign trucks around, now there's a truce between Iraq and Iran. We'll tuck in behind the leaders. Maybe the customs will be bored by the time they reach us."

And so it turned out. The swarthy unshaven Turks at the border post waved the trucks through after a cursory glance at the manifest. The Iranian customs men, equally swarthy and even more unshaven, did stamp each passport, even glancing up to see that the photograph roughly resembled the owner of the passport, and one of them undid the lashings of the lead truck and peered vaguely into the dark interior. But that was all. As Yardley had anticipated, there was a long column of DAFs and Volvos and Mercedes six-, eight- and ten-wheelers, all waiting to roll into the smitten country and swap their goods for petrodollars. Even the fundamentalist regime could not continue to demand sacrifices from its people after the fighting had come to an end.

Sharqi had been back at her desk in the Shams ol-'Amareh—The Building of the Sun—within the complex of the Ghulistan Palace, for two days before the summons arrived. A surly janitor, formerly a revolutionary guard and supposedly an executioner for the mullahs, walked into her room without knocking and told her she had to see the Deputy Minister, at once. He slammed the door on his way out.

In the Shah's day, she thought, the man would have stood with eyes downcast when she passed him by. He would have considered it above his station to look one of the wealthy middle classes straight in the face. Now the revolution and the gun had reversed it all. Dressed in a little brief authority, she said to herself, as she gathered a notebook and the file on her latest Swiss visit. Oh God, please let it be brief.

She ran lightly up the two flights of stairs. A dignified dignitary would have waited for the elevator, and might have waited a long time. The building had been constructed a dozen years before to house a special Ministry of Tourism, which one of the many sycophants surrounding the Shah had persuaded him to pay for. The idea had been to encourage tourists from the West, in particular the United States, to visit Tehran and Mount Demavend and Isfahan and Persepolis in the south and pay homage to the wisdom and the lineage of His Imperial Highness, the Shah-in-Shah. In fact, as she and "the hundred families" knew all too well, it had been just another con game to remove millions of dollars from the country's treasury and pour them into the coffers of the "families," who owned the construction companies through nominees. And so it had been jerry-built. There were large cracks in the ornate facade and the elevators only worked sporadically; even worse now, since no spare parts had arrived once the Revolution took place.

She tapped at the door, paused and then walked in. Her boss, Bahram Sohrabi, sat behind a large mahogany desk, gleaming in the fall sunshine that streamed through the large windows to his right. There were no papers on his leather blotting pad, but alongside there was an ornately chased brass tray with a copper high-necked coffee jug and two small porcelain cups—the best Royal Doulton, she guessed. "Ah, Sharqi," he said, "come in and sit down. Coffee?"

She smiled and nodded. As he busied himself, pouring the thick Turkish coffee with exquisite care, she looked at him guardedly and tried to assess the atmosphere. She knew his type so well; it was a far more sinister and dangerous type than the out-and-out fundamentalist mullahs. His father had been a rich man under the Shah and the son had been educated at the Sorbonne and Heidelberg. There were hushed rumors that on his return to Iran, before the Shah abdicated, he had been connected with SAVAK, the dreaded secret police force. And yet father and son had managed to play both sides off against the middle. Sohrabi Senior had maintained links with Ayatollah Khomeini during his exile in France. So when the Revolution came, the family bobbed up again. The father had had a series of minor heart attacks and was no longer active in politics, but he had developed private links with Ayatollah Rafsanjani, who seemed a good bet to lead Iran when Khomeini finally died.

Bahram Sohrabi wore a kind of linen caftan over what was clearly a Savile Row suit. His neat black semibrogue shoes were as clearly hand-made. Once, going through a series of invoices for art purchases, she had come across receipted bills from Huntsman, the London tailors, and Lobb's, the Royal Warrant shoemakers in St. James's Street. She had quickly pushed them back into the obscurity of the files. She suspected that his broadly knotted silk tie was by Sulka. When in a good mood, he liked to be called "Barry." Otherwise, it was "Mr. Bahram" or, worse still, "Mr. Sohrabi." Which would it be this time? she wondered.

Again, in a reproving mood, he would talk to her in classical Farsi. When being informal or trying to flirt, it would be a mixture of slangy English and German. His few words to date had been in English. A good sign?

He handed the fragile coffee cup across the table. "So how did it go this time?" he asked, still in English. "You had a swinging time in little old Switzerland, Sharqi?"

"Hardly swinging, Mr. Sohrabi . . ."

". . . Barry," he interjected.

"Barry. The sales ran for two full days. In the evenings, I talked with different New York and London dealers. It's always useful to know what may be coming up for sale, even weeks and months ahead."

"Of course. We have every confidence in you. If we hadn't . . ." He shrugged and with a lopsided smile turned his hands palm upward. "Now tell me what you bought for the greater glory of the sacred State."

She ran through the list from her notebook: a set of sixteenth-century Isfahani paintings on ivory disks, some silver filigree bracelets from the Nasr-i-Shirin period and three Bokhara silk prayer rugs, which were at least two hundred years old. The total cost had been six hundred thousand rials, about eighty thousand dollars at the official rate. They both knew full well but were too discreet even to mention it to one another that this represented over three quarters of a million dollars at the real devalued rate of the rial.

"You appear to have bought shrewdly, as always. Spot on, as we say. But what happened to the bronze bust of our noble ancestor, Darius? I thought that was the main reason for your visit."

"It was false, Barry. A phony, as they say." Damn, watch your tongue, she said to herself. Don't let him see you're mocking him. She hurried on, "That nice man from Bonhams—you know, I've mentioned him before—put me wise. He's an expert in metal founding. He suspected it was machine turned. At the inspection before the sale, he showed me a row of grooves around the base, where the metal had been clamped to hold it steady against the machine."

"You don't think he may have been bluffing? And bought it for himself more cheaply?"

"No. I sat next to him when that lot came up. He didn't bid. In fact, the bust never reached its reserve and was withdrawn."

"And he didn't buy it afterward—at the reserve price?"

"You are very wise, Barry. But no, I'm sure he didn't. That was the first day of the sale. I'd have heard from the other dealers on the second evening if he had. Word travels fast in the art world."

"Not only in the art world, *Liebchen.* I often think of you when you're away, a young girl among all those experienced men. A babe in arms—and a beautiful babe. It must be difficult, a single woman all alone, a *jeune veuve* with no man of her own. And those dealers, eating and drinking in the best hotels, away from their wives and families. Who could blame you if there were soft music, a glass of champagne too many, an eager man to comfort your solitude."

She could have smacked the leering smile right off his face but she carefully put down her coffee cup and clenched her small fists in her lap.

"The reality is quite different," she said coldly. "I can assure you. Several of the male dealers are homosexuals. Most of the others are happily married men, twenty years older than me. Besides, when I have the honor of representing the Islamic Republic in a foreign country, I know that in a small way I am an ambassador. To behave as you have suggested would not only bring dishonor on myself but, worse still, on my country as well. I may not have been born to the true faith but, as you know, I have deliberately chosen to follow it for the rest of my days."

"Come on, Sharqi. I was—what do they say?—pulling your leg. But, chaste as indeed you are, I think you must have made at least one small conquest. A handsome young man, who must have been a European, was seen saying goodbye to you at Zurich Airport."

If she had still been holding the porcelain cup, she would have dropped it with a crash on the parquet floor. She must have been spotted with Flood at the airport. If only she had been wearing the *chador,* the formal black veil that covered the nose and chin of a devout woman. But now female ministry officials only wore it in public; inside the building they moved around unveiled.

Somehow she managed to hold her face together and then even produced a half-smile. "Oh good heavens," she said, "yes, there was a man at the airport, but I didn't think he was handsome. He was the representative of Novaire AG, the company that sold us the new air-conditioning equipment. You know what the Swiss are like, so thorough in everything. He wanted to make absolutely sure we left none of the old equipment in place. Everything must be removed, even if it's still in working condition. Otherwise, he kept on saying, the guarantee would not stand. They are a very boring people, the Swiss, but highly efficient."

He was nursing his coffee cup in his thin brown fingers. She had never noticed before the black tufts of hair on the back of his knuckles. He was like some hairy wild animal underneath the silk shirt and the Savile Row suiting; she repressed an inward shudder.

"Do I detect an unspoken conclusion to that last sentence?" he asked. "Unlike the Iranians, who are interesting but not highly efficient?"

"That is your interpretation. A mere woman is not competent to make such important pronouncements."

A corner of his mouth lifted and he bowed his head slightly, like a fencer acknowledging a hit. "Tell me more about this new equipment—so important that a director of the company presumably—you haven't told me his name, by the way, should feel it necessary to arise early in the morning and escort you to the airport."

"He did *not* escort me. *He* arranged to meet me there before my flight took off. And his name"—she made a pretense of riffling through her notebook to find the right page—"was Fleuve."

"That sounds French. I have been told that Zurich is a German-speaking canton."

"Indeed it is. But Monsieur Fleuve comes from the French-speaking canton of Vaud, the town of Savigny. Or so he told me. He has not lived long in Zurich."

He nodded. "And the new equipment?"

"It was being packed and loaded onto the trucks the day I left. If the two trucks started the journey next day, they should arrive here in another three days."

"Excellent. Please ensure that I am informed when the installation begins. I shall be most interested to inspect this efficient Swiss manufacture. And always remember, Sharqi, that our country has many enemies abroad. The utmost vigilance is called for—always. Why, even in that neutral, peace-loving country, Switzerland, two—shall I say, 'friends'?—of the Iranian Republic were found brutally murdered in a Geneva hotel the other day. A hotel, I gather, quite close to the one where you were staying. Did you hear about the tragedy?"

She was able to shake her head with complete conviction. "How ghastly! No, I heard nothing about it. Perhaps I'd checked out by then?"

"Perhaps you had." He stared at her face and then her throat and her breasts. "Perhaps you had."

Forty miles inside Iran, the route swooped south through the high valleys to Shahpur and Rezaiyeh, then along the enormous lake and farther south to Mahabad. The two trucks then swung northeast, aiming for Tabriz. A Persian driver had told Miller that the truck park outside Tabriz was the best equipped, with proper showers and hot food.

The whole team had gathered around for a break. Miller said with a snigger, "From what he hinted, you can get a bit of the old spare at that park. Dusky maidens giving their all for Allah—and a hundred-rial note. I could go a round or two with one of 'em. What do you say, boss?"

Yardley said, "No way. The least you'd get is a dose, if I know anything. We can't afford invalids on this job. It's only another couple of weeks."

"Couple of weeks," Miller said. "Feels like a couple of years! Christ, in the Marines they used to say, 'If you can fuck, you can fight.' My motto is 'If you can fight, you can fuck.' "

"You can't do either," Lysol said. "You heard the officer. Keep it stuffed inside your pants, or I'll find you a mountain goat to play with."

There was some general joshing, but Yardley noticed that Archie Morton looked annoyed at Miller's jeering tone and edged away so that he did not have to sit next to the man. Yardley knew Morton to be one of those quiet easygoing men who tended to live and let live until they were really roused. Miller must be quite abrasive, he reckoned, to have stirred up old Archie to that degree. He didn't want antagonisms flaring or deep divisions formed before the going got tough. The strain of being cooped up in the basement of the Palace for hours and days on end, surrounded by enemies, would be pressure enough when the time came. So, the following morning, before they left Tabriz, he suggested they should switch passengers around, with Nick joining the second truck and Miller taking his place in the first. Even then, he had to tick Miller off twice for teasing Peter Shaw unduly. Then Miller started to make comments about Jacques and the stink his Gauloises made. He kept pretending to cough and flapping a handkerchief in front of his face to ward off the fumes. Jacques took one hand off the wheel, gave him a two-fingered salute and said in a rasp, *"Foutes-moi le camp,"* and Miller kept quiet for a few miles. But Yardley knew that there was still a problem to solve.

From Tabriz the road, improving in breadth and surface every mile, ran east–southeast to Tehran, three hundred miles away. Averaging forty miles an hour, the twosome convoy could have reached the capital in one day's hard driving. But it would mean getting there after dark, having no close look at the approach roads and the center of the city itself. For years, Yardley, and indeed the rest of the team who had served in the British forces, had drummed into them the old slogan, "Time spent in reconnaissance is seldom wasted." They would have little enough chance to reconnoiter once in the truck compound in the heart of the city. Foreigners found walking the streets and noting traffic flows would quickly become objects of suspicion. So, after driving down the long valley with the river Zenjanrud flowing alongside the highway, sparkling in the crisp fall sunshine, he decided to stop for the night at Karaj, the last town of any consequence before Tehran, some twenty miles away. They would drive in as slowly as they dared on the morrow, noting all points affecting the eventual getaway.

It was Jacques and Claude's turn to prepare the evening meal. Miller, as the Farsi speaker, volunteered to look for a merchant selling fresh eggs to supplement the canned rations, and to see if there might be a hotel where some of them could take a bath. Yardley sat in the cab of one vehicle, jotting down points in his notebook. Peter Shaw sat alongside him, polishing his gleaming instruments and looking for nonexistent specks of dust. He was like a well-trained puppy dog, Yardley thought with affection. He's happy as long as he can sit quietly with his master. He made a mental note to get one of the others—not Lysol, who had blotted his copybook early on; perhaps Archie Morton—to become another uncle figure for the little man. If anything happens to me, he thought, we don't want him adrift, feeling there's no protector for him.

Baring cut into his musings by tapping on the cab window. Yardley opened the door. "What is it, Nick?"

"That Marine's been gone some time, skipper. You don't think . . .?"

"Christ, no wonder he volunteered to take a look round. Jesus, why can't the guy just jerk off, if he's that horny? Here, will you go and check him out? Don't take Archie, he might kill the Marine. Take Lysol. Don't be too long, half an hour at the most. It'll soon be dark."

"Right, skipper." Yardley watched Baring slide away, speak quickly to Lysol and then the two of them loped off toward the town. Fucking hell, he thought. If Miller's tangled with some respectable woman and the local gendarmerie has nabbed him, we're off to hell in a leaky bucket. That would look great back in the National Security Council. A major operation grounded before it got going, because one of the team was thinking with his dick.

Twenty minutes later—it was the longest twenty minutes of his life, far worse than waiting in a bombed-out shop in Beirut—he could see three figures approaching through the gathering dusk. Baring seemed to have a comradely arm around Miller's shoulders but he was in fact supporting the man, who held his hands delicately laced across his stomach, as though holding it in place. A trickle of blood ran down from the left corner of his mouth and a dark bruise was swelling below his left eye. Baring pushed him forward, to confront Yardley. Miller stood, head down.

"We got to him just in time, boss," Baring said. There was a cutting edge of contempt in his voice. "Just. He was about to start the leg-over act with one of the girls. Girls?—she could have been ninety, hidden under that veil. There would have been a nasty little scene. Two or three of her menfolk were gathering. I waved a few dollars around, that quietened them. One spoke a bit of French and I explained our friend was gone in the head. So everyone shook hands and the dollar bills disappeared."

"There wasn't a fight?" Yardley asked.

"No way."

"So how come the damage?"

"Let's say Lysol and me had to persuade him to come quietly."

"Miller!" Yardley shouted.

The man looked up.

"Stand to attention when I speak to you! I warned you before—no tangling with the locals. You're being paid—well paid—to do a tough job. When it's over, when *I* say it's over, you can go fuck everything in sight. But not before. You read me? I don't give a goddamn you're the only one who speaks Farsi. You stray one inch out of line again, the Royal Marines Bugler will be blowing the Last Post in your memory. I'm not having you, or anyone else, endangering the whole team because his prick is stiff. You got anything to say?"

Still head down, Miller muttered, "No."

"No what?"

"No, sir."

"Okay, go and clean up. The rest of you, let's have some food. I'm starving."

After supper, while they were sitting in a circle round the Primus stove, whose roar and blue flame gave the illusion of a family hearth—all of them wearing greatcoats or heavy sweaters because the night was chill at over five thousand feet altitude—Lysol surprised the others by pulling a battered book out of a bag and offering to read a couple of passages. Baring swore he was positive Lysol couldn't read and he accused Archie Morton of having taught him when no one was looking. Yardley had already told them all that the trucks would be parked in a special compound close by the Tehran railroad station and that they were booked into a modest, second-class hotel, the Piruz, three hundred meters away.

"I thought we were going to swank it in the Intercontinental, boss," Morton jestingly complained.

"That was the original idea, granted. But when Flood and I looked into it with a large scale map, we saw the Intercontinental's miles away to the north. The railroad station's to the south of the city—with the bazaar about a mile to the northeast and the Ghulistan Palace literally just north of the bazaar. We'll need the trucks most of the time and there's no secure park near the Intercontinental, where we can dump them at night. So to save all that traveling to and fro . . ."

"Oh, sure," Morton said. "Long as there are no fleas."

"Ah, the bazaar," Lysol exclaimed. "Listen, fellow nomads, I'll read to you from my book."

"What's the title?" Baring asked. "*First Steps in Reading*?"

Lysol tried to quell him with a glance. Without success. He said loftily, "How about *Fall of the Peacock Throne*? That grab you? By some punter named Forbes."

"I knew a Forbes once," Morton said. "Guards officer. He was so fucking stupid even the other Guards officers spotted it. They kicked him out, so he joined—what was your Regiment, Lysol?"

"Coldstream Guards," said Lysol.

"Must've been another Forbes I'm thinking of. My guy was thick as two short planks—but not stupid enough for the Coldstreamers."

"Let's have some quiet," Yardley said. "We'll be here all night if we don't let Lysol read his stuff. Up the Guards!"

"Right up," Baring muttered.

"I'll ignore that last remark," Lysol said loftily. He cleared his throat. "I will begin. 'All that is Oriental, exotic and mysterious in Tehran comes in the area a mile or so south of Rudaki Hall. Four hundred years ago, this was a walled town, and even after 1779, when the Qajar shahs began to use Tehran as their capital, they chose to build their Ghulistan Palace within the walls just north of the bazaar. Not until 1874 did a Qajar shah replace the old wall with a new one, about a mile in every direction outside the original one. It reached what is now Shahreza Avenue on the north and defined Tehran until Reza Shah, removing all the walls, extended the avenues and added new ones in the 1930s.

" 'In the color and excitement of its bazaar, Tehran does

not have to concede points to any other city in the Middle East. The bazaar starts as a plunge: down stone steps from Buzarjomehri Avenue into a maze of passages—six miles of them—between dusty two-story brick buildings set close enough together to support zinc roofs over the lanes. Inside light comes from rather un-Oriental ring-shaped fluorescent tubes dangling by their wires. The bazaar has a rough system: in one passageway the stalls sell nothing but jewelry; in another, shoes; in another, clothes; in another, rugs. But elsewhere it's a jumble of merchants side by side selling abacuses, samovars, T-shirts, compasses, perfume, prayer beads, barber's shears, toys, grocer's scales and suitcases made out of beer cans.' "

"There," Lysol concluded, "they don't write 'em like that anymore."

"How old's that book?" Yardley asked.

"Can't exactly say, skipper. Some clown tore out the pages in front of the title page. Probably got caught short. It's soon after the Shah's abdication, I reckon. 1980-ish?"

"I doubt whether the bazaar's changed that much. Comparing the up-to-date map with one from the Shah's time, it's clear all the place names were changed after the Revolution. Pahlavi Avenue—that's the big one running due north, up past the Sheraton and the Hilton—wasn't the flavor of the month with the ayatollahs."

"There must've been a bit of bombing, missiles and so forth, during the war with Iraq. I saw a TV news bulletin showing houses smashed and on fire from an aerial attack." This from Miller, who had sat silent throughout the evening.

"You're right," Yardley said. "We'll just have to keep looking and trying to sort out the geography. From the map, the U.S. Embassy is about two miles north of the palace—but it could be two hundred. If the op comes unstuck, we're totally deniable. And the British Embassy doesn't even exist right now. There's some talk of renewing diplomatic relations, but that's all. The Swiss are supposed to be looking after British interests and they won't want to get involved in a diplomatic incident. If the shit hits the fan, there's no one to turn the fan off."

"So what else is new?" Baring said.

Lysol began to sing "The Whiffenpoof Song" softly, almost to himself, and the others chimed in with the chorus, "Baa, baa, baa."

10

"How sweet is mortal Sovranty"—think
some:
Others—"How blest the Paradise to
come!"
Ah, take the Cash in hand and waive
the Rest;
Oh, the brave Music of a distant *Drum!*

Next morning, the two trucks drove in on the Otoban-e-Tehran Karaj, a broad highway, if not the autobahn, after which the city fathers had named it. There were wide *maidan*s, open spaces to right and left, until they turned right on Mohammed-Ali-Jenah and circled round the Meydan-e-Azadi. Still to their right was the international airport. A descending aircraft roared across their vision two hundred feet above them as it prepared for touchdown. It was not till they veered left on the Qazvin Serah that they were properly inside the built-up area of the city. The early-morning sun shone warmly on the yellow brickwork and plaster that prevailed throughout Tehran. Here and there, the team noted evidence of bomb damage, particularly to the east of the airport. A row of large houses on the corner of Hashemi and Ayatollah Saidi leaned drunkenly against each other, with the top stories blown out and smashed windows like empty eye sockets. Miller, who was in the leading cab with Yardley and who was obviously trying hard to get back into the leader's favor, said, "Must've been an overshoot, boss. All the guts in the world, those Iraqi pilots, but not so hot with aiming missiles."

"You reckon?" Yardley said. "We had a briefing at Bragg; said there were cases where the Iranians had faked a bit of damage. Blown up several of their own houses, and then blamed the opposition."

"Could be. But see the angle? Looks like an east-to-west strike. Like the Iraqi jets overshot the airfield and clobbered the buildings on the perimeter."

"You could be right. Here, watch for a right fork in a minute. We turn off onto the Helal-e-Ahmar and then after about six hundred meters we come to a big turning circle, the Meydan-e-Gomrok. We make a right there onto a street named Kargar and then we should be a few hundred meters from the railroad station. At least, that's what the map says."

It was after nine o'clock in the morning and the traffic was building up. Diesel-driven old cars throbbed all around the two trucks, there were donkey carts and even a pair of supercilious camels laden with panniers on either side as they swayed along; and bicycles everywhere, weaving in and out of the traffic, shrill bells ringing to add to the cacophony of blaring hooters and voices. There were conspicuously few women on the sidewalks; those who did go demurely down the street were wrapped to the ankles in long dark gowns and each wore a black strip of cloth over her head and the inevitable *chador* across her features.

They navigated to the railroad station and then followed the signs, in German, French and English, to the international truck compound, close by the railway sidings. An aggressive-sounding official in a muddy green uniform barked out various queries, but his face lit up in a half-smile when Miller answered in Farsi. He motioned them to a couple of slots alongside the perimeter wall. Miller explained that they were on an official task for the Ministry of Culture and the official became almost human.

"Do we bribe him?" Yardley asked.

"In the Shah's day, you bet. They all lived on baksheesh in the good old days. Now, I guess we gotta watch it. Maybe a present when we leave. We'll wait for him to tell us."

The second truck nosed into position parallel with the first. The whole team descended and stood around, stretching and shaking the cramps out of necks and shoulders.

"What now, boss?" Morton asked.

Yardley spread the large scale map across the hood of his truck. "Gather round," he said. "Keep your voices down. Any of these guys round here, making like truck drivers, could be in the pay of the mullahs. English isn't a popular language in these parts, so watch it. We're here." He indicated a yellow space close to the sidings that opened out from the station like the ribs of a fan. "If we cross the railroad bridge and there turn right into the Meydan-e-Rahanan—what you guys call a roundabout—and then go a block due north on Vali-ye-Asr, we come to the hotel. It can't be more than eight hundred meters, say half a mile. Do us good to take a walk after all that sitting around. So let's take our bags and go check in. Except Jacques and Claude. I'd like you both to check the vehicles, make sure everything's locked up and all the equipment lashed down, and then you bring up the rear. *D'accord?*"

They nodded in unison.

"The rest of us'll go in pairs. Here, Peter, you come with me. Everyone behave normally and don't march. We don't want to look like Lysol and his bloody Guards trooping the color, or whatever they do.

"After we've checked in and had a wash, we'll do the tourist bit. It's only a mile or so from the hotel to the palace. So let's get a feel of the place, find out where we can park the trucks when we start, all that stuff."

Baring and Lysol chanted together, "Time spent in reconnaissance is seldom wasted."

"Okay, you wise guys."

Walking to the Ghulistan Palace later that morning made Yardley think of New York, but a bombed-out, crumbling New York, more like the slums of the Bowery district than the groomed wealth of Park Avenue or the luxury of Fifth Avenue between Forty-eighth Street and the Plaza Hotel. To modernize the city he had conquered, Reza Shah drove broad avenues north and south through the medieval streets. You could still see the unfinished edges of houses where the bulldozers had torn gaps for the arrow-straight avenues to drive through. But, unlike New York, the east–west streets did not run straight from river to river. In the area skirting the bazaar, between Vahdat-e-Eslami and Khayyam, there were narrow alleyways, cul-de-sacs, the open space of hospital grounds and then more little streets twisting and jinking at right angles. There was the smell of fires and cooking and outdoor sanitation, the sweet smell of rotting and decay.

Peter Shaw drew closer to Yardley as they walked silently through an area unchanged since biblical days, except for the wailing of radio sets tuned to some local station.

And then suddenly all was light and brightness and beauty. They had reached the palace. The word *ghulistan* means "rose garden" in Farsi. The building was set in a park four hundred meters long by two hundred meters wide, with arbors and serene lakes, pools and miniature waterfalls. Massive trees surrounded the palace and there were indeed rose gardens and graveled paths. The sky was a clear-washed blue and the fall sunshine glinted and splintered on the walls that were covered in blue and yellow tiles. The tiles were grouped to show designs of lions and castles and pastoral scenes, with everywhere the rose motif weaving in and out. The other members of the team had caught up. Silently, they drank in the splendid scene. Even Lysol could think of nothing funny to say.

There was a small line at the entrance to the palace itself, a gaggle of children with a turbaned teacher and a few adults who looked as though they had come in from the countryside to see the sights of the capital. The team showed their official passes, after waiting at the portico that enclosed a divan carved from alabaster and marble, with dragons breathing fire and other weird monsters chiseled on its flanks. Inside, the main hall was even more breathtaking than the exterior. There were glass cases displaying countless heaped-up jewels, richly colored carpets hung on the walls, and in another central case the Pahlavi crown with its egret-feather crest, bedecked with dazzling diamonds. It blazed at them: a notice on the outside case stated simply—in Farsi, English and German—that the crown contained over three thousand individual diamonds.

They crowded round it like children at an apple-bob. Jacques sucked in his breath in a long hiss. Nick Baring said casually to Shaw, "What do you make of the security, Peter?"

The expert took a long look and then said, "Nothing to the locks on the showcase. Ten minutes' work is all. But there must be an electromagnetic field inside the case as part of a circuit connecting the base to a central alarm system. Break the circuit and every bell in the place will go off. Sorry, Nick."

"To immobilize the main circuit?"

"There'd be a master alarm switch somewhere. Probably

in the director's office and, if they've spent the money, connected to a master board indicating the position of every piece in the place. That would work on a back-to-back system linked to the local gendarmerie, switch off here without using the daily code sets *their* bells ringing and they come running. With a little beauty like the Shah's headgear here, there is probably a mercury trembler switch under the base—lift the crown from above and the trembler release opens the circuit and, dingaling!"

"You guys at Chubb's didn't set up this little lot?"

"No—since our time. Far as I can remember, the ground floor here was all covered in dust sheets and muck when we were working in the basement. But that was ten years ago. There was some talk of laying pressure pads under sections of the floor but I don't think it materialized. The Shah was supposed to have made over the palace to the people in 1971, but it wasn't a proper museum when we were here." Shaw reveled in holding their attention.

Baring said, "Pity. I wouldn't mind that crown in my wheelhouse. Make a nice souvenir."

"Forget the Shah's bowler hat," Lysol said. "I'd just like to get out of here with my head still on my shoulders."

"Spoken like a true coward and gentleman," Baring replied.

Where the walls were left uncovered, mosaic mirrors added to the dazzling splendor. They were constructed with four small triangular pieces of glass, cunningly fixed to form a pyramid; the pyramids, repeated endlessly, reflected light in all directions with the effect of slowly twirling a cut diamond in the light of a bright torch. At the far end, the throne room—now lacking the Peacock Throne—had so many carpets on the floor that they overlapped like tiles on a roof.

And then Bob Yardley's heart seemed to skip a beat and plunge on to catch up the rhythm. The sound of a woman's shoes was echoing off the marble floor somewhere and he turned to look for the approaching heels, and there she was. It was Sharqi Zachin walking toward them, looking beautiful and in charge. Yardley wanted impulsively to go and greet her, take hold of her, but he stood his ground. A suppressed wolf whistle came from one of the men behind him and he felt like ripping his tongue out. Sharqi was explaining something to the man with her, gesticulating with both hands and then pointing to Yardley's group. The man, wearing dark brown robes and a white turban, was nodding in obedience.

"Good morning, gentlemen, welcome to our fine museum." She stopped in front of Yardley. "And you must be Herr Robertz?" She offered him her hand in brief courtesy and then clasped both hands together in front of her waist, and that's where they stayed. The robed man consulted a list of names on his clipboard and found Robertz.

"Good morning, madam, that is correct, I am Mr. Robertz and these men are my engineers and work crew. May I present them to you?" As he reeled off the men's names, the list of names was again being scrutinized.

"And this is Mr. Hashemi, our chief maintenance engineer." The brown robe did not offer a hand, and the thin catlike face under the turban remained suspicious. "My name is Zachin, *Miss* Zachin, I am the curator here." Her charm swept over them causing the men to shuffle their feet and move awkwardly, their masculine politeness masking a stronger sexual interest. Hashemi spoke sharply to Sharqi in Farsi, her retort, with a stern look, clearly put him down and he strode off toward a passage at the end of the chamber.

"Mr. Hashemi is right," she said in a controlled voice. "You have work to do, and must want to get started."

She led them to the passage taken by Hashemi. "Let me take you down to the basement and show you what has to be done."

She conducted them along the passage and down a flight of steps. The basement was enormous, at least a hundred and fifty feet in length and half that distance wide. It ran the whole length and breadth of the palace. There were naked electric lights, looped on wires from the dusty stained ceiling. Dust and dirt lay thick on the stone floor. In the center of the vast room was a black rectangular steel cube, stretching from the floor almost to the basement ceiling. It was the vault containing the safe that contained the Peacock Throne.

Hashemi stepped from the shadows and Yardley was suddenly nervous at the attention his men were paying to the vault. "This contains your air conditioning, Miss Zachin?" He spoke loudly and placed his hand against the vault.

"Oh no, Mr. Robertz." She made a dismissive gesture. "This is of no interest to you, your work is over here." She indicated for them to follow her over to a corner. "This is the old air-conditioning apparatus that must be removed before you install the new one." In the corner was a large antiquated oil-powered system encased in a stainless steel frame that towered above them. A control panel with levers and dials stood to one side and cast-iron pipes linked it to a big compressor bolted to the floor and another large unit containing four giant fans behind a wire mesh.

Yardley spoke in a businesslike manner. "Well, lads, we have one hell of a job here." Jacques and Claude were looking behind the apparatus, the others looked on in silence. They all realized that the equipment was far larger than expected. Yardley turned to Sharqi. "We'll need to bring the trucks into the compound tomorrow morning. Is there a convenient place, perhaps against that wall over there, for us to park close by? And a better access to the basement?"

"Yes," she said. "Mr. Hashemi has agreed that you could remove the steel grille from that ground-level window on that far wall, it will give you a very large opening for moving the equipment in and out. But it will mean guards being posted each night, our security chief, Mr. Gulami, has insisted on that." Her last statement got everyone's attention.

Hearing his name used, Hashemi stepped forward and started chattering in useless French, obviously wanting to run the job. Sharqi quietly interrupted him. "Mr. Hashemi is responsible for the maintenance of the museum and is rather put out by your presence here. However, I have explained that the new system is electrical and sophisticated and demanded that it be commissioned by the manufacturers. Also the language problem requires that you discuss your needs and problems directly with me, Mr. Robertz. I trust that will not be so uncomfortable for you as it is for Mr. Hashemi?"

"No." Yardley replied. "No, not at all, Miss Zachin." God, you're a cool one, Sharqi, he thought. I'm as edgy as hell and she's calmly putting all the ducks in a row.

"I suggest that you join me in my office upstairs and we talk over your work schedule. I will instruct Mr. Hashemi to show your drivers where to park and to explain the work necessary on the window." She exchanged with Hashemi in Farsi, the officious little man clearly enjoying his moment of authority.

"Nick, accommodate him, will you?" Yardley kept his voice low. "Treat him gently and keep everyone together."

At last they were alone, and Yardley could not hold back.

"Are you all right? My God, it's good to see you, this place is so full of menace I've been worried sick about you."

"Bob, oh Bob, it's lovely to see *you,* but please don't ever show familiarity with me here, it is dangerous beyond your understanding. There are eyes and ears everywhere and we must use these moments to coordinate your actions." She spoke with suppressed emotion, the strain showing briefly in her eyes. With Yardley so close, it was going to be harder to carry on the deception.

To the onlooker, the two of them appeared to be continuing the formality shown in the basement. As they walked through the vast building and up the long stairs to her office, Sharqi disguised their intimate talk by stopping from time to time and pointing out items of interest here and aspects of the water garden there. The tall handsome "European" and the beautiful dark curator were an obvious couple and were being observed from all directions.

"My office is bugged, so keep it strictly business in there." She stopped and acknowledged a passing employee. "I must warn you about Gulami, he runs the security here and is very dangerous."

"With him and Hashemi we're going to have our work cut out to pull this off." Yardley's voice sounded anxious.

"Hashemi is a problem because he is jealous of his position and likes to curry favor with Gulami, but I can keep him away from you most of the time by delegating work in another part of the museum. Yes, you must be careful of him, but Gulami is the real danger. You'll know him because he swaggers around as though he owns the place and he has a cast in his left eye. His uncle is an ayatollah, a man of real influence. This Gulami was in charge of an assassination squad in the early Revolution days, or so they say. He's a nasty piece of work and he's full of hate, but he's no fool. So please watch for him and be polite, if you can. The reason you have not seen him when you arrived is because he was checking your papers and passports with the ministry, but he will confront you, nothing surer."

They entered her office. It was comfortable and warm with a feminine touch. She invited him to view the city panorama from her wide ornate window and then rang for coffee. She unrolled an electrical plan across her desk and then sat in her chair and looked at him. He turned away from the window and slipped into a deep chair opposite her. The way he moved, the warmth and concern that came from him and the strength in his eyes, tugged at her heart. Feelings were swimming inside her that both excited her and added to existing fears. They sat looking into each other's eyes, saying nothing, just soaking up the moment. The door opened and a young boy entered with the tray of coffee.

"Miss Zachin, I am concerned about completing the work in the time we have, the old unit looks difficult to remove, is there any chance of working at night?" Yardley spoke as he accepted a cup of coffee from the boy.

"There may be a problem with that, I would have to ask my boss," Sharqi replied. "It would mean the security men working overtime, and as we already will have two guarding the window, Mr. Gulami may object. My boss listens to his objections."

They talked for ten more minutes for the benefit of the listeners. Yardley imagined the ear of Gulami not very far away. Then she escorted Yardley out.

Back at their own hotel in the early evening, Yardley called a council of war. It was an old-fashioned hotel and the hot water pipes rumbled and grumbled; when the taps were turned on, there would be a spurt of almost boiling water, then a puff of steam and then a rusty trickle. But at least the place was relatively clean and quiet. They had managed to book four twin-bedded rooms on the same floor, there were no elevators, and the team had split up into its regular pairings—the twins together, Baring and Lysol, himself and Shaw and Miller and Morton. Miller seemed anxious to get back into favor and was volunteering for the unwanted jobs and being overtalkative.

He had taken heed of Sharqi's warning about listening devices and felt paranoid about the room's security, so they now sat at two tables on the roof patio, huddled around an oversized coffeepot. They were alone, with the bent television antennae and a collection of discarded rusty tables and chairs. The sun was running for cover and the Islamic prayer ritual was crying out across the city. In the distance could be heard the eerie sound of a mass rally of fundamentalists chanting. Every so often the chant was interrupted by a weird slapping noise, it reached them as an amplified echo.

"Merde!" Jacques spat the word out along with his Gauloise. "I have not heard a sound like that since the Congo, when those bloody Bakongo rebels, out of their brains on

daggar, were working themselves up to attack, they used to beat their chests with platted grass until the blood ran."

"What they are doing is much the same," Miller spoke with certainty. "They're being worked up by the mullahs, whipping themselves with leather thongs, fucking flagellation—maniacs!"

"Well, you've all seen the site," Yardley said. "Let's talk it through before we freeze our nuts off up here. We've got about a week to carry out the official job. What do you say, Jacques? You and Claude are the experts."

Jacques scratched his bristly chin. "Five days, *mon chef,* yes? Two days to remove the old piping and break down the old unit, three days to put in the new *apparat.*" He pouted his lips and made a loud kissing sound, "It will be tight, that old unit has been there for a long time, I think we need six days, maybe seven—but no more, *le plus.*"

"How does that leave you, Peter?" Yardley asked.

"It all depends," Shaw answered. "From what that nice girl said, we could have problems with the guards."

Miller cut in. "Nice girl? I'd like to give her a good fucking, hey lads?"

"Shut up, Miller!" Yardley snapped. "Save your whorehouse bullshit for your own type, I don't want to hear that kind of talk about Sharqi again, and that's a fucking order, get me?"

"Sharqi, boss?" Lysol had asked the question for all of them, and they were waiting for an answer.

Yardley leaned forward, his shoulders hunched. "Yes, her name is Sharqi Zachin and she's one of the team." A surprised murmur went through the group. "She's one of Flood's people and our inside track here. The woman is taking one hell of a risk with us, her neck is on the line and don't forget, by telling you, I've increased that risk. If any of those sons-of-bitches see the slightest look of recognition from any of you, she's dead."

"So *she's* the capable lady," Lysol said. "Our man Flood is certainly one for understatement."

"I reckon the picture's clear, Bob, in all respects." Baring had heard enough. "Let's do the business."

Shaw continued, "If those guards are sniffing round the whole time, I can't get to work. All the vaults Chubb's sets up have a fail-safe method built in, like I explained at the briefing. It's for emergencies, in case someone gets shut in, there has to be a quick way to open up the vault. I can't recall exactly where the spot is in the surface of the vault—it's over ten years since we constructed it. So it could take me ten to twelve hours on the stretch to find it. Then once I've opened the vault, there's still the safe to deal with. I installed the coded locks, but I didn't set the dials myself. Far as I recall, it's a twelve-digit code. That gives almost four hundred and sixty million combinations. See my problem? Even with my acoustic equipment—it cuts the odds by a factor of a thousand, perhaps—that still leaves nearly half a million possibilities. You've got to give me at least twenty-four hours—uninterrupted—to work that out."

Yardley thought hard. Then he said, "There's only one thing to do. We have a large metal packing case, large enough to hold the throne when the time comes to lift it out, on the second truck. You, Peter, and let's say Nick here, will have to climb inside it before we leave the truck compound tomorrow. Then we'll lower you into the basement along with the other equipment. I'm sorry—but you'll just have to stay inside the packing case for the rest of the day. Jacques, and you, Claude, make sure they have a bucket, a thermos of hot coffee and some food; make the thing as comfortable as you can. Once our crew pulls out at the end of the day, Nick can keep watch and you, Peter, will have the whole night—twelve hours, if need be—to sort out the vault first. You may have to do it the next night and consecutive nights if need be. Sorry, chaps, but that's it. If Peter here doesn't open up the vault and then the inner safe to reach the throne, we're stuffed."

"What about lighting?" Morton asked. "Peter'll need a torch or something to work in the dark in that basement. They're never going to agree to leave the lights on. The war may be over but there's still a blackout in force."

"Good point. The mullahs have to keep the population in fear of a surprise Iraqi air attack, to prevent the flame going out on their Revolution. Torches are out, there will be a minimum of two security guards on that window and you can bet your life Mr. Gulami will be on the prowl, you'll have to use the NV equipment, Peter."

"But Bob," Shaw spoke apprehensively, "I've never worked with night vision gear before, it'll be pitch black in there and I'll need both hands for the acoustics."

"No problem, old bean," Lysol said. "With the Sopelem

goggles you could find a lady's nipples in the dark and play with them for hours, with both hands."

"Lysol's right, Peter," Yardley reassured him. "The NV device you were shown in Château d'Oex was a basic single image-intensifier. We've brought with us the Sopelem TN2-1 Binoculars. They fit onto your head like oversized ski-goggles, and only weigh 470 grams, you won't even know they're there."

"I've been thinking, boss . . ." Lysol began.

"What with?" came from Baring.

". . . before I was so rudely interrupted, when we pull out the old stuff, could we heap it up, sort of casually, around the vault? It would shield Peter from view and give him a chance to apply his stethoscope without attracting the guards' attention."

"Great idea," Yardley said. "That okay with you, Jacques?"

"Très bien, mon chef," said the Belgian. "We first unload the packing case and lower it into the basement, putting it next to the vault, then break down the old plant and stack it along the side of the vault nearest the window, next we unload the new plant and move it into position for installation. I can work on the new air conditioning with Miller, Morton and perhaps Lysol, while Claude and you are seen to be breaking up the old shit for loading. *Ça va?"*

"Okay, that works," Yardley agreed. "Nick? When Peter breaks through, you take my place on the old iron and stay close to keep an eye on him, I'll then be able to float as a supervisor and fend off that termite Hashemi, and watch for Gulami. Any further questions, lads?"

No one spoke.

"Fine," he said. "Reveille is oh-seven hundred tomorrow morning. We'll RV independently at the truck compound at oh-eight-thirty. The rest of the evening is your own and, for Christ's sake, keep a low profile. These people are suspicious of strangers, particularly foreigners. So keep out of trouble."

Yardley felt like being alone and declined an invitation from Baring to join him and Lysol at a small bistro across the street. They assured him they would look after Shaw and he went to take a shower, changed into a fresh shirt and left the hotel.

He strolled along Molavi Avenue and then up Vahda-e-Eslami Avenue to the Park Hotel at the corner of its wooded park. Checking his watch, it was only nine o'clock and he needed a drink and some civilized behavior. Pushing his way through the swinging doors of the hotel he searched out the restaurant bar and sat down at a table where he could watch the people come and go. A good scotch was what he really yearned for but he knew it was either unobtainable or crazily expensive—and he didn't want to draw attention to himself by ordering it. He settled for a coffee and a glass of *arak,* that universal Middle Eastern drink. The waiter brought a small jug of water with the order and with a smile, lingered for the tip. He left Yardley to add the water to the spirit, a few drops would turn the colorless *arak* a milky white. He hoped to God that the potency of the spirit would kill whatever germs might be lurking in the water. It would be ironic if, in the midst of his most important op, he was laid low with dysentery—the notorious "gippy tummy." There was a saucer of dry biscuits on the table and alongside it a small bowl of Caspian caviar. To middle-class Iranians, caviar must be what peanuts or potato crisps are to an American or a Brit. He was only sorry that, as far as he was concerned, it tasted like a fishy kind of Jell-O with tiny beads embedded in it, and not a wonderful luxury.

He lingered over the thick black coffee and the *arak* and absorbed the activity going on around him. The people were more relaxed in here than on the street, some attractive women laughed with their men and gave an impression of attempting some sort of normality. The interior of the place could have been a Sheraton or a Hilton, people were dressed in a clever mixture of Eastern and Western clothing, careful not to go over the boundaries that would inflame the fundamentalists, but the nervousness was there, you could smell it.

The waiter came by and Yardley reordered. Sharqi was on his mind, injecting herself into every thought he was having about the mission. He had never been on a secret operation before where a woman was involved. And here was a young beautiful woman in the midst of it all, and one he could feel himself falling in love with. Hell, he thought, that damned general back at Rangeley Lake in Maine sure dropped me in it from a great height. But somehow, even though it doubled or trebled the big potential risk, he was secretly glad about Sharqi. His mind swept back and forth between her personal life and her involvement in his operation; at times he felt she had a better grasp of the intrigue they were all framed in than he did. Was there another man in the background? Here in Tehran? After all, she had said her marriage had been more a brother and sister relationship; ah, what the hell, no woman, especially a good-looker like her, can be expected to keep it in the ice box until he happened along. But sipping his *arak* and trying to rationalize his thoughts did not push that aching feeling away. The waiter was back. He paid the man and left; shit, he had a job to do.

The work had begun in earnest early the next day. The two trucks were driven slowly through the narrow streets and into the grounds of the Ghulistan Palace, to be parked side by side alongside the basement wall. The position was well away from the public entrance and was not overlooked by any windows opposite, the biggest danger being that anybody could approach their side of the building out of sight, suddenly rounding the corner and be on them without warning. Baring and Shaw had already concealed themselves inside the large metal container. The second truck had a built-in self-loading HIAB crane fitted behind the driver's cabin, which Claude manipulated with a flourish. Two stabilizing legs had been dropped and pinlocked at the rear of the truck and Jacques was standing atop the container calling for more slack in the chains. Claude deftly pushed one of three levers in a cluster of hydraulics he operated from a standing position next to the driver's door, and extended the arm almost into Jacques's stomach.

"Merde! Attendez! Attendez!" Jacques shouted. "You want to take my balls off with that thing?" He gathered the four chains, attached one to each corner and looped them onto the arm's hook. Claude carefully took up the slack and slowly swung the container, with its human cargo, off the truck and down through the gaping hole in the basement wall.

"Your Swiss German speaks perfect French, Mr. Robertz." Yardley spun around to face the voice. Gulami stood two feet away, having approached unseen while everyone was concentrating on the swinging container. "Almost as if it is his native tongue."

Yardley collected himself without expressing surprise. "And I must compliment you on your perfect English, sir, and good morning to you, Mr. Hashemi, I am delighted to see you this morning."

The ratlike features, still beneath the white turban, were trying to see around the shoulders of Gulami. Yardley willed his pulse rate to slow down and offered his hand to the arrogant-looking security chief, conscious that the men had stopped working behind him.

"I believe you must be Colonel Gulami, sir, the officer in charge of security at this beautiful museum." Massage the man's ego, Yardley thought. Christ you're an ugly bastard.

The cast eye seemed to wobble, the good eye widened in response to Yardley's flattery. "Yes, I am security chief here, and *Mr.* Gulami will do." He did not accept Yardley's hand and looked beyond him to the trucks and each of the men. "I see only six men in your crew, Mr. Robertz, where would the other two be?"

"Ah yes." Yardley was ready for this one. "Our electrical engineer has become ill this morning with a sick stomach, something he ate last night I think, so I felt it better that he remain at the hotel, one of the crew has stayed with him. Fortunately they are not vital to this work until we begin to install the new equipment." He turned and waved an arm at the men. "Come on you guys, get back on the job."

"But Mr. Robertz." Gulami's voice was filled with cunning. "Will that not slow down your schedule? I understand you have only five or six days to complete your work."

"I hope not, sir. If I see it getting critical perhaps I can ask Mr. Hashemi here for some extra hands-on labor." Bluff, just keep bluffing.

"You will have to consult Miss Zachin about that, I am sure she will want to check her figures and reduce your exorbitant Swiss labor costs accordingly." The spite gave him pleasure. "I will position two of my men here at seven o'clock each evening, you will leave at that time and report to the main guard office as you go." With that he walked away, taking Hashemi with him.

Yardley climbed down the wooden ladder into the basement. His legs felt a little shaky, this man was going to be a real problem.

"Doesn't miss a trick does he, boss?" It was Miller. "He was cursing us foreigners under his breath as he walked away, used some very ripe Farsi expletives, he did."

"Call the lads down here, will you, Miller."

They gathered around him, beside the container resting on steel rollers on the basement floor. "You all heard the man," Yardley said. "That is Mr. Gulami, he's trouble, and he's no idiot."

"I could arrange a nasty accident for him, boss," Miller said. "It'd be a pleasure."

"Sure you could, Miller, old boy," answered Lysol. "Suddenly the chief of security goes missing. Use your head, man, it would really bring the heat onto us."

"Lysol is right," Yardley said. "We keep our cool and our eyes open, don't speak to him unless it's absolutely necessary, and if it is, humor him. Right, lads, back to work."

The work soon fell into a steady routine. As the old piping was removed and cut into lengths with an acetylene torch, it was stacked up in heaps near the vault. The metal container had also been positioned, with the aid of the rollers, next to the vault. The work was dirty and the basement soon filled with dust, which meant they all put on dust masks that covered their mouth and nose, serving to muffle their voices and hide their faces. It all helped to keep people at a distance. By the end of the first day the old fans had been torn from behind their filthy metal grilles, clogged with the dirt and dust of several decades, and lifted, with their housing, onto the heap. Gulami had revisited the site, and tried to exercise his authority by ordering them to restack the old material away from the vault but he had given up trying to talk over the noise of the work and the flying dust choking his throat. On a prearranged signal, they all grabbed something and begun hitting it against some metal surface as he entered the basement, just to help the noise reach an impossible level. They established a rhythm of taking an hour for lunch with a twenty-minute tea break either side, outside in the yard. A small hestamine stove was set up for boiling water and they took it in turns to wander at irregular intervals to the end of the building—to stretch their legs and watch for Gulami's people. Feeling it safe enough at the second tea break, which coincided with the afternoon prayers, Yardley opened the small door of the container.

"Nick? Peter? Come out and stretch your legs, get yourselves orientated to the basement and eyeball the vault."

Shaw was first out and his face showed the tension of being shut in. Baring emerged and put his arm around Shaw's shoulders. The dying rays of the afternoon sun sinking behind the museum wall gave the basement an unfriendly feel.

"Bob, we can't hear a thing in that box and we lose track of time." Baring sounded concerned. "That's not good for Peter here."

Yardley could see Shaw getting into a state. "I tell you what, Nick, I'll get Jacques to drill a small hole next to the handle of this door, at least you'll be able to see and hear something."

"Can he please do it now, Bob?" Shaw's voice was shaking. "Before we go back inside. I don't think I can stand it."

"Hey, Bob! Bob!" The whispered shout came from Morton at the top of the ladder. "Gulami is coming, he's got the woman with him."

"Quick, both of you back inside," Yardley said urgently.

"I'm not going back in there!" Shaw gritted his teeth and clamped his arms by his side, thumbs pointing to the ground. "I will *not* go back in there."

"Get a move on!" Again Morton's muffled shout. "They're almost on us."

"Peter," Yardley tried the calm approach. "Pull yourself together, I will . . ."

Baring didn't wait for Yardley, he picked Shaw up bodily in a viselike grip and threw him into the container. Following the flailing locksmith through the small door, without turning he said firmly, "Close the fucking door."

Yardley closed it and pulled the handle down to the locked position. As he reached the bottom of the ladder, Sharqi looked over the top, her hair falling down, framing her face. The gray light behind her silhouetted her in the opening and as he climbed up to her, his nostrils caught that distinctive perfume.

"Is everything all right in there, Mr. Robertz?" She spoke calmly, and it calmed him.

"Everything is going fine, Miss Zachin," Yardley replied as he crested the ledge and stepped out into the yard.

"Mr. Gulami has voiced some concern about the buildup of materials in the basement and the possible danger of using the cutting torches. Is there any danger of fire?"

Yardley lifted his face mask, it made her smile at his dirt-covered features. "No risk of fire, Miss Zachin, there's nothing down there that's flammable."

"But I have seen the sparks, they fly everywhere." Gulami stepped forward, speaking loudly. "Look, there is a burn in my shirt, I am certain it happened this morning."

Yardley could see the burn hole was typical of cigarette ash but took his chance. "I am very sorry, Mr. Gulami, the flux from the cutting rod sometimes throws a spark shower, but it is harmless to anything in the basement. Your shirt is nylon I think and the low heat of the spark . . ."

"My shirt is silk, Mr. Robertz," his indignant tone raised a chuckle among the men. "I insist that . . ."

"Mr. Gulami, you will not insist," Sharqi said. "Mr. Robertz, I think it would be a good idea if we sealed the door at the bottom of the stairs leading to the basement, so none of my staff can enter and accidentally come to any harm. Your only access will have to be as now, using this ladder."

"That's no problem to us, Miss Zachin."

"Mr. Gulami, please issue instructions that no one should come into this area without your permission and see to it that the stairs door is locked." She turned back to Yardley. "Mr. Robertz, would you please come to my office first thing in the morning, I wish to discuss your schedule. I was very sorry to hear of your man falling ill. Nothing serious, I hope?"

"No, nothing serious." Yardley found her coolness exciting.

As they walked away, he was suddenly reminded of just how vulnerable she was. Lysol's words penetrated like a bullet: "He hates her, boss."

The sound of the drill forcing its way through the steel door had calmed Shaw down and he had pressed his face against the inside of the door for several minutes, as if the hole close to his lips were bringing fresh air and escape. Baring had checked the night vision goggles and adjusted the straps to fit Shaw's head comfortably. The PS 31 battery would give them sixty hours of continuous operation, it should be more than enough. He had Shaw wear the mask and straps during the day so he got used to moving his head at a regular pace, as a coal miner would in his helmet. He was now happy with the soft leather pad fitted snugly around his eyes and conditioned to seeing the world through the small binocular lens that hinged down to meet the pad. The action of pulling the lens unit down to his eyes switched on the light-intensification tube, and he could see almost as clear as day, except the day was green.

"I'm going to open the door now, Peter." Baring was carrying the bag with Shaw's acoustic gear, over his shoulder. "You all set?"

Easing the door open, Baring prayed Jacques had swamped the hinges with grease. He slipped around the end of the container and looked for the guards, he couldn't see them, but he was sure they were there. The head of Shaw appeared, looking a little like something from a horror movie. He was able to move easily through the various rubbish lying around them and went over to the vault. As Baring kept guard, he began to explore the surface of the vault inch by inch, delicately tapping the tuning fork and listening with his stethoscope. In the silence of the basement he was worried that the ring of the fork could be heard, but Baring reassured him he couldn't hear it standing six feet away. Shaw toiled laboriously for hour after hour, the fail-safe weak point, which was only the breadth of a stout knitting needle, evading him. He concentrated like a sonar operator hunting for a killer submarine, only pausing to wipe away sweat and mark the end of each line of his tracing. The first night, he drew a blank.

Five o'clock in the morning brought a cold chill into the basement and the sound of morning prayers wailing from loudspeakers throughout the city. They shut themselves back into the container, and Shaw sank onto the mattress, taken from one of the trucks, to fall instantly into sleep. Baring lifted the NV goggles from his head and stowed them in their case. You're a sturdy little bugger when you want to be, Peter, he thought, as he looked down at the exhausted figure. You sleep, mate, I personally need a stiff shot of whiskey. He lay down on the other mattress and was soon asleep.

Yardley jumped down from the truck as Jacques turned it off the driveway toward the yard. "Carry on as usual, I'll be with you as soon as I've spoken to Miss Zachin." He made his way to her office.

Greetings and coffee passed formally, and a contrived conversation between them had Sharqi threatening to withhold payment to Novaire AG if the schedule slipped and the museum had to supply workers. The eavesdroppers heard a firm but charming curator dealing competently with a foreign contractor. She then ended the meeting and accompanied him back to the site.

"Sharqi, I wish there was a chance for us to talk about what we're into here," Yardley spoke softly as they paused to admire the fountain.

"Not possible, not here in Tehran." She smiled artificially for the benefit of those watching. "Have you ever been to the Museum of Modern Art in New York? There's a painting there by Munch of a face with the mouth wide open, giving a silent scream. That's what this place reminds me of. Everyone's watching everyone else. If you inform on someone, they'll be automatically arrested, and most likely punished. It doesn't matter whether the informer is getting his own back on an enemy or whether there's a good reason. It's a nightmare city. This week Ayatollah Mossaveri's up and Rafsanjani's down. Next week it'll be the other way round. And their followers go up and down with them."

They moved on across the grounds. "And I'm doubly suspicious. I'm a Jew who converted to Islam. I didn't have a choice, but my people don't see it that way. And the fundamentalists look on me as a turncoat. Not really one of them. So I am fair game for any ambitious informer, like Hashemi or Gulami. And the fact I can travel abroad and enjoy life in Europe makes me even less popular. I am aware of the risks I am taking and I worry terribly about you. Here, they will lock you away and throw away the key if any hint of suspicion is pointed toward you. The Englishman, Cooper, is example enough of what they will do. He is an innocent but they lock him in Evin prison without trial, to use him as leverage against the British government. The Interior Minister Ali Mohtashami has kept him there for over three years and wants him hanged for spying. All part of his ugly game to keep the Revolution anti-Western. There's no love here for the Americans and the British, and Gulami already suspects your crew's Swiss nationality. So you see you must work fast." The anxiety in her voice had risen.

"Sharqi." He allowed his hand to brush against hers. "We all know the dangers, but what scares me is what happens to you when we pull out. Sooner or later someone, somewhere, is going to make a big play of having scooped the Peacock Throne from under the mullahs' beards. Could be it'll be displayed in Times Square or on Capitol Hill. What then? Ms. Zachin, curator and negotiator for new air conditioning—bingo!—number-one suspect. Think about that!"

"I have thought about it, and it frightens me, but . . ."

"It stands to reason," he argued. "A lot of planning has gone into this op, government people are involved. Not to mention putting eight of us, and you, at risk. If no one gets to hear the throne's been taken, what's the point of it all? We're all deniable, but the throne isn't. Someone has to make capital out of it. And I don't want you here, all alone playing patsy, when the balloon goes up."

"Dear Bob," she said, pausing to look at him. "What you are saying is right, but we must succeed with your objective, that is the priority. It's lovely that you worry for me, but please, your talk unnerves me. Look, your man is an expert, isn't he?"

"Yes, one of the best."

"Then once the throne is out, he will leave the safe itself and the vault the way they are now."

"Sure."

"Well, if the ayatollahs and the mullahs and the revolutionary guards have not been able to open the vault in the last ten years, they're unlikely to do it in the next few weeks. I am scheduled to travel to a Christie's sale in London at the end of the month and then on to Monte Carlo, to inspect some jewelry, a week later. That will take me out of harm's way. Mr. Sohrabi would expect me to attend both occasions."

"Then what?" Yardley's caring was making him impatient. "Will you stay out? Can we meet?"

"Yes, I want so much to meet you, away from here." She had to end this cryptic exchange between them; it wasn't the time. "I can be in London in a little more than two weeks. And then the mullahs can go and jump into the Caspian Sea!"

He smiled, but he wasn't fooled. At the back of his mind was the thought of the two Hizbollah hit-men and the flowerman in Amsterdam. The Ayatollah's reach extended far and wide.

The work progressed and the tension mounted. The old plant proved stubborn to remove and the team found themselves with a tough, sweating job on their hands. Inside the container, after a second night of failure, Baring was doing his best to lift Peter Shaw's spirits. The little man was also showing signs of a real attack of dysentery. On the third morning they smuggled him out of the grounds in one of the trucks, on the pretext of taking the cutting gear for repair. Yardley insisted on his spending a day in bed at the hotel swallowing pills to cement his guts. Baring made sure he was seen about the site that day, working as if he was fresh on the job. He ignored the fatigue pulling at his nerves and the three-day stubble on his face. His anger was obvious to everyone, when Claude returned with the truck during the afternoon tea break without Shaw, who had refused to leave the hotel. The loss of a night at the vault increased the dangers for all of them. Yardley made Baring promise not to take his anger out on Shaw when they returned to the hotel, and suggested perhaps one of the others should take over as nursemaid. The Rhodesian calmed down and volunteered to stick with it.

Sharqi visited the site each morning and afternoon, sometimes accompanied by Gulami, whose suspicions had not relaxed. The man operated on instinct, he wasn't a trained security expert and typified the revolutionary zealot who had been elevated to a comfortable job of authority as payment for denouncing a pro-Shah sympathizer. The end of the fourth day saw most of the old material prepared for loading. The Belgian twins began to move the new equipment into the basement to add to the clutter around the vault, and to delay having to remove the container. It meant leaving the second truck parked across the opening overnight. As they left the museum that evening, Yardley went alone to the guard house with the crew's passes. He had established the routine to avoid a head count and cultivated a friendly rapport with the staff.

That night Shaw cracked it, he found the secret spot. Baring had to clamp a hand over his mouth to prevent the locksmith's excitement being overheard by the guards. Shaw's determination had returned and he attacked the vault with a tireless energy. Backward and forward, up and down, he knew he was close, and then the minute change of decibels reached his ears. Got it! They retreated back into their hide.

"You little beauty, Peter," Baring whispered close to his ear. "I knew you'd do it." They shook hands and did a little jig.

Shaw removed the goggles and took hold of Baring's arm while his eyes adjusted to the dark, his face was a wide smile.

"I need to push my prong through the spot, Nick, interrupt the fiber optics and open the trip circuit to the vault's lock, it'll make a noise." Shaw wanted to get on with it.

"It'll have to wait until morning, Peter, we can't risk it now." Baring sensed his words deflate Shaw. "Give me the goggles, I want to check on the guards. You wait in here."

Baring returned a few minutes later and explained to Shaw how the two guards were taking turns to steal sleep in the cab of the truck. It was still too risky. They would wait for daylight.

It was with a smile of relief that he gestured to Yardley with a thumbs-up a few hours later. Shaw still slept as Baring showed Yardley the spot. Using the cover of the noise in the basement Shaw could lance the circuit in a single strike and spring the lock in a few minutes.

"That's great, Nick," Yardley said. "You looked whacked, can I spell you for a night or two?"

Baring refused. "Peter and I are a team now. Let's leave it, but thanks. That little guy's got some guts. He'll do me."

Yardley thought there had been worse citations when the medals were handed out.

They were interrupted by the sound of the basement door slamming shut.

"Shit!" Yardley said. "That's supposed to be locked. Quick, check the container door is closed."

Sharqi came quickly down the basement steps and said hurriedly, "My boss, Mr. Sohrabi, has decided to inspect the work. He'll be here in under half an hour. Can you make even more mess? He likes to keep his feet clean, and I don't want him taking too close a look."

Yardley swiftly passed the word around. When the elegant minister appeared at the top of the basement steps, the cacophony of banging that greeted him was like the Anvil Chorus from *Il Trovatore.* Clouds of dust hung in the static air and Claude was adding to the chaotic scene by dragging and scraping the old iron fan housing across the uneven flagstones of the basement floor. Sohrabi wrinkled his nose fastidiously and remained a few steps down from the top, gazing down at the dirt and the din. Sharqi, accompanying him, beckoned to Yardley, who ran up the stairs.

She said, "Mr. Sohrabi, may I introduce Mr. Robertz, who is in charge. Mr. Robertz is an installation expert from Switzerland."

Sohrabi held out a languid hand and said, *"Guten Tag, Herr Robertz, velkommen nach Tehran."* There was a pregnant pause, then he tossed his head back and laughed. "I am afraid that is the only German in my repertoire, please do forgive me."

Yardley let his hand drop and steadied his voice. "I am very happy to converse in English, sir. I'm afraid I don't speak any Farsi."

"You are very courteous, Mr. Robertz. I know you Swiss are so good with languages. In fact, I believe one of your men does speak Farsi, Herr Gluck, isn't it?"

The bastard means Miller, thought Yardley, "Yes, Mr. Gluck does pride himself in learning a few words of local dialect when we visit a customer's country. It has proved very helpful on the road."

"An excellent choice of man for your team." Sohrabi spoke with a hint of mocking. "Monsieur Fleuve chose well, don't you think?"

Yardley dropped his eyes to the ground, it was all he could do to avoid glancing at Sharqi. The question raced through his mind, Who the fuck is Fleuve? His brain seemed to seize solid and he could feel Sohrabi's stare burning a hole in his forehead. Shit! Sharqi, get me out of this one.

She did. "Monsieur Fleuve was also very concerned that you did not have time to visit your family before coming on this urgent job, Mr. Robertz. He is new to his position, but assured me he would make it up to you on your return."

Lysol helped out by performing vigorously near the bottom of the steps, a thick cloud of dust came wafting up the stairway. Sohrabi sneezed, then took out a silk handkerchief and elegantly blew his nose. "I think we must leave you to your rather dirty work, Mr. Robertz." He flicked the tiny specks of dust from his trousers. "I suspect you will enjoy washing this dust from your throat this evening, now that you have acquired a taste for our *arak.*" As he turned to leave, he smiled and said, "As the Americans say, have a nice day."

Yardley felt a chill travel the length of his spine as he watched the retreating backs. He thought, What the hell was that all about? He had the nasty feeling the minister had just played with him, as a cat plays with a mouse; and his other paw was itching to stroke Sharqi. He crushed the thought and turned back to the basement. Shaw was his biggest problem right now, Baring had told him of his mood swings, about the perpetual tic, a slight tremor above his left eye, that had developed as if his self-control was almost snapping. They must hold him together until he opens the bloody safe.

Click, click, click. "That's it, Nick, pull the prong out!" Shaw didn't care who else heard his shout, the exact second was vital. Clunk! "Okay, done it, we're in."

They masked their work and walked away from the vault. Shaw's face was etched with the strain of being cooped up in the container and the pressing knowledge that they all depended on his skills. Tonight he would crack the safe combination, if it killed him.

Being closed up that night didn't worry him. He put on the goggles and sat waiting for Baring to let him out. Two hours later he still struggled with the combinations. As he had explained it, there were four main combination locks that had to be set in turn from left to right. Unless rotated in the proper sequence, a special fail-safe mechanism overrode the dials. He was close to fathoming the far right and the dial next to it, but the left-hand dial, the master one for tripping the others in their order, was defeating him. He wasn't sure he was going to make the distance, his hands slipped with the sweat and his eyes hurt from the concentration. He had begun to see green even when he took the goggles off. Baring watched over him, protected him, and saw his nerve going. He laid a hand on Shaw's shoulder. Click! Click! He felt Shaw's tension release. They were in.

11

Think, in this batter'd Caravanserai
Whose Doorways are alternate Night and
Day,
How Sultán after Sultán with his Pomp
Abode his Hour or two, and went his
way.

Next morning, when the rest of the team arrived at the basement for the day's work, they carried an air of expectancy. The previous evening had been spent in the bazaar district, shopping, drinking coffee and soaking up the ethnic atmosphere, a spontaneous suggestion from Jacques that Yardley was glad he had agreed to. As they had threaded their way along Bazar Cheh-ye-Mo Ayyer and crossed the modern Khayyam Street to plunge back into the ancient world of Pachenar Street and the labyrinth of alleys that eventually led them back out to Molavi Avenue, he had observed them more relaxed. Later, gathered round their last drink of the night, they had laid odds that tomorrow was to be the day Peter opened that tin of beans.

"I don't see the guards anywhere," said Lysol as he climbed down from the truck. His words were almost drowned by the mullahs' prayer ritual, singing out from the Emam Khomeyni Mosque, a short distance away on the other side of Panzdah-e-Khordad street.

"Ahhh, maybe they are *les pédes,*" scoffed Claude. "And they have a little, fucking, in my truck!"

Yardley got down and walked to the ladder; the gray morning light filtered into the basement and threw long strange shapes across the floor. The men grouped together near the hoist controls and listened to Claude describe how he wanted the old metal fed to his chains. The morning was cold and they moved and shuffled to keep warm in the shadow of the building. Yardley found himself walking to the ladder. Something wasn't right, he could feel it. Halfway down the ladder the noise reached him—ping! ping! ping! He could not see through the shadows, so he continued down the ladder, his instincts suppressing the urge to call out to Peter Shaw. It can't be Peter, he thought. Reaching the floor, he found the electrical lead and ran his hand along it a few inches to find the light switch. This turned on a single bulb, powered from the truck battery above, that they had rigged up because of the constant power cuts suffered by the museum's main circuit. The bulb, hanging at a lazy angle from a hook on the container, dumped its dim light in a cone on the floor. Yardley saw Gulami standing there like a cheap cabaret artist in a dingy dockside club, and dangling from his outstretched hand was the chromium tuning fork. As Yardley approached, Gulami tapped the instrument repeatedly against the door of the container. Ping! ping! ping!

"Good morning, Mr. Robertz," he said with a broad smile and dead eyes. "You are off to an early start this morning I see."

"Ah, Mr. Gulami." Yardley's voice failed to hide his alarm. "Yes, we are impatient to finish our work here."

"You are not enjoying your stay in our beautiful city, Mr. Robertz?" Gulami asked. "Our glorious Revolution does not excite you?" His lips twisted across his neglected teeth, and saliva collected at the corners of his mouth. Being cool did not come naturally to him.

The sound of Yardley's men beginning to descend the ladder shortened his script. "I am very curious, Mr. Robertz." His voice seemed to rise a few octaves. "What would this instrument be for? I have not noticed any of your men using such a tool until now, and such an expensive-looking tool to leave lying about. Would you not agree?"

Lysol now stood alongside Yardley, and grasped the situation immediately. "My feeler gauges, sir," he said. "I worried all night that they were lost. Thank you for . . ."

"You work, how should I say, a night shift, Mr. Schuler?" Gulami interrupted sharply. "I do not think so. I walked here after you left last night and this tool was not where I found it this morning. My guards assure me none of you returned here after handing in your passes. We have a little mystery, I think."

Inside the container, Baring held Shaw hard against the wall. The sound of the fork drumming on the outside had reached them and seemed to magnify in volume as it repeated over and over. The small hole in the door acted as an amplifier, bouncing the fork's tune off the inside walls of their cage.

"The fork, the bloody fork." As he moaned the words, Shaw had scrambled to his bag and rummaged through it, searching hopelessly in the dark. "It's not here, Nick, I've dropped the bloody fork!"

The panic in his voice became shrill. He grabbed the night-vision goggles and put them on, yanking the lens down in front of his eyes. The expected green-colored vision did not appear.

"They're not working, they're not working!" His panic now took hold.

"Calm down, Peter, calm down." Baring spoke evenly and reached across and took off the lens cover. "There, you can see now, okay?"

Shaw continued to panic, crawling everywhere looking for the fork that he knew was outside, in someone else's hands. "We're dead, Nick, we're dead! Don't you understand? We're dead!"

Gulami had heard him as clearly as the rest of them. A frozen silence hung between the three men, and the security chief's eyes widened with realization, his hand wavering between the whistle at his pocket and the gun at his belt.

"Ça va, mon chef?" Jacques arrived next to Yardley, speaking calmly as he saw what was happening. His arm moved like lightning from where it hung by his side, a faint click as the long blade sprung from its handle, and the knife was buried its full length into Gulami's chest. The naked eye had not seen it fly the six feet through the air to get there. It hit Gulami with such force that the shock held his body rigid, his eyes stared at them and his scream never arrived. He was dead.

Lysol stepped forward and grabbed Gulami's head from behind as he folded to the floor. Bending his head down to his chest meant the last rush of blood from Gulami's mouth did not leave its traces on the flagstones, but on a fresh silk shirt.

"Get that container door open!" Yardley's order was to no one in particular. The rest had arrived and Miller jumped to the door. As he opened it he beckoned Baring to come out. First the frightened Shaw climbed out followed by an alert Baring who asked with an inquiring look if Gulami was dead.

"Yes, he's finished, Nick," said Yardley. "Get him inside the container, quickly. As of now we're in deep shit."

Baring pulled the small door closed behind him, Gulami's body safely shut away. Shaw sat on a discarded pipe close to Yardley, trying to reconcile it all.

"Has he told you?" Baring asked.

"Told us what?" Yardley spoke as he searched for solutions.

"Last night he cracked it." Baring smiled at him. "One Peacock Throne coming up." He strode across to the vault, cleared away the pipes they had stacked to hide their tampering, and slid back the hatch. Yardley and the others followed him, in a bewildered silence. One by one they slid past the heap of old pipes and into the vault, stepped across the narrow space in between, through the opening—it was high tensile top-grade steel over twelve inches thick—and into the vast safe surrounding the throne. The sight that greeted them stunned them all. Even in the internal dusk, the thousands of pearls and precious stones along the sides and back made a milky glow. The cabriole legs, the steps up to the immense divan-type seat, the back with its carved doves, gleamed and shone with refracted light, like some enormous jewel glimpsed at the bottom of a dark pool. Lysol took a step forward, as if to ascend the throne, but Morton put out a restraining hand.

"No, mate," he whispered, awestruck. "They say you get piles from sitting on a cold surface."

"What?" Lysol looked at him, a little confused. "Oh, oh yes, of course, old boy," he said and stepped back.

"Que faire?" asked Claude. "What is to be done?" His question snapped them back to reality.

Yardley had been thinking hard. "Everybody back outside on the double." He stole a last glance at the throne, measuring its size in his mind and followed them out. "We'll have the throne out of here tonight, tomorrow morning at the worst. Lysol, take Miller and Morton and move Gulami's body into the safe. Now! Nick, when they're done, you help

Peter close the safe and the vault, and mask his work, including the earlier bit on the side of the vault. Jacques, give them some grease to rub over the touched areas and throw dust on it to make it conform to the rest of the shit in this place. And Nick, for Christ's sake, let's make sure Peter's memorized the digital code, or written it down. We can't go through all that again."

It was a race against time now, and each of them knew it. Any time now, certainly before the morning was out, someone was going to come asking for Gulami. Perhaps he reported each morning to a superior, or lunched with his family. It was academic; he would be missed, and the hue and cry to follow would center on the basement. Peter's breaking into the vault and any evidence of their stay in the container would have to survive a thorough search of the basement. Five minutes of frantic activity had it all in place, the mattresses back in the trucks and all hands back at work on the air conditioning.

"Jacques, how's it going? How long before the new system's up and running?" Yardley called up to the Belgian as he worked methodically on top of the large power unit. He had phlegmatically shrugged his shoulders at the morning's events, lit another Gauloise and gone back to his installation.

"*Comme çi, comme ça.* There is—what you say?—an airlock in the return pipe. We bleed it, adjust the thermostat and the magnets in the motor, then—*peut-être?*—she functions."

"How long, Jacques? How long?"

"Tomorrow? The day after?"

"Gotta be tomorrow. We can't hold the situation more than a day."

"Okay, *mon chef.* Tomorrow it will be."

Yardley became aware of a strange tranquillity sweeping in from outside. The violence of the early morning had been accompanied by the song of the mullahs, and the abrupt halt to the constant wailing caused him to hunch his shoulders, as if reminded of the hush just before the scream of incoming shellfire. He looked around him and saw the whole team working with a fresh urgency, cutting, stacking, heaving, and Peter Shaw buffing with cleaning rags to put a shine on the new equipment. The old equipment was laid out to be lifted onto the trucks as if building a jigsaw. His thoughts were broken by Sharqi entering through the basement door, and he went to greet her. Thankfully she was alone, and he got straight to the point.

In an urgent whisper he outlined what had taken place. Her face went pale and her voice shook. "Was it absolutely necessary to kill him?"

"Of course it was damned necessary!" Yardley snapped back, and then regretted it. "He was throwing an angle on us from the start, and this morning he got there."

"My God!" Sharqi's hand went across her mouth as the full ramifications of the event hit her. "Gulami takes lunch with Colonel Tudeh today, he does so the same day each week at the office of the Criminal Investigation Bureau in Shahid YarJani Street, a short walk from here. They are family friends and equal swine, so I am bound to get a telephone call to ask where he is."

"I need time, Sharqi, just a little more time." Yardley took her arm briefly. "You have to find me that time."

"How much time?"

"They're gonna be onto Gulami early afternoon, so use your judgment. If you sense they'll come looking for him, work it so their search begins in the basement. We can't risk loading the throne until they've cleared the damned basement, understand? We will load a few items into the container and leave it sitting with the large doors open. Once they've inspected it we're clear to fill it. First thing in the morning that chair goes in followed by some heavy metal and we seal her up—then straight onto the truck. We'll load the other truck this afternoon."

"Yes, that's clear to me." The fear in her voice receded. "What about commissioning the new equipment? There must be an orderly handover to Hashemi. It is vital to avoid suspicion."

"Time that for ten o'clock tomorrow morning. I don't want him near the place before then, okay?" She nodded and nibbled at her bottom lip. "Good girl, and don't worry, we'll pull it off." He wasn't sure he believed himself.

Their eyes held momentarily and then she turned and left the basement. The hours dragged by, minute by aching minute. Yardley strolled around the team as it worked. None of them needed telling what to do. He had explained the new plan to each of them and now it was a matter of finishing the job, maintaining the charade and toughing it out.

The midday prayer time had come and gone. The crew had finished lunch, a ten-minute coffee break round the stove, and were loading the large pieces of the old housing onto the truck. Claude took charge of the hydraulics and the rest manhandled the equipment down in the basement, guided it over the crane truck, and anchored it down on the second truck parked alongside. Below, Jacques and Shaw worked frantically to bring the new system on-line. There was suddenly a commotion at the top of the basement stairs, and simultaneously a squad of six security guards, armed with Soviet AK 47 rifles, rounded the end of the building and formed an offensive line to cover the trucks. They all stopped working.

"Merde!" Claude muttered under his breath. "The sheet az hit the fan."

Three people came hurrying down the stairs—a bearded mullah in the uniform of brown robe and white turban, an officer in a camouflage combat suit and a worried-looking Sharqi bringing up the rear. Yardley went over to meet them.

The mullah looked him up and down with dark suspicious eyes, but said nothing. The officer barked out something in Farsi. Sharqi stepped forward and interpreted.

"Colonel Tudeh wishes to know what has happened to Mr. Gulami."

"Mr. Gulami?"

"Yes, the chief of security. Has he visited the basement today, Mr. Robertz?" Sharqi spoke authoritatively.

"Yes, he has, Miss Zachin, he was here first thing this morning. That has been his routine for the last week. He had very little to say, as is usual, and left."

She turned to the other two men and translated Yardley's remarks. He sensed that the mullah at least understood English. The officer was becoming more agitated and again directed a barrage of Farsi at Yardley.

"Colonel Tudeh is demanding to know the exact time Mr. Gulami was here this morning and wishes you to point out which of these men is Herr Gluck." Sharqi's voice had remained steady, but her reference to Miller's false name was heard by all of them. Gulami had obviously been discussing their phony Swiss passports with the colonel.

"Miss Zachin." Yardley kept his voice calm and turned to the officer. "Colonel Tudeh, with respect, I do not recall the exact time he was here. I can say it was before eight o'clock and I remember that the Koranic recitation was broadcasting from the holy mosque for some time after he left." He had purposely made it long so Sharqi would have to split the translation.

She got the hint and translated carefully for the colonel. The mullah stroked his beard and looked up at Yardley, who towered several inches above him. He seemed about to say something, then gave a wolfish smile and bowed his head. Yardley bowed as well. Sharqi and the officer kept talking, then he looked hard at Yardley and started conversing with the mullah in rapid, insistent tones.

"Mr. Robertz," Sharqi said quietly. "I have explained to the colonel that Mr. Gulami came to my office after visiting the basement and took coffee. We had discussed your work and he had left my office to go to the Export Customs Office in Shahid Raja'i Street to check on your documentation for removing the old equipment. I had also asked him to collect the staff payroll from the Mellat Bank in Esrafil Street on his way back."

They both feigned great concern between them.

"You don't think perhaps poor Mr. Gulami may have . . ."

"Yes, Mr. Robertz," Sharqi said a little louder. "I fear Mr. Gulami may have been attacked and robbed."

The two Iranians looked sullen and indicated to Sharqi they wished to return to her office. Without acknowledging Yardley they took their leave. As they mounted the basement steps the colonel shouted an abrupt order. Outside the squad of security guards broke ranks and filed down the ladder into the basement. They made a thorough search of the place and made no secret of their dislike for the foreigners. Satisfied, their squad leader ordered them up the steps into the museum. The sound of their search could be heard progressing throughout the building.

Standing among the crew, Yardley spelled it out. "We're on borrowed time, you guys, Sharqi has bought us that much. There are two hours left before they close us down for the day. I want every job completed, including the system online, Jacques, before that closing bell rings, the container positioned to receive the throne and the winch prepared. We'll sweat it out in the hotel tonight. In the morning we load and be wrapped up before the ten o'clock commissioning ceremony for this heap of junk. Okay, let's get on it!"

"Bob, one thing more," Baring said. "What do you make of that bastard's reference to Gluck?"

"I know what it meant," Miller said, through clenched teeth. "I served here as a Marine instructor, remember? I reckon one of Tudeh's people is following up a make on my passport photo."

"As I said"—Yardley's expression spoke volumes—"We're all on borrowed time."

Bleary-eyed and stiff, the team stood around in a huddle at dawn the next morning. The cold night air at the altitude of six thousand feet had penetrated through the open basement window. It was raw and bitter cold—"Like a fucking tomb," as Lysol put it, as he stamped his icy feet and squeezed each hand under the opposite armpit, to bring the blood back to his blue fingertips. The added tiredness did not help. They had spent most of the night buried in the bazaar, pretending to play tourist, to avoid any spontaneous police visit, or harassment at the hotel. Yardley had settled their bill in cash rials and given a generous tip to the manager so they could get out of Tehran as soon as the transport papers were rubber-stamped. Seeing that Miller had succeeded in engaging the two night guards in friendly conversation round the stove, Yardley gave the nod to the others, and they began.

Lysol and Baring positioned themselves along one side of the throne, Morton and Jacques alongside the other and Yardley put his back against the front. Shaw bent low next to him, holding the metal hook that was attached to a small-gauge high-tensile wire that ran across the floor of the safe, out through the vault and into the container. Yardley glanced along the wire and his eyes met the gaze of Claude waiting ready at the winch, welded into the far wall of the container.

"Ready?" Yardley whispered loudly. "Lift!" Five of them heaved upward, the throne raised slightly off the floor, Yardley kicked back with his right leg at the steel roller, forcing it beneath the platform. Shaw dropped the hook into the wire strop and held his arm up. Claude saw the signal and took up the slack wire on the winch. Winding the ratchet's handle furiously, he pulled the throne forward. As it rocked against the roller, all of them rushed to the rear and pushed.

"The rollers, Peter!" Baring hissed. "Straighten the other bloody rollers!" Shaw scurried back and closed the seven rollers together in a neat line. The throne platform tottered on the brink of falling back. "Push! For fuck sake, push!"

The wire strained and threatened to snap, then the platform tipped forward and dropped heavily onto the rollers, sending one of them rebounding across the safe. It was too late to be cautious now, Miller had just better keep them occupied. They guided the throne as fast as they could along the rollers and through the two doors, toward the container, waiting with its large double doors thrown wide. Shaw fed the rollers, as they appeared out the back of the throne's base, to the front and they kept it moving. Claude yelled a warning that it was going to catch the container's roof as it entered, but luck was with them. A tight fit would have been an understatement. As they inched the throne forward, the container appeared to be swallowing it, like a boa constrictor gorging itself on a carcass, until it was finally devoured. Claude climbed out over the structure and Shaw gathered up the ramps from the safe and vault doorways and threw them in behind it. They had made good time and now stood looking at their catch. Even in the low light of the single bulb, the throne glimmered and glowed like the iridescent scales of a salmon breasting a river torrent. They were all struck dumb by the extraordinary beauty of the thing, the feeling they were holding in their hands a priceless object, the eighth wonder of the world.

"Better get that tarpaulin over it, lads," Yardley said softly.

"Yes, come on, Nick." Lysol took hold of the canvas. "This royal apparition stands out like a smuggler's beacon."

Yardley gave orders. "Morton, Jacques, get Gulami's body into the safe. Peter, you close up the safe and the vault, sew them up as tight as a nomad's water bag. Let's go!"

Miller came down the ladder. "They've pushed off, boss, prayer time." He gave a nervous chuckle. "Bloody hell, I said mine when you dropped that damned thing. I had to spill coffee on one guy's balls to keep their heads turned."

"Well done, Miller," Yardley said. "Give them a hand with Gulami and then all hands on the loading." He was beginning to warm more to Miller, the man seemed to keep his head when the chips were down. They're all good, damned good, as cool as you like. If we come out of this it should be commendations all round, especially those two Belgians. And, Christ, Shaw included. You couldn't ask for a better bunch. Please God, they'd all come through to enjoy a celebration before they broke up and went their separate ways. Laughter reached his ears, and the three men emerged from the vault.

Miller spoke out, beckoning him over to the vault door. "Hey boss, if they're ever smart enough to open this box themselves, what'll they find?" The Marine tossed his head back and laughed, gesturing for Yardley to take a look.

Where the throne had been, now sat an old chair. Propped up in the chair was the ashen corpse of Gulami, stiff in death, and looking like a shrunken puppet alone in a large empty toy box.

Yardley nodded, and stepped away. Perhaps he'd been premature about Miller. He didn't like his sadistic streak, but, hell, this wasn't a school for morals. Since that stupid episode back on the road, the guy had done his stuff. If he got his kicks from setting up corpses behind closed doors, so what?

"Okay, men," he said. "This is it. Let's move this sucker."

The container had been sealed; and all but the few pieces that were to be stuffed behind to discourage curious customs officers thinking of taking a look was loaded. Yardley's watch said eight-twenty and that meant most of the arriving staff was now inside the building and preoccupied with the beginning of their day. As they had prearranged, all but Baring and himself climbed out of the basement to join Jacques by the truck. Claude, like a master organist, shifted levers and nosed the hoist down through the opening and extended the arm out toward the container. Baring stretched the wire strop encircling it to meet the hook swinging at the end of the arm. Gradually, with the aid of the rollers the container was dragged toward the window. Then it was time to lift it. Withdrawing the arm, Claude removed the center section to shorten it and told Jacques to position the other truck so that its higher deck overlapped the rim of the hoist truck's deck by a few inches. The chains went taut, and the container was lifted gently from the basement floor. Yardley and Baring turned it end-on to the hole as it swung free. The hydraulics began to complain in a painful groan as Claude edged it up to ground level, then the truck tipped under the weight, the wheels farthest from the wall lifting off the ground. As the deck rose two to three inches it met the deck of the second truck, and held. Claude kept it coming, ignoring the fact that if the decks slipped apart, the truck would crush him against the wall. His face streamed with the sweat of concentration as the metal box was carefully eased through the aperture into the light of day. The crew steadied it as two-thirds of it emerged and Claude lowered it the few inches to the ground and let the chains fall slack.

"Okay!" he ordered. "Move that other truck out of my

way, and two of you raise the rear legs." He clambered up onto the container and freed the hook, then dropped into the cab and repositioned the hoist truck so he could swing the load up over the side and place it on the truck's deck. The operation was quick and smooth. Yardley let his breath out in a long sigh and looks of congratulation circulated among them.

"All right, get the rest of that housing loaded, and that's it," Yardley said.

And just then he heard the sound of a powerful engine. A big blue Mercedes car was approaching along the driveway of the palace gardens. It pulled up behind the trucks, effectively blocking their exit. Mr. Sohrabi, in a well-cut Savile Row suit and wearing expensive Ray-Ban dark glasses, stepped out from the back, as his driver leaped out and held the door open for him. Sharqi got out of the other side. There was a slight frown on her face.

Sohrabi came over to him and said, "Not leaving us already, Mr. Robertz?"

"Good morning, sir." Yardley extended his hand in greeting. "No, not quite, we like to clear the job away before handing over to the customer, sir. It is the Swiss way."

Sohrabi smiled, that smile that Yardley had seen a lot of over the last few days. "Ah yes," the minister said, "The Swiss way, everything *just so.*" He walked to the opening in the wall and perused the surroundings. "We have sweepers to carry out such menial tasks. We do not believe here that—as they say in the West—Jack is as good as his master. Is that not so, Sharqi?"

"Yes, Mr. Sohrabi," she answered dutifully.

"I'm afraid it is not a saying familiar to Switzerland, sir," Yardley said politely.

"Mmmm, I do not suppose revolution is familiar to Switzerland either, Mr. Robertz," he chuckled to himself. "I understand the commissioning of the new equipment is scheduled for ten o'clock. Would you care to join myself and Miss Zachin in her office for coffee?"

"It would be a pleasure, sir, but your Mr. Hashemi is due here shortly. I would like to attend his introduction to the new system, if you do not mind, sir?"

"I understand, Mr. Robertz, very conscientious of you. And then you must leave? Ah yes, you explained before that an urgent job calls you elsewhere." He turned to Sharqi. "I must be at the Ministry of Justice by ten-thirty. Come, we will discuss those other matters. Perhaps when you are finished here you can walk across to Khayyam Street and join me there." He placed his hand in the small of Sharqi's back as if to walk her away, and turned suddenly to face the crew, grouped near the truck. "Miller!" he shouted loudly. "Which one is Miller?" They all froze, Sohrabi's eyes picking each of them out in turn, searching for reaction.

Yardley willed Miller to keep his cool. "Miller, sir?" he queried calmly, "I don't have a Miller, Mr. Sohrabi—a mistake perhaps."

Sohrabi ignored Yardley and remained staring at the men. Yardley could feel the sweat gathering under his armpits. He could sense other members of the team stirring. Lysol flung a quick look at the second truck, measuring the distance to the compartment concealing the weapons—no chance.

Yardley broke the tense silence. "That reminds me, Mr. Sohrabi, do I assume we collect our passports from the gate in exchange for our passes, with exit visas already stamped?"

"No, Mr. Robertz, you do not!" The game of cat and mouse was being taken further. "The name Miller was contained in a rather worrying report from Colonel Tudeh that arrived on my desk this morning. A preliminary procedure in his investigation into the disappearance of the security chief at this museum. A mystery, an unacceptable mystery. As is his suggestion concerning an Englishman named Miller. No, Mr. Robertz, your passports will be returned, but your exit visas will not be issued until you arrive at our northern border. I trust you will have a pleasant journey." The smile again. "Come, Miss Zachin."

He nodded formally to Yardley and waved a hand at his driver. Taking Sharqi's arm, he walked her off toward her office, leaving the driver to reverse the Mercedes and crawl along behind them. Yardley's heart was in his boots. It was possibly the last time he would see her, and there she goes in the grasp of that scum, the man who could order her death. Death for all of them.

"Mon chef." Jacques took his arm, his voice understanding. "It is hard, but we must move."

"Yes, Jacques, I'll be right with you." They all heard the emotion in Yardley's voice.

Hashemi arrived with two assistants and a great display of understanding of the new system took place. It basically involved turning two switches on and off, but Jacques patronized him and congratulated the maintenance chief on the speed at which he had learned. Yardley had stood back. He seemed to feel very tired, or was it just the strain of Sharqi, playing on his emotions? He watched the crew ready themselves for the trip, to fight their way out if they had to, and admired Jacques's patience, as he explained the thick service manual to the objectionable mechanic.

Sharqi entered the basement on the stroke of ten o'clock. Thankfully she came alone. She crossed the floor and stood next to Yardley, without announcing herself to Hashemi, still engrossed in Jacques's instructions.

She spoke deliberately. "We must complete these formalities quickly, and you must leave the city as fast as possible. That horrible Sohrabi is becoming convinced that something is not right." She nodded an acknowledgment to Hashemi as she talked and he came toward them. In a whisper she said, "We have no time to talk now, please be careful."

"Miss Zachin." Hashemi bowed his head in greeting. "I am very satisfied that everything works," he said, and then broke into Farsi dialect.

Sharqi heard him out and watched him demonstrate the operation of the system and approved the product support package and service agreement. Making some ceremony out of the occasion, she shook hands with all the crew and formally signed the acceptance papers. As the shiny new air conditioning hummed away in the background, she officially handed the maintenance manuals over to Hashemi, who accepted them with a display of self-importance.

It was agreed that Hashemi's men would replace the large grille in the wall and, with that, the little ceremony came to an end. Yardley walked Sharqi to the bottom of the steps.

"Sharqi," he said, "I can't leave you in this mess, I . . ."

She turned abruptly to face him. "Go, Bob, do not discuss it, go!" Her face was taut and the words came out aggressively. "Another time or place perhaps, but not here and now. For God's sake, see the danger you're in, the danger talk like this puts me in!" Her face suddenly softened and she took his hand. "Please go, and go safely." She mounted the steps and left the basement without turning to look back.

Yardley planned to accompany the truck with the throne secreted at the back and, apart from Claude the driver, had chosen Nick Baring and Lysol as the other two escorts. He had felt a little guilty at having to relegate Peter Shaw to passenger in the other truck, but Peter was now indeed one of the team. His success at opening first the vault and then the safe had made him the man of the hour and sent his self-confidence rocketing. If they all got back to Switzerland safely, Yardley suspected there might be problems in pushing Shaw off to South Africa. The others were professionals. They would break up with a handshake and go their separate ways, some back to regimental duty, others to rest until the next mercenary job came along. They'd all remember this caper and the other guys who took part, but as time went by and other operations succeeded it, walking off with the throne would become one of several; a big one—perhaps the very biggest—but not all that different.

But to Shaw, it would be the highlight of his circumscribed life, the one glamorous moment when seven tough fighting men depended entirely on his skills to win the day. Even the cold-blooded killing Nick had had to do on the road from Marseilles would change its horror into excitement. So he would not want to let go, to be pushed off, sent packing to a strange country where he knew no one and would yet again be back on his own. Yardley's thoughts were oscillating between concern for Shaw and the threat bearing down on them from Sohrabi. The matter of Miller's face being recognized from old SAVAK files, the Shah's hated secret police, was still percolating somewhere in this paranoid city and it would soon come to the boil. The thought gripped his guts and he pushed it away, the whole crew felt the danger. Shaw was a more comfortable worry and the problem he presented was safely beyond the border.

I'll have to do something, he thought, but let's get out of this rathole first; and all of us in one piece, heads and balls in their right places.

Claude had already swung the leading truck onto the driveway leading to the main gate. Yardley said to him, "Left at the gate and then first left. We go right along the side of the palace garden. Then round that big roundabout—it's the Meydane-Emam Khomeyni, sounds like Big Brother himself—and north on Ferdowsi. We pass the main gates of the British Embassy on our left and a couple of hundred yards on, you come to another roundabout. Make a left on Enqelab and then we go straight along toward the airport. From there on, we go out the way we came in. Okay, Claude, nice and easy, *n'est-ce pas?*"

Claude took one thick fist off the steering wheel and bunched it. *"Avec Vaseline, mon chef,"* he said with a twist of the lips.

The trucks nosed their way along the busy streets. Yardley knew all too well that it was not over yet, not by over six hundred miles. A typically crazy taxi driver could easily skid into one of the trucks, or one of the holy men who walked along the streets wearing a black turban, deep in the Koran or in their devotions, might suddenly step out blindly from the curb and be crushed under the huge front wheels. And then the police would gather, questions would be asked, the trucks and their passengers thoroughly searched; and when that big container was opened up, the emblem of Iran, the one shining symbol that any schoolchild would recognize, would be revealed in all its shimmering opulence. He left the scenario at that point. What might happen next was too nasty to consider in detail.

So, under his apparent coolness taut as a violin string, Yardley watched the Tehran landmarks crawl past the window of the cab, as they crept out along Enqelab Avenue. It was the upper-class, academic area of the city, with first the wide expanse of the Polytechnic University and then the even bigger and more spacious Tehran University. Away to the north was the Emam Khomeyni Hospital and last, as they were nearing the airport roundabout, the Sharif Industrial University. Whatever wrongs that old man with the burning, deep-set eyes and the wrinkled bearded face had brought to the troubled land of Iran, he had at least brought a healthy desire for learning. Yardley wondered briefly whether Peace and Tolerance were on the curriculum.

He breathed more easily once they turned west onto the *otoban* leading to Karaj and Qazvin. It was past noon but he had decided to postpone the first break until the trucks were well clear of the city. He had said to the others, "Let's get some miles under our belts before we stop. There's that small town we came through on the way in—Abyek Sofla—about halfway between Karaj and Qazvin. We'll grab a break and a hot drink there."

There was not the usual jokiness and chaffing when the team reassembled for the first break. The team walked about instead of lounging against the sides of the trucks, they drank their tea in quick gulps and tore into their sandwiches with impatience more than hunger. Even Nick Baring seemed infected with the general eagerness to get on with it. Yardley knew the feeling only too well. Once in Beirut he had finished a one-man patrol early and had been forced to wait for forty-five minutes in a stinking dark cellar in a bombed-out building close to a Hizbollah headquarters. He had lain, huddled in one corner, in God knew what filth and excrement, holding his Browning pistol in his lap, a full clip in the butt and a round in the chamber and his right thumb hooked over the hammer. Every noise in the area, the bumping of a heavy weight above his head, the scratching and rustle of a rat exploring the far side of the cellar, assailed his ears. His shoulder blades were clamped together in tension. Once he nearly betrayed his hiding place by blasting away when the rat gave an unexpected squeak. It had been a long, long wait.

The traffic was heavy on the highway and an icy rain lashed down from the mountains to their north. At one point just short of Qazvin, the road was under repair and there was single-lane traffic for five kilometers. The leading truck was waved through at one holdup point but the second truck was halted at the barrier. Once clear of the obstacle, Yardley told Jacques to slow down and give the others a chance of catching up. It was the first time in over two thousand kilometers that the two trucks had been forced apart. He felt naked and defenseless to be split away from the trusty second half of the team. Nearly half an hour went by as they seemed to crawl along, being overtaken by truck after truck, but none of them the one he was getting desperate to see. At last, there was a double flashing of headlights behind them.

"Ahh," Claude sighed and mumbled to himself, *"Je suis bien content que vous soyez là, mon cher."* And blasted two long welcomes with the truck's Klaxons.

"What's up, Claude?" Yardley demanded.

"My favorite brother is behind us, I am very glad to see him."

With the end of October approaching, the night had begun to draw in early. The rain had stopped but it was growing dusk when they were still fifty miles short of Zanjan. The six-thousand-foot altitude contour ran close to the main highway, according to the map, and the temperature was falling. Yardley dared not risk the chance of black ice on the road and a possible accident. So he decided to stop for the night at the truck compound on the outskirts of the town of Zanjan. Driving sedately, both trucks came to a safe halt alongside each other. Yardley ordered a cook-up and set a guard roster for the night. They now all carried their side-arms concealed under their clothing. One more day's hard driving and they would be at the Turkish frontier—with safety just a wooden barrier away. And then he recalled Sohrabi's trump card—the exit visas that were the key needed to lift that barrier. Could he and the team fight their way across the border? Stop bloody worrying, he told himself. If they had to, they would.

Sharqi was in her elegant apartment in the rich Abbas Abad area of north Tehran. Her apartment was on Sohrvardi Avenue, which under the Shah had been called after his queen, Farah. In the overcrowded city, pullulating with humanity, it was an oasis of peace and space. There were a few noble Bokhara rugs on the floor, staining the pine floors with warmth and color, and some antique Isfahan paintings on the whitewashed walls. She was in a bathrobe, having just taken a shower and washed her hair. She was wondering whether to plug in the air dryer and risk blowing the main fuse—at this time in the early evening the pressure on the antiquated electrical system was greatest, with lighting on and neighbors beginning to cook their evening meal—when the telephone rang.

As she answered it, she immediately recognized the voice of Sohrabi.

"Sharqi," he said, "many apologies for calling you at this hour. Are you alone?"

"Of course, Mr. Sohrabi," she said abruptly.

"Forgive me again. I was not implying . . . I thought there might be a servant there."

"I do not have a living-in servant."

"I see. You have booked your flight to London in four days' time, have you not? In case you had already begun to pack, I wanted you to know right away that you will not be going to London on this occasion."

"Not going?"

"I fear not. There has been a slight change of plan. The Ministry of Foreign Affairs has decided that an Iranian presence in London at this moment in time is not required. But cheer up, Sharqi. It is only a postponement. I am sure there will be other opportunities for you to spread your sweetness and light, as they say, in the cultural centers of Europe."

"But, Mr. Sohrabi, the Christie's auction is very important. There are artifacts from the period of Darius coming up."

"I'm sorry, Sharqi. I am only the bearer of bad tidings. No doubt our minister will make alternative arrangements for bidding at the auction."

"But there's no one who knows the scene the way I do!"

"None of us is indispensable, Sharqi. Let us always bear that in mind. And, if I may say, arguing does not become you."

"I'm sorry, Mr. Sohrabi."

"So am I. By the way, how is the air conditioning working at the Ghulistan Museum?"

"Excellently, thank you."

"So your friends appear to have done a good job. That must be pleasing to you."

"For the record, Mr. Sohrabi, they are not my friends. My contact with them was a professional one throughout. And anything that helps the museum pleases me."

"Happy the man who comes into contact with you, dear lady! Well, I must not keep you. I am sure you have a busy social life. Oh, I nearly forgot, would you do me the kindness of calling at my office tomorrow morning. At eleven o'clock. For coffee, of course."

"Are there any notes I should make in advance? Or papers you wish to see?"

"No, nothing like that. A general discussion, that's what we need. Goodnight, Sharqi, pleasant dreams."

She replaced the telephone. Her left hand was wet with sweat and shaking slightly.

She walked up and down the room, thinking furiously. She had to be under suspicion. She knew, and Sohrabi knew full well, that there was no one else who could take over her job of bidding at an international auction with only a few days' notice. Had the minister wished to groom a successor for her, she would have had to train the man or woman, most likely a man, and then take him to several auctions and teach him when to bid and, more important, when not to, over at least three or four major auctions. Without resorting to vanity, she knew that she had done an excellent job for the ministry over the past few years, which made her supposed crime all the greater. If she had behaved irresponsibly or bought the wrong items, they might punish her by denying her the trips abroad; but she was sure it was not for that reason. Something to do with Yardley and his team? There was no way they could have discovered as yet that the Peacock Throne had been stolen. If there had been and she was thought to be implicated, there would not just be a suave telephone call. By now, her front door would have crashed in and the revolutionary guard would have dragged her away by her hair.

Perhaps the phone call had been genuine; perhaps there really had been a change of policy high up in the Majlis, the Islamic Assembly, and her ministry had no choice but to accept the directive. She had seen too much of the mullahs' government at close hand to think it was swayed by a sense of logic or realism. A dream, a supposed vision during prayer, or simply power politics would be enough to reverse any so-called cultural policy.

She stopped her pacing up and down. Sohrabi could be playing games. There had never been any intention of canceling her flight to London. He was just pretending it was off—the evil man was capable of anything. His invitation for coffee in his office tomorrow morning was purely to demonstrate his power to her, to tell her that he had succeeded in having the trip reinstated. Typical of Sohrabi—dancing between the silken threat and currying favor. She'd soon find out.

Her instincts would not let it rest and the various options raced around in her head. She could telephone Rustum, yes, Rustum Rosenbah, an old friend of her family and one of the few other Jews to have survived the fundamentalists' purgation. He worked as chief liaison officer for the Personal Identification Bureau, at Iran Air. She glanced at her watch. My God! Five-fifty. Would he still be in his office at the airport? Her hand grabbed at the telephone. Nervous fingers made her misdial several times, but finally the number was ringing. It was a terrible line, two loud clicks hurt her ear and she thought she heard her own breathing echo in the receiver. She dropped the handset as if it were red-hot and then fumbled it back onto its cradle. The phone was tapped! The fear seemed to grip her by the throat and she found herself wiping her hands continuously down the sides of her bathrobe, but they stayed wet with perspiration. Stop it! Stop it! Think, woman, think! Her bottom lip became stuck in her teeth and she could taste its blood. The public phone down in the porter's hall, use that.

She scrambled into a pair of old jeans and threw on a sloppy pullover, snatched up her diary and keys and raced out into the hall. The elevator was occupied so she ran down the stairs, searching for his number as she went. The five floors down to the lobby felt like twenty. The number rang and he was on the line, charming and chatty. She cut him short: "Rusty, dear friend, I know we have not spoken enough recently, but please listen to me." She tried to normalize her voice and manufactured a chuckle. "Can you check my flight details to London for me? I have been told of a postponement but not the new flight number." As she waited for him to call up the information on his computer, her legs threatened to give out and she held on to the edge of the phone booth.

"Sharqi." His voice was low and cautious. "It appears that there is no rebooked flight."

"Oh, well, the ministry have issued a temporary change of policy, so I . . ."

"Sharqi." Now his voice was almost a whisper. "It is not temporary, Sharqi. Your exit visa has been withdrawn. You come up on my screen as a detain and notify."

"What?"

"That is what shows, my dear."

She was actress enough to give a kind of carefree laugh. "Oh, Rusty, sometimes I despair of this country . . ."

"Sharqi!" he cut in warningly. The silence between them said it all. "Take care, my dear, bless you." His voice trailed off and the line went dead.

She held the handset against her forehead and rode out a shiver that traveled from her feet to her head. It had to happen sooner or later. As she replaced the handset, a calmness came over her and pushed the fear ruthlessly to one side. So be it. She went across to the elevator and rode back up to her apartment. Sohrabi's suspicions had reached the point of no return and there was not a moment to lose.

She dressed rapidly in tweed slacks, a woolen sweater and a pair of strong walking shoes. From behind a rack of shoes in a cupboard she lifted out a small satchel and hung it on her shoulder. Wrapping her head in a dark silk headscarf, she took a waterproof topcoat from a hanger, scooped up a single red shoe from the rack, and without a backward glance, left the apartment.

Outside, she slipped around behind the building and collected her bicycle from where it was chained to the security railing. With the collar of her coat turned up, she cycled out of the front gates and into the busy traffic flow of Sohrvardi Avenue. Hunching her shoulders against the rush hour noise and fumes, she rode south along the avenue, glancing left and right at the corners of the first few intersecting streets that ran with mathematical precision due east and west off the avenue. She did not notice any unusual parked cars or solitary men lounging about that would tell her that surveillance had been widened to block her escape.

She turned left into Andisheh and Panjom streets, using their narrowness to check that she was not followed. It would take her about ten minutes to reach her destination close to the sinister Savar Police Station, and the neighboring ugly blocks of Shaar Prison. The procedure she was following had been rehearsed, for such an occasion, drilled into her by a bossy instructor at the short training course given to her clandestinely during one of her many trips to Europe. Becoming an agent against Khomeini had not been a difficult decision. Just as she had kept a survival bag packed, she also had a car hidden in a lockup garage near the prison. Through a friend of a friend the lockup had been found, conveniently located behind a gas station on Hamid Street. A mechanic at the station was paid indirectly to keep an eye on the car and start up the engine from time to time to maintain a healthy battery. She had driven past the garage on occasion and cycled to it from her apartment, but never entered or approached it. She now prayed that the powerful Fiat was there and in working order. The mechanic was one of the Bakhtiari tribe from the southwest; life had been better under the Shah, and being paid for protecting someone's luxury car helped redress the suffering brought on him by the new regime.

She pedaled to the end of Panjom Street and skirted some houses by taking a back alley running along their rear. As she passed the third house from the end, she threw the red shoe over the wooden fence into the small back garden, and coasted out of the alley into Shari'Ati Street. Reaching Hamid Street, she rode along the line of vehicles waiting to buy gasoline, and turned in behind the station. No one took any notice of her. Discarding the bike, she fished in her survival bag for the set of keys, one for the garage, the other two for the car. Her heart was thumping as she pulled up the overhead door. The dusty radiator grille of the Fiat was a very welcome sight. The engine fired instantly and she headed the car out and away from the bustle of the gas station. To avoid getting stuck in the traffic lining up for gas she turned left into Sorush Street, and past the police station with lights burning in every window. The police car pool was humming with activity. One car accelerated onto the street and closed right up behind her, lights blazing and siren wailing. She fought the urge to scream and panic. It pulled out wildly and shot by her. She grimaced.

The die was cast, she was now a fugitive. Sohrabi would give Colonel Tudeh his head and he would be let loose, to bring back to Sohrabi hers, in a sack if necessary. They would calculate immediately that the only route she could take would be north to the Turkish border. All other directions would take her toward hostile or unwelcome countries. But some luck was riding with her. Perhaps she could catch up with Bob Yardley and his team. If not, the car was running well enough to get her where she had to go. The catalog from Sotheby's in Geneva that Flood had slipped to her at Zurich Airport had held the coded coordinates and cryptic message for an alternative way out, if only she could make it.

Only a few weeks earlier, shortly before the uneasy truce with Iraq, missile-firing enemy aircraft had swooped low over the city. One of the targets must have been the military university just north of the prison. When the all-clear went, she had seen an ominous cloud of smoke and dust rising from the area of her secret garage and, casting caution to the winds, had cycled furiously until stopped by a police barrier. The missile had missed the garage by fifty yards, but the blast had blown an armchair from a neighboring wrecked house onto the roof of the garage. The chair balanced freakishly across the roof's apex, swaying in the breeze. A servant had placed a ladder against the wall and brought it down. The onlookers clapped and shouted with glee; it was a sense of relief that, whatever the damage, they themselves were alive and unharmed. And Sharqi had been doubly relieved that her hiding place and her ticket out had not been blown to ruins. Yes, her luck had held; and now she needed all the luck she could get.

She hardly dared breathe until she had rejoined Doktor Ali-ye-Shari'ati Avenue and turned north, leaving the menacing spectacle of the police station and prison behind her. The flow of traffic along the avenue seemed to harass her and she felt all the other drivers knew she was on the run. For a heart-stopping moment the car's engine convulsed and almost stalled and her eyes flashed to the fuel gauge. In her rush she had not thought to check it and the relief of seeing it showing full almost made her burst into tears. A nervous laugh escaped her throat as she told herself not to be pathetic. As she approached the overpass that would lead her onto Bozorg Rah-e-Resalat, the east–west highway that would take her toward the airport, the traffic congested into a single lane. Rubble from a recent air raid had spilled across the road and had only partly been cleared away. It was every man for himself when it came to filtering into the single flow and Sharqi found her way blocked by a Cadillac limousine edging aggressively into the tight space. She let the driver have his way—confrontation was the last thing she needed. The two cars sat momentarily side by side. Sitting in the rear of the Cadillac were two robed mullahs. They were discussing an article in the *Abrar,* the Tehran daily newspaper, in the glow of an interior light, and appeared to be disagreeing. One of them looked out and across at her, glaring in an expressionless manner into the Fiat. Their eyes met, and she went numb—he must recognize her. The bearded politician liked what he saw and a lecherous smile spread over his face. A cold shudder welled up from inside her. Then the Cadillac was gone and impatient horns blared behind to push the Fiat forward. Angrily she accelerated into the lane, past the obstruction and up onto the highway.

Corrupt, hypocritical pigs, she thought. To hell with this benighted country, where power, corruption and the Koran go hand in hand. The Ayatollah preached Islamic purity, that women should model themselves on Fatima Zahra, daughter of the Prophet Mohammed, that the Revolution was for all. That hairy-faced monster had just mentally undressed her from the comfort of his Cadillac! She felt better for her anger and switched on the car radio. Even the incessant caterwauling of the Arab music made her smile. She said a little prayer to herself—Please let me get away safely to a civilized place.

The traffic thinned out beyond the river and consisted mainly of heavy trucks as she joined the Qazvin *otoban* near the international airport—the road north that Yardley and his team had taken nine hours earlier. Subconsciously she speeded up and felt confident to hold the car's speed at seventy-five miles an hour. It was some distance before she stopped glancing continuously in the rear mirror and let the tension gripping her whole body trickle away. She knew that, even now, the guards might have smashed in the door of her apartment and found that the bird had flown. Somehow it didn't matter anymore, and she let the darkness beyond the city lights consume her.

Sharqi had not eaten since lunchtime but, strangely, she felt no hunger. There were some hard rations packed in her survival bag, but they were for an emergency, as was the 9mm Walther automatic pistol and the wallet of mixed currencies. She decided against stopping in the religious city of Qazvin and drove on through the night toward Zanjan. The lights of the city came into view and the perimeter lights of the truck compound were easily distinguishable in its approaches. The compound meant gas pumps and she decided it would be wise to top off the Fiat's tank, maybe buy some food, then push on through the city. Twenty minutes later she was driving out the other side of Zanjan and feeling comfortable with her plan of action. She picked and nibbled at the piece of cold chicken lying in newspaper on the seat beside her, as she drove, and smiled inwardly at some of the compliments offered by the rough, but kind, truckers back at the compound. She remained completely unaware that Bob Yardley and his men were resting in their vehicles there.

Rainer knocked lightly and entered Flood's office. "Excuse me, sir, I know you do not wish to be disturbed but you have an urgent call from the Middle East on the secure line. I think you should take the call." He walked the handset from the desk to Flood's fireside table, and left the room.

Flood set aside the thick dossier he had been studying and picked up the phone. "Yes?"

"Good evening, Flood, I trust I'm not disturbing any more than just a business preoccupation?"

Flood instantly recognized the gentle voice of the old professional. "Not at all, you old rascal, it's nice to hear from you. And how is that lovely new wife of yours, not finding you too hot to handle, I hope?"

"Do you ask for me or for yourself, my antipodean friend?" They laughed together and then in a more serious voice: "My call is about another of my ladies. We have learned tonight that our Cinderella has lost her shoe and run from the ball."

"Tonight?" Flood checked his watch and calculated the time in Tehran. Christ, their network had moved fast to get the signal out of Iran so soon.

"Yes, tonight. I fear she will not make it in time, but at least we know that your people are on the road north."

"Are your chariots going to get there on time?"

"Yes, with a section of our elite 'Jonathan' unit on board. Our boys could load their 1553B data systems with all the detail needed to hit the spot on time with accurate fuel. Amos still thinks the greatest threat is from their Soviet ZSU-23s. A forty-round burst from that quadruple 23mm cannon and it's over."

Flood was relieved to know that the Israelis' giant MH-53 assault helicopters carried the Elisra SPS-20 self-protection system and the APR-39 radar warning kit. They would be able to suppress and confuse the ZSUs' J-band fire-control radar all right.

"Has he deployed any stand-off jamming platforms?"

"Yes, I understand they're taking along a Hughes MD500 Defender to lift in the intercept party and to provide stand-off protection on the way out. I'm not too concerned about the inbound leg. We've got the penetration of Syrian airspace down to a fine art and the J Pave-Low III terrain-following equipment makes it a party for those young pups. But the exfiltration will be something else. They'll be tired after five hours nap-of-the-earth flying and one in-flight refueling. To repeat the same coming out plus the possibility of trouble on the ground, I must tell you, my boy, it has me worried."

"Well to cheer you up, I can tell you that this end has gone fine and Amsterdam is waiting like a baby for its bottle. And don't worry, my man can handle it on the ground."

"Ah, that is typical of you, Flood, but I know you worry for Sharqi, and your boys."

"That's the business we're in, old friend, and it's long time you gave it all up and enjoyed your beautiful Eva. Give my best regards to Amos. If he pulls this off he'll remain one of my favorite generals."

A few pleasantries later, Flood replaced the handset, and gazed into the flicking flames of the warm fire. He knew exactly what was going on out there, he'd been in it enough times himself. Pouring a deep scotch from the crystal decanter, he took it with him to the chart on the far wall. He studied the map for several minutes and then moved the magnetic marker to a position beyond Zanjan.

Yardley and Lysol took the last spell of guard duty—six to eight A.M.—that morning. It was a bleak dawn and he pulled his duffel coat tighter around him as he paced up and down. Neither of them spoke, it was no time for a jolly chat, and each was deep in his thoughts as they made sure no one approached the trucks and their precious burden. It would be a hard day's drive to reach the Turkish frontier by nightfall. The traffic leaving the compound and going north was heavy and it would take a good hour for the convoy to spread out and get up some speed. Should they stop short and aim to leave Iran at sunup the next day, when the border guards would be at their lowest ebb, and thus risk another twelve hours in hostile territory? Or aim to go over just before the frontier post closed for the night, when the security men and customs officials would be bored and tired and ready to wave a last convoy through. The latter sounded the best bet. And if it came to a firefight, God forbid, the night darkness would give them an edge and conceal them once they had broken through. Somehow he knew, as they all did, that their exit visas were not going to be a simple border formality.

And what of Sharqi? She had another four days, no, three now, to sweat it out before she climbed aboard that plane for London. He had hated leaving her behind. It seemed almost a cowardly thing to do, but his first duty was to get the throne safely to the military air base outside the city of Erzerum, a good one hundred and eighty miles inside Turkey. Three more days, with luck, and the mission would be over. And not a goddamn day too soon. He'd had enough of General Bradford and that slippery Rodel to last him a lifetime. Once he'd handed over the throne to the reception committee at the air base, whoever that may be, the NSC, the CIA, official X, who gives a shit, they could all go and jump into the Potomac River. For him it would be the first available flight to London, and that reunion with Sharqi.

The rest of the team was beginning to stir. Jacques made some coffee and Miller went off to negotiate some unleavened *chupatti*-type bread. They wasted little time eating the brittle slices and downing the hot coffee. The trucks were refilled with diesel oil and were rumbling out of the compound onto the highway soon after seven o'clock. That put them near the front of the traffic. Even the early-rising Germans and Swedes had been slowed down by the bitter cold and were obviously resigned to taking longer to reach the frontier.

As the miles ground by, their spirits began to rise. The closer they were to the border, the more the expected fight would be on their terms. That was all any soldier ever asked for. Lysol began to hum to himself and developed it into a tuneless melody. Baring put up with the noise for so long, then couldn't resist a verbal attack on Lysol's lack of talent.

"Cut it out, you two, I'm trying to think," Yardley moaned.

"What with?" they both chorused. Lysol added, "Seriously, skipper, how do you rate it?"

"Once we're past the guardroom at the Erzerum air base and have handed over this old chair, I'll reckon we made it."

"I guess we all reckon to agree with that, Bob," Baring said matter-of-factly, "Mr. Sohrabi's reception party should be quite a gate crasher."

"He may have been all bluff," Lysol suggested, "the little pseudo-*podestà*."

"You know better than that, Lysol." Baring gave a quizzical glance. *"Podestà?"*

"Ah, Nick, my colonial friend, of suspect learning and a bush childhood." Lysol was enjoying himself. "Let us just say an appointed governor of a medieval municipality, of Italian origin . . ."

"Oh knock it off, Lysol." Yardley sounded irritated. "What's up ahead is all we need to know about Mr.-fucking-Sohrabi, okay?"

"Okay, boss. Point taken."

They could guess who was on his mind, and fell silent.

The sun was up, casting a long shadow ahead of the leading truck and lightening the distant mountain peaks as they drove through the funnel of ranges on either side of the highway. The road ahead was clear and Claude had the monster truck rolling at sixty miles an hour. The second truck with Jacques at the wheel followed close behind, the twin brothers driving almost as one, denying any outsider the chance of coming between their rigs. Conversation among the team remained light, and Shaw, who now had nothing to prove, fell in and out of sleep. Once on the road north of Zanjan, all of them became engrossed in preparing their weapons, distributed in the darkness of the compound. The automatic pistols and Heckler & Koch MP5s were easy to conceal and were comfortably small to handle inside the driver's cabins. Baring rested his slightly longer Franchi inverted between his lap and the dashboard, and fed the specially loaded cartridges into the magazine. He'd grown fond of the gun's balance and the rate of fire he could achieve after doing a little doctoring with the pump action's return spring. Perfect for in close. Yardley couldn't help but notice how his men checked and rechecked their weapons, professionals, used to working alone without any support. Their only backup if a weapon malfunctioned was their bare hands. There were no reinforcements in this game. He reckoned at this rate they would see the border in about five hours.

The road followed the Zanjanrud, a fast-running river at this time of the year, and twisted its way back and forth between the railway and a buried pipeline, all paralleling each other northward. In places it reminded Lysol of his time in the Oman. Their talk on that subject was suddenly interrupted by Claude applying the brakes and waving his hand out the window to warn Jacques he was slowing to a full stop. They had rounded the bend to be confronted by a wooden barrier across the road, three hundred yards ahead. A group of armed men gathered at the barrier, and one of them had his arm raised for them to halt. Claude brought the giant DAF to a stop almost on top of him. A sign hanging on the barrier displayed the words *"Bozorg Rah Dar Dast-e-Sakhteman,"* and the men were wearing the assorted uniforms of the revolutionary guard. Yardley jumped down and called Miller forward to translate. The Marine parleyed with the man, who seemed to be quite apologetic for stopping them, but was demanding something from Miller all the same. Yardley could hear him saying, *"pol down, pol down"* and *"after rah ahan, after rah ahan."* It seemed to make sense to Miller.

"Boss, he says the main bridge is down this side of Meyaneh. Seems there was a big storm in the mountains overnight and the flood water washed away one of the piers. Least, that's what I made out, his accent's a little unfamiliar to me. We have to make a detour, across this railway line and along that road over there." Miller pointed to where a road could be seen climbing into a mountain pass. "It takes us to some dump called Hasanabad, where we'll reach a fork and have a choice of two roads up to a town called Chow-something, which then puts us back on a better road to Meyaneh. It's about a one-hundred-and-thirty-mile detour, the guy says."

"Holy shit!" Yardley said as he opened the map to the right fold. "We could get in a mess up there." He studied the twisting route to Hasanabad, which climbed past a trig point nearly eleven thousand feet high and then, after the town, went south a short distance before dropping down to cross a deep gorge and the River-Sarug before climbing back up and north to the mountain village of Chowqati—again nearly at ten thousand feet. "Miller, ask him why we can't take this northern fork directly to Chowqati? It would save us about thirty miles."

Miller returned to the truck. "He says our trucks are too big for that road, and we must take the more gradual contour route—quicker in the long run."

Yardley discussed the route with Baring. They agreed that although it would add a good seven, possibly ten, hours to their journey time, that could be an advantage. It was not yet nine o'clock in the morning. It would put their arrival time at the border well into the night.

The guard in charge of the barrier shouted something to Miller. He walked back to the barrier and talked to the man, who got a little excited and pointed to the trucks. Miller came back to Yardley and said, "He wants to detach two men, one to each truck, and have them navigate us through the detour."

"The hell with that," Yardley shouted. "We're not having bloody Iranians aboard!"

"I've argued with him, boss, he . . ."

"Well, go and argue some more!" Yardley's anger was showing.

Baring said quietly, "Easy, skipper. We don't want to start anything here. Compromise with the bastard, take one man, what we do with him up in the hills is another matter."

Yardley thought that made sense. "Okay," he said. He walked forward to the barrier. "Tell him we'll settle for one guard, it's all we have room for; that's final, no argument." He looked into the eyes of the guard doing the talking, and saw a highly trained threat. He turned on his heels and returned to the truck. "Lysol, you drop back and take Miller's place in the number-two truck, I want him up here with me to translate what our new passenger has to say. The man could speak English, so keep the chat to a minimum. Miller? One man only. Let's roll!"

The two trucks swung off the highway, across the railway line and down the narrow road leading west. They rode in silence, unsure what new threat this situation would bring. The metal top road ran reasonably straight across the high plateau, then began its twisting path along the Quezel Ovzam River and up into the higher mountains. Claude was able to roll along at sixty miles an hour initially, until they reached the fork in the road Yardley had noted on his map earlier. The guard said nothing, but insisted with his jabbing finger that Claude take the left turn toward the village of Kahriz and then west to Hasanabad. Yardley shoved his map in front of the guard's face and pointed to the shorter road up to Chowqati.

"Miller, tell him I want to try the shorter route."

"Haram, haram!" the guard muttered aggressively, and punched Claude on the shoulder, then pointed impatiently along the road to Kahriz.

"The man's angry, boss," Miller said. "He's just said the Chowqati road is forbidden."

The truck labored up the passes as it climbed from seven thousand feet to close on ten thousand, following the zigzag contours on the bleak uplands. The metal road broke up in places and, in some stretches, was nothing more than a dusty earthen track a few feet wider than the trucks themselves. Kahriz was nothing more than a few mud houses and a leaky oil tank using a discarded tractor as a pump. Jacques dropped back a short distance to avoid having to struggle constantly with the low gear ratios.

Once over the saddle of the mountain range, the trucks willingly rolled down toward the valley floor. The passengers felt relief as well. At last it seemed as if they were getting somewhere. The drivers now had to engage their lower gears to assist with the trucks' braking action. Claude was continually stamping on the brake pedal as he pulled and heaved the long vehicle around each corner. It was slightly easier for Jacques because of the warnings given to him by the lead truck's brake lights. Several times they had to pull up abruptly to avoid flocks of sheep and goats crossing the road. The herdsmen took no interest in them whatsoever.

In both trucks someone had commented on the lack of other vehicles, let alone other trucks, on the road. When they had left the main highway, a line of them had already formed up behind the DAFs. Why weren't any of them coming up in their dust?

"You know, boss," Miller said. "Some things have been bothering me since we left the highway."

"That makes two of us, Miller," Yardley replied. "Let's have yours first."

"Well, that sign hanging on the barrier for starters. It basically read, "Highway under construction." That's not the usual sign for repairs or an accident. And that guard's accent has bugged me from the start. As for this bloody heathen"—Miller nodded at the guard—"the only word he's muttered is their word for 'forbidden,' hardly the popular slang used by the average squaddie."

"I hear what you're saying, Miller." Yardley observed the young guard, staring blankly straight ahead. He had noted, as with the leader at the barrier, that he was alert, lean and fit.

Suddenly, as they came around one long curve, Claude was forced to hit the brakes hard and bring the truck to a juddering halt. Behind, Jacques almost rammed into the rear of the lead truck. His "dead man" braking system locked the rear wheels of the DAF and moaned in protest as the rig skidded to within a few inches of Claude's tailgate. In the front cab they could see the gray Fiat car, sideways across the road. Yardley could swear he saw armed men behind it, before the car was enveloped in the thick cloud of dust thrown up by the sliding trucks.

The guard who had been riding shotgun jumped down from the cab. He then backed away toward the car now reemerging from the dust, waving his AK 47 in short circles as if to threaten the three foreigners. He shouldn't have done that. Miller promptly shot him through the neck.

"I knew that little fucker was all wrong!" Miller shouted, and then he was gone. Ignoring the height of the cab, he made a dive for the ground and rolled. Claude went out the other side, leaving Yardley to scramble the best he could over the central gearbox to make his escape. Miller came up off the ground, using the shelter given by the shoulder of the road, where it met the cliff face. Three selective bursts from his MP5 shattered the Fiat's windows, ripped open a rear tire and made two heads disappear down behind it. Claude gave Miller covering fire as he worked his way to a sizable boulder, instinctively trying to widen their field of fire. They felt naked, their only protection being the large front wheels of Claude's truck which he had left turned outward. To move back would make them blind to any advance. Baring and the others had grabbed weapons and moved forward to Yardley's position, hugging the sides of the trucks.

"What the shit in hell is going on?" he shouted. "Who are they?" He held the shotgun by its pistol grip vertically against his cheek. From his position he could see that Miller was vulnerable. "Miller?" he shouted. "I'm going forward, move your ass back here!"

As Baring jinked forward toward a narrow ledge just below the level of the road opposite Miller, he blasted four rounds in the general direction of the car. Its hood flew off and the driver's door seemed to disintegrate. He just made it. A vicious flow of bullets stitched their way along the road, narrowly missing his legs, then abruptly stopped and reappeared in a repeat performance on the other side of the road, this time digging their way toward the running form of Miller. They found him.

Miller let out a choked scream as the bullets ripped open his side and shattered his leg. "Nobody move!" The shout came from Yardley. "They've got a light machine gun up there."

A strange silence seemed to fall over the violent scene. Men with wide eyes, crouched in the dust, watching for the slightest move. Fingers hovered against their triggers. The only noise was the last distant echo of the machine gun's deadly song fading far away down the valley.

"Boss," Morton whispered, "that's a bloody Galil assault rifle up there—Israeli."

"What? Are you sure?"

"Damned sure. I instructed on foreign weapons at Hereford. That son-of-a-bitch is a Galil mounted on a bipod."

"Claude, mon cher," yelled Jacques. *"Attender serait inutile."*

"I say, old boy," Lysol cut in, "speak the Queen's English; this isn't bloody Dien Bien Phu, you know?"

"I said to my brother, To wait would be pointless."

"I said nobody moves!" Yardley repeated his order.

A gun barrel appeared over the car waving a white rag tied to the end. "Major Yardley, Major Yardley?" came a shout in English.

Yardley was galvanized by the shock of hearing his name. Without pausing to think he shouted back, "If you think there's a Major Yardley here, why don't you come and look for him?"

"We've no time for such games, Major Yardley. Nor have you. My name is Captain Negev of the Israeli Defense Force. We are here to relieve you of . . ."

His voice was suddenly drowned by the wild buzzing sound of a Hughes MD 500 helicopter sweeping around the corner at road level. It reared its nose and then seemed to squash into a hover, turned menacingly to face them from a standoff position out over the long drop to the valley. The Israeli markings were clearly visible.

"Bob, Bob, can you hear me?" The female voice was barely audible above the din of the helicopter. The pilot appeared to be talking to someone and backed away, but not beyond the range of its underbelly mini-gun that tracked back and forth, covering their position. One squirt with the trigger on his cyclic control and the pilot would rip them apart. "Bob, Bob, it's me, Sharqi. Please listen to the captain, no more shooting, please."

"Sharqi?" said Yardley. "What in hell is she doing here?" A moan from Miller lying out in the road and the impatient clunk of metal weapons in the hands of his men shook Yardley out of his surprise. "I'm coming forward," he shouted.

The captain emerged to meet him halfway, first ordering Sharqi to stay where she was, behind the car. As the helicopter bobbed up and down holding its hover it threw up dust around them. The captain spoke into a small radio and it maneuvered to a position behind the trucks. Everybody waited.

"That was an unfortunate incident, Major Yardley. Your man acted irrationally, and perhaps my man a little carelessly." He turned and waved forward the medic in his party.

"Irrationally, Captain?" Yardley was angry and a little confused. "You damned idiot, these men have years of combat experience, they don't stop to ask fucking questions. What's going on here? And what's she doing here?"

The young captain turned and signaled Sharqi to come forward. As she approached nervously, he said, "Sharqi, tell the major what this is all about. I wish to attend to my men and do what we came for." He walked away.

Yardley looked at her. The distrust he felt prevented him

from moving close to her. "He called you Sharqi. A baby captain in the Israeli Army shoots up my trucks and calls *you* Sharqi. You'd better explain pretty damned fast."

"Bob, listen, please listen. Flood has all the facts and this is part of his operation. He always closes out an operation in his own way, don't you understand?" Her voice was becoming more desperate as the disbelief remained on his face.

"Mossad recruited me. My father was executed—remember my story as I told you in Lausanne? I have been a sleeping agent in Tehran since then. I was activated for your operation. It is vital that we succeed here, please understand; I could not tell you my role, the whole operation has been need-to-know. No one could calculate us meeting and having close feelings for each other."

Her pleas began to penetrate his emotions. "Why didn't you tell me before I left Tehran? I've been worried sick about you."

"I couldn't, and in your heart you know I couldn't."

Her bravery swelled in his heart. "So you did it for Israel?"

"It is my country," she replied.

He took her hand lightly. "Well, we'd better get on with it then."

He realized that Baring had already reached the right conclusions and was organizing the repositioning of the trucks. The MD 500 lifted out of the way. Lysol, Morton and two Israelis were attending to Miller in the middle of the road. The body of the dead soldier had been gently carried beyond the car. Yardley sighted the captain ordering his men to push the car over the edge of the ravine and taking information from another young officer. He walked toward them and recognized the second officer as the guard who had been commanding the barrier party way back on the main highway. He had been in the group that had arrived with the small helicopter.

"Captain, I suggest you tell me your plan of action here." They stood toe-to-toe with Sharqi off to the side.

"You hand over the throne to us, Major Yardley, and we lift it out of here."

"The hell I do! My orders are clear about where that piece of furniture goes."

"Bob," Sharqi interjected, "call Baring up here, he will confirm this."

"Nick will? What's he know about all this?" He didn't wait for a reply. "Nick? Get yourself over here."

Baring trotted over to the group. "Yes, Bob?"

Yardley clenched his fists. These were not the rules he was used to. With restraint he said, "Sharqi says you know about this."

"I knew about the intercept, Bob, but not how it would materialize. Yes, I knew the Israelis were involved." They glared at each other. He continued softly, "Look, boss, Flood and I go back a long way. He had to brief me fully or I wouldn't have signed on. But it was strictly need-to-know in case any of us fell into an Iranian interrogation cell."

Yardley nodded in resignation. "Okay, what happens now?"

"We give them the bloody throne. That was Rodel's plan all along, not to risk it at the border or to deliver it to your own military. They have a greater game of intrigue to play with the thing."

"So we've done the hard work and those fucking Israelis just walk away with it?"

"Major," said the captain calmly, "you must assume that we are all in this one together."

Yardley smiled to himself. It wasn't so bad; Sharqi was safe and getting rid of the prize made things easier for them. That Flood's a cunning bastard. "It's all yours, Captain."

"Thank you, sir."

"Nick, all hands to the truck. But hold on. Captain, do you intend taking one of the trucks?"

"No, sir. We have brought our own." He took a small radio handset off his belt, and activated a button. Looking at Yardley, he said, "This is a PRC-112(V) transceiver, sir. Its single-burst transmission will be interrogated by an ARS-6 Personal Locator Receiver in one of our CH-53s about three minutes' flying time from here. Our pilot can home right in on us."

"Very impressive operation, Captain. Our people don't have that little toy in service yet. We still use the PRC-90 Locator." Yardley grinned with the rest of them. "I guess your boys in the States have been helping themselves again."

There was still the danger of an Iranian air patrol descending on them and they worked urgently to prepare for the transfer. The truck was rolled a short way down the road to where it widened enough to take the helicopter. The old material at the back of the vehicle was tossed over the ravine, and they waited.

Baring saw it first, a good distance away, flying fast and

low along the valley floor. It disappeared, then reappeared several times as its flight path twisted around the inhospitable terrain toward them. The Belgian twins whistled in wonderment. They had never seen nap-of-the-earth flying like it anywhere. The huge camouflaged machine seemed inches from the ground, its massive rotor blades almost brushing the mountainsides as it closed on them at 175 knots. Just as it looked as if it would ram into the blind canyon wall far beneath them, its blunt snout tucked up, as if to smell its prey, and without any check in speed it rose in a power climb to their perch. From their viewpoint at the roadside they were looking down directly into the top of its rotor. Then the monster was there, its huge menacing form painted in a dust color, its lines broken up with splashes of green and bristling with numerous add-on systems for early warning devices, the Pave-Low III and other electronic and countermeasure equipment. The noise from its three engines was deafening and the long in-flight refueling probe protruding from the side of its nose appeared to be sniffing them out. The machine slid sideways as the auto-hover slaved to the Locator searched out the exact spot on the road. One of the captain's men stood facing away, as if ignoring the brutish approach, his arms raised. The helicopter danced about his head, then settled down in front of him, its rotor blades continuing to churn through the air. The rear ramp was already lowered and two crewmen ran down and across the short space to the back of the truck, then signaled everyone to give a hand. Steel runners were used to link the ramp with the truck and a cable attached to the container carrying the throne. Without ceremony it was winched across and into the cavernous belly of the helicopter.

"Time for us to go, Major." The captain shook his hand. "You too, Sharqi, let's go." He strode away and left them. His men were emplaning and loading the casualties into the big bird.

Sharqi gripped Yardley by both arms and kissed his forehead. "You'll have no trouble at the border now. London in one week, Flood will tell you where. Take care." And she was gone, running up the ramp. An Israeli crewman swung a rear-facing 0.50 caliber mounted machine gun into place and the giant rotor lifted them off. The small MD 500 leaped up to follow.

12

The Moving Finger writes; and, having writ,
Moves on: nor all thy Piety nor Wit
Shall lure it back to cancel half a Line,
Nor all thy Tears wash out a Word of it.

Seven weeks had gone by and Christmas was only a few days away. Flood was driving the Porsche in a relaxed way, southbound on the lakeside road to the east of Annecy. Baring sat quietly beside him, his fingers tapping a silent accompaniment on the passenger door's armrest to Bach's Concerto no. 5. The evening was beautifully clear, with only patches of high cirrus cloud between them and the stars. The Brandenburg Concertos fitted their mood and their surroundings, and Baring always felt a lift from the orchestral ritornello in the fifth. Their conversation had started out on the reflective side and with the help of speed and good music had progressed to the convivial. A synergy flowed, built on mutual respect, and Flood's role as mentor rarely entered their dialogue overtly.

He veered hard right when he saw the sign to Talloires, went down the hill on the narrow road between two walls, continued slowly across the village square and on down until, just short of the lake, the headlights picked out the gateway entrance to the great hotel Au Père Bise.

He swung between the posts into the parking lot and pulled up next to a highly polished Bentley Mulsanne. The wide tires crunched on the swept gravel.

"It's not so long since you've been here, Nick?" Flood asked.

Baring was leaning back in his seat, in no hurry to get out. "You know the answer to that," he replied. "In fact I parked the car right here when we took on those Corsicans next door in the Hotel L'Abbaye. I'm glad tonight is a more agreeable reason for being here."

"When Roger Rodel phoned to say he was taking Christmas leave and wanted to give us a celebratory dinner, I suggested this place. Deliberately. For old times' sake, and because it happens to be one of the three best restaurants I know in France."

"I'd agree with that, but pricey."

Flood held his hand out, palm downward, and waggled it to and fro. "It can be. And tonight perhaps it should be, as our fat friend Rodel is picking up the tab." As they climbed out and walked through the garden and past the verandah, which was closed in wintertime, he went on, "Normally, the two-hundred-fifty-franc meal is enough for me. But knowing Rodel, he will insist that we go for the seven-hundred-fifty-franc menu, hoping we'll decline of course. He likes to impress. I think we'll oblige him, and accept."

Baring laughed and said, "I bet he's an expert at hiding pricey meals in his expenses. He's just hidden a million-dollar operation from the American people."

They went through the French windows into the main dining room. Rodel and another man were sitting at a table in the far corner. Baring said urgently, "You never said there'd be someone else here."

"I didn't know. Rodel said nothing about it. If it's not kosher, we'll leave."

"What? And kiss goodbye a seven-hundred-and-fifty-franc chef's delight."

Rodel stood up to greet them. "Ah, the heavenly twins, Flood and Baring. Let me introduce my other guest, Sir Denis Stiffkey. Sir Denis is a Whitehall warrior—one of our senior friends who has helped greatly to put the word 'special' into 'special relationship.' "

As he shook hands, Flood saw a tall, elegant Englishman, impeccably dressed in a charcoal gray lounge suit with a thick chalk-stripe. His graying hair was worn slightly long, with a small horn brushed up above each ear. He knew the type well. They looked wet and helpless, as though they needed a servant to tie their shoelaces, but they could be cold and deadly.

The others were drinking *kir royales*, so he and Baring had a glass each and then another. Before they had a chance to state a preference, Rodel insisted on trying the seven-hundred-and-fifty-franc menu. A hidden smile crossed the table. By the time they had finished two exquisite bottles of Puligny-Montrachet for the opening courses and were well into a magnum of Château Latour for the meat dishes, Flood decided it was going to be a good party. No wonder, he thought. The USA was running a multibillion-dollar annual deficit. Rodel alone must be responsible for a large chunk of it. Sir Denis kept them chuckling with a flow of "Unattributable, don't you know" stories of Whitehall "moles" and the earnest attempts to revise the Official Secrets Act.

"That's what the Brits call being economical with the truth," Rodel observed. "What a wonderful phrase! Could you imagine George Shultz using it?"

"Could you imagine George Shultz *having* to use it?" Sir Denis said lightly.

At the end of the sumptuous meal, he and Baring each ordered a *marc de champagne,* while the other two settled for a Delamain. Rodel, who was sweating greasily on his forehead and scalp, sat back and lit a large Havana cigar. Once it was glowing to his satisfaction, he held it between the second and third stubby fingers of his left hand as he swirled the cognac round and round the *ballon* glass he was cradling in his right hand. He said, as if addressing a meeting, "Gentlemen, I think congratulations are in order. I reckon we've pulled off a damned good op and showed those fucking mullahs how to play chess. A toast!" His drink splashed onto his shirt, unnoticed, as he started to get up.

Baring moved faster and quietly stood up. "A toast to absent friends." He raised his glass toward Rodel as he spoke.

Flood and Sir Denis replied by raising their glasses, but Rodel continued. "Absent friends?" He gulped back his cognac. "Absent friends, Nick? Bullshit! Mercenaries, a goddamn jailbird—and don't tell me you're mourning for that dead Israeli kid!"

Baring set down his glass, spread the fingers of both hands on the table and leaned across, his face inches from Rodel.

"That rolled off your tongue too easily, Mr. Rodel." Baring's eyes were cold. "You think it's clever to write those guys off as just another bunch of paid brush strokes on your big canvas. Miller's dead, you son-of-a-bitch. He died in a hospital in Haifa after the Israelis did their utmost to save him. And that 'Israeli kid' died doing his job, *your job.* That mess wouldn't have happened if the team had known the Israelis were in the picture!"

"Gentlemen," said Sir Denis, "let's take it nice and easy. Hard words could curdle this delicious glass of marc, which, mine host, if I may say, is almost empty."

Flood placed a restraining hand on Baring's arm and with a subtle nod, gestured for him to sit down. Rodel gratefully picked up Sir Denis's cue and waved a fat paw at the wine waiter. Then he said, "I'm sorry, Nick. Apologies. It was the drink talking. Didn't mean to offend."

"To be fair, Nick," said Sir Denis in the same calm, detached manner, "you must, I'm sure, appreciate why Roger couldn't bring up the involvement of Mossad in all this."

"I do, Sir Denis. It was fortunate that Flood had explained the big picture to me. I'm less sure of your involvement."

Sir Denis smiled. "Let us just say that our interests crossed and although we were somewhat nervous for a time, we are very pleased with the results. We have been suffering a blessed logjam with the Iranians for some time, no leverage at all, and apart from the hostage problem have known from intelligence that their Shi'ite extremists were about to launch a terrorist offensive in Europe, particularly against British targets. That is why we decided to get our hands on the flowerman. We knew he was controller."

"Jesus, when I learned what you Brits were up to, I had to break it up fast." Rodel now spoke in a more level tone. "If the flowerman had reached Geneva, our plan would have been down the tubes. As you know, Nick, his family connection with Ali Mohtashemi, the hardline Iranian Interior Minister, effectively made him an extended arm of that zealot's policies. Mohtashemi is opposed to any attempts at relations with the West, any moderation in Lebanon, where he controls those Hizbollah freaks, and over three hundred Iranian revolutionary guards garrisoned in Baalbeh, in the Bekaa Valley, *and* he's a key figure in the power struggle for the succession to Ayatollah Khomeini. A major obstacle to the man we want to see in power, Hashemi Rafsanjani."

"Rafsanjani is a pragmatist among Tehran's Islamic ideologues," said Sir Denis. "He's as cunning as a fox, ruthless, but he is prepared to wheel and deal. He persuaded Khomeini to accept UN Resolution 598, which established guidelines for an indefinite cease-fire with Iraq and that takes power. But when we try to negotiate with him over the Beirut hostages, he's impotent to use his power over Mohtashemi, who controls Iran's Lebanon involvement. So you see, we all have a very real interest in Mohtashemi's demise."

"Three weeks ago," Rodel broke in, "the flowerman was introduced to a very lucrative deal—the sale of the Peacock Throne. He was filmed in the company of two other Iranians he was convinced had escorted the throne out of Iran with the Shah in '79, negotiating the selling of twenty-five of the precious stones to two Jewish diamond merchants in Antwerp, Belgium. At the eleventh hour a certain lady, whom you both know, walked on stage. That convinced him that his uncle's ministry was part of it."

"Sharqi?" Baring asked.

"Correct!"

Rodel continued, "We had to undermine the Mohtashemi and Ayatollah Montazeri clique, the main opposition to Rafsanjani gaining absolute power. You'll remember it was Montazeri's nephew, Mehti Hashemi, who exposed our Iran-Contra setup by leaking it to the Beirut Ash-Shiraa newspaper."

Flood spoke. "But, Rafsanjani had him shot for treason, didn't he?"

"That's right," said Rodel, "but Montazeri survived all that and the clique held on to Khomeini's favor. We knew then that we had to give Rafsanjani a trump card with staying power. A long grip on their balls, you might say." He was enjoying holding the floor, and paused to have their glasses filled. "We linked them in to ripping off the nation's treasures and, worse, hocking them to Zionist devils, by editing a surveillance film of a guy called Najaf Abadi, once a close aide to Mehti Hashemi, meeting with the flowerman in Amsterdam. With the film in the can, we arranged for a copy, along with the combinations to the palace safe, to fall into Rafsanjani's hands." Rodel couldn't control the thrill it gave him and giggled out loud.

"And what a surprise when they opened the safe," said Baring.

"I have it on good authority," said Sir Denis mischievously, "that they found the body of the chief of security inside. A certain Mr. Sohrabi found himself in a foxhole with the fox." He paused for effect. "I believe Mr. Abadi and Mr. Sohrabi were executed two days ago."

As their glasses clinked together, Flood said, "Here's to the Ayatollah's belief in the 'swift justice of Islam.'"

"I guess the Israelis get to keep the booty?" asked Baring.

Rodel laughed. "No way—we'll be giving that back to our *friend* Rafsanjani. Goddamn awful shame after all the trouble we went to. Do you know that goddamn chair has been valued at over forty million U.S. dollars?"

"You'll do *what*?" Baring said incredulously. "And after *who* went to all the trouble? I don't recall seeing your sweat and fear down in the basement of the Ghulistan Palace. But I do recall Peter Shaw's sweat and fear and downright guts!"

"My dear Nick," Sir Denis intervened, sensing Baring's mood. "It's the age-old game of political currency. With a new administration in Washington, it will be the time for goodwill gestures all round. As I implied earlier, getting a result is what counts. Speaking of Mr. Shaw, what became of him and the rest of your team?"

"Uh-oh," said Rodel, "be careful how you answer that, Flood. Sir Denis is always at work for his masters."

"Come now, Roger, that's most ungenerous of you. This little chat is totally off the record."

"Peter Shaw is loving life in Johannesburg," Flood said. "He's now technical director with a major security company, contracted to the government. And found himself a nice girlfriend. A rather amply proportioned Afrikaans widow, who will probably mother him to death."

"Well, I hope someone has told him not to honeymoon in his native England. I seem to remember he owes Her Majesty's Government something like six years' penal servitude."

Sir Denis's dry humor served to lighten the mood around the table. "And the rest?" he asked.

Flood said quietly, "They went their ways. Archie Morton went back to London. He never strays far from his SAS regiment. The Belgian twins returned to Brussels and have just been hired for another covert operation. Rupert Lycett-Smythe, well, poor old Lysol, as we call him, has had to hang up his webbing. His elder brother, and heir to the title, was killed in a car accident while we were away. So Lysol looks like inheriting. There are no other male relatives, so he's going to have to find a wife and carry on the line. No more covert adventures for him. Sad, really. He loves the life."

"Major Yardley, the team leader?" asked Sir Denis. "One of yours, wasn't he, Roger? A Yank, I mean. I kept hearing bits and pieces about him through my SAS friends. He sounds a good man."

"A very impressive soldier," Flood said. "Agreed, Nick?"

"Sure. I'd go with him any day."

Flood went on. "He telephoned me the other day to wish me a Merry Christmas. He's having a ball. Resigned his commission and has settled in Israel. It appears Sharqi Zachin plucked his heartstrings. The man has taste, and he's smart enough to marry her."

"Oh, he'll be down the aisle before you can say 'gefilte fish,' " joked Baring. "When I told him Flood had cleared the decks for me with the Marseilles mob and he could use my ketch for the honeymoon, he said a strange thing and then rang off. 'Thanks, but no thanks. This is what comes from taking a swim in Rangeley Lake.' I wonder what the hell he meant."